DIRTY LYING FAERIES

THE ENCHANTED FATES SERIES

DIRTY LYING FAERIES

DIRTY LYING DRAGONS
AUGUST 2023

DIRTY LYING WOLVES
SEPTEMBER 2024

DIRTY LYING FAERIES

SABRINA BLACKBURRY

by wattpad books

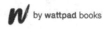

An imprint of Wattpad WEBTOON Book Group

Content Warning: sex, language, violence, mention of past murder and infanticide, mention of past pregnancy loss, fated mates, one bed, mental health, magic

Published in Canada by Wattpad WEBTOON Book Group, a division of Wattpad WEBTOON Studios, Inc.

36 Wellington Street E., Suite 200, Toronto, ON M5E 1C7 Canada

www.wattpad.com

First Wattpad Books edition: August 2022

ISBN 978-1-99077-851-3 (Trade Paperback edition)
ISBN 978-1-99025-919-7 (Hardcover original)
ISBN 978-1-99025-920-3 (eBook edition)

Library and Archives Canada Cataloguing in Publication information is available upon request.

Printed and bound in Canada

1 3 5 7 9 10 8 6 4 2

Cover design by Tiana Lambent
Images © Nicola Bertellotti via Shutterstock
Author Photo by Malinda Mathis

To my Upstarts. You know who you are, stay troublesome.

And to my first reader, my first editor, my sister, Olivia. Thank you.

CHAPTER ONE

THEA

"Is that really what you're going to wear?" Candace looked at me questioningly. She tapped her perfect pink manicured nails on her desk.

"Apparently not," I mumbled.

"Correct." Her straight blond hair brushed the tops of her shoulders as she tilted her head. She was dressed to kill in a little gold cocktail number.

"Are you going to tell me what's wrong with it?" I asked, craning my neck to see my backside in her mirror. The gray dress fell to my ankles, paired with my only black flats. My hair was up in its usual messy brown bun.

"Thea, that whole dress is a disaster. The silhouette is all wrong for your waist to hip ratio, the darts in the top do nothing for your chest, and flats to a formal event?" She stood dramatically, chair legs squeaking as they slid across the tile floor. "I'm going to have to dress you."

"No."

"Yes," she insisted.

"I don't even want to go. I'm only there for you and the fancy food."

"All the more reason to look good." Her heels clicked across the tiles as she excitedly threw open her closet doors. "The Candace Lewis entourage has to be as hot as Candace Lewis herself."

"I'm your entourage now?"

"Just get your butt over here." She pulled out several things from the piles of clothes in her extensive wardrobe, pondering them for a moment before discarding them atop a nearby armchair. "Where the hell is that designer gown I just bought?"

"The red one? Candie, that has, like, no back to it."

"Yeah, that's kind of the point." She shoved herself between two large coats. "If I had your yoga-babe shoulder blades, I'd never cover them up."

"I can barely hear you through all that fabric," I said. "Isn't something backless a little too cold for December?"

"Fashion is pain and all that. A-ha!" She emerged triumphant, holding up a long red gown. "Get that monstrosity off and put this on."

"The things I do in the name of friendship." I slipped my dress off and let it fall to the floor. Candace was on me in one fell swoop, sliding the red satin over my head and smoothing it down my body. She stood back and eyed me from top to bottom.

"Gorgeous." She clasped her hands together, flashing a wicked grin. "You look absolutely *devastating*. I'll get some black pumps!" She dove back into her closet.

Turning to the mirror, I *felt* devastating. The neckline plunged, but not quite out of my comfort zone. The satin squeezed every drop of curve it could from my hips, flaring out as it brushed the top of my thighs. It was hands down the most flattering garment I had ever worn.

"Here, put these on. Match it with this ruby lip gloss, and for god's sake, Thea, run a brush through your hair." Candace checked her reflection next to mine.

Biting my tongue, I pulled a brush through my hair and slipped the hair tie back over it once it was more neatly in place. "Happy?"

She squinted at me and stuck a decorative silver hair pin in it before nodding her approval. "Yes."

With a laugh, I turned to the side and eyed the new ornament in the mirror. "What would I do without you?"

"You'd die a book hoarder in a dark basement apartment surrounded by antiques and tears. Now, let's go."

L'Atelier Rouge, or the Red Studio, was an oversized greenhouse in the middle of an elaborate garden. What was surprising was that it managed to stay that way, undeveloped as the offices and skyscrapers of Seattle went up around it. Once the workshop of the artist Marcel Dubois, it was painted—you guessed it—red. The studio had been preserved as a museum, with a modern art gallery built on its grounds. It was a classy place, for sure. Much classier than our ride anyway.

"How did you wangle an invitation again?"

I felt a little silly pulling up to a charity event in the same dented van I'd had since high school, but Candace insisted I drive so she could *drink her weight in overpriced wine.*

"I told you already." Candie reapplied her lipstick in the mirror. "My boss couldn't make it, so she gave her tickets to whoever gave her the best article this month."

"I thought you were joking; Georgina hates you."

"Hate is a strong word," Candie said, snapping her lipstick lid closed. "And I'm her best journalist." Candace opened her door and I followed her lead until we were both on the sidewalk in the frosty night air.

"Shit! It's freezing," she complained.

"Fashion is pain," I deadpanned.

Candace glared at me, then walked as quickly as her heels allowed toward the front door. Mercifully, the snow from the previous day had been cleared off the sidewalk, or I would have ended up on my butt in these shoes.

"Are you sure we're dressed appropriately?" I eyed a stylish couple walking in—they reeked of money, and I could swear they were staring as they passed.

"Relax, I work in fashion journalism. I think I can pull together a couple evening wear looks." Candace smoothed her skirt and took the last few steps to the door in excitement. She practically dragged me to the front door, where a man in a suit was collecting tickets and scratching names off his list. Candace ogled the other guests while I tried my best to turn invisible. Dying of embarrassment was starting to sound like a good option when the guy at the door stopped to rave loudly about Candie's amazing boss and her tickets. I don't know how he'd become such a fan of a magazine editor, but it didn't look like we would get out of hearing about it until the lady behind us cleared her throat in annoyance, moving the process along.

Inside, the extravagance of it all sank in. Soft yellow light cast a golden glow throughout the room. Some wore jewelry worth probably more than my whole year's paycheck. There was a champagne fountain in the center of a huge buffet table. Even the waitstaff was dressed in black tie as they glided around balancing trays of drinks. Somewhere a piano was playing seasonal music while couples danced across the marble floor.

"Candie, this is way out of my league. How am I supposed to talk to anyone here?" I whispered.

"Relax." She sauntered over to a table loaded with refreshments, and I followed close behind. "You're here for the food and the exhibits, right? Just grab a plate and enjoy the art. Actually, you should find a cute piece of ass and dance—you look absolutely delicious in this lighting." Her eyes began to scan the crowd dangerously, and the very real threat of Candace plucking a dance partner *for* me was starting to creep into play.

"Dancing is unlikely, I'll go with the food." Giving her the side eye, I did have to admit the table looked delicious. "And you're going to be where?"

"Rubbing elbows with the rich and famous." She winked. "I'll let you be a bridesmaid in my posh celebrity wedding once I land one of them."

"Of course, I'll be a bridesmaid in your very plausible celebrity wedding."

"Have fun. Thanks for driving!" She blew me a kiss, then scooped a glass of champagne from a passing tray and waded into the crowd. Taking her advice, I turned my attention to the food.

And holy hell, *the food.*

Different kinds of fruit and cheese and meat were everywhere. Pastries with complicated decorations were stacked high on porcelain trays. I had to stop myself from breaking off the head of a carved chocolate swan—tempting as it was, it was probably meant to be a display. Even the plates looked expensive, monogrammed with gold-leafed edges.

Loading up on appetizers I'd probably never have the chance to try again, I walked over to the art. Whoever put all this together had an eye for detail that I appreciated. The food was amazing, the soft piano was perfect, and the decor was stunning, but the art was terrible. Painting after painting of tortured gray blobs lined the walls of the main gallery. Maybe I didn't know much about modern art, but this looked like something my two-year-old niece could have made at daycare.

Taking slow steps along the wall, pausing at each canvas to try to find something interesting, my mind wandered as aimlessly as my feet. After most of my snacks were gone, I looked around, trying to find Candie. From the safety of the wall, I watched her on the dance floor as she glued herself to a guy with too much gel in his hair. Between dances she socialized with anyone near enough to participate, asking them questions about their clothes in typical Candie fashion. She was reveling in the attention; I could see the victory in her eyes. Candace had two passions in her life: fashion and people. With a smile, I popped a miniature cherry tart into my mouth as I watched her. As different as we were, she was thriving in her element, and I was happy to be here when she wound down, enjoying the food and a quiet walk by myself through the gallery. Candace spotted me against the wall and winked. Laughing, I got out of there before she could pull me onto the dance floor.

Moving out of the main room, onto a different exhibit, I pretended I was in a world-famous museum, surveying the treasures around me in the secret hours after the visitors were gone. It was the Dubois permanent collection, not one of the ever-changing special exhibitions that passed from gallery to gallery, but the namesake of L'Atelier Rouge. Most of the guests had probably seen these paintings before or didn't care in the first place, but I'd never seen them in person. So, I walked and munched on crostini, regretting Candace's choice of footwear. After a while I paused against the wall in a particularly dim corner to rest my feet, hide, and eat.

"Beautiful," said a gravelly voice just over my shoulder. The sound startled me; I whirled around to see a man in a *finely* tailored suit standing there. His dark hair was long and pulled back, his emerald eyes filled with amusement. Broad but not bulky, tall and poised enough to join the art on the walls, this creature was walking sin.

"What?" I replied, swallowing.

"The paintings. Don't you think so?"

Setting my plate on a table behind me, I hoped he hadn't seen me stuffing my face. "Yes."

His laugh was a low, comfortable sound that crawled up my back. "Much better than the gray eyesores out front, but I suppose that's what's 'in' now."

I snorted and immediately felt the heat rush to my face, slapping a hand over my mouth.

"Is this your first time at L'Atelier Rouge?" he asked, blessedly not laughing at my reaction. His low, confident tones were right up my alley.

"It is." Was this man somehow the only other introvert at this party? Maybe, since he wasn't in the main room with the rest of the guests. Or maybe he liked the atmosphere here. I know I did, that's what drew me to museum studies.

"Marvelous. Would you enjoy a private tour?" A wicked playfulness danced across his lips.

"Do you know much about art?" I asked, approaching one of the paintings. A soft smile spread across my face, cautiously interested in where this was going.

"I should hope so." His eyes glinted as he closed the distance I had just put between us. "I own the gallery. Please, call me Devin."

"That explains it. I'm Thea, it's nice to meet you. A tour would be lovely; I'm not as familiar with modern art, but this collection is beautiful."

That seemed to take him by surprise. "Should I assume that you are familiar with other eras of art then?"

My eyes shifted to the nearest painting, a forested landscape. Warmth crept up my neck in a telltale sign that I was dangerously close to becoming flustered, either from shyness or an attraction to Devin or both. "Only lightly compared to you, I'm sure. I just finished my history degree in the spring. Museum studies."

Devin's brow raised and he gave me a reassessing gaze. "How interesting, I've been giving some consideration lately to displaying more of the gallery's history."

"Considering the original studio still stands I think that's a wonderful idea," I said excitedly. "Do you have other remaining artifacts? Information about the original owner? Any surviving photographs would be an amazing addition to the displays. All of that would make an interesting—*oh*." Biting the inside of my cheek to stop the enthusiastic babble I was spouting, I cleared my throat. "A tour would be lovely."

Devin's polished composure dropped a bit in favor of an abrupt sound of amusement. "A conversation for another time, then." His eyes moved from me to the painting I had stepped in front of earlier, causing me to still as he leaned in slightly to nod in its direction. "This series contains some of Dubois's earliest landscapes, this one being one of the first uses in his entire body of work to harness this technique regarding water texture."

The tour was more of a conversation, and it flowed easily between us. There was something captivating about the paintings that made one want to keep staring into them. Magical, whimsical little details that drew your eye across the canvas in a natural flow. When my eyes weren't caught by the paintings, I found them drifting toward Devin as we went, glancing at his strong, sculpted profile as he spoke about the history of the pieces.

He led me through the exhibit, showing me painting after painting with a comfortable curiosity between us until we reached the farthest wall. It was like I was in a trance—following his every word through the quiet gallery.

"Here, you can see the difference in his later work. For instance"— he made a sweeping motion with one arm—"this was one of Marcel's last pieces. Near the end of his life, he claimed to see things in the forest. Fairy tales come to life."

The painting was a dark line of trees behind rows of gorgeous pink lilies, the sun shining on the grass. Behind the branches, a blackness contrasted against the sunny field. Eerie eyes peered out from behind tree trunks. They were so imperceptible that I almost wouldn't have noticed them had they not been pointed out to me. It struck me as odd, considering the realist nature of the other paintings.

Devin moved, and the gentle scent of his woodsy cologne brushed my nose. He stepped back and motioned to another painting. From this viewpoint, the paintings took on fantastical elements. Wings, ears, eyes, all hidden as though Dubois himself were seeing them only from the corner of his vision. And Devin was invested in each painting, knowing the history of it, where the landscape sat, and when in his lifetime Dubois had painted it. He was fascinating to listen to, and my hungry curiosity only grew as we explored the collection.

"This one is a personal favorite." The latest painting depicted a little girl holding a bouquet of wildflowers as big as she was. Her smile was missing a front tooth, and it wasn't until I looked closer that it appeared her ears were *pointed*.

"What do you think?" He took one step closer to me, not uncomfortably close but near enough that I could feel the warmth of his body in the otherwise cool gallery. Letting out a slow breath, I calmed my nervous attraction and did my best to focus on the subject matter.

"He was a skilled painter," I said, stepping back and licking my dry lips. "If perhaps a bit eccentric in the end."

Devin's low tones gave way to a burst of laughter that lit up my chest. Immediately I regretted stepping away when I could have stayed next to him instead.

"Eccentric is an excellent choice of word." He straightened his silver tie, checked his watch, and offered me a hand. "I'm afraid I've prattled on enough. I appreciate that you allowed me the pleasure of a tour; few show much interest in Marcel anymore."

"It was a pleasure."

Devin took my own outstretched hand and kissed it gently. My arm flared to life as though it had been asleep until now, and our eyes locked. My focus on Devin and the paintings sharpened, as if I hadn't been using my senses properly before. A hot coal of attraction landed in the pit of my stomach. "I assure you, the pleasure was all mine," he mused, letting go of my hand. As my fingers fell, I clutched them absently over my beating heart.

"Thea!" Candace called from the other side of the room—wine glass in one hand, heels in the other. She was off-her-ass drunk.

"Oh no," I groaned.

Devin chuckled, taking a step back. "I sincerely hope we have the opportunity to do this again sometime; I'd love to explore your ideas on how to go about organizing a few displays throughout the collection. I'll leave you to your friend to enjoy the rest of the party."

While I would rather have watched Devin go, the short blond spectacle in the doorway shouted, "Thea, dance with me!" then slurred, "Who'sh the hottie?"

"The *owner*. You're drunk."

"His ass should be under one of these damn spotlights," she said, a little too loudly. Several heads turned our way from the main room behind her.

"How are you already this drunk? We've only been here for, like, thirty minutes."

"Psh, it's been *hours*. Look!" Candace held her phone to my face so I could see the time, and I gaped at the numbers across her lock screen.

"That's impossible." Pulling out my own phone, I swiped through to find the same time displayed.

"No, *you're* impossible." Candace swung her arm out, sharing a few drops of wine with the pristine white floor.

"Come on, Candie, we're getting you home," I mumbled, taking the wine glass from my drunk friend. "I think we've both had enough for tonight."

CHAPTER TWO

THEA

"I don't want to go yet," Candace whined, trying to push my hand away as I reached for her seat belt. "That girl with the vintage Tiffany ring let me try it on. I want to go baaack."

"Here." I took a pastry that I had pilfered from the snack table on the way out and stuck it in her mouth. "Eat that and please don't throw up in my van."

"Mm-mmhrm phff," she said, unintelligibly, as I buckled her up. "More of these?"

Smiling, I handed her another pastry, and walked around to the driver's side door.

While the van warmed up I gave the gallery one last look, seeing a silhouette in a window on the third floor, high off the ground. My fingers tightened on the wheel. Perhaps wishful thinking on my part, but I could have sworn it was Devin. We drove off, leaving the strange party and the enchanting gallery owner behind.

—

The roads were quiet, and in half an hour I had Candace inside her warm apartment building. I was digging out my copy of her key when she began swaying her arm in front of me, a series of numbers scrawled across her skin.

"Look what I got tonight."

"Are you serious right now?" I turned the key and half dragged Candace through her front door.

"One HUN-dred percent, baby!"

"Why didn't you just put the number in your phone? This isn't middle school anymore." I caught her as she stumbled and helped her over to her bed. I unzipped her cocktail dress and let it slide to the floor. "Only you would find a booty call at an art gallery."

"No, it's—it isn't a booty call." She giggled as I tucked her into bed, the bubbliest drunk I'd ever known.

"I will remind you that I knew you in high school." I moved her shoes so she wouldn't trip on them in the morning and grabbed a wipe from her bedside table. "Let me see your face."

She sputtered and pushed, fighting me as I wiped off her makeup. "Ugh, too rough."

Eventually I was able to clean her face, and then mine, before getting her in bed and turning off the light.

"Good night, Candie."

"Nooo, are you leaving? Stay with me, pleeease!" She was half out of bed again.

"Stop! Stop," I said as I rushed back. "Fine, all right, I'll stay here tonight."

Candace giggled and made room for me on the bed. I dropped the red gown next to hers with a sigh and crawled in.

"For someone so put together, you sure are a hot mess when you're drunk," I said.

"Yeah? For someone who needs to get laid . . ."

She paused. "You . . . need to get laid."

"Go to sleep," I told her flatly. She snuggled in next to me, clutching me like a teddy bear, and I pulled the covers up to our chins. "I swear, if you throw up on me . . ."

Silence.

"Hey." I looked over—she was out like a light. I stifled a laugh. I could pretend to hate dealing with her drunk ass all I wanted, but she indulged me when I wanted to peruse a bookstore or see a new exhibit with little complaint, and the occasional designated driving wouldn't kill me.

"Night, Candie," I whispered.

I considered leaving, but she'd entwined herself around my body and would probably wake up if I moved. Oh well—it was after midnight anyway and sleep sounded really good about now.

But I couldn't.

A pair of playful green eyes wouldn't get out of my head. My fingers still tingled where Devin had kissed them. Something felt significant about it but I couldn't say what. Maybe I was excited about the gallery or about Devin or both. After a while spent counting sheep and trying to get comfortable, I gave up and watched the moonlight through the windows. The occasional car passed by—a soft hush whispered through the glass every time one drove through the icy slush.

He was trouble. Too smooth, too much my type.

Focus, Thea. You don't need that kind of distraction in your life. It's not like a little bit of shared interest is going to lead to your dream career. He probably wasn't serious about hearing your ideas anyway— that doesn't happen to the quiet ones like you.

He smelled wild, like cedar trees or a campfire.

Stop it.

What would it feel like to run my fingers through his hair?

Throwing off the covers, I peeled myself away from Candace, needing air. Pulling open a drawer to borrow a pair of sweatpants and a hoodie, I willed my feet to move quietly through the studio apartment. Candie had decorated her small and expensive ideal home with her favorite name brands. And the location was great—I looked out the window and could see a thin slice of Elliott Bay. I pulled on my coat and went up to the roof.

The chill hit me right away and I tightened my coat around my shoulders. A gazebo with benches and a picnic table had been built up there for the tenants. As I sat on one of the benches, my breath clouded in front of me, but the air was doing wonders to cool down any part of me trying to stay hot and bothered.

"—heard that he already picked one."

"What court do you think she'll—"

"—about time we got another—"

Curious, I stood and walked to the edge of the building. The streetlights below glowed yellow, and another car splashed through the slush on the road.

"—another ignorant human—"

Peering over the chain-link fence that bordered the rooftop, I saw two women sitting on the hood of a Mustang. One of them was a pretty blond; the other had snow-white hair.

I squinted—was their skin a little blue? They were wearing almost nothing, despite the freezing temperatures.

"—probably another brat for Spring."

The brisk night carried the sound so well from the street to the rooftop. Suddenly, one of them, the blond, turned and stared right at me. Watching me, she grinned and whispered something to her friend. They both broke out in laughter. I jumped back from the fence like it was on fire. Embarrassed of getting caught snooping and weirded out by their odd conversation, I'd had enough fresh air. Back inside and downstairs again, I climbed back into bed with Candace and soon fell into a deep, restful sleep—eyes in the forest and glimpses of pointed ears and teeth filling my dreams.

CHAPTER THREE

THEA

"You're being too loud," Candace moaned from beneath the covers.

"I'm doing yoga, not playing the drums." I stretched my legs apart and my arms high in a warrior pose.

"You're doing it too loud."

I held my body in place for a long count, then relaxed and eased into a downward dog. "You could always join me."

She snorted.

"Suit yourself. Do you want me to get you anything before I leave? An aspirin for the hangover?"

"Candace Lewis does not get hangovers," she grumbled.

"Mm-hmm."

"I will *allow* you to bring me some water."

"Of course, your majesty." I dropped to the mat, and then hopped back up to go to the fridge, grabbed a water bottle from inside, and threw it at the lump of blankets.

She yelped and then popped her head out, squinting at me. "Rude!"

"You do realize it's almost noon?" I slipped on my shoes and grabbed my coat, still in the borrowed hoodie and sweatpants since my maxidress wasn't my first choice of December work attire.

"Afternoon shift?" She yawned.

"Half shift, one to five." I set some aspirin out on the counter anyway, despite her protests. "See you later."

The door was almost closed behind me when I heard her grumble, "Who the hell wrote on my arm?"

I looked around outside for the Mustang I'd seen last night, half wondering if I had imagined it. But if it had been there, it was now gone, along with the strange women. I had to scrape a layer of ice off my windshield, but at least the sky was clear and I was soon on the road, headed for work.

The drive was peaceful, even with the weekend traffic slowing everything down. At a particularly long red light I looked up and watched my school lanyard swaying from the rearview mirror, taunting me as I drove to my low-paying job that had nothing to do with the four years I'd spent earning a history degree. That only brought my mind back around to last night, talking to Devin in a gallery setting. It wasn't my dream museum, but damn it felt really good to talk to another academic for a while. My love for Candace was far-reaching, but I couldn't make her fawn over an old census book any more than she could get me to be enthusiastic about our New York Fashion Week sleepovers.

And Candie's bicep didn't strain under her coat sleeve.

Beeping behind me snapped my eyes to the now-green light, and I hit the gas pedal.

Pulling into the parking lot of the car wash, I turned off the engine and laid my head back against the seat. It was an automatic wash, so at least I wasn't getting messy—just taking care of the cash register and letting the guys at the other end do the detailing. Eventually, resigning myself to the next few hours in a booth, I slid out of my van.

"Sweatpants today, Floor Sign?" A redhead with a short beard and coveralls slid over my hood, leaning in a pretend-sexy pose. I laughed and headed toward the office.

"I told you I own more than leggings, Alan. And when are you going to stop calling me that?" I opened the door and the girl on shift before me practically ran past us, barely waving good-bye.

"Have a nice day, Beth," I mumbled, walking inside.

"I'll stop calling you that when you stop doing this." Alan dramatically performed his interpretation of the stick figure on the *Caution: Wet Floor* sign.

"It's called *yoga*, and it's good for you." I put on my company jacket and clocked in on the ancient computer.

"Sure, it is, Floor Sign." He winked. "How was the fancy party?"

Sinking into my chair and kicking it around in one slow circle, I said, "The crowded party was not for me. But, oh my *god*, I wish I could eat like that every day. The food was out of this world, they had this cheese pastry thing that was still warm and had toppings pressed into them, and these little cherry tarts that melted in my mouth in one bite."

"If it's food you want, I can help with that." He leaned against the doorway. "My cousin is pouring drinks for this new place out east of here. They're having a friends-and-family practice night before they open in a couple of weeks. If you aren't doing anything the Wednesday after next—"

"I don't know," I said. "I usually go to yoga if I have Wednesdays off."

"You can't miss one day? Aren't you, like, an expert in posing for floor signs by now?"

My lips parted in shock as a car pulled into one of the self-serve vacuums and a man stepped out with curling horns on his head. "What is he wearing?"

"What?" Alan asked, following my line of sight. "Who?"

Blinking, I watched the guy put coins in the vacuum as it started up, and when he turned to his car the horns were gone.

"You okay?" Alan asked.

Shaking off the trick of the light, I faced Alan again. "All good, just tired I think. So, the restaurant, I'll go. Text me the address."

"Sounds good." He winked and trotted through to the detailing station. Letting out a sigh that ended in a laugh, I closed the door and straightened up the register area.

We were unusually busy that afternoon—December was typically one of the slowest months for a car wash. Not only were we slammed with customers but my eyes kept playing tricks on me. Things were fuzzy. Aspirin didn't help, and neither did washing the window of the booth inside and out. Something about the angle of the sun was just messing with my brain or something, because I kept seeing blurs and flashes of colors. Horn guy wasn't the last I saw of the bizarre costume accessories either. Flashes of Dubois and his more eccentric paintings came to mind every time I thought I saw glowing eyes or pointy teeth, and I was already trying not to get a headache from whatever was going on with my eyes. I was beyond ready to leave when Katie came for the evening shift; I barely offered her a tired wave before clocking out.

"What's with everyone today?" I grumbled as I got in my van, willing the engine to warm up when the sun had already disappeared an hour ago, "Jingle Bell Rock" blaring through the speakers while I waited. At the sound of scraping I looked up to see Alan clearing the ice from my windshield with exaggerated strokes and a stoic expression plastered on his face. Finished, he patted the hood and stood back, saluting. At least he was able to break my mood.

"Bye, you weirdo!" I called through a small crack in the window.

"Farewell, Floor Sign!"

The ride home was as weird as everything else that day. Twice I saw people with extra parts, one with horns and one with wings. Both times I swerved to avoid them, but when I did a double take they were gone, earning me more confusion and a few honked horns at my driving. They simply looked at me and laughed as I passed as if I was the one making a scene and not them. By the time I pulled into the parking lot at my apartment complex

I was exhausted—too exhausted to make dinner. I waded through the slush to the café next door and mentally apologized to my budget for eating out again, but it was already after five and I was hungry.

"Howdy, Thea," a chipper girl with freckles called from behind the counter.

"Hi, Melanie. No Heather today?" I glanced around, searching for the tall, dark, laid-back woman who owned the café, but she was nowhere in sight. Instead, I walked up to the counter and inspected the menu. Not that I needed to—we both knew I was going to get tea and soup.

"She's in the back, did you need her?" Melanie wiped her hands on a towel and propped her elbows on the counter in front of me. "Or can I get you some tea?"

"No, I'm just curious. I'll take a black tea today, please. I'm just zapped from—" The sound of a dish smashing caused both our heads to whip toward the kitchen.

"Heather! Oh my god, are you all right?" Melanie rushed over to a broken pair of mugs at Heather's feet. Her apron was splattered with coffee, but her concern seemed to be on me. Heather crouched down to help pick up the broken pieces.

"I got it, Mel. I thought I saw a bug." Heather swept her long black hair over her shoulder, shooing Melanie away with her other hand.

"Ew! Where is it?" The waitress squealed, hopping to her feet and backing away.

"No, it was . . . something else." Heather's voice wasn't quite even.

"Do you need a hand?" I leaned over the counter for a better look, and when Heather looked up, I could have sworn there was a bright, unnatural gold in her eyes, and I balked in surprise. She quickly ducked her head down again. Was there a costume convention going on or something that I missed? Maybe it was the lighting messing with me.

"Don't worry about it, guys. Just a pair of mugs, we have more in the back." Heather stood with the broken pieces cupped in her apron. She started back toward the kitchen.

"Hey, Heather. Did you do something different with your contacts?" I asked, the strange color appearing again before blurring out.

"Contacts?" Heather paused in the doorway and raised a hand to the corner of her eye. "Yes, I'm . . . trying out colored ones."

"Ooh, can I see?" Melanie asked, moving in close.

"Maybe later, Mel. Can you get the broom?" Heather avoided Melanie and went in the back to dump the broken mugs. When she came back out, she was looking at the floor, watching her employee finish sweeping up ceramic bits. "What can I get you, Thea?"

Weird.

"Just a black tea for now, please," I said.

"Right, coming up." She put everything together on a tray and started steeping the tea bag for me before sliding it all to my side of the counter.

"So, what's new with you lately? Do anything interesting this week? Last night?" Heather's full interest was on me now as she waited for an answer.

"Are you okay?" I asked.

"Fine, fine. Anything new?" She perked up.

"Not really. I'm going with a coworker to some new restaurant next week." I scratched my chin. "I went to a party last night. Candie got a pair of tickets to a charity event at L'Atelier Rouge and wanted me to go with her."

"L'Atelier Rouge?" Heather's face fell.

"Yeah. Heather, are you sure you're okay? You look a little pale."

"Never better." She pulled off her apron and tossed it behind the counter. "Hey, Mel, take over. I have that dentist appointment tonight."

"You're going to the dentist?" Melanie put the broom away and returned to the counter. "After business hours?"

"I'll be back later."

The sudden movement of Heather sweeping her jacket off a hook behind the counter and sliding her arms through it in one fluid motion startled me. She disappeared through the back door with barely a wave.

"That was . . ." Melanie stared at the door. I nodded in agreement with Melanie as I took another sip of my tea, the two of us staring at the door where Heather had rushed away.

"I think I'll have tomato soup."

"Sure, one sec," she said, and turned back to the counter. Today was just getting weirder and weirder.

CHAPTER FOUR

THEA

Finishing my soup and hurrying to beat the light snow, I crossed the parking lot to my building. Inside my apartment, I kicked off my shoes and changed into pajamas, dropping Candie's sweats and hoodie into the laundry so I could return them clean. On that note, I sent her a text.

> I borrowed some clothes but I'm washing them now. How's the hangover?

With the fluffy snow outside I threw back my living room curtains and sank onto the couch with my laptop. I spent some time job hunting, like I usually did after work. Which led to feeling stressed, which led to being hungry, which ended with me grabbing some cereal and streaming videos.

A glance outside told me the snow had stopped a while ago and the city's lights sparkled with the season—Christmas lights twinkled, menorahs were lit for their last days, and wreaths hung from doorways and inside shop windows. And in the parking lot of my building someone very large stood with an eerie stillness.

They were the biggest person I had ever seen and were standing mostly in shadow. Some kind of fog obscured the details, or maybe it was my blurry vision again. Within the depths of the enormous silhouette I saw a pair of red eyes. *Glowing.* Of all the strange things that had happened today, this was the most off.

I yanked my curtains closed as goose bumps crawled down my arms. I bit the inside of my cheek and scolded myself for being such a baby. I'd been living away from home for years, I wasn't going to suddenly throw my reason out the window now.

Still, it was better to be safe than sorry. Going to the closet, I pulled out a bent piece of iron pipe that my brother brought me from a job site when I first moved to the city. I remember laughing at him when he'd handed it to me, telling me to keep it by my front door. But now setting it on the couch next to me, I felt mildly better. Opening the curtains again, I saw the figure was gone. My brows knit together as an odd phrase from the night before came to mind:

Near the end of his life, he claimed to see things in the forest. Fairy tales come to life.

It had been quite a day; this was what I got for stuffing my face and staying up all night. Still, I'd had a good time. A playful smile crossed my mind and suddenly my thoughts were completely on L'Atelier Rouge.

Flipping my laptop open, I searched for articles about the painter, Dubois. But all that came up were routine pieces about the opening of the gallery, some student papers about a couple of his early paintings, and an awards page—L'Atelier Rouge had won some prestigious art standards.

"That's it? Nothing about his condition?"

No biography, no records, not even most of his works. You would think a painter would have a few articles at least speculating on his mental health or physical ailments. But my researcher's curiosity was getting the better of me. It seemed impossible that there was nothing on a known figure from the area's history. It was doubtful that my new vision problems were the same as his, but whatever it was that had convinced Dubois he was seeing fairy tale creatures was sure to be fascinating. If I really wanted to sate my curiosity, I would have to go back to the gallery. Devin did say he would be interested in this kind of collaboration.

And I was doing this as a project, not just to see Devin again. It wasn't just an excuse. Okay, it might be an excuse. Or both. It could be both. *Fine.* I wanted to go talk to the charming gallery owner again; after all, he did say if I had questions about Dubois that I could ask him.

A twitch had me rubbing the heel of my hand at the corner of my eye, trying to relieve the irritation. They were tired and sore from rubbing them all day. Whatever had irritated them was wearing me thin.

Next up: searching for optometrists in my area. Settling on one that let me schedule online, I double-checked my work calendar and booked the appointment. This blur thing was not going to fly, not when I was only in my twenties.

Lying back on the couch, I glanced at my open tabs and my mind drifted back to Dubois. What did he think he was seeing? I began a new search and focused on the stranger things he'd painted.

Fangs

Supernatural fangs

Pointy ears

Wings

The results gave a rather expansive list, which I should have guessed. I'd filled my head with enough fantasy books to last a lifetime when the most interesting thing to do in my hometown was to go to the library. But the last article I clicked on checked all the fantastical boxes and could describe what Dubois thought he was seeing. Closing my laptop, I let out a halfhearted laugh.

"Yeah, right. Faeries."

CHAPTER FIVE

DEVIN

Sometimes I regretted having a damn doorbell. You would think being a lord of one of the four fae courts I could command those under me to leave me alone, but there was always something that needed my attention. An endless stream of responsibility.

It had been a long weekend—dealing with humans, arguing with the other court leaders over petty squabbles, beginning the changeling's transformation, though that had been quite a pleasant surprise this year. And now, just when I had gotten home . . .

Whoever was outside had better have something important to say or I would be filleting a faerie. Passing by the hallway mirror, I checked my appearance—my glamour was firmly in place. As usual, I looked impeccably human as the doorbell rang again.

"I'm coming." I continued down the hall and yanked open the door to see one of my Winter Court fae standing there with a chip on her shoulder. "What?"

"I—were you asleep?" Heather's expression had gone from visibly upset to surprised.

"I was trying to, seeing as I hadn't slept since before the party. What is it?"

"Pick a different one," Heather snapped, the previous upset was on her face once more. She flipped her long black hair over her shoulder and stood straight, nearly matching my height with her shoulders squared and her fury on full display.

"Pick a different what?" I crossed my arms and leaned against the frame. "You have one minute to get to the point."

"A different changeling," she said.

"That's not possible, the change has been initiated."

"She's one of my best customers, and she's my *friend*. She absolutely does not deserve this." Heather shook her head. "She shouldn't even have been a candidate! Pick a different one."

"You know it doesn't work that way. Good-bye, Heather." I tried to close the door, but she stuck her arm inside at the last second.

Her hands became claws. "Your glamour is slipping," I said.

"There has to be another way," she demanded.

"You know there isn't. Don't be stupid; it isn't becoming of our kind."

"At least tell me why." Her voice cracked.

An ache was already starting in my temples. There would always be a soft spot for Heather as one of my more unfortunate changelings. "Come inside."

We entered the sitting room, where I sank into one of the matching black sofas, tossing a lazy gesture for Heather to take the opposite one if she wished to sit. "What's this really about, Heather? Is her situation bringing back bad memories for you?"

The anxious fae remained standing, fidgeting with the zipper on her jacket. "No, it's not that. Thea shouldn't even be a candidate in the first place, who nominated her?"

"Lady Georgina's Summer-Court-pain-in-my-ass found this one. When I agreed to turn the yearly changeling, she was the one who insisted we take turns locating candidates." Recalling the report, I ticked the list off on my fingers. "No family, almost no friends, no strong connections to humanity that can't easily be erased. And compatible traits with the Summer Court. Reckless, impulsive, emotional. They haven't had one in a while, so the changeling was accepted."

"That's not Thea at all." She narrowed her eyes. "Wait. Was Thea the only human there?"

"Of course, she . . ." I said, remembering the obnoxious one who interrupted us. "No."

"Who else?" Heather demanded, and I turned a stony expression her way, ice creeping across the floor from my feet even as the air took on a biting cold. The overhead light flickered.

"You will contain yourself before the Lord of the Winter Court."

Heather closed her eyes, reining in her outburst. "You're right, I'm upset."

"I know," I offered more gently. "Let me think about last night."

The icy hold in my sitting room dissipated. Thea had been all I could see last night. Her affinity was palpable, there was no denying she would have a strong change. But Heather was correct in that there had been another human there.

"A petite blond was with her. She had some affinity as well, I suppose." Though not nearly as strong.

"Short? Tan? Probably a pink manicure?" Heather clenched her fists.

"Yes, yes, and I don't know," I grumbled.

"Candace," she hissed, standing up. "You got the wrong girl!"

"Stand down," I growled, a dangerous glint taking over my expression. Heather flinched.

Heather fell back into the couch, her palms landing on her knees and her knuckles white. "Thea . . ." she whispered.

I felt a small ripple of guilt at Heather's pain, but there wasn't anything I could do about it now. Due to the emotionally volatile nature of the fae, it often felt like half my job was keeping them in check before someone lost control and made a mess that I had to clean up or worse— broke the delicate glamour that shielded us from the humans. That would be a real pain to sort out.

27

"If it was a mistake, I will look into it," I said.

She wiped her eyes with her sleeve. "What if her body rejects the change?"

"It won't."

"How do you know?" she asked.

"Because I *sensed* her. From *outside* the building. It was overpowering—I barely noticed it on the other girl." I ran my fingers through my hair. "She's a strong candidate, as far as that's concerned."

Heather shot me a determined look. "Give me permission to tell her about the fae."

"No. She may not have been our intended target but the responsibility to nudge them into our world still falls to me. We won't tell her immediately; that will end poorly."

"If she dies because of this . . ." The muscles in her jaw tightened then relaxed as Heather got off the sofa and strode to the door. She looked at me over her shoulder, as though she had more to say but, instead, she bowed her head sharply as she shut the door behind her. I could hear her motorcycle rev to life a moment later as she sped away.

A decanter of bourbon on the mantel began to look like a tempting dinner. I ignored it and waved away the frost creeping across the room's surfaces. I put on a pot of coffee before sitting down at my desk, opening my computer, and flicking through my emails until I came across Georgina's last message. *Dammit.* Thea was indeed the wrong human.

My brow creased as I skimmed the report—this Candace Lewis was exactly our usual candidate. Her connection to the human world was weak, her one friendship with Thea being the last string that she would miss were she to be changed. Unfortunately, Candace wasn't the one who'd stood out last night. And hell, did Thea stand out. I'd felt her potential before she'd even parked her van. She exhibited open fascination with Marcel's paintings, and the way she relished every bite on her plate made me remember a time when things could still be new and fascinating. And this wasn't even faerie food—I wondered what expression she would make if *that* crossed her lips. She breathed life and pleasure with her every movement. Liveliness—was that the nature of a fae from the Summer Court, or was that simply Thea?

I sat back in my chair and frowned. This was a problem. We had nothing on this Thea; she hadn't even offered up her last name. We would have to do this the old-fashioned way. I got up and wandered back to the kitchen to see if the coffee was ready, absently swiping through my call history until I landed on Arthur, my right hand in the running of the Winter Court. He answered immediately.

"What's up, boss?"

"I need you to look into something." I walked upstairs and into my closet, sifting through my dress shirts.

"Sure, what do you need?"

"I want a full background on the changeling." I pulled out a shirt and started matching ties.

"Didn't Georgina give you that? Or do you need something more specific?"

"Ignore Georgina's candidate. We found a natural changeling last night and I need to know what I'm dealing with. Check the gallery's footage for a Thea. I expect the report on my desk by morning."

A pause at the other end. "Of course, Lord Devin."

I tossed my phone on the bed and finished dressing. The solstice was coming, and regardless of who the courts had voted on to become the next changeling, Thea would be the one to change this time. If this girl was as strong as I thought she was, I would need to prepare. We all would, because a natural changeling could become anything, and our courts would have to adjust.

CHAPTER SIX

THEA

My van rolled into the parking lot, making tracks in the fresh morning snow. The gallery had been open for half an hour but there were still only a few cars in the lot. With any luck, Devin would be available to talk.

With one last glance at the university lanyard hanging from my mirror, I grabbed my bag and got out. I smoothed down my long sweater and walked up the front steps. It was no backless designer dress this time, but I wasn't here to impress Devin; I was here for academic reasons. Purely professional. Really.

A woman just inside the doors greeted me as I approached. Her name tag read *Stacia*.

"Hello, Stacia, my name is Thea Kanelos." Shit. What was Devin's last name? Did he tell me? I cleared my throat and powered through. "I met Devin at the party a couple nights ago and was wondering if he's available? He told me I could find him here during business hours."

"He's in the office today, let me find out for you. I'll be right back." She walked over to a small open room that seemed to serve as a gift shop and information desk all in one. Slipping behind the counter, she picked up the phone and made a call.

While she called Devin I stepped back and took in my surroundings. Maybe it was the music or the decorations or the company but two nights ago it felt so much more enchanting. Today, with the bright light of day streaming through the windows, it held excitement and possibility. Something I was equally as enthralled with.

"Mr. Grayson will be down in just a minute." Stacia was already walking back toward me and she gestured to a staircase that was roped off around the corner behind the gift shop room.

"Thank you." I couldn't hold back my smile as I walked over and stood near the stairs. As I rounded the corner, Devin was coming down. My breath caught in my throat—I had to swallow to get it to work correctly again.

"Hello, Thea," he greeted me with pleasant surprise. "What brings you back to the gallery?"

"Is this a good time? I was hoping to ask you a few questions about Marcel Dubois."

His eyes glinted in amusement. "Piqued your interest, did I?"

"You did," I said. "Would you have a moment to talk?"

Devin checked his watch. I admired how he dressed just as sharply today as he had at the party. "My schedule is clear for the next half hour, and if we run out of time, would you care to arrange another meeting? Maybe over lunch?"

"That sounds great. I mean, for my research, of course."

He raised one eyebrow. "Research?"

"I became invested in Dubois after our conversation, and I was hoping you maybe knew some more about him or knew of resources I could turn to." Heat crept up my neck and across my face as I realized how weak that excuse sounded once I said it out loud. "And you had mentioned the gallery's history and I thought you might have something of interest. Academically."

A grin spread across his face. "I've always had respect for those who dedicate themselves to preserving the stories of humanity. Speaking of which, do you have a specific area of interest?"

My face lit up. Almost no one wanted to hear me go on about the subject. "Westward expansion. Everything that happened between here and the Mississippi—another reason Dubois has stuck with me, I guess. Do you know if he arrived before or after the Denny Party? I know he was a very early settler to the area, but strangely enough I can't find much on him apart from his paintings."

"You know, I can't recall. There is something in my office that might help you though. Come with me." Devin offered me his hand. I didn't know what to do, but thankfully he did, lightly holding my hand as he escorted me upstairs to his spacious office.

What an old-fashioned move, I marveled. Not that I minded.

Once we were through the doorway, I got a better look at how Devin operated. If he was the one who decorated this place, which I had a sneaking suspicion he was, he was a man of taste. It was all aged leather and solid wood furniture, but with large windows and glass side tables to break up the heavy pieces. He had quite the collection of books on shelves that lined two walls, and a few personal pieces of art hanging behind his desk.

He went over to a barrister's cabinet and, taking a key from his desk, unlocked the top glass and pulled out a faded leather journal. "This was Marcel's diary. Not many take an interest in him beyond his art; you're the only other person to touch it in some years."

Devin held out the book, and I took it from him and delicately started flipping through the yellowed pages, turning to get better lighting. "Is this the only copy?"

"No, I had a few copies made a while back. Paper this old won't last forever, though you would know that more than most. Here, let me give you one." Devin went back to the cabinet and shuffled through some other books.

"I can't accept something like that. Could I at least pay for the printing?" I asked.

"Nonsense. In fact, if you come up with anything interesting, I'd love to work with you to add some history to the exhibit downstairs." He returned with a much newer print of the diary, and I handed him back the original.

"That sounds like an amazing project for the gallery." I flipped it open and saw Dubois's photocopied handwriting. It would probably do me and any future readers a lot of good if I typed this up instead.

"That's the hope," he chuckled.

While we spoke, I flipped through the pages, occasionally passing sketches of more fairy tale creatures. "He really did have hallucinations, didn't he?"

"Marcel?" Devin asked, looking over my shoulder. "That depends entirely on your perspective."

I landed on a page depicting a winged being with pointed ears in a flower field and held it up for Devin. "You almost sound like you believe in the faeries too," I teased.

He laughed, so close to me that the rumble from his chest was almost tangible. My heartbeat jumped up to the level of light aerobics while I tried to clear my head.

"Maybe I do." His warm breath tickled my ear. "I believe Marcel truly saw all of the things he painted."

"I admire your imagination, but I'm going to be a little tougher to convince."

"Should I take that as a challenge? I happen to have a hobby of convincing lovely historians to believe in fairy tales."

Whatever answer I may have come up with fell away from my thoughts. His closeness, at the party and again in his office, was endlessly distracting.

"Next weekend then? Lunch?" he mused, pulling a business card from his jacket pocket. "There are a few questions I'd like to ask you as well, regarding the gala."

"Okay." I tucked the card inside the book.

Devin checked his watch. "Regretfully, I do have another appointment, but I'd love to continue this line of inquiry. Promise you'll text me?"

"Promise." The word left my lips, and a sudden chill came over me. I shuddered and pulled my arms tight, wrapping them around myself.

Devin's sharp eyes gleamed in amusement. "Something wrong?"

The feeling passed and I let my arms drop. "Just a chill."

"Yes, that does happen in these big, spacious buildings. The winter solstice is almost upon us, after all."

I walked out of Devin's office with the book tucked safely in my bag. I savored the encounter—it wasn't every day someone wanted to talk history with me, especially not someone who looked like Devin. Waving good-bye to Stacia on my way out, I stepped back out into the cold, December day. My face fell when I reached my van. Someone was leaning against the driver's side door dressed in some kind of costume—blue hair with a feathered jacket.

"Hey!" I called, hurrying over. But when I rounded my van all I got was an eyeful of blurred vision and the beginnings of a mild headache. I couldn't find signs of anyone having been there, and there were no foot-prints in the fresh snow apart from mine. I climbed inside and locked the doors, then tested my eyesight on several different objects around me. No hazy vision. Nothing.

No one in the parking lot but me.

CHAPTER SEVEN

THEA

The snow had mostly melted save for little pockets next to buildings and under cars where the sun didn't reach. The unfortunate design of my apartment building meant there was still a lot of slush to walk through as I made my way to Heather's Café. Before leaving the parking lot, a sudden haze at the edge of my vision startled me. Next to a nearby bus stop I saw a pair of strange people making out. Then they were gone. I could have sworn one was wearing horns and the other prosthetic ears. Pointy ones. They'd both dressed like it was the peak of summer and not December.

I shook my head and walked on. *Nope.* Not going to question it today. There must be a cosplay convention nearby or something. It was just weird to keep seeing costumes while researching Dubois. What was more disturbing was how I was getting used to seeing these things now, and that bothered me. I tucked my hands inside the sleeves of my sweater until I'd safely reached the door to the café. The little bell overhead announced my arrival.

"Hey," Melanie called from behind the counter. "Black or green?"

"Green, please." I walked over to the back-corner booth. I set up my laptop and flipped the diary open to where I'd left off. I quickly fell into a rhythm and didn't notice Melanie until she set the mug in front of me with a clink.

"Big project?" she asked. "Wait, you graduated. Are you going back for round two?"

"Oof, no. I couldn't afford that, my savings are dwindling as is. No, I'm working on some research on a painter. For fun, mostly, although the owner of L'Atelier Rouge may use it to enhance the exhibit. Have you heard of it?"

"Nope." Melanie leaned over enough to get a good look at the page I was working on. "But it sounds cool. Is that an elf?"

The sketch was of a long-eared beauty lounging on a tree branch. "Dubois had hallucinations. He would see faeries and things, and they made it into a lot of his paintings. The diary is really telling so far."

"Let me know when you're all done, I'd love to check it out. Soups of the day are tomato and clam chowder—can I get you anything?"

"Tomato and a grilled cheese, please."

"Sure thing." Melanie walked off and I went back to the slow work of deciphering Marcel's handwriting. I had just started to type when Heather slid into the booth across from me. She sighed loudly, still wearing her leather jacket and sunglasses.

"Hey," I said. "Busy day?"

"You have no idea," she said. "I heard you talking about Marcel Dubois, what's the project?"

I slid the diary to Heather, and then pulled my tea close, adding sugar and milk. "You know about Marcel Dubois?"

"Somewhat." Heather tilted her head, studying the diary. "Can I flip through it?"

"Sure, that business card is my bookmark so don't lose that."

Heather flipped the page. "You met the gallery owner?"

I took a long sip of my tea before answering. "I did."

"And did he tell you anything? Any interesting or wild stories?"

"No, we just talked about Dubois mostly."

Heather paused on a page with a large sketch more detailed than many others in the book—which was saying something as Dubois was meticulous. I leaned forward to get a closer look, but she closed the diary and slid it back to me.

Heather drummed her fingers on the table. "Thea . . ."

Melanie came up to us then and placed a plate in front of me with a steaming bowl of soup and an oozing grilled cheese sandwich. "Anything else, hun?"

"No, thanks."

Melanie beamed and turned away to help another customer.

Melanie left, and Heather ran nervous fingers through her hair as she turned back to me. I'd never seen her so anxious before. "You should know more about the fae if you want to know how Marcel's mind worked. You should get answers from Devin."

Startled, I sat up in my seat. "You know Devin?"

"Yeah, and you should listen to him before you get into this too deep." Heather's face changed, even under her sunglasses. "Please, Thea. Promise me you'll talk to him."

"I will," I said, unsettled.

"Good." Heather nodded, then slid out of the booth and walked away behind the counter.

I looked down and flipped through the diary in search of the detailed sketch that Heather had landed on before. When it didn't come up right away, I returned to the page I was working on. I'd get to it eventually anyway. Taking a big bite of grilled cheese, I returned to Dubois's words:

The faeries, be them in good humor or otherwise of a dubious nature, seem to be comfortable intermingling with the human people of the town. Should one fail to be wary of their surroundings, I fear it an easy fate to fall into the whims of the fae folk.

CHAPTER EIGHT

THEA

I slid into a familiar wooden chair, plopped down my armful of books, and opened my planner. Yesterday at Heather's café I got a lot of the diary typed up, but today I wanted to learn. Thank goodness my school let alumni continue to use some of the library facilities. If I couldn't afford rent, I sure as hell couldn't afford all the books on faeries I wanted. And being surrounded by the filled wooden shelves and the dinged-up study tables was a strange kind of comfort.

Grabbing my phone, I sent Candace a text since she still hadn't replied to my last one. It wasn't unusual to miss a few days of texting when either of us was busy, but I wanted to return her clothes and catch up.

Busy week?

She didn't respond, but I didn't expect her to, either, it was the middle of a weekday. Maybe my text would remind her she hadn't responded to the last one. Dropping my phone in my bag, I shifted my attention to the tasks ahead. Worrying wasn't going to help; I could always follow up with her later if she was busy. Besides, I had a task in front of me, and that was a kind of comfort too.

Scanning my planner for the week ahead, I scratched out today's reminder for my eye appointment. They couldn't find anything wrong with me and recommended a therapist instead of an optometrist. With a huff I flipped to the notes section and started scratching off the books I'd found from the list I'd put together the night before, then set to work reading.

Faeries, as it turned out, were fascinating. Once I'd started reading, I couldn't stop. Or maybe that was the researcher in me—it was difficult for me to put down material on a new subject until I had at least a grasp of the broader concepts. And the more I dove into the mythology of faeries—or fae, as Dubois called the beings in his paintings—the more connections I found in the artist's work.

Dubois had good reason to fear them. Fae were dangerous. Not like the cartoons and coloring book versions I'd seen as a child. They weren't tiny; they didn't fly around on little butterfly wings and do good deeds. They were bad news. The stealing-babies-and-torturing-people sort of bad news.

And they had so many rules. Rules about lying, rules about favors, rules about etiquette. There were different rules according to different books, but there was quite a bit of overlap too. The most important things I could find were about being in debt to a fae and how dangerous that could be. Even something as little as a "thank-you" could land you in hot water. That debt was magically binding, and you could be asked to do anything to repay it—from giving up your most prized possession to murder. The fae were especially careful not to owe one another a debt; their powers could make things messy very quickly. If I were hallucinating a bunch of fae in the trees around my house, I'd be freaking out too. Hell, I'm freaked out now with all the costumes in town.

When afternoon light filtered through the big window, I pulled the diary out of my bag and opened it to a specific passage to reference. The business card fell out. I picked it up, flipped it over, and read it for the hundredth time. The raised, shiny black letters of Devin's name, his phone number beneath.

Devin. Handsome, charming, witty, and with an appreciation for history. Lunch. I should schedule that lunch. Even Heather had told me to learn from him if I wanted to dive into more of this Dubois work. I went to text him, ready and eager, and then froze. How to start.

Hey it's Thea

Delete. Too casual.

Hello, Devin. This is Thea Kanelos. We talked about Dubois and you lent me a copy of his diary.

Delete, delete, delete. *He's not an idiot, Thea. It's only been a couple of days, give him some credit.*

Hello, this is Thea. How about lunch the day after tomorrow?

I put my phone face down on the table and tried to concentrate on the books I'd gathered. It vibrated a moment later and I snatched it up like the last roll at Christmas dinner.

Thursday is perfect. Meet me at the gallery and think about what you'd like to eat. I'm paying. One of the benefits of owning a business is being able to write off any meal as a business expense.

A laugh bubbled up as I read his text. I had to choke it down when a few studious heads turned my way. *Sorry,* I mouthed to the girl studying at the next table as I packed up. My concentration was shot anyway, so there was no point in sticking around. Double-checking that I had all my notes, I deposited the books on the librarian's cart and slipped out into the slushy parking lot.

Paying more attention to my feet than my surroundings, I slipped on an unfortunate piece of ice and slid right into a streetlight, a feat I was wholly clumsy enough to accomplish in the middle of an empty parking lot.

"Ouch!" I grabbed the pole for stability and hefted my bag back over my shoulder, only to jump at a sudden burst of cackling. My back stiffened. I looked . . . up.

Perched atop the pole was a naked woman painted lavender and wearing what appeared to be a large set of dragonfly wings. She laughed until she cried. An inelegant noise came from my throat as I fell backward and landed on my butt, clutching my bag.

"Oh, honey, you have so much farther to go, don't you?" The woman winked at me, then stood to her full height and jumped off the pole.

"Wait!" I scrambled to my feet to, I don't know, catch her? To be beside her as she died from impact? But she stretched out her wings and flew away without touching the ground, still laughing at my fall. Somehow, she was real. And she was *flying*.

Pulling my phone out I tried to take a picture. This was my chance to capture a piece of the bizarre scenes that had been plaguing me for days, but my hands were shaking so hard that all I got was a few shots of one leg before the woman disappeared into a blur of gray sky. My heart hammered in my chest while I stared at the empty air where she had disappeared. I pulled myself up with the pole while I looked around frantically for more blurring. A fog, a haze—anything to tell me I hadn't just interacted with someone who had actually disappeared.

I wiped water drops off my phone's screen with my sweater and looked at the picture I'd taken. No matter how hard I looked or zoomed in, the woman's foot was no longer lavender but a light brown. No, that couldn't be right. She had definitely been lavender.

My anxiety overflowed and I laughed nervously. I couldn't stop until I reached my van and got inside. The contents of my bag nearly spilled out when I tossed them onto the passenger seat. I swiped through the photos again, taken in rapid succession. Still nothing, just three pictures of the same naked foot.

Not a hint of lavender in sight.

CHAPTER NINE

THEA

My poor nails were chewed down impressively in the hour since I had left the library. Now I was sitting in the work parking lot having a panic attack. I stared at them while seated in my van, waiting for Mom to pick up the phone.

"Hey, sweetie," she said a moment later.

"Hey, Mom."

"What's up, is everything okay? You sound like you used to around finals," she teased.

My planner was in front of me, propped against the steering wheel. "Just doing a quick medical check for a thing. Does our family have any history of epilepsy?"

"Epilepsy? No. What's this for?"

"I'm thinking about switching to a new doctor's office and I need my history. What about Parkinson's, is that what GiGi had?"

"No, she had dementia."

"Anyone with a history of, say, schizophrenia?"

"What's going on, are you all right?" Concern had crept into her voice.

"I'm not trying to scare you," I said. "These are all just hypotheticals. You know me, always prepared."

She let out a singsong sigh. "Don't scare me like that; that's what your brother's for."

Fair enough. George's pranks got him into more than enough trouble as a kid. Mom still blames all her gray hairs on him, but I'm just glad his antics settled down once he got married and had kids. Though, he does still tease me every chance he gets.

"Hey, what time do I need to be there for Christmas?" I asked, changing the subject and scratching off those three suspects on my list of reasons a person might hallucinate. "We're doing it on the Saturday, right? I forget when George and Marsha are leaving."

"Small dinner at about five on Saturday, then the big meal for lunch Sunday. George, Marsha, and the kids are leaving Sunday night to get to her parents' house before Christmas Day. Oh, and Dad didn't listen when he went out to get it and he bought a bird twice the size I need, so I hope you're able to take some leftovers home."

"Always."

"Good. Oh!" A beeping in the background—the kitchen timer was going off. "Can I put you down? I need both hands for these pies."

"I'll let you go, Mom. See you then."

"Love you, talk to you later!" And she ended the call.

Looking at my list, there remained brain tumor, infection, or delirium, but some, like drugs or Alzheimer's, were easy to eliminate. Unless it was early-onset Alzheimer's. *Crap.*

Acute stress. That made the most sense—I had latched onto this Dubois project so hard I was now hallucinating faeries. Maybe completing the project would help. I nearly jumped out of my seat when a car horn blared right next to me.

Alan's beat-up Chevy, which was older than me, pulled up beside me at the car wash. Inside, he shifted around, trying to pull on his coat before opening his door. He finally got it on and came around the front of his truck.

"Sorry, Floor Sign. My elbow hit the horn."

"Christ, you scared me!" I shouted through the window, slouching back in my seat and finally releasing my breath.

"Sorry," Alan said again as I climbed out of my van. "Hey, everything okay? You look exhausted."

I'm sure I did. The bags under my eyes could take a family of four on vacation, which is where I wanted to be right now—not hallucinating about fae.

"It's fine, just tired." I shouldered my bag, closed my door, and started toward the booth.

"You sure?" He hurried to catch up, zipping his coat.

"Yeah, I just have a lot going on right now. Wait." I stopped suddenly and Alan nearly ran me over.

"Whoa!"

"Sorry," I mumbled, pulling out my phone and flipping through the pictures. "Hey, can you tell me what this looks like to you?"

I shoved my phone in his face. Alan moved back reflexively before taking my phone and staring at it. "Is that a foot?"

"That's it? Nothing weird about it? No colors?"

"Skin colored? It just looks like a foot to me. Why is it in the air? That's kind of a cool optical illusion." He handed the phone back. "You sure everything's okay?"

"Yeah, it's just a research thing. Thanks."

"Are we still on for next Wednesday?"

Wednesday? Oh.

"I think so. I mean, yes." An excuse to not be alone with my hallucinations? Yes please.

"Cool." He flashed a grin and started off toward his detailing station. "Let me know if I can do anything, seriously. You got friends, use 'em."

As I walked into the booth, the girl on shift before me was putting on her coat. We traded places and I settled into the chair to wait for the next customer. At a car wash. In December in the Pacific Northwest.

Pulling the diary from my bag, I started reading. My notes and questions were piling up. What I really needed at this point was someone to talk to about them. Dubois would write for days on end and then nothing for months, and the deeper into it I got, almost all of it was about the fae. I flipped through the pages, stopping on a drawing of a familiar face. Apart from the fangs and ears, I could have sworn it was a picture of Devin.

Was this his great-great-great-something grandfather? And what was with the fangs? I read the entry under the eerie drawing, wondering if Dubois was projecting his hallucinations onto people he knew. Which led me to wonder if I was doing similarly.

The fiend that had been courting my daughter for months appeared again. I only saw him from afar, but he saw me, and smiled. If only she had never tasted the faerie food she would never have fallen into this trap. Would I have never tasted the food, too, for I would still be in blissful ignorance of the wickedness around me. I fear that once you see them it will not fade with time. I miss you, my darling daughter. Please come back to me.

Odd. And if this was indeed a distant relative of Devin's, a family connection could explain his interest in preserving the Dubois exhibit. My head shot up, and I grabbed my planner. It flopped open to my bookmark, where I'd written down my lunch date with Devin in two days. Not a lunch date, a professional meeting. Either way, Devin had answers. And I know Heather told me to be careful, but she also told me to ask him about the fae. No matter what happened, I was willing to risk caution for some answers before it all drove me over the edge.

CHAPTER TEN

DEVIN

Impatience was not something a fae of several centuries experienced often, and yet, the thought of lunch with Thea brought out this rare feeling as the week crawled by. Today in particular there was plenty of busywork at the office, but I couldn't pass more than a few moments without staring at the time. Finally, I saw her van pull into the parking lot. I rushed out my office door and down the stairs to meet her just as she was opening the van door.

"Devin," she said warmly, tinged with something akin to relief. "It's nice to see you again."

"It is." I held her hand as she stepped out of the van. "Have you thought about where we should go?"

"Honestly, I'd do anything for a burger right now if you like that sort of thing."

"Perfect, I know just the place. I'll drive."

There was no missing the look on Thea's face when we reached my car in the parking lot. The polished black two seater with a luxury interior made quite the impression. But if she didn't want to say anything about the difference in our vehicles, I wasn't about to bring it up. If anything, I was eager to see how the fae could improve her quality of life. Where that rusted van was concerned, I was sure we could do far better for our newest changeling. Once she was settled, the drive to the restaurant was quiet but peaceful. I'd decided on the steakhouse I often used to persuade wealthy donors when I wanted to do something expensive in the gallery but didn't want to dip into my own pockets to do it. Thea seemed unfamiliar with the location, and something inside me was pleased that I was the one bringing her here.

Inside, we were seated quickly at a table with white linen and polished silverware. The tables were spread out and the light lunch crowd gave the dimly lit restaurant a more intimate appeal than I had anticipated, something her sharp eyes did not miss as a soft flush crept up her neck and across the bridge of her nose. After ordering our food, Thea pulled out a notebook and her copy of Marcel's diary, flipping it open.

"Has the diary been helpful?" I asked.

She looked up after marking a passage on the open page. "Yes, it's been wonderful. I actually want to talk about something I found in it."

Thea slid the book toward me. My face fell when I saw what she had encountered. A few decades had passed since I'd last read the thing, and she had found the one important drawing I had forgotten about. Even from across the table I could see I was looking back at myself, my glamour partially revealed.

"Is this a relative?" she asked.

I feigned curiosity, before sliding it back to her. "The drawing looks just like me, doesn't it?"

"It really does, and I was hoping to ask you a few questions. We have a shared friend who told me you would be able to answer them. Are you close with Heather?"

"I've known her for a long time. She told you I would have information?"

"Yes, about the fae."

Folding my hands together on the table, it was difficult to keep my expression neutral. "Ask away. There is not a question about the fae that I would not know."

She hesitated before asking her first question. "Do you really believe in them?"

"I do, and the things Marcel saw as he painted his life's work still walk here today."

Watching Thea closely, I saw goose bumps had formed on her arms. She tucked a lock of brown hair behind one ear, her heartbeat elevating slightly.

"Has anyone ever told you how strange that sounds?" she asked.

Leaning forward, I answered her softly. "Many times."

Many, many times have I had some version of this conversation. Another turning of the seasons, another changeling for the courts.

Her eyes darted to the notebook again. "All right, so if I wanted to learn about the fae, what would be something important to know for starters?"

"I take you for the studious type. Have you already begun your research?"

"Some."

"It might be easier if you ask me about a detail and I answer yes or no."

She pulled out a pen and checked the first item off a list she'd made. "They can't tell a lie?"

"Correct."

"They're evil? They steal people and hunt them for sport, that kind of thing?"

"Not so much anymore, but they can be as good or evil as any human. Simply . . . amplified."

She glanced up at me with her big brown eyes before drifting back to her list.

"They organize themselves into four groups following the seasons?"

"The courts, yes. Though, there are some unaligned to any court. Those are known as wild fae. Be cautious around them, they can sometimes grow corrupt, a twisted fae that has lost all reason and can be dangerous."

"Dubois wrote a little bit about that," she murmured with a frown. "Okay, do fae really live forever?"

"Unless they die of unnatural causes, their body will not age past what might look like a young adult to an adult in their prime."

She hovered over the sketch in Marcel's diary. It gave me pause.

Our food came then, interrupting us. Thea moved the diary to her bag and scooted the notebook to the edge of the table to make room.

"If you continue to study the fae, you might find yourself seeing them too." My words were calculated, prodding. Just how far along was our new changeling?

She froze, caught on my words as though I had unearthed some secret she had been struggling with. I felt a pang of guilt—I liked the curious Thea, the way she looked at something, touched something; the way she moved and laughed. I regretted my part in what she would experience in only a few days.

She picked her next words carefully. "Seeing them? Like, hallucinations?"

Oh dear. She was further along than I thought.

"Something like that," I answered, pausing to sip my drink. "By the way, I was thinking about creating an interactive exhibit with the greenhouse. It was Marcel's original studio, after all. It's been locked for years, but I've been considering allowing some access around it, especially if you've been finding things of interest we could share with our guests."

"The greenhouse? Oh!" She pulled a folder from her bag and slid it to me. "So far, I've got this much gathered on the dates and construction of it. I included a few other points of interest alongside the founding of Seattle for a comparative timeline. I was thinking that a visual of this with a few photographs could help. I have printed references but if you'd like I'm sure I can help find something else."

She was insightful, bringing up ideas for the gallery that I hadn't considered. Her knowledge of art was lacking, but her enthusiasm for the history behind it was bountiful as she showed me what she had worked on so far. And she was charming. The way she held her wrist when she ate, the way her eyes sparkled as she laughed. What kind of fae was she destined to become? Something warm and loving like her could fit in any of the courts. Something about that bothered me for reasons I couldn't pinpoint. Maybe I simply wanted to see her in my court for selfish reasons.

We were deep into our lunch before either of us noticed the time. With our plates cleared and the check paid, I walked Thea to the car. I opened her door and leaned in, speaking directly to her ear, taking in her scent.

"I'm having another party at the gallery, on the solstice. I would love it if you came."

She shivered deliciously. I had to pull myself away as she got in. I went around to the driver's side, giving her time to think.

"What kind of party?" she asked once I'd started the car. I looked over; she was flushed.

"Dancing, food. I think, if you come, you will find many valuable resources in your search for faeries."

She licked her lips. I watched her carefully, before returning to the road ahead.

"I'll be there."

CHAPTER ELEVEN

THEA

My mind kept wandering on the drive home after Devin and I had parted ways after lunch. I was really into Devin, I could admit that to myself, but the fae thing still bothered me. He was too clever to fall for hallucinations, but he seemed genuine when he spoke on the subject, and a part of me was scared and another part excited. And then there was Heather, who'd backed up his claims.

Then Candie.

Normally she would be the first to hear about one of my dates, or whatever pseudodate the lunch had been, but I still hadn't heard from her. A couple days was one thing, but it was starting to stretch into uncomfortable territory.

I fished my phone out at a red light and put it on speaker, clicking Candace's number.

"Hey, it's Candace Lewis, you know what to do." *BEEP.*

I left a message and ended the call as the light turned green. The whole situation was weird. Today was the day—I would figure it out.

It took me a minute to find the number for Candace's office.

"Georgina Beaumont's office, how may I direct your call?" The voice on the other end was pleasant and about as sincere as a week-late birthday card.

"Is Candace Lewis in today?" I asked.

The pause on the other end lasted long enough that I almost repeated myself. Then—

"Candace Lewis is no longer with the company."

Click.

What? I tried calling again but hit a busy signal. No, not a busy signal—they'd blocked my number!

"Dammit." I threw my phone to the seat next to me, my pulse quickening in my neck. Had she been fired? Is she too depressed to message me back? Ashamed? Writing for fashion was her dream job—I can't imagine how she would feel to lose it. Maybe she was in her apartment; I mean, where else would she be?

I pulled into a spot in front of her building, grabbed my bag with her clean clothes to return, and fished out my key to her place. Not many people were around, and I didn't see any faeries. Frowning, I tucked away the part where I had just admitted the hallucinations were fae and went inside the building.

The hairs on my neck stood up as I walked through the hallway, and it wasn't the winter air. Stopping at her door I knocked, maybe a little more urgently than I normally would have.

"Candie?"

No answer.

"Candie, I'm coming in." I unlocked her door and went inside, flipping on the lights before the keys in my hand clattered to the floor.

Her studio was completely empty. The bed, the wardrobe, the desk—gone. No leather purses on hooks by the door, no designer coats draped over the backs of bar stools. No bar stools, for that matter.

"What the hell?" I walked around, hoping to find any trace of her. A shampoo bottle in the bathroom, a box of cereal in the cabinets—anything. But there was no indicator that Candace Lewis had ever lived there.

She was gone.

I sat on the cold floor, staring blankly out the window. Several possibilities crossed my mind in terms of what might have happened, from having the place sprayed for bugs to repainting the walls, but none seemed to fit, because the Candace I knew would just move in with me for a few days.

Stress. It had to be acute stress I was experiencing. My best friend was ghosting me or something. I was going to have to face my family at Christmas and tell them I still wasn't doing anything with the expensive degree I got, and to top it all off I was crushing on a guy while my eyes were playing some nasty tricks on me.

I moved to stand up when the light caught something nearly invisible on her tile floor against the wall next to a bit of dust. Still half sitting, I stayed there frozen while I stared at it. Iridescent and translucent, something reflected the light in pink and yellow hues as the sun shifted over it. Slowly, I straightened up and walked toward the strange item. It was about as big as my shoe, and I picked up what looked like a torn-up piece of dragonfly wing.

With a shudder I dropped it and backed away. Too big. It was too big to be from an insect, and page after page of sketches from the diary flitted through my mind. Staring at it, my stomach turned over itself until I built up the guts to grab it again and put it in my bag.

Faeries. I was at a crossroads where I either had to look for help with what I was seeing or let go of the notion that I was hallucinating at all. I had seen them, talked to them, even tried to take a picture of them. But this, *this* was unexplainable, and I'd held it in my hands. And they had been in Candace's emptied apartment.

Devin. He knew about the fae. He kept saying it, and I knew he kept saying it, but I wouldn't listen. Pulling my phone out, I scrolled my contacts until my thumb hovered over his number.

The fiend that had been courting my daughter for months appeared again. I only saw him from afar, but he saw me, and smiled.

That sketch. Was it really of Devin's ancestor or . . .

Heather. Heather knew something about this whole ordeal.

Shoving the phone in my pocket, I made a run for the parking lot and started my van. Deep, slow breaths dragged through my lungs as I fought to stay calm. The drive was a stressful blur until I pulled into the café parking lot. I slammed the door behind me and took two steps toward the café before turning around and making a run for my apartment.

That pipe from George. I had kept it by the door every day since I'd seen the figure with the red eyes. With the fae running through my mind, all the warnings about their repulsion to the metal surfaced. I was glad to shove it in my bag. Turning right back around, I sprinted for the café.

"Hey there, welcome to—Thea, are you okay?" Melanie put down the menu she had just picked up. Heather's head whipped my way.

"Thea!" Heather scooted out from around the counter, setting down the latte in her hand. "Mel, take that to Table Five. Thea, come with me."

I followed Heather blindly as she pulled me into the small kitchen in the back. She spun me around and gently placed a hand on each arm while searching my face. "You can see them now, can't you?"

See them? See . . . oh.

My breath was short and sharp. "S-see what?"

Heather frowned, closing her eyes a moment before looking at me again with gentle sympathy. "Thea, you're seeing things that others can't. Faeries."

My heart nearly stopped. I choked out a sob while tears clouded my vision.

I'm not alone.

"Shit. Come here." Heather wrapped me in a hug.

Moving my hands free enough to dig in my bag, I pulled out the piece of wing, half expecting it to not be there only to have my stomach turn when I pulled it out for Heather to see. Heather's arms fell away. She stared at it with a wince, but with none of the surprise I expected.

"Tell me now. What you know." I asked, my throat tight.

The rope of muscle in her neck tightened as she went stiff. "I've got orders not to tell you."

"Orders?" I asked, a helpless whine creeping into my tone.

Heather asked, "Where did you find that piece of wing?"

"Candace is missing." I handed the wing over to Heather, who scrunched her nose up as she took it. She frowned. "Her apartment is empty. Cleaned out except for that."

Heather closed her eyes and squeezed the iridescent marvel in her hands. "I think I know how to find her, but I need to talk to Devin."

"Devin? What does he have to do with any of this?"

Heather sounded strained when she answered. "Everything."

We left the café and stepped out back to Heather's motorcycle. She pulled the helmets off the bike and put hers on while I stared at a pair of them—fae—across the street. Pink skin, one with wings and the other with impossibly long hair nearly dragging the ground behind her.

"Thea?" Heather went to hand me the extra helmet, then saw where my attention had wandered across the street when I didn't reach for it. "I see them too. Two of them, one Spring and the other Autumn."

Squaring my shoulders, I took the helmet she offered. Soon enough we were winding through the streets. The highlight of the trip was when a fae appeared in a car next to us. I clung hard to Heather's back. She looked over and flipped them off before our light turned green and we sped off.

We stopped in front of a small, cute apartment building. Heather helped me off her bike and walked me up to her door.

"Home sweet home." She unlocked her door and let me walk in first. The place was small but cozy. A big painting of a motorcycle took up most of the wall over the sofa. Her kitchen was tight but the bar stools looked vintage and very comfy, and it smelled like roasting coffee beans.

Heather took out her phone and sent a text while she talked, setting it on the counter when she was done and turning to me. "Grab a seat, let me get an answer about Candace and then I can tell you everything. I think."

"You think?"

"Orders," she said, and finished her text. "Here, let's get you comfy while I wait a sec for a reply." Heather pulled me to the couch and cocooned me in a soft blue blanket.

"Who are you messaging? Do they know about the fae? Could they know where Candace is?"

"Shh, one at a time. You have to trust me, remember? I'm definitely doing the most I can until I'm allowed to say more."

With me wrapped up tight, she moved on to putting a record on an antique record player. The room filled with soft, soothing music from eras gone by. When her phone vibrated on the counter, she snatched it up.

"I can't believe you didn't talk to her!" Heather snapped.

Fixated on the phone call, I couldn't take my eyes off Heather's expression for any sign of trouble. My knuckles were white with how hard I gripped the blanket.

"Are you kidding me? She's already seeing everything and now Candace is missing." A pause. She rolled her eyes. "Yes, *everything*."

Heather flashed me a gentle smile before arguing on the phone again.

"It can't be impossible, it's already happened. Look, she's at my place right now. Give me permission to talk to her about it."

She leaned against the counter. "No, not yet, but if I keep flexing this hard, I'm not going to be able to do it at work tomorrow. I don't have your reserves of mag—uh . . . I mean . . ." Heather hunched down and talked quieter. "Just tell me what you want me to do."

She nodded, listening as she began to move around the counter and do something at her kitchen cabinets. The clinking of dishes and running of water were the only things I could hear while she held the phone to her ear with a shoulder.

"Fine, we'll do it your way, but I still think it's a mistake. No. No. Fine. Yes, I'll text you later. Bye." Heather ended the call, then sank into the couch next to me.

"Who was that?" I asked. "Do they see things too?"

"My boss, and yes," she said, gesturing to the mug of hot chocolate in front of me. "Sorry, I don't keep tea at home."

I scooped up the mug, letting the warmth seep into my fingers. "Thanks. Is Candie okay?"

Heather winced, nervously tapping her knees. "Yes, she's being taken care of now, I promise. She's safe from any harm."

Some of the tension left my shoulders. If Heather said Candace would be okay, I would trust her. I'd feel better if I could see Candie, but I'd trust Heather.

"Now, the fae. You're a historian, right?" Heather asked softly. "Let's look at this logically. If you were cataloging an unknown item, what would you do to learn more about it? Humor me. What does an archaeologist do?"

"They might start with detailing the features of the object. You know, write down its size, weight, texture, material—those kinds of things."

"Great, let's start there. If you could touch one, talk to one, would you be able to say they were real? If you had cataloged proof?"

"I guess, under the circumstances, I'd have to."

"I want to tell you some important things, but I need you to be open to what I have to say."

My hot chocolate, which had become my new center of gravity, was resettled in my hands. Heather pulled the blanket around my shoulders again, her movements still a bit tense.

"Do you want to talk to one?"

"Isn't that a bad idea? Aren't they cruel?"

"Is that what your research has told you?"

There was no thinking clearly right now. As I glanced down at the notebook in my bag, Heather took the hint and pulled it out for me. My fingers were shaking as I turned the pages, but not as badly as they had been earlier. Reaching the page I had written my most condensed thoughts on, I decided to trust researcher Thea for my answers and not panicky Thea. "There are mean ones, but also nice ones."

"What if I were a fae? Would you think I'm cruel?" Heather asked.

My hands stilled as I looked at her. "You've been my friend for years. If you were mean, I'd have found out before now. I trust you."

She relaxed. "Can you promise to keep that attitude if I do something strange?"

Nodding, I put the mug down for fear I'd drop it. "Yes."

Heather took a deep breath then reached for her eye. She tugged at something. She pulled out a contact lens and set it on the table, and when she turned to me again—her eye was gold. A completely unnatural honey gold.

"You're one of them," my voice came out a strangled whisper.

She removed the other lens and set it down. "No. Not quite. I was born human. I had to get these contacts for . . . you know. My eyes are the hardest part of my glamour to keep up, and you were already seeing through it."

My stomach dropped. The day after the party, when she dropped those mugs, then ran off.

Heather reached out to me and I flinched. She snatched her hand back, the hurt on her face evident. She stood up and stepped back, removing her leather jacket and hanging it on a peg by the door. Slowly, she let out a breath and her skin changed. Her features sharpened, her ears pointed, and she turned a shimmering bronze. At that moment she looked more like a metal statue than a living person. Her nails grew longer, claw-like, and her glossy black hair shimmered like the rest of her. Her golden eyes brightened even more, solidifying her otherworldly appearance.

"Like I said, I was born human. I grew up on a farm an hour or so outside of the city. I had a normal human dad, a normal human mom, and a normal human sister. When I was about nineteen, I was chosen to be a changeling."

I balked, horrified. "Aren't those stolen babies?"

"No, not anymore. Once upon a time I guess, but not anymore. Now they choose adults, and they carefully consider the lives that would be disrupted. The fae can coax the change in a human with the right amount of affinity and turn them into a fae. It means I was touched by faeries, given faerie food—"

"What's faerie food?" It was a subject that I had read about but with little in the way of answers.

"Food that faeries prepare with magic mixed into the process."

"Then the café . . . ?"

"No. You have to make it with careful intent, and I do not prepare faerie food for humans. I never want to. Anyway, I was exposed to the faerie magic enough that eventually I turned into one during one of the four days of power: the spring equinox, the summer solstice, the fall equinox, and the winter solstice. When you're close enough to turning, it will happen around one of those days."

"So now you're a fae. But why?" I asked.

"Population. Breeding is difficult for fae, and normally they choose changelings that would see life improvement. People with no families, few ties to humans who would miss them, usually miserable with their current situations. My family was already gone when I was changed. That's how it's usually done, until now."

"What do you mean until now?" I asked.

"Thea, you are starting to see them just as I did before my change."

Nausea hit me hard. My breaths were coming in short bursts. My head reeled as I stood. "I'm going to change? Can't it be undone?"

Heather shook her head, heartbreak plain on her face. "I'm sorry, you can't undo it. On the winter solstice, you will change."

"Into a fae." I clutched at the blanket for any sort of comfort while it all sank in.

"Into a fae," she agreed. "But I'll be here with you. I promise."

CHAPTER TWELVE

DEVIN

Fucking Georgina.

Ice clawed at my office walls as I ended the call with Heather. Thankfully, Thea was in her care for now and could reveal the fae officially. As impossible as it seemed for a changeling to be so far along already, it was clearly time for Thea to be let in on it.

The fact that Candace had been abducted was another matter entirely. Waving a hand, I cleared the ice from my walls and the temper from my voice. It was time to deal with the Summer Court. The phone rang several times before she picked up.

"What is it? I'm busy." She snapped.

"Hello to you, too, Lady Georgina. What have you done with the missing girl?"

"What do you mean?" Georgina asked, feigning innocence.

"The changeling you submitted."

"She's not missing, she's with me."

"Georgina, she's not the changeling this year. I haven't begun the change on her."

"You what?" Georgina raged. "I've already wiped her presence! She's with me now. What do you mean you didn't start her change?"

I pinched the bridge of my nose and then grabbed my keys and left the office. "Did you get the email I sent out the day after the party?"

There was a pause. "I didn't read it."

"Georgina."

"It's the same damn email every year!"

"You have the wrong girl locked up in your basement, don't you?"

"This isn't the wrong girl; this is the girl we all approved of at the last meeting. Get your ass over here and fix it, Lord of Winter!" She ended the call.

I cursed the Lady of Summer as I walked to my car. Seattle was portioned into districts where the courts could stretch their power without us overlapping. The conflicting natures would otherwise be oil and water, causing undue aggression between us when we needed to stay united to protect ourselves from the wild fae. The dark ones, the mad ones that did not belong within the courts but craved to take control of it from us.

And now, instead of remaining within my own space to handle my court's affairs, I had to set foot in her blistering presence to clean up a mess.

Entering Summer Court territory, I pulled up to Georgina's ridiculous castle of a house and pushed my way inside. Two idiots from Summer Court appeared shocked at the sight of me. They were probably supposed to be standing guard outside but were instead hiding inside for warmth. They looked just a touch drunk as well. I couldn't blame them; I'm sure the cold was as uncomfortable to them as the hot sun was to anyone from my court.

"Lord Devin." One of them bowed his head. "We weren't expecting you."

"I am aware. Move."

The mansion was decorated lavishly, not one speck of dust on the pristine white marble below. Fires roared in every room, fending off as much of the snowy cold as possible. Gorgeous fae draped themselves across the furniture, singing and drinking and generally being very *Summer Court* about everything. The corner of my mouth twitched. I billowed my winter chill around me like a sweeping wind, causing more than a few of them to shiver as I passed.

The door to the basement was guarded better than the entrance had been. I recognized the big one.

"Samson." I nodded. He was one of Georgina's more capable followers, one she relied upon heavily to retain order among her fae. Something had mangled the tip of one of the wings he usually displayed proudly. Something had mangled part of it off. I raised an eyebrow at him, but he did not offer an answer as to what could have done the damage.

"Lord Devin." He bowed his head. "Lady Georgina is dealing with our current situation."

He opened the door and I descended into a finished basement with cool blue walls and more modest furnishings than what was found upstairs. Entering the basement, I immediately saw Georgina and a couple of her fae conversing in hushed tones outside a door.

"Hello, Georgina," I said. "Always a pleasure to be in your illustrious presence."

"Devin. Still a bastard, I see." She glared sharply.

She was gorgeous in a sleek business suit. Her ruby eyes shot daggers at me as I approached and her even redder hair was pulled into a slick bun, reminding me of Thea. I wondered what her hair looked like when she let it down.

"Why are you grinning like an idiot?" She narrowed her eyes at me.

Startled that drifting thoughts of the changeling would lead my expression to slip, I changed gears to flatter the Lady of Summer. Mostly because I knew it irked her.

"Seeing you is always cause for enjoyment, Georgina."

She raised her chin, staring me down despite being much shorter. "It won't be after I'm done with you. You've royally messed up my plans."

"Have I?" I droned.

"What happened to changing the girl I selected?" she hissed.

"It was just as I reported to you, Artemis, and Nikola. I mistook a different human for the candidate and changed the strongest human in the gallery," I said. "With the swapped changeling, I proposed we meet over this issue at a later date."

"What do you mean a 'stronger candidate'? I have been preparing this one for two years!" She was shouting by the time she reached the last two words, her face flushed.

"Did you not read my message?" I asked, a mild throbbing beginning to form at my temples.

She stiffened, growing defensive. "I assumed it was simply a message of confirmation over your part in the change."

With a heavy sigh, I bit back my annoyance. "Then it would seem we have both made an error this year, because the woman in that room is not our changeling."

"This is ridiculous!" She seethed. "Go fix your mistake then!"

"Temper, Lady of Summer," I insisted. "I'm not doing anything without talking to the others. We have a decided precedent of one changeling per year, and as I'm the one performing the act of the change on the cusp of my court's solstice, you'll have to settle for patience while we sort this out."

"I will show you a precedent if you do not get in there"—she thrust her finger to the door behind her—"and change this girl right now!"

"Georgina," I frowned. "You kidnapped a mortal. We swore to put an end to the old practices. No children, no kidnapping, and one changeling per year."

She scowled. "I acquired a girl, who should have been a changeling by now."

"And I don't suppose you were going to lay claim to her before the court leaders could meet?"

"I would never." We locked eyes. "All four of us have the right to explain the situation to our changelings, we just choose to let you do it since you begin the process."

She wasn't wrong, it was within her right. That is, if she had actually made contact with the changeling.

"Get on with it!" she snapped. "I would change her if I could, but it's your season, not mine."

Of all the years for her to start being responsible. But headache aside, if I could ease the transition for this human, I would. "Let's see this mortal then, but you get to explain to the others why we have a second changeling. Can she see the glamour yet?"

She hesitated. "Some."

"Could she before your people got their hands on her?"

"Does it matter, Devin? She can bloody well see it now, so get in there and fix it!" Georgina threw open the door behind her, nearly taking it off its hinges. She gave her two fae a look and they scurried upstairs, dismissed.

I recognized the girl immediately upon stepping through the doorway. She glared up at me from atop a bed, the room's sole piece of furniture, looking more feral than when I last saw her. Yellow hair sticking out at odd angles as it pulled free from her braid, a flush on her face, and scratches on her arms. I wondered how they knew each other. If Thea was a thinker, this one was a fighter. Was Thea always looking after this one or was their relationship more symbiotic? I shook my head—I'd deal with Thea later. Right now, I had to focus on the problem at hand.

"Candace," I said.

She froze. "Who the hell are you?"

"My name is Devin, and I'm here to help you."

Realization dawned on her. "Devin-from-the-party, Devin? Did you kidnap Thea too?"

"Who is Thea?" Georgina snapped from behind.

I held up a hand to silence them both, dropping the room a few degrees before pulling it back up. Candace stopped, goose bumps crawling up her exposed arms. "I have not and do not plan to harm one hair on Thea's head. Right now, we are discussing your situation."

"Are you letting me go?" she said, eyes painted with hesitation.

"Unfortunately, that is not something within my power to give you."
I closed the gap, still giving her some space. Yes, she smelled like fae now.
Stronger than the night of the party but not nearly as strong as Thea.

"Then why are you here?"

"Has Georgina told you what is going on?"

"She's the one who had me kidnapped!"

"You have not been kidnapped, you impudent brat," Georgina hissed.

"*Enough.* You aren't helping." I shut the door in Georgina's face and
turned back to Candace. My action had earned me a bit more curiosity in
Candace's eyes and a fraction less hostility. Clearing my throat, I eased my
tone of voice. "All right, let me try this again. Georgina has something to
tell you, but I highly doubt you'll believe me or her. You have a transition
before you and it's happening whether you like it or not, so I'm going to
provide you with the most painless path available."

In a flash, I was kneeling next to her, one of her hands in mine. I
kissed her hand, just as I had Thea's, and let her yank it back.

"Ew, pervert. You're with Georgina, why should I trust you?"

"Do you believe in fairy tales?"

"Not since I was five," she snapped. "What does that have to do with
anything?"

"Come on now, after everything you've seen?" Watching for a reaction, her back stiffened. So, she *had* seen through the lesser fae, to at least
some extent. My heart went out to her, but there was nothing I could do
to stop her progress. As I spoke, I lessened my hold on the glamour that
would let me appear wholly human. Eyes aglow, ears elongating, fangs
lengthening. Candace took it all in, her eyes darting from one feature to
the next as I spoke.

"Start believing again, because you are on the verge of joining our
world," I urged. "The process has already been set in motion, so your most
comfortable path ahead will come if you embrace the change. Your friend,
Thea, is preparing to do the same."

Candace looked ready to take a swing at me and run away at the
same time. She leaned back before she spoke again. "What's going to

happen to me now? Georgina was a terrible boss, but this tops the charts." Tears beaded at the corners of her eyes, but she fought furiously to contain them. A fighter, this one. "What does she want?"

"Believe it or not, she wants you to be happy." I shook my head and backed up to the door, firming up my glamour to appear human once more. "I truly wish we could have done this under better circumstances, but for now I will leave you alone."

"You're leaving me here?" Pain crossed her already disheveled features, and I paused at the door, a softer expression falling on my face.

"My best advice is to watch out your window"—I nodded to the lone window just above her—"and allow yourself to believe the impossible."

"What does that mean?" she asked desperately.

"You're fae now, though I don't think these words will truly hit you until you've completed your change. Whatever abilities you now possess, we'll show you how to use them, and we will take care of you. We will always take care of our own."

"Who's we?" she asked, and then the door opened. Our eyes turned to Georgina.

"*You*," Candace hissed. "You bitch!" She lunged toward her boss, snarling. Georgina stood perfectly still as Samson appeared in time to catch Candace.

"Let me go!" she screamed. "This bitch is behind everything! The tickets, the party, the freaks that kidnapped me!"

"You bit me!" Samson growled.

"And I'll bite off the other one, too, if you don't get your hands off me!"

A grin threatened to creep onto my face as I put the pieces together of what had happened to his wing.

"Where are you going?" Georgina asked me, watching as Candace struggled in Samson's arms.

"I did my part, she's all yours. You had better teach her as gently as you can, circumstances as they are. You owe her that much. Don't forget, it's on you to tell Artemis and Nikkos about this." I waved a hand as I left. "See you at the solstice."

Georgina did not say another word to me—she only had eyes for Candace. For all her ruthlessness, she did care deeply for her court, and Candace was a clear Summer Court candidate if I'd ever seen one. Candace would be well taken care of. Once she calmed down.

CHAPTER THIRTEEN

THEA

Heather was a blessing. She spent the night with me, talking through my fears until the late hours and even sharing some of her history. She got me to calm down and focus on getting through the next few days. It helped that I knew Candie was okay, and Heather got some more information about her situation while I was at work, ensuring she was safe. Candace, I was told, was going to change too.

On some level, it was great that Heather understood what I was going through. On another, I couldn't stop staring at her fae features, dreading my change. On paper, becoming fae had a lot of perks. A fae could live for hundreds, maybe thousands of years if they didn't die from an outside cause, which was both shocking and impressive. I wasn't sure how to feel about the life span as it pertained to me, but I was at least starting to accept it. Fae also had influence on the space around them just by existing. An aura of whatever magic made such a creature in the first place and limiting human touch was important so as not to affect anyone with side effects like I'd gone through. Seeing things, hearing things. Heather had mastered navigating her café without actually touching anyone, and now that I knew her secret it was amazing to watch her work around it. The idea of magic was a delight to the childhood Thea that spent her time absorbed in books, but really, I just hoped it wasn't anything dangerous that I could hurt myself or others with. And possibly the most intriguing thing I found out was about the glamour, a subtle magic that hid a fae's supernatural appearance from those weaker in magic than themselves. Some fae could hide their features from other fae, and most fae could flex it hard enough to even disappear from the human eye, a trick I'm pretty sure had been used on me when I was seeing them in the streets.

Regardless of how I felt about the whole thing, my human days were literally numbered. My dream to work in a museum, write a published article, buy a house and decorate it how I want, see my niece and nephew grow up and take them on fun trips, and have a family of my own. None of that could possibly look the same anymore, and I felt that loss deeply.

The one thing I struggled with the most over the week was seeing them, knowing they were really there. When I wasn't working, I was at the café staring out the big windows. People watching. Fae watching. I tried to pick out which court they belonged to and how powerful they were based on how clearly I could see them. Some seemed surprised that I was watching them. Others just smiled and waved. Heather would point them out when business was slow and tell me if she knew them and what they were like. She suggested calling one in to meet but I refused, not quite ready yet. I knew I would have to face them eventually, but I wasn't ready to pop this bubble of relative peace.

A week after I'd found out the truth, my phone buzzed and I jumped in my seat, almost spilling my tea. Snatching up my phone and staring at the screen, I felt a flicker of disappointment cross my heart when it wasn't Candace or Devin, neither of whom had talked to me all week. The former probably didn't have her phone or she'd have called by now, and the latter hadn't messaged me at all. The fact that I was disappointed about Devin's lack of contact raised a few questions I wasn't prepared to dive into just yet. Heather had alluded that he was a fae but refused to speak much more about it.

After the initial pang of disappointment evaporated, I frowned at the message from Alan as I read it.

still on for dinner?

Alan. Shit, it was Wednesday. I'd been more than a little distracted over the last couple of days.

"What's up?" Heather's worried glances were never far from me when I sat in the café.

Holding up my screen, I explained the dinner I had planned. Heather listened, and when I finished she slid into the booth across from me.

"You should go."

"Are you sure that's a good idea?" I asked.

"This isn't the end of your life, it's a change to it," Heather said, not for the first time. "I still go about my life, right? Go, enjoy dinner. You need the distraction anyway."

The time flashed at the top of my phone screen—I still needed to shower and get dressed.

"Okay." Maybe she was right. Heather reached out to squeeze my hand, then retreated from the booth to attend to her other customers. My thumbs moved across the keys, answering Alan's text.

Yes, I'll be there. Do you have the address?

i'll send it. see u there

I plugged the info into my Map app while I walked back to my apartment to get ready.

—

The restaurant wasn't hard to find, just off one of the main roads east of Lake Sammamish. It was a bit of a drive, but it felt good to get out where there were so many trees. It was new, a wooden lodge that looked plucked from a ski resort. I pulled up, the tires crunching through a light layer of snow, and quickly spotted Alan's truck.

"Floor Sign, over here." He waved from the entrance. People were already filing inside, eager to escape the cold. An older woman did a double take at Alan as he called me by my nickname.

"You're terrible." One side of my mouth tugged upward as I wrapped my arms around myself, the first sign of amusement I had felt in days. "Aren't you freezing out here?"

"Nah, not too bad, but let's get inside before my beard grows icicles." He held the door for me. Inside was warm, with one of those little electric fireplaces dancing in the wall behind the hostess. There wasn't much room left on the benches, so I took a seat and Alan stood next to me.

"Which one is your cousin?" I asked, taking off my coat once I warmed up some.

Alan pointed to an open section over on the far side, a round bar area with stools around it. In the middle of it all, a shorter, stockier Alan was pouring drinks while talking to a couple.

"Oh wow, you could be brothers."

"Yeah, all the Wallaces look like this." He posed dramatically. "It's a curse to look this good."

"Pfft." I covered my grin with both hands. Heather was right, the distraction was good and Alan was the best at lightening the mood.

It wasn't long before we were called, and we followed our hostess to a corner booth. The seat backs were tall, blocking off most of the view around us save for the floor-to-ceiling windows along the wall. Candles were lit on every table. This was going to be a dating hotspot the moment it officially opened.

The waiter handed us menus and set two glasses of water on the table. "Good evening, folks, thanks for coming to our practice opening tonight, we really appreciate it. You'll find a survey by the candles if you'd like to help us out with feedback of your experience. Let me tell you about tonight's special and I'll let you look over the menu."

I glanced up from the menu, then froze. Our waiter was one of them.

"Tonight, we have a hickory-smoked salmon with steamed broccoli and butternut squash. I highly recommend it. Can I start you two off with something to drink?" He had a dazzling smile but slightly too many sharp teeth. Pointed ears, violet eyes. Blood rushed in my ears as my heart pounded at the sudden encounter. Not that Alan was seeing any of this.

I covered the lower half of my face with my menu. Heather and Devin both said they weren't evil. But they also said they weren't not evil. But . . . I had to face these encounters eventually.

"I'm Ron's cousin," Alan said, oblivious to the distress I was hiding behind my menu. "Can you tell him to surprise me? Bartender's choice."

The waiter nodded then turned to me. "And for you, miss?"

"I . . ."

Just act normal and get through this dinner. Nothing but a normal interaction with a waiter, no reason to treat him differently. I put the menu down.

"Can I recommend the house wine?" he offered, his face turning at the edges with just a hint of mischief. Oh, he knew—the wicked gleam in his eyes gave him away.

"Just water, thanks," I murmured.

"Excellent, I'll be right back." He nodded and headed to the bar.

"You can get more than just water." Alan looked at me. "Are you sure you don't want anything else? Tea?"

"No, I'm all right, really."

"All right, just say the word if you don't feel comfortable."

Well, that ship has already sailed.

"No, no, I'm fine. Oh look, they have lasagna. That's right up my alley."

Alan accepted my answer and moved on to his own menu. Holding in a sigh of relief, I scanned the room. As far as I could tell our waiter was the only fae. My hand slipped into my bag and my fingers brushed against the pipe. I still hadn't taken it out of my bag, and now I was glad that I hadn't. Not that I thought I had it in me to do anything with it, but it made me feel better to have it nearby.

He returned a minute later with a glass of amber liquid for Alan and took our orders before quickly departing. I resisted the urge to keep looking around and turned to Alan instead.

"It's a nice place," he said. "I'm surprised they took on Ron, but I guess he cleans up okay."

I glanced over to his cousin. "He looks like he's having fun."

"Yeah, but I'm still gonna mess with him. Family obligations, you know. Is this better than yoga?"

Right then a girl came by and set down a basket of garlic bread sticks before moving on to the next table, and my face lit up.

"Oh yeah, garlic bread wins any day." I took a bite; it was amazing. "Okay, I'm now officially glad I skipped yoga."

We fell into comfortable conversation. Alan was going to college part time while working at the car wash. He talked about some of his classes, his cousin, my ancient van, his family's mechanic shop, his grandma's recent cruise, and other little things that helped me forget what was happening to me. Until our food came.

"Here we are, folks." The fae came out with our plates and set them down in front of us. "Can I get you anything else? I can put in a ticket for the pumpkin spice cake. It'll be ready for you when you're finished with your main course. We've got to take advantage of the last days of fall, after all."

"No, I'm good." I narrowed my eyes at him, trying to decide whether he was up to something or if mischief was just the look of him.

"Very well." He smiled at me, showing all of his too-many pointed teeth. "Enjoy."

Watching him go, I still couldn't shake the odd feeling he gave me. Alan was happy to dig right in, but I gave my food a little more thought first. After a quick investigation of my plate and finding nothing off, I started eating. Alan and I continued the light conversation from before with short interruptions while we ate. We were almost done when he came back again.

"Everything all right, folks?" He waltzed over and placed two steaming mugs in front of us. "Apple cider, on the house. A pre–grand opening thank-you."

"Thanks." Alan took his and was about to drink. My eyes flew to the fae; his smug grin set off alarms in my head.

Do not thank the fae.

My attention went to the mugs on the table. Another off-menu item, and this one wrinkled my nose.

"Wait!" I stood up, bumping the table as I did. I gasped as Alan took a sip. His eyes locked onto mine—he could see my panic.

The waiter backed away with a grin. Alan had thanked him, but what about eating their food? Was this fae food? How can you tell?

"What was that?" Alan's eyes darted from me to the waiter to the mug.

"It's, um . . ." I sat down, my face flushed with embarrassment. "It looked hot. I didn't want you to burn yourself."

Alan turned to the waiter, but he was already heading to the kitchen. I didn't touch my cider while Alan finished his. Unsure of what to say, I figured he had already taken a drink of it and whatever was going to come of it would come no matter what I did at this point.

We didn't see our waiter again, one of the other servers brought us the ticket. Alan's cousin came by to talk to us for a while once everything had died down. Most of the tables were empty now while staff were busy cleaning or huddled talking near the bar.

The whole night, which had started on such a good note, was now soured by whatever off feelings I had from the fae. But Alan didn't notice that I was forcing my smile, or at least pretended not to for my sake as we said our good-byes.

Alan made sure I made it to my van before he got into his truck and started the engine. Turning mine on as well, I sat back and waited for everything to heat up when I saw the crisp piece of paper in my passenger seat.

Sitting up, I looked around the parking lot. For what, I didn't know—just that I was unsettled to have something left in my van that I definitely hadn't left there myself. Reaching out with caution, I picked it up and read the sloppy scrawl of black ink on it.

Don't trust them.

~C

CHAPTER FOURTEEN

THEA

Heather and I had made plans for me to spend the night with her—the night before solstice—after I got back from the restaurant. I borrowed a lighter from a smoker outside my building and burned the note I'd found on my windshield—I didn't want it around me, nor did I want any of the fae to find it. I didn't suspect Heather—I'd known her too long for that. But that didn't stop the unnerving chill that had settled in the back of my mind as I drove to Heather's apartment.

Heather was ready with movies, pizza, popcorn, and an amazing photo album that contained everything from her family farm in the 1940s to pictures of the café through the ages, Heather in retro fashions to match. She was so excited to spend more time together that she didn't notice my stomach was perpetually in knots from the cryptic note. We stayed up late and I passed out on the couch sometime around three. Heather tossed a blanket over me and went to bed. I drifted in and out of sleep all night, with strange dreams I couldn't remember upon waking. There was no doubt in my mind they were about the impending party, the only part of which I was looking forward to was finally seeing Candace and making sure she was okay.

We got up around ten the next morning, and my last day as a human officially began.

I called in sick to work while Heather scrambled us some eggs. I also shot Alan a text to make sure he was feeling okay. Whatever that fae was doing, if he was even doing anything, I didn't want Alan to get involved. Thankfully, he seemed fine, as he shot me back a *I had a great time, thanks for coming* and I was able to focus on my egg without Heather prodding me for what I'd been worried about. We were still eating when Heather's attention snapped to the door. She was already up and walking toward it when someone knocked.

"Fae hearing." She tapped her ear and opened the door to a pair of fae who wheeled in a rack of clothing.

"You can just leave it by the window." Heather pointed.

"Hey, Heather, what about these?" A petite fae woman stepped through the door carrying a huge stack of shoe boxes.

"Can they all fit on the counter?"

"What is all this?" I asked.

"Gifts from Lor—from the Winter Court." Heather eyed me then turned to the nearest rack of fabric. "The Lord of the Winter Court is in charge of the party tonight. He wanted to make sure the changelings had something to wear."

"Oh. Nice of him," I murmured, not really sure what else to think.

Changelings. Heather was giving me all the information I would need, as Candace was across Seattle being given the same by another fae more familiar to her, apparently. I was worried about her; of course, I would worry in this situation. It's not that I didn't believe Heather when she said Candie was fine, but I wouldn't really be okay with it until I could see her for myself.

"Don't look so down, we've got dresses to try on." She pushed me into the bathroom. "Shower, I'll have everything ready when you're out."

She lifted her hand from my back and her voice softened. "God, you feel like you're about to pop."

"Pop?" I asked.

"I just mean you feel ready. Go on, enjoy the shower. Use up all my hot water and a whole bottle of the shampoo you liked."

Huffing out a laugh, I closed the door as Heather left me to clean up. I took my time, letting the steam smother me. After, I borrowed Heather's comb and, wearing only a towel, peeked my head out the door.

"Do we still have company?"

"Come on out," Heather said. "They've left. I thought you'd rather it be just us."

"Definitely preferred." I stepped out of the bathroom, enjoying the quiet of her cozy apartment that was now filled with clothing options I would have to sort through. I eyed the pile of shoes on the counter with resignation.

"Hair first." Heather had a mirror and supplies waiting on a clean portion of the kitchen counter. She patted a stool for me to sit on. She brushed out my hair and we managed to wangle it into some kind of updo. Candace would have been a big help here, but I was still more than thankful for Heather.

She finished and we moved on to dresses. Deep reds, icy blues, minty greens, neutrals of all kinds, and even a few metallic shades. An overwhelming set of options that Heather quickly halved by shoving one of the racks at random into the hallway. In the end, we chose a soft pink two-piece. The top was lace with a sweetheart bodice, the skirt had a high waist with more lace, and it flowed down to my ankles. I should have chosen it on looks alone but secretly I chose it because it was made of something stretchy and if I was going to go through a stressful ordeal, I was going to do it comfortably.

"You look amazing." She wore a blue velvet dress of her own that showed off her long legs.

"You're not so bad yourself," I said, eliciting a musical laugh from her that lifted my nerves, if only for a moment.

"All right, then. Grab your coat and let's go."

—

The ride to L'Atelier Rouge was cold but it didn't bite too hard. A charge was in the air, or on my skin—or both—like something was about to pop. Just as Heather had said earlier. We pulled into the gallery's lot and I took off my helmet. Heather checked my coiled hair for any loose strands.

"Are you ready to see the four courts actually interacting? You can put some of our practice to use—see if you can figure out which is which on sight."

My pulse was high and my posture tense, but I gave Heather a slight nod and she steered me gently up the front steps.

Fae of every kind drifted into the gallery, their dress not at all indicative of the season. Wings and fangs and horns. Everyone could have been a normal human under all the colors and textures draped over them like a jumbled jigsaw puzzle. Bile crept up my throat at the thought that this had all been hiding in plain sight my entire life. The staring would be the death of me. Too-big eyes and longer-than-normal teeth would be my new normal, even as I felt their hot gazes trying to peel back my layers, figuring out what was about to become of me. My eyes scanned the faces for the two people I knew would be here other than us: Candace and Devin.

Devin. He was obviously a key player, but I had pushed away the thoughts of it. We hadn't spoken since the day we'd had lunch, and my stomach was in knots trying to figure out if I was relieved he hadn't contacted me, or disappointed.

"Deep breaths," Heather's grounding voice urged beside me. She pulled one of my arms through hers and kept her hand on top of mine.

Deep breaths.

With every three steps I took I sucked in air, and in the next three I released it. In and out, moving through a sea of dancing, laughing, chattering fae. They crowded us, wanting to know my name, if I was the changeling, if being with Heather meant she had found me. Several were shocked as they had already met Candace. At the mention of her name, I craned my neck, searching for my best friend through the crowd, but she wasn't in sight.

"Give her some air," Heather told the surrounding fae. "You know the rules. You can meet her properly after midnight."

That drove most of them away and Heather took us deeper inside the building where the gallery had been completely transformed. Silver decorations were everywhere and blue paper lanterns were suspended throughout, giving off warm light. A crackling fireplace twice as tall as me and three times as wide took up most of a wall that I could have sworn was empty a week ago. And the fae—they were everywhere. They were beautiful, frightening, curious, and otherworldly all at once.

"And this must be Thea." A musical voice turned our attention, and the fae around us moved back with respect. A stunning woman, youthful in appearance but with ancient violet eyes. She carried herself with incredible confidence, a bold orange gown hugged her body, her black hair crowned on the top of her head in small braids.

"Lady Artemis," Heather said, bowing her head. Startled, I tried to mimic the action and once I bobbed my head back up, Artemis held her piercing gaze on me as though she could see right through to my heart.

"Thea, this is the Lady of Autumn. She is one of the four powerful fae that watch over the courts here in Seattle."

"You bring a tide to the courts. Perhaps beyond," Artemis said, her unsettling stare still holding me in place. "It will be interesting to see how things reshape once you have settled."

I was startled and completely unsure of how to respond—the words that came out of my mouth were whatever popped into my head first. "I don't want to make any waves."

Artemis huffed an amused sound. "You will see in time, young one. I suggest you find a glass of wine for your nerves before midnight."

Not waiting for a response, Artemis turned to walk away, the crowd parting for her as she went.

She gave me goose bumps. Turning to ask Heather a question, I found her staring at her phone.

"My boss would like to meet you." She pocketed her cell and took my arm through hers again. "There are a few last-minute things to explain before midnight."

Heather took us to the foot of the staircase I had been to before when

I'd met with Devin in his office. As we ascended the stairs, a growing feeling in my chest told me we were heading to his office. It didn't take a genius to wonder what the odds were that Devin would be the one standing behind that door.

For some reason I was nervous to see him. Or maybe nervous to know what his part in all this was. Heather opened the door and let me walk through first. Stepping inside, I saw him for what he truly was. He was in front of the window with his back to us and turned around as we entered. Pointed ears, fangs; his eyes, which were a deep green before, were practically glowing now with the light of the moon behind him. A sketch crossed the shadows of my mind. A drawing from a diary written well before I was born. That was never Devin's ancestor: it was Devin.

"You're fae." Shocked to see it despite the knowing fear in my gut, I stepped back. My instincts were telling me I wasn't just in the presence of another fae like Heather but something else, something old and powerful akin to the way Artemis had made me feel.

Somehow there were four of these fae in Seattle; to have them in one room must be suffocating.

Devin nodded to us and Heather gently pulled me inside, shutting the door behind us.

"I am," he answered, then frowned. "And you aren't." His eyes slid to Heather, an eyebrow raised in question.

Heather shrugged. "No change yet."

Devin looked at me with concern. He stepped forward, pausing when he saw my shoulders stiffen. He cleared his throat. "Are you all right? Were you hurt?"

I shook my head. Heather tugged at my wrist, trying to get me to sit down next to her.

"Good." Devin stared at me for a long moment, his eyes a mix of both hope and sadness. He'd been one of them this whole time. What about our connection—was I the only one who'd felt it, or was it all fabricated from the beginning?

"Was anything you said to me the truth?" I asked quietly.

Devin's face stilled, a mask of indifference. "Heather, please leave us."

Heather stood up. I shot her a panicked look as though my lifeline between this strange culture of fae and the human world was leaving me. And in many ways, that's exactly what Heather was for me now. She'd shown me that the fae were more than the frightening tricksters the old fables made them out to be. That I could possibly navigate this transition and actually find a balance that I could live with.

She gave my shoulder a squeeze as she passed. "I'll be right at the bottom of the stairs. Devin is the best of the fae rulers, I promise you're safe with him."

"Heather," Devin warned.

Heather put up her hands. "I'm going, I'm going." She slipped out then, leaving me to face Devin on my own. My stomach was in knots, my fingers picking at a stray thread on the arm of the chair as I glanced up at Devin.

His expression softened once we were alone. "Every word I said to you was true; a fae cannot lie."

"Heather can lie," I said. "She lied when I first started seeing her eyes."

Devin crossed his arms and glanced out the window. "Heather was not born fae as I was. The changelings don't have to adhere to the rules as we do."

"Will that be the same for me?" Devin nodded. "What if I don't change?"

"You will."

"How do you know?"

Devin turned to me again, his eyes meeting mine. "Because I initiated it."

The room fell quiet and cold, the pause between us growing uncomfortable until I broke the silence. "What are you talking about?"

"You're a natural changeling," he said. "We haven't introduced you to our magic slowly, which is the normal method. You take to it exceptionally well. The one chosen this year was actually your friend, Candace. Slowly exposed to Georgina's magic for the past two years."

My mouth fell open. "Her *boss* Georgina?"

Devin nodded. "The Lady of Summer, my counterpart from another season. But even with all of Georgina's preparations, the moment you walked into the party it was *you* I sensed radiating the feel of a change-ling. My job is to initiate the process of the change. It's my fault you're here now. I began your change with a kiss, giving you the last little push of magic to tip over the edge."

A kiss? My mind sifted through the tipsy haze of the gala, landing on our parting moments when Devin had lifted my hand to his lips and kissed it. I instinctively rubbed the spot where it had happened. Devin followed my movement then looked away.

"It was not my intent to choose the wrong person, but as it has happened, I swear I will ensure you the most comfortable transition into our world that I can."

Tears welled in my eyes. "This was a mistake?"

"Thea." My name was a whisper on his breath. He reached forward but stopped himself.

Good. I wasn't ready to interact with him yet. Was any of it real? I thought there was a chemistry between us, but now I wasn't so sure. There would always be the possibility that Devin only spent time around me because I was a changeling. "You've uprooted my life, you know that?"

"I know," he said, his voice a low rumble. "I never intended to. Our goal is to change someone whose life will turn out for the better, not worse. And I meant it when I said I will do anything within my power to settle you comfortably. We will ensure you have anything you could want—we fae leaders take care of our changelings."

"You can't give me what I want!" I bolted to my feet, moving away from him, clenching and unclenching my hands as I tried to keep my breath even. I hadn't meant to raise my voice, but now that I had, all my frustration was spilling out. "What if I wanted to grow old with my brother? What if I wanted to settle down with a nice normal human at some point? My spouse would wonder why I still look twenty-three when they're fifty. What if I wanted to be a grandma someday, and pick my grandkids up from school early and take them for ice cream? Exactly how am I supposed to do any of that now?"

Devin didn't answer, but he did look guilty as hell.

"Please," my voice cracked. "Tell me what's going to happen tonight. I don't think I want to stay in this room any longer than I have to."

Devin closed his eyes, clearly this was hard for him too. "You will be placed in a court. It won't be difficult—you'll know exactly which court you belong in when you change. At midnight you will finish your transformation if you haven't already, and the fae lords and ladies will hold an audience to let you and Candace make your choices. Afterward, the lord or lady of your court will settle you into our world. You'll have already heard most of the fae rules from Heather; there shouldn't be too much more for you to learn."

One of the courts. I knew I'd fall into one of them, but now more time with Devin was a possibility. But only a 25 percent possibility.

"May I go now?" I asked softly.

"I truly wish you the best," Devin said. "I will see you at the choosing."

I walked out of his office. My throat stung. I thought I was finally okay with all this, but to find out that it was Devin of all people who was responsible for my situation . . . I didn't know what to think. An accident. A mistake. I suppose lives often change drastically because of such moments, but this situation was more than I could have imagined.

Heather was down at the bottom of the stairs just as she said she would be.

"Hey," she said, "how'd it go?"

Instead of answering, I threw my arms around her neck.

"I don't want to be a faerie." My throat tightened as I tried to pull myself together. "I want to go home and have a mug of tea and pretend this isn't happening."

Heather wrapped her arms around me, rubbing a hand down my back. "Hey now. I thought we were through this part. What happened with Devin?"

"I'm just upset." I pulled back and wiped the corners of my eyes. "It's not really the fae, it's . . ." *my heart.*

"Thea!"

I spun around, knowing who it was without even needing to look. "Candace!" I ran to her and she engulfed me in a hug.

Her arms had an orange glow to them, and it wasn't just a bad spray tan. The blond in her hair was gone, replaced by a more vibrant yellow. She pulled back and held my hands in hers. I could see the changes on her face. Her features were a little sharper, narrower, and her ears were pointed.

"You changed already. Are they treating you well? Did they do anything weird to you?"

"I changed last night," she said. "They're technically treating me just fine."

"Technically?" I held her a little tighter. "Do you need us to get you out of there? I heard it was your boss."

"No, no. Now that I know what's going on I'm fine. Once I changed it took a couple hours to calm down."

"Understandable," Heather murmured.

Candace nodded. "Yeah. Anyway, once I did, there was no more denying what they were saying, you know? So I'm getting settled into a new house. A suite in the main mansion, as long as I'm a Summer Court fae like they suspect."

"And you're okay with it?" I asked.

"Oddly, yes. This isn't even the worst uprooting I've gone through."

Her words reminded me of her time in the foster system, and I grimaced. "Oof."

"It is what it is. But enough about me, why don't you look any different?"

"She hasn't changed yet," Heather said. "But she will tonight. Do you feel it yet?"

"Yeah, I think so." I rubbed my arms. "I have goose bumps that aren't there, and I feel . . . electricity?"

"What do we do now?" Candace asked.

"You two enjoy yourselves." Heather put an arm around us both. "Tonight is as much about you as anything else. Eat, drink, dance."

"I think I can do that." A familiar gleam overtook Candace and she reached out a hand. "Dance with me?"

If I wasn't so overwhelmed I would have laughed. Candace was taking this in stride, and I was still stuck inside my head over it. "Do I have to?"

"Yes." She gave me that look that meant she was going to be stubborn about it, but at the edges of her confidence I recognized a sliver of the softer Candie. The Candie that needed someone to hold her when things were hard or new. Maybe I wasn't the only one still adjusting.

"Okay." I had barely answered before she pulled me into another fierce hug. She unwound from me and locked our hands so she could pull me to the open space where other fae were already dancing.

Settling into an empty space, we began to move, and I took in all the changes. She was more fluid in her movements, and the lines of her face were familiar but somehow foreign at the same time. "You're so different."

She looked away, her mouth moving to the side in thought. "I know."

"I didn't mean it in a bad way. If you've got to turn into a magic being, you might as well be as vibrant on the outside as you are on the inside."

We stood there a moment as the orchestra changed songs. I rolled my shoulders in discomfort, the prickly feeling growing stronger the later into the night it became.

"We can talk tomorrow. Tonight, let me just dance it away," Candace said, renewed vigor in her voice.

"Okay." I squeezed her hands and she tugged me deeper into the mob of fae.

CHAPTER FIFTEEN

DEVIN

After Thea left, I waited a few minutes before leaving my office. Coming down the stairs, I could see the main gallery and all the activity. The Winter fae I had placed at specific points to ensure nothing got out of hand were at their stations. The courts were mingling tonight. There was a novelty for them to be thrown in together and not just with their own kind. A once-a-year celebration of the changeling was also a time when most of the Seattle court fae gathered in one place, and that would always risk clashing powers. I made note of where in the room the other three fae rulers were. Always aware of our balance, they would be as keenly aware of my presence as I was of theirs. Especially tonight, when my court's power came into the forefront of us all.

At the bottom of the stairs, I began to look for someone specific. Spotting Heather at the edge of the main gallery room, I followed her gaze to the changelings dancing.

"You really messed up with her," Heather murmured as I approached.

"She'll get over it. They all do." I inhaled crisp pine air—she'd just been here.

"Right, I forgot, Lord Devin doesn't make mistakes."

"I see your worry has dissipated now that you see how safe her change is going to be." I raised an eyebrow.

"You didn't tell her anything!"

"There was no way of knowing she would start seeing things so early. It's highly unusual. Besides, she had you and it all worked out in the end," I argued.

"Better than how Georgina handled Candace, I guess."

"True."

"I mean, what a disgusting way to find out." Bitterness crept into Heather's voice.

Looking at her, it clicked. "Is this about Candace, or is it about you and Arthur?"

"I'm not talking about him."

"It was decades ago, and you both misled each other."

"I said I'm not talking about him," she seethed.

We stood in silence, which was my preference. I was already irritable from two days' worth of meetings with Georgina, Nikola, and Artemis, not to mention decorating the gallery. When this was over, I was going to take a long vacation.

"She's taking it well." Heather broke the silence, her words softer now. A couple moved off the dance floor, leaving just enough of a window for us to see clearly, Candace and Thea. My heart skipped at the sight of her.

"Magnificent," I whispered. Heather looked at me from the corner of her eye.

"What does that mean?" she asked.

"She radiates it." I waved at the dance floor. "One way or another, she was meant to be a part of our world. A miracle one of us didn't catch a hint of her before. I can't believe you aren't feeling it already."

"I can't believe you care enough to comment."

"Of course I care. A powerful fae in your court is always something to fight for." I started for the far end of the gallery, leaving Heather behind. "Keep an eye on her," I said over my shoulder. "The last thing we want is the wild fae to get their hands on her."

I walked absently toward the four thrones set against the back wall. The crowds parted, giving me a generous amount of space. I resisted watching Thea and instead continued to my seat. Artemis was already on her throne, being waited on by her people, while Georgina and Nikola were nearby having a heated debate about something unimportant, no doubt.

Artemis acknowledged my presence with a slight nod. "Leave us." She waved away the fae tending to her.

The Lady of Autumn was the most imposing of us, though the other courts likely thought I held that title. But of the four of us, she was the oldest and the most powerful.

"A lovely solstice, Devin."

"I can only hope to accomplish a portion of the extravagant autumn equinox you hosted a few years ago," I said, taking my seat.

"You are a flatterer and a snake." She grinned like a hellcat. "But it was splendid, wasn't it?"

"There you are, Devin. I thought you'd still be sulking in a dark corner." The Lord of Spring walked up to us, dressed in white and gold. His wild blond hair flowed over his shoulders. "Are we taking bets on the changelings yet?"

"Why bother?" Georgina joined him. "It's about midnight, we'll find out soon enough."

I thought about saying something regarding the Summer fae that was already obviously hers when my head snapped to the dance floor.

"Don't you think so, Devin?" Nikola had said something, but Artemis hushed him.

"What is it?" she asked in a low tone.

"I don't know." My heart was racing, my back tense. "The changeling, where is she?"

"Which one?" Nikola asked.

A startled scream parted the crowd instantly. The orchestra fumbled to a halt.

"Thea?" Candace called, looking around. "Heather, help!"

But there was no help to be given—she was changing.

"She's powerful," Artemis murmured. I stood.

Thea froze, kneeling. A glow had begun at her forehead and was crawling down her skin. She looked like living moonlight. She let out a small whimper and grabbed her head. Her light brown hair dulled then ignited in a rose-gold hue. Her light eyes joined her skin, glowing, glimmering, a blinding unnatural blue. She dropped her hands from her head, exposing twin protruding horns—small antlers like those of a deer and no longer than my finger.

"Holy gods," someone hissed. Candace and Heather stood frozen next to Thea as she sat on the ground, panting. Her eyes darted to me, and my heart nearly burst at the sight of her as I felt an undeniable thread form between us. In the silence of the gallery the whole of the fae courts heard me speak:

"Oh . . . shit."

CHAPTER SIXTEEN

THEA

My breath was still ragged from the change. My skin felt tight, like when the air is too cold and dry but at the same time my body was hot. The room was too much—too much body heat, too much sound, too much light. Everything here was so much more than my senses had ever been bombarded with before. I stared at my foreign hands—slender, pale, glowing softly as if I was bathed in a dim light—and my brain struggled to claim them as mine even as I watched them move at my will.

Devin took a cautious step forward as Heather and Candace helped me stand. I let out a small cry as the sensation of their touch brushed my skin. Even my dress was overwhelming, and all it did was sit on me just as it had for the last couple of hours.

"What's wrong?" I asked, panic rising at the strange responses around me.

Heather stared at the Lord of the Winter Court—and she wasn't alone. All eyes were on Devin. Meanwhile his sharp green eyes were fixed only on me, and my breath hissed out as I felt a tug of my heart toward him, as if connected by a thread.

Grunting, I clutched my chest. "What is this?"

Scents engulfed me. I breathed in husky cedar, the air crisp with it, like after it had snowed. Was it coming from Devin? My new, sharper eyes focused on his features. I could completely see through his glamour now. Everything I'd seen in his office was now intensified—the curve of his ears, the glow of his eyes. His lips were almost sinful. His eyes settled on mine.

"A thread of fate," Devin answered, our eyes locked. The audience reacted strongly, and Heather stiffened next to me. My heart thudded. Something was going on, and Devin was at the center of it.

"Thea." He raised his hand slightly. Closed his mouth and swallowed. "We're sorting them. Now."

"Oh," Artemis said from her seat next to Devin's. "Oh my."

"Now, Devin? It's still a few minutes to midnight," said a fae with fiery red hair cascading around her, wearing an emerald dress that looked fresh off the red carpet. My stomach roiled as I recognized Candace's boss, Georgina.

"Do it now!" Devin's voice shook the quiet of the room. He was clearly in some sort of panic and the nagging tug at my heart thrilled at the sound. The lords and ladies drifted to their respective thrones, their faces varying degrees of amusement. Devin looked pained as he peeled his eyes from me and took his own seat.

"Come on, you two are going to pick your courts." Heather took my elbow as I winced at the sensation and led us toward the thrones.

"Right now?" Candace asked.

"Lord's orders," Heather mumbled.

We walked, and I stumbled, to the back of the gallery. My slightly altered shape was disorienting. I felt bombarded with sensations, and my fingers itched with unfamiliar pressure.

"Candace, approach the thrones," the Lady of Autumn commanded, with her air of smoke and leaves and windy nights.

I resisted letting go of Candie, but she had to step away.

"Artemis, why are you starting with her?" Devin snapped. I was surprised by how clearly I could hear him from where I stood. I could hear my own heartbeat, too, which I didn't like one bit.

"She was the first to turn. A rule we have not used in centuries, but a rule nonetheless." She did not take her eyes off us. "Candace, from these four thrones you feel our power. Let your magic speak and give yourself to your court."

Candace looked briefly between the thrones and went to stand before Georgina. I was sure she would hate her former employer as much as she did when still human, but I guess the pull of the Summer Court power was too strong.

"I can't really fight it, this is the one," she said confidently. Georgina smiled victoriously, placing a hand on Candie's shoulder. Then the whole room turned to me. The pressure of their eyes was heavy, but none as heavy as Devin's.

"Thea, approach us." Artemis turned her eyes to me, and I wobbled forward. "Thea, from these four thrones you feel our power. Let your magic speak and give yourself to your court."

I looked longingly at Candace. I could feel the warmth, the sun and grass and ocean waves emanating from her. Georgina and Candace were definitely creatures of the sun. But I didn't feel anything like that myself. If anything, I was repulsed by it.

Okay, not that one.

On the next throne sat a blond man with flowing hair and a lazy, amused expression. He was blossoms and spring rains and songbirds. But still no pull.

Two down, please let it be the next one.

Next was Artemis. She whispered earthy scents, wet leaves, and howling winds. I could feel cool fall evenings radiating from her, but I didn't feel any pull to it.

And then there was *him*. Devin hummed an icy chill. Both gentle falling snow and roaring storms at the same time. He was the evergreens that thrived in the cold. The crisp stillness in the air, and the dark night full of cold white stars.

There was most *definitely* a pull, and it was overwhelming. More than the thread tugging incessantly in my chest, my whole body wanted to sink toward that comforting chill like it was a giant pile of blankets and I hadn't slept in days. Something told me the weariness in my bones would find comfort there.

I could feel it. Taste it. I wanted to run to it. My arms prickled with winter sensations. I wanted to dance in the moonlight, leaving swirls of footprints in the snow. The cold didn't bite like it had only a few minutes ago. My new skin was comfortably warm, and something told me that nothing would chill me to the bone ever again. Even if I hadn't felt Winter's pull, I still felt a pull toward Devin. In his bright eyes I saw only longing; the urge to run to his arms was strong. Something was . . . wrong. Candace hadn't acted like this strange pull existed between her and Georgina.

I turned to Artemis. I would not be trapped by Devin a second time—he had already tricked me once and my heart was crushed for it. I felt the cool, earthy presence from the Lady of Autumn, and stepped forward.

"Lady Artemis?" I whispered, my words not at all sure, and took a small bow. "I think I should be with the Autumn Court."

She leaned back on her throne, lacing her fingers together in her lap. "No," she said. "Even if you weren't lying to yourself about where you belong, which I think you are, I will not have my court come between Devin and his mate."

Devin had called it a thread of fate, but I had come across the word mate in my fae research. A strange bond between fae. I'd read a few passages about it, but they all conflicted and hadn't seemed relevant to my plight. I hadn't given them much thought. Now I wish I had.

Whispers flew through the room behind me. I tried to ignore them. I turned to Georgina; the heat from her and Candace was sweltering. I'd suffer there. Even without the suffocating Summer presence, I took one look at the crafty Lady of Summer and knew I'd be miserable.

The Lord of Spring smiled lazily when I turned to him. My face was pleading but he simply shook his head, and my resolve crumbled. I turned again to Devin. His face was a mask of stone, but his eyes couldn't hide how anxious he was.

"Do I have to choose a court at all?" I asked the four thrones. More than one fae in the crowd murmured.

"No, you do not," Artemis answered, shooting an arm out in front of Devin as the latter leaned forward. "Though I would counsel against it. You, child, are not meant to be a wild fae. You would be wise to choose."

Fine then. I was stubborn, but I wasn't stupid. "All right then. I choose . . . the Winter Court." I sucked in a breath as a burst of approval hit me—a sensation, I could somehow tell, that had come from Devin.

He stood from his throne and smiled wide. "Then let the celebrations resume!" he ordered, and the music began immediately.

Laughter and cheering reverberated throughout the room. The suspended tension I was swimming in a moment ago now swept away. The Summer Court glowed as they surrounded Candace and pulled her toward the music. They reveled in their new sister. I knew in my heart she belonged there—the delight on her face was evidence enough. At first, she tried to find me in the crowd, reaching for me, but she was quickly overtaken by her court and lost in a sea of energy.

The Winter Court was calmer. A swarm of curious fae gathered, pressing in around me but not threateningly so. While Candace was surrounded by warmth and light and noise, the ones gathering in front of me were curious and calm and thoughtful. With offers of warm welcome, compliments, and outreaches of friendship, this was the nature of the Winter Court. They were genuinely glad to look at me as one of their own, much as the Summer Court had been with Candie, but with an air of uncertainty thanks to whatever this situation was between Devin and me. Heather pushed to the front of the crowd and wrapped her arms around my shoulders.

"Damn." She squeezed me. "That was intense."

"Yeah," I agreed. My hands shook as I hugged her back. "You're one of them. I mean, us. Winter."

She hugged me tighter. "I'm so happy to be with you right now."

I didn't say anything and just buried my face in her neck. She was cool to the touch, but I found it refreshing. I felt a small pulse of something then. Magic? It must be—I felt it wafting from the fae around me to varying degrees. We were one in a way that was so very strange and yet so natural to me at the same time.

I sensed Devin behind me. The fae parted to let him through. I stiffened.

"Don't be too mad at him," Heather whispered. "It will just hurt you both."

I didn't understand what she meant.

"Thea." His voice was somber. "Please, turn around."

I did—I couldn't help myself. Up close he was even more beautiful. His midnight hair was slightly blue, now that I saw it with my fae eyes, and pulled back from his face. I wanted to trace the strong lines of his jaw, his ears, those dangerous teeth. I desperately wanted to be closer to him, and at the same time I was still overwhelmed and upset.

"We need to talk. Will you come with me?" I got the feeling he wasn't one to throw around the word *please* lightly.

To be honest, I was a little afraid to be alone with him. I knew we had this thing between us to discuss, and I was still woefully in the dark about what it entailed. But the last conversation we had ended bitterly and I didn't know what would happen if I ended up in an argument with the leader of my new court.

"Do I have to?"

He offered me his hand, and I stared at it a moment before accepting. A warm, fuzzy energy buzzed between us. Like the force I felt from Heather but stronger. Much stronger.

All eyes were on us as he led me away. Looking at Heather, who was forcing a smile, and at Candace, lost in a sea of wild celebration. I took a deep breath and tried to settle myself somewhere between the polarizing desires of my heart and the upset of my mind.

"Where are we going, Lord Devin?" I asked as politely as I could, mimicking Heather's way of speaking to him.

"Call me Devin." He faced me. "You don't need to call me Lord. You're my . . ." He paused. "How about a drive? We can go wherever you want. Your favorite place."

"And leave the party? Can you do that?"

"There's no one here who can stop me," he said. "Except you."

Except me. I looked down at my faintly glowing hands, not sure I was ready for a drive just yet. But talking was okay, I could handle that. Here in the crisp white tile of the gallery it felt too bright, too crowded. There were fae everywhere—just out of arm's reach but too close. Curious eyes, passing servers with trays of drinks, the loud music—it was too much, the party was still going. Would it be weird to talk outside? There probably wouldn't be anyone standing out in the cold when a thought hit me. More of a feeling or intuition. "I can't freeze anymore, can I?"

"No," he answered softly. "And you're really not going to like the heat."

"I guess I didn't like it too much anyway." I played nervously with a strand of hair that had come loose from my updo. The texture of my hair seemed somehow smoother. I looked down at it and was startled by its color.

"My *hair*!" I no longer sported my mother's fawn-brown hair; instead my new reality was something that shimmered metallic and pinkish.

Devin reached out for me but stopped himself. "Are you all right?"

"I don't honestly know," I said. "I think I need a mirror. Get all the surprises out at once."

"There are mirrors in the bathroom, or the car visor," he suggested. "Or I can . . . drive you home."

It seemed painful for him even to offer that. Hell, it was hard for me to hear and I still sort of wanted to get away, but I might as well work this issue out now.

"Can we talk outside? I'll wait on the mirror until after we sort all this out."

His face lit up. "Of course." He offered me his arm. "Right this way."

CHAPTER SEVENTEEN

DEVIN

A thread of fate. The powers that draw gatherings of fae to one place and separate us to the courts are as fickle and unknown to us now as they have been from the beginning of time. And sometimes, rarely, a thread of fate connected two fae into a messy entwining of hearts.

There was no denying my attraction to Thea before, but now it was so much more than a serendipitous encounter. It was a natural attraction ready to pull us together the moment she had enough of her own magic to give it life.

And she was stunning. Her general shape hadn't changed much. Her features had sharpened, and her ears came to a newly formed point. But her other new features were undeniably fae. Beautiful and elegant and uniquely hers. If I was attracted to her before, the bond was now making her entirely distracting to my senses.

Thea walked next to me as I brought us through the sleeping gardens to Marcel's old studio. It didn't go unnoticed that her wide, curious eyes darted around the rose beds and up the path.

"It must be beautiful when everything is in bloom." Her voice was low, warm, comfortable. I could listen to her forever.

"You're welcome to see for yourself any time," I offered.

She scrunched up her nose at me. "Why do the faeries have a gallery anyway? You've clearly been here a long time—Dubois drew your picture in his diary."

"His greenhouse is built on a faerie gate." When she drew her brows in confusion I elaborated. "If the term is unfamiliar, do not blame Heather. The older fae have called them gates for a long time, but the term does not arise often. The gate—not that we can see it, as it's more of a feeling rather than a physical portal—is a place where the land's magic seeps through to our world. She did tell you there are other fae communities, yes?"

She nodded, and I continued. "The connection to Earth's magic is powerful here. A gate will pick and choose many things, including to draw the fae to it."

"Not all fae." It was half statement and half question.

"No, not all fae. There are many who roam freely with no call to a gate at all, but we thrive in community and the wild fae are typically not that strong." And not that good-natured, but there was no call to frighten her.

"But you don't thrive enough to make your own children, you have to steal them from humans," she said coolly.

I steadied my face from showing a reaction, though it stung to hear her ire against her new people. "Yes, unfortunately. It has been my duty to turn changelings for many decades now. A decision was made to turn a single human every year, and I volunteered to begin the change as my season of power approached. Adults, I might add. The practice of taking children has never sat well with me, though other parts of the world still practice the old ways."

Shoulders dropping, her face smoothed and she rubbed her temples lightly. "That wasn't fair, I shouldn't have said that. I'm just . . . it's a lot right now."

We reached the greenhouse door and stepped inside. The space was cluttered with easels, paintings, sketches, and supplies. Tools and long-ago dried paint jars, exactly as Marcel had left them. Thea's inquisitive nature couldn't keep her focus on me as her attention wandered to Marcel's relics. Amused, I shut the door behind us to keep out the wind and watched until her attention returned to the conversation at hand.

"Why?" she asked, barely audible. "Why turn humans? Why do you need to keep building your population when you don't age and die like humans do?"

"We protect the gate, and the humans in it, from darker fae. They may not feel the draw of the gate as we do but even a wild fae can feel the thick magic here."

Nodding slowly, she left my side then and started to wander the greenhouse.

"If we had a smaller presence here," I continued, "there would be war for the faerie gate, and I promise you the humans would suffer for it."

"That sounds terrifying."

The sounds of reverie in the gallery that had trailed after us changed as the orchestral music shifted to a slower melody. We still hadn't discussed this thread between us, but even if it wasn't pulling us together, I did enjoy her company. My hand hovered in the air between us, a silent invitation to dance.

She paused, considering it, then placed her hand in mine. Her touch was warm, and more than inviting against my skin. If the shiver that ran through her and the hitch in her breathing were any indication, I would say the same was true in reverse. Setting a hand on her hip, I led us in an easy dance to match the music.

"You and the rest of my court are under my protection. This gate has been here for centuries, and it will not fail now. Not under me."

We danced for a silent moment and I watched as she stared up through the glass to the night sky beyond. "So, this thread. I feel it, there's no denying that. I've read a bit about it but it wasn't exactly the focus of my research."

I nodded, and we spun softly as a violin sang out. "Ask me anything."

"You called it a thread of fate; I've also seen it referenced as a mate bond. What is it?" A soft flush crept up her neck as her eyes failed to meet mine. "That sounds like some heavy stuff to drop on a girl."

"You've heard of the concept of a soul mate?"

"Yes."

"To us, it is simply a tangible resonance of that concept. The perfect missing piece, shaped by fate or destiny or whatever higher power you want to wrap your head around. Two hearts as a pair of magnets, shaped to seek each other out."

I began to trace the line of her jaw, and she leaned into my touch before catching herself in the act.

"I don't like that there's no choice in the matter." Her voice trembled.

"There is a choice. There is always a choice," I said.

"What does that mean?"

Another crescendo from the gallery. Moving deftly around the open center of the greenhouse I turned Thea in my arms, her touch responsive as she moved and came back around to face me. "You feel it, even now. This thing between us won't go away just because one wants it to. The pull will keep pulling until we've acknowledged it, and then it will settle into something else entirely."

"Into what?" she asked incredulously.

I gave a short laugh, not missing that she watched the movement of my mouth as I did. "I can't say for sure as this is a first for me as well, but I hear it's much less strenuous."

"Don't you have to make the same decision?"

"What if I told you I found you enticing the moment we met?"

Her lips parted, surprised.

"I find your company enthralling. Your excitement, your expressive face, your clever mind. Even the way you move as you walk."

Moving my hand more solidly onto her back, I dipped her backward with the song as her eyes widened and her hand at my shoulder gripped me tightly.

"All enchanting."

Her attention was suddenly fixed to the side, out the window of the studio, her heartbeat fluttering.

Bringing her upright again, I resumed leading the dance. "Not everyone finds their bond, and I won't be so foolish as to take this lightly. Not when I was already attracted to you."

"Oh," she answered weakly.

"Time and distance usually mean the odds are against a pair finding one another, and yet here you were, right under my nose," I mused.

The music died to a halt, and so did our dance. Before letting her go completely, I raised her hand in mine and kissed the same fingers that had begun her change, my eyes locking hers in place as she watched every movement. Her hand wasn't what I wanted to kiss. I would much rather have claimed her mouth and told this bond exactly how agreeable I found it. But for now, the sight of her throat moving as she swallowed whatever answer she had to my kiss would be reward enough.

Thea stepped back, but not far. Absently touching the back of her fingers with her other hand. "This pulley feeling, will it go away eventually?"

"Yes and no." I settled myself into leaning against one of the shelves, arms folded over my chest before they reached out to her again before either of us were ready. "We can acknowledge the bond and let it fall into place, but this 'pulley feeling,' as you call it, will only be replaced with a firmer connection. You won't have the urge to run to me and do unspeakable acts, but you will always feel my presence within the city, and we'll know one another's strong emotions."

"Who says I want to do any unspeakable acts?" She frowned.

"Certain desires must be consuming your thoughts, because that's exactly what I'm battling myself." I smiled, feeling particularly wicked at the scandalized look on her face.

"How does one acknowledge the bond then?" She looked away.

"A kiss should do it," I said.

"Didn't you already kiss my hand?"

Reaching out, I cupped her chin gently, rubbing my thumb on her soft bottom lip. "Here."

Thea moved her face out of my hand just enough to speak, and I resumed crossing my arms. "You're really not bothered by all this? You didn't have a choice in me any more than I had a choice in you."

"Rare though it be, I've seen the bond before and I have faith in it. But you set the pace; it's you who's new to this world."

"What happens if I don't accept the bond?"

"You'll feel as you do right now, forever."

She frowned at that. "And if we accept this first part, but ignore it after?"

"Then we ignore it."

"And you'd be all right with that?"

Pain flashed through her eyes, and it broke my heart. I most certainly would not be all right with it, but I would deal with it. "Think on it. It doesn't have to be dealt with tonight. If you're comfortable, I would love to take you to dinner sometime."

Please, I want to see you smile.

She tilted her head my way, her pale blue eyes fixed on me. "I really don't think I'm ready for . . . all this. It's overwhelming, and I can't begin to pick apart what bits of me hate you for turning my world upside down and what parts of me are attracted to you."

"I understand."

"Can I go home for the night?" she asked. "I think I can give you a better answer soon."

"Of course. Heather drove you?" She nodded. "I would love to drive you if you'll allow it."

"Assuming I'm safe from harassment now?"

"No one in this city will touch you. You're Winter Court now, and you're under my protection. Especially while you're learning our ways, and indeed until you've mastered glamouring."

Displaying an example of my meaning, I slacked my hold on the power that contained my ears, teeth, the glow of my eyes, showing Thea more of my true self than I had shown anyone in a long time. Once she had a good look, I regained my tight hold on my glamour and appeared to all the world human once more. "That's how we keep ourselves disguised in human form."

And with the bond between us, none in the city would be so foolish as to make her uncomfortable, or out her new fae form—it would be too risky, for all of us. "Come on, I'll take you."

"Thanks—oh!" She slapped her hand to her mouth, eyes wide.

I chuckled. "You will never owe me a favor, Thea. But please be careful. Other fae will most certainly be glad to have you in their debt." She took my offered arm without pause. Something deep in my chest purred with satisfaction as I led her out through the greenhouse.

"I should say good-bye to Candace and Heather." She looked to the illuminated gallery. "I'll be right back."

Thea let go of my arm, leaving a cold emptiness at the absence of her touch. She disappeared back into the yellow glow of the party, leaving me to the dark.

"I've never seen you such a mess." A dark fae walked up beside me, both of us watching the door.

"You'd be in the same state." I scoffed.

"Yeah, rightly so. Mate, huh?" He folded his arms. "Do we have a Lady of Winter then?"

"I'm not pressuring her into anything."

"I wouldn't have expected you to. But the gate won't let one of the courts hold all the cards, and she feels potent. Fit to burst with some kind of power, whatever it is."

"You think something will happen to balance it out?" It seemed plausible—nothing in the nature of the fae came without balance. An evening of powers, a rounding of numbers. Two powerful fae, bonded by fate; it would stand to reason we would see something come of it.

"Heather was around earlier. You still haven't spoken to her," I said, dodging the conversation.

"And I'm not going to."

"You think you have forever until you don't, Arthur," I warned. He fell silent.

Something was tugging me toward the party. Thea had intense feelings about something—I could sense her by the doorway. Arthur slipped away as she reappeared.

"Okay, let's go," she said, and I led her to my car.

Traffic was almost nonexistent on the main road. We continued for a few minutes, not saying anything.

"Text me if anything unusual happens." I pulled onto her road. "Fae can have any number of abilities, so don't be distressed at something strange, just contact me. You'll need to learn to glamour, that can come once you've gotten some rest. We can also discuss an option for you to move closer to the court while you adapt if you like. I'm sure you're tired, we can talk more tomorrow."

Thea said a quiet okay in response, and then looked out the window, her new fae features giving her a softer look of concentration than what she'd displayed as a human. Slowing for a red light, I said. "Don't bother the other courts. There are some off-limits areas of town that belong to them, as well as some safe areas belonging to the Winter Court only. Mostly just small areas around our main populations, nothing near your apartment. I'll send you a map."

"I'll do my best to memorize it this weekend. I do have to go somewhere Saturday, how will that work?"

"I'll make sure you know what you need to know in the morning. Glamouring, a few rules."

She nodded, then watched in silence as we pulled up to her apartment. "Th—ugh, I need to get used to not saying that. Let me try again: You were kind to give me a ride. It's good to be home."

"My pleasure." I gripped the wheel all the harder. I wasn't ready for her to leave.

She slid out of the car, sweeping her dress out of the way as she closed the door. I let out a slow breath and closed my eyes, taking in the scent she'd left behind.

Tap, tap, tap.

I blinked—she was at my window. I rolled it down, straightening in my seat. "Yes?"

She leaned into the car. I froze. Swiftly, she pulled me forward by my tie and placed her lips on mine.

CHAPTER EIGHTEEN

THEA

My heart pounded as I kissed Devin, thrilling the thread between us. It was a slow, sweet kiss that filled me with warmth. Pulling him by the tie, that was absolutely a Candace move. But it was worth channeling her if it gave me the backbone to reach out and make the move I wanted.

His hands tightened on the steering wheel, the scent of him in my face and making my head swim. A snap startled me—a small gasp escaped my mouth against his and Devin took full advantage of it. Moving his tongue against my parted lips, I welcomed him in as we deepened the kiss. The string at my heart pulled tighter and tighter as if screaming for more.

When the pull between us felt impossibly needy, asking for more than I could physically give it, everything suddenly went slack. It was like a light switch had turned off. The pull was gone; in its place was a gentle warmth coming from Devin. I felt his heart, his adrenaline.

Letting the tie slide through my fingers, I leaned back so I could see him. My lips left his, and his hungry expression was slowly replaced by his mask of calm. That made one of us. My breath was burning sharp and fast as I panted down air; my chest rushed to keep up.

"That's better," I breathed. "I wasn't going to be able to sleep with that thread dangling like that."

Devin was surprisingly speechless, and my eyes flicked to the top half of his steering wheel, which had broken off in his hands. That explained the snap I'd heard.

"Goodnight, Devin," I whispered, stepping back from the car.

Devin ran a hand down his face, tossing the broken piece into the backseat. "Goodnight, Thea."

The thrill of my own actions moved through me as I turned and walked to my front door. Even walking I could feel where he was, feel that he hadn't moved his car yet. A compass came to mind. I was glad he was the type to make sure I got to my door first, but I liked to think he was also still recovering. Because that kiss? That kiss was more than anything else I had felt before.

How did I feel about it being with Devin? That was still up in the air. Was I attracted to him? Definitely. Even before the thread business between us, I hadn't ever wanted to reach for someone as much as I'd wanted to reach for him. But was I still upset about the whole changing accident? Hell yeah I was. But that was a problem for Tomorrow Thea. Tonight Thea needed to release that damn string enough to catch her breath and clear her head.

I shoved my key in the lock and let myself in, desperate for a shower and the impending panic attack in front of the bathroom mirror. When I flicked the lights on, I screamed.

A figure stood at the back door, the emergency exit in my kitchen at the opposite end of the apartment. Even with the eyesight I was still adjusting to, they were too quick for me to get a good look as they fled.

Reaching for my bag, I realized it was back at Heather's and so was the iron pipe. I took a step back, my eyes flicking from the disturbed papers across my table to the open doors to my bedroom and bathroom. Whoever that was, they had gone through my things.

"Thea!" Warm hands pulled me back against a hard chest, and I knew who it was before I looked up into Devin's hard expression as he looked around. "What happened?"

I took a breath, sharper than intended, as my throat tightened. "There was someone here, at the back door."

Without a word, Devin moved around me and ran for the back exit. *Don't trust them.*

My heart tightened and I put a hand over it. The note in my car had told me not to trust them. Them, the fae. Watching Devin, I didn't think the note meant him, or at least whoever *C* was surely didn't mean all of them. Did they? But whoever was in my apartment was undoubtedly fae, and that was terrifying.

Devin came back to me, placing a hand on each of my arms. "What did they look like?" he asked softly.

"I don't know, they were so fast and it was dark and—" I shook my head, tears welling in my eyes. "Fae, it was a fae."

His worried grip softened as he pulled me in for a hug. I held him fiercely, the tears starting to overtake me.

"Probably a wild fae." His chest rumbled as he spoke, and I found it comforting as my fingers gripped the fabric of his coat. I felt so violated, someone had been in my apartment, a place that should have been safe from strangers.

Devin pulled away from me but not fully arm's length. "Does it look like they took anything?"

I shook my head. "Things aren't exactly where I left them, but my laptop and the furniture are the only things of value, and those are still here."

He nodded, pulling me out of the doorway. "You can't stay here tonight."

Devin was right; there was no way I'd feel safe.

"Pack a bag, I'll take you somewhere. I'm happy to invite you to the heart of the Winter Court—no one would be able to get close to you there. Or Heather is only a call away—she can meet us at her place and you can stay with a friend."

I opened my mouth, almost ready to run to Heather for comfort, until a thought struck me and I shivered. *What if they came for Heather too?*

Was it me they wanted specifically, or something I had? Either way, my presence could put Heather in harm's way and she lived alone otherwise. And what would happen when she left for work and I was at her place by myself?

Candace was now in the Summer Court's stronghold, my parents' house was over two hours away, and I didn't have anywhere else to go.

"The Winter Court . . ." my voice was a strained whisper. "It's safe?"

Devin put one warm hand on my cheek, rubbing his thumb on the corner of my eye where it was still wet from my shocked tears. "There's nowhere safer in the city, and I'll be close by."

"Okay," I said. "Please, take me there."

Devin's expensive car should have tipped me off that he would live somewhere expensive too. It was an odd thought to cross my mind as we pulled up to what appeared to be a private road with huge townhomes and immaculate lawns, but it definitely distracted me from the stressful events of the night. We stopped at the end of the road, where one detached house stood by itself, and Devin pulled into the driveway.

"These homes belong only to our court. No other fae come here, and with such a concentration of glamour, few humans would come down this road."

"And it's okay for me to stay here?"

His expression softened. "It's more than okay; the court will be happy you've come. I'm happy you've come."

We got out of the car and I slung my bag over my shoulder, only to have Devin take it from me as we walked to the front door. "Is there a spare room or a couch then?"

Devin paused at the door, horrified. "A couch?"

I shrugged.

Devin shook his head, unlocking the door. "There's a bed for you here. Welcome to my home."

The moment I stepped inside, I could tell it was Devin's home even if he hadn't told me. Everything smelled like him, a masculine earthy scent that reminded me of the pine-covered mountains. Every wall was white and the floor that wasn't covered in dark hardwood was covered in crisp marble tile. A sitting room to my left had a fireplace and a set of matching modern sofas all in black, white, or blue. In fact, all the furnishings I could see were modern with clean lines and sharp corners as though the house had been staged for a magazine cover.

"This way." Devin brought my bag up the stairs to the right, and I followed him to the top, where he opened the last door down the hallway.

The room was simple—one big bed with white bedding sat under a large window, and the other furnishings were sparse but stylish. It was more like stepping into a hotel room than a guest room.

Devin set my bag at the foot of the bed and moved to the doorway before pausing. "I'll be just down the hall. If you need anything, please let me know."

"I think I just need a shower and some sleep," I said.

"Of course." Devin hovered a moment, unreadable as he took in the sight of me in the room. He inhaled as he closed his eyes a moment, then shut the door behind him as he walked out.

I took my laptop out of my bag, set it on the bedside table, and brought the rest of my things into the attached bathroom. Ignoring the mirror until I was good and ready to face my reflection, I stepped around the glass wall of a very big shower with my shampoo bottle and froze. There were already shower items here. Were they guest amenities? Picking up a full bottle of shampoo, I decided that must be the case, but I still used my own things. Something familiar would go a long way for me tonight.

My mood was greatly improved with a shower, despite the frown that stayed on my face while I washed around something that had sprouted from my head. I remembered feeling it at the time but had forgotten until the shower. Fresh and clean as I stepped out of the shower, I knew it was time to face myself. I purposefully avoided the mirror until I had set everything on the counter. Then my hands gripped the counter as I looked up.

A strangled sound choked in my throat at the sight of myself staring out of blue eyes I didn't have before. My hair I was prepared for, having seen it as pieces had fallen around my face throughout the eventful night. It was the antlers that caught me completely off guard. They were very small, little baby antlers if anything, protruding from my head maybe three or four inches. I allowed myself to stare for another several minutes before turning away. Not staring back at my mom's hair and chin or my dad's brown eyes would take time to get used to, but there was nothing I could do about them now. I wondered what stretching would feel like from now on. Would warrior pose feel different on my yoga mat now that everything felt stretched out? Letting the thought go, I didn't want to dwell on it until I had to.

Combing my hair slowly, if only to occupy myself while it dried, I sat on the edge of the bed and stared out the window and watched a light snow begin to fall. Once I was done, I turned out the light and crawled into bed.

Devin. Devin was everywhere in this house, and the fabrics of the bed had absorbed his scent too. Or maybe that was from the strange bond between us, or just the way my nose was now. The feeling of warmth that had settled between us was like a compass. It told me he was in the other room down the hallway, a mere wall separating us.

I should have been more upset. I should have been worried about the break-in at my apartment or the fact that I wasn't even a human anymore, a feeling that would certainly take time to acclimate to. Instead, I found comfort in this home that smelled like earth and pine and snow.

After the longest night of my life, sleep came fast, and my dreams were filled with wicked green eyes.

CHAPTER NINETEEN

DEVIN

"You've found nothing?" I growled into the phone, feeling the air drop to an icy chill in my kitchen. Once I was certain Thea was asleep upstairs, I used the rest of the night to coordinate efforts to find out what had happened. Even now as the sun peered through the windows, some of my more skilled court fae were looking into it.

"None. Wherever they went, they didn't leave a trace," said Arthur. "At this point our best bet may be to refocus on watching instead of pursuing."

To think that a wild fae would appear in the home of our brand-new changeling on the winter solstice, the night my court came into power. Fury rolled off me, even as ice crunched beneath my feet. Taking a breath, I waved it away, erasing any trace that I had let my powers slip.

"Do it," I said. "Regroup and focus on watching the territory. I trust your judgment."

"I'll call if we find anything. I'll send a report tonight regardless."

I would much rather have investigated myself, but that meant leaving Thea here alone. This street may be the heart of the Winter Court, but I still couldn't bring myself to leave her side, not when she might be in danger. I could feel her; she was still in bed. *My* bed. Having her in the safest room in the whole of the court made me feel better. Not that I had slept anyway—I would make do in my office. For all the rooms in my home, they were furnished for storage or work, but I'd never anticipated needing a guest bed.

We had much to do today, and it was time to let Arthur perform his duties and me to perform mine. I had a new changeling to care for, and it had nothing to do with the fact that we had a mate bond between us. The Lord of Winter does not shirk his responsibilities, even when the situation turns complicated.

I showered in the downstairs bathroom, thankful for yesterday's delivery of clean clothes that was still sitting on the kitchen table. I hadn't brought it upstairs yet, too busy with the solstice preparations.

Pulling on a pair of black slacks, trying to comb the damp hair that brushed my shoulders, a thrill of panic hit me at the same time I heard a yelp from upstairs. Strange, to feel a pull from outside of my body connected inside my mind all at once and knowing Thea was at the other end of it. Dropping what I was doing, I ran up the stairs and to the bedroom door.

"Is everything all right?" Keeping my voice even was difficult, and my hand hovered over the doorknob, awaiting her answer.

"Yes," she said, her voice muffled through the door, and I could feel her approach thanks to the bond. Taking a step back from the door, I gave her space to open it. She was in a similar state as me, her hair damp and combed back off her shoulders. She wore a sweater several times too big for her. Her eyes flicked down to my state of half dress, and they came back up with a blush across her face. One side of my mouth curled up in amusement, and she averted her eyes.

"I, um, poked a hole through my sweater."

I frowned. "What?"

She tapped the end of one of her new antlers sheepishly. "Poked a hole. I forgot."

Looking down near the neckline, sure enough, a hole had torn through the yarn, disrupting the stitches and leaving an unsightly gap. Snorting a laugh, I pushed the door open gently and she let me in. Striding to the closet, I pulled out a black button-up and offered it to her. "We can find you more clothes but take this for now."

Her head snapped from the shirt in my hand to the closet, then back to me. "Is this your room?"

Tilting my head, I unbuttoned the shirt in my hand as I spoke. "It is, does that bother you?"

"Me? Doesn't it bother you? I could have taken the guest room." She removed the ruined garment, leaving her in just the tank top she wore underneath it.

"I don't have such a room in my home." I finished unbuttoning the shirt and draped it over her shoulders as she stared at me. "You were exactly where I thought you would have the safest night's sleep while I worked."

"You didn't sleep?" she asked, alarmed. "I feel like I just imposed big-time."

"You didn't."

"Then what are we going to do tonight?" she asked. "I can't go back to my apartment yet, can I?" A pang of fear crossed her face.

"No, of course not."

"But you only have one bed."

"If it bothers you, I'll just buy another one. I have another room downstairs that could be converted to a bedroom where I can stay. It's nothing but storage right now."

"But—"

"Thea," I said, my voice lower and firmer than I had intended. "I want you here, and even better, I'm glad you slept in my bed."

Another flush of emotion from the direction of Thea's warmth. Just a hint of lust. Her lips parted in surprise, and my eyes followed the motion with a spreading grin.

"Did you sleep well, bond mate?" I asked, low and with clear intent to tease.

Thea caught her breath and stood up straighter, pulling my shirt tighter around her shoulders. She looked me up and down, a mix of curiosity and scandal on her face. "Now who is thinking unspeakable things?"

Her reaction was unexpected and I chuckled as I took her fingers in my hand. "You're entangled with a fae now, darling. Unspeakable things are what I excel at."

Kissing her hand exactly as I did the night we met, I was rewarded with her fluttering heartbeat. Letting her hand go, I backed up to give her space. "What are your commitments for the next few days?"

"I was supposed to go have Christmas with my family tomorrow. Now I'm not so sure I can. And after that, a Monday morning shift at work."

"Whatever your current employer is paying you, I would like to triple it if you'll come work at the gallery with me."

"What?"

"Did you think all our conversations about bringing a historical element to the gallery were in jest?" I asked.

"After everything that happened? Sort of."

"I do not make jokes about L'Atelier Rouge," I said. "You are a clever delight of passion when it comes to your projects. I'd be mad to ignore what you could bring."

She let out a strangled laugh. "So that's it? I just . . . *have* a job?"

"Of course. Even if you weren't the changeling, I thought we were in the midst of a professional transaction. I had every intention of hiring you to coordinate this new archival development at the gallery."

"Okay," she murmured, first looking down, then meeting my eyes. "Yes, please. I'd love this opportunity. I won't let you down."

Reaching out to tuck a loose lock of rosy-golden hair behind her gently pointed ear, I smiled. "I'm glad. As for your Christmas festivities, I'm happy to teach you what you need to know to navigate it as a fae, and as one more precaution I would like to go with you if possible."

"To my family's Christmas?" she asked. "I can still make it work and see my family?"

"I'm not going to stop you from seeing your family; this is the last holiday you'll have with them before you need to start taking new precautions."

A pained expression crossed her face, and it hurt to watch. "It's just sinking in, that's all. I was thinking about my family. Can I really not touch them anymore?"

"You can," I urged gently. "Just . . . sparingly. Too much direct contact over time will still put them in contact with fae magic. A little is unavoidable for most humans, but too much could cause side effects. Seeing fae details, confusion, things like that. It's how we prepare a typical changeling in the first place."

"I see." Her jaw tightened and relaxed as a slew of thoughts passed behind her eyes before she looked up at me again. "I don't know what it's going to be like after this year, so I want to make the most of this one."

"Of course."

"But you want to come?" she asked again.

"There is a lot you don't know about the wild fae and what was possibly searching your apartment," I said. "I want to go, not only for safety reasons but also"—I leaned in close, her enticing scent filling my lungs as I whispered in her ear—"I want to be close to you."

Thea placed a hand on my chest, whether to steady herself or to pause the moment I wasn't sure. But she wasn't pushing me away, and the delicious sensation of her flushed heat between us was addictive. Still, I moved back to give her air. My point had been made; now the decision was hers. I am a patient fae, I could wait as long as she wanted me to.

"Okay. Teach me what I need to know and we can leave tomorrow."

CHAPTER TWENTY

THEA

Devin was nothing if not distracting when he was teaching me how to glamour. Spending the morning learning how to pull in my magic, which was weird enough to hear in the first place, I finally figured out that the pulsing feeling of pressure I felt from the other fae was the potency of their powers. Heather was a warm pressure when she hugged me, and Devin filled the room. The difference would have been comical if it weren't so eye-opening.

But once I got the hang of pulling it into me, it was an easy flex to hide the magic away and my outward appearance would be as it had been before the solstice. Unfortunately, that led to another problem entirely when the only thing to focus on without the distracting pressure in my way was the hot compass that was Devin.

My stomach was in knots all day, wondering what we were going to do about the bed situation that evening, now that I knew I'd taken Devin's room. I was torn between my mother's voice in my head yelling at me to be a good guest, and the urge to know what it would feel like to climb in bed next to the smooth, charming fae, a thought that intrigued me as much as it shocked me. In the end, Devin spent the night out of the house to take another look around my apartment, leaving a few fae to keep an eye on things in his stead. I slept in his button-up since most of my clothes were still at my apartment, the added bonus being that Devin's shirt still smelled like him—an intoxicating scent that shouldn't have been as much of a comfort as it was.

And after a long day being bombarded with new skills and information, I found myself waking up early. Mom had been shocked when I told her I was bringing my "boyfriend" but glad all the same. Devin kept watch as we went back to my apartment so I could pack more clothes, ones with larger head holes, and the presents I had bought and wrapped for my family. When I put them in the back of my van next to a pile of wrapped gifts that hadn't been there yesterday, Devin simply smiled and ignored my questioning look. After that, we set off for my parents' house.

It was snowing pretty heavily on the drive. My skin was cool, but I hadn't felt that uncomfortable winter chill since my change. I didn't even have to turn the iffy heat on in the van. Devin argued in favor of bringing his car until I explained that not only does his car still need to get the steering wheel fixed, but it would stick out like a sore thumb in a small town, and I wanted to avoid as much attention as possible. Where I came from, *attention* was code for *small-town gossip*. So, my van it was, but he insisted that he drive to keep an eye on things. The wild fae came to mind, so I didn't argue.

The drive was fairly dull with no interesting scenery, just alternating patches of trees and suburbia outside of Seattle until you hit alternating patches of trees and farmland. Devin and I didn't talk much. It wasn't uncomfortable, but I got the feeling we both had a lot on our minds and we just needed time to process it all.

Passing one of my personal mile markers, a broken-down red truck in a field that had been there since I was a kid, my phone rang. Devin's eyes drifted to where I sat in the passenger seat, then back to the road.

"It's my mom," I said, then answered. "Hello?"

"Hi, sweetie. How's the drive?" From the sounds of it, my mother was busy mixing something.

"Good, I'm about an hour out. We just passed the red truck."

"We're ordering pizza since I'm going to be cooking all day tomorrow. What toppings do you want?" She stopped mixing and I heard the creaking of old cabinet doors.

My eyes drifted to Devin. I bit the inside of my cheek, picturing the powerful fae eating something as mundane as pizza. "What toppings do you like?" I whispered.

"Whatever you like," he answered, keeping his eyes on the road.

"Olives and mushrooms. Are you cooking something now? I can hear you," I said.

"Cookie dough. Jack and Amy wanted to make some, but they got bored halfway through."

I smiled as I imagined my brother's young kids "helping" in the kitchen. "Are George and Dad watching the game then?"

"Yes, and I guess it's not going well for their team." As if on cue, angry shouting erupted in the background. "Keep it down, you'll disturb the neighbors! Sorry about that. If you need to stop for gas, get it before you get to town. Hanson's ran out this morning; their delivery is late but should be here tonight."

The side of my mouth jerked up, picturing my mother on her morning gossip run, picking up this information while doing her errands.

"Thanks, I think we're good, though. Mom?" The phone crackled, the sound gone. "Mom?—AH!"

A black figure too large to be a dog, too oddly shaped for a deer, darted across the road. I dropped my phone as Devin cursed and hit the brakes. Tires screeched and I slid sideways and we crashed right into something that brought the van to a halt. Devin had somehow managed to reach a hand around the back of my head before it knocked into the window on impact. The angry whirling of snow picked up, making it hard to spot the figure.

I unbuckled and reached for my phone on the passenger side floor. "Mom?"

Nothing. No reception either. Pulling it away from my face, I looked at the dead black screen with a crack across it. "Dammit."

"Stay here," Devin ordered, his face hard and that pulsing feeling rolling off him. Anger too. It caught me off guard the few times I had been able to feel an emotion come from outside my own head, but this was one of those moments where the bond between us told me Devin was pissed.

I pocketed the broken phone and watched out the window, but the snow was swirling and I couldn't see much. My eyes flicked down to the bag at my feet, and I pulled out the pipe. It felt good to have something in my hands when that big . . . *thing* was still out there.

Gripping the pipe like a club, I opened my door. Devin had told me to stay in the van, but I could tell we had hit something when we crashed and I wanted to take a look.

Snow crunched underfoot as I made my way to the front of the van and stopped by the broken fence post. There was a huge dent in the side of the vehicle, just behind the headlight. It was ugly, but it shouldn't stop the van from running. What was one more dent, considering how rough the rest of the vehicle already looked.

"Great." I scanned the farm. This wasn't the only broken fence post, and the field looked like it hadn't been taken care of in quite some time. Still, my van had just broken part of it, and I should probably give them my insurance information.

But not right now. Right now, I could feel Devin at the road ahead where we'd seen that thing come out of the trees. There was no way it was human, and I wasn't about to delude myself after everything I'd seen in the past weeks.

My eyes wandered back to the farmhouse, and I wondered if it was just run down or if it was abandoned entirely. Then I froze, movement in one of the windows stopping my feet and my heart at the same time. Something was there, and it had glowing yellow eyes.

A sudden hand on my shoulder caused me to absolutely freak out after what I'd just seen in the window. "Thea."

"Ah!" The pipe in my hand felt solid as I turned and swung at Devin. I was so distracted that I hadn't noticed that the warmth that was the other end of the bond was standing next to me. Devin reached up and caught the pipe with his hand well before it could connect with his head, and I dropped it into the snow.

He swore, scowling down at his sizzling palm.

"I'm so sorry!" I said. "I didn't mean to, I thought I saw something."

Looking to the window again, the figure was now gone.

"Give me your hand," Devin said with kind urgency. Pulling it out of the sleeve of my sweater, I held it out to him. He rubbed his fingertips over my palm. Frustrating heat hit me at his touch, and I had to ignore the warmth flooding my hand and other places.

"Are you burned?" he asked.

That caught me off guard. "Burned?"

He flipped his own hand over and I gasped at the sight of angry red welts, and it hit me. "Oh my god, it's iron."

"Yes, it is." Devin shook his hand in the cool air, his face stern as he stared at the pipe between our feet. Shrugging off his coat, he bent down and used the coat to pick it up, turning to me with an intense expression. "Iron is a burning poison to us; you shouldn't be able to touch it."

Looking down at my smooth palms, then to Devin's angry red one, I didn't know what to say. He took the pipe, still wrapped in his coat, and tossed it into the back of the van.

"I found nothing. But the scent of wild fae is all over this place, among other things."

"Other things?"

"Do you think we are the only living, breathing fairy tales in this world?"

I shook my head, startled by the implication.

"Right. There is definitely something else living around here. Stay away from this stretch of road if you can help it. For my sanity and your safety."

Climbing back in with shaky hands, I pulled the door closed and locked it. Devin got in the driver's side and pulled my hands gently in front of me so that he could see them again. He ran the thumb of his good hand over one of my palms, then met my eyes.

"You keep iron with you?" he asked.

"A leftover precaution from before I changed." His worried look was scaring me. "You're hurt, I'm so sorry."

"I'll be fine soon, it's you I'm . . ." Shaking his head, he let me pull my hands back. "We'll have to look into that when we get back."

My eyes drifted from the farmhouse to my hands to Devin as he started the van and pulled back onto the road. Another unsolved mystery. *C*, the farmhouse, my apartment, my unharmed skin. Just how many more questions had to pile up before I was buried in them?

CHAPTER TWENTY-ONE

THEA

An hour away from the creepy farm sat a small town of fewer than two thousand people. There was only one school for all grades, and downtown, if you could call it that, was three blocks' worth of stores and a little town hall. If you needed to go to the hospital, you had to drive about forty-five minutes to the nearest one. Mom had stayed at home while my brother and I were growing up. Dad was the local sheriff. Now Mom spent her days quilting with the church, and Dad was getting ready to retire next year.

I directed Devin down the familiar street lined with neatly trimmed yards and matching white mailboxes. My family's brick home was decked out in blinking white lights and giant plastic ornaments hung from the leafless maple tree in the front yard. The driveway was already full, my brother's giant truck taking up one side, my dad's patrol car the other.

"This is it," I said. "This is where I grew up."

It was an oddly emotional moment for me. Even seeing movement in the living room window, knowing my family was there and ready to celebrate, tugged at my heartstrings. No one was any the wiser that the little girl of the family had gone and gotten herself turned into a faerie. My throat tightened as a light turned on upstairs.

Devin's warmth leaned over to my side of the van. "The changes are not as big as you expect, at least until it becomes apparent that you aren't aging. They will still love you, and you will be able to see them for a few more years before we have to figure something else out."

"But not touch them," I added, my words bitter. It was one of the things that could push a human to the fae world. Food, and touch.

"Give them each a big one." Devin pulled one of my hands to his lips, kissing the back of my hand as he had taken to doing. "Make it count."

He sounded sad, remorseful. I knew it was all one big accident and he thought at the time that he was changing a human with no connections, but it still stung. It was hard to blame him, but it was still easy to be upset about it.

Outside the van, I slung my duffel bag over my shoulder and gathered my heap of poorly wrapped presents. Devin's were gathered neatly in a large bag and he not only handled his own things with ease, but he took part of mine as I protested. Making enough of a fuss, I probably alerted the whole house that we had arrived. I didn't even have to knock—the door flung open and my nephew appeared in the doorway, staring up at me.

"Aunt Thea?"

"Yes, Jack?" I smiled.

"Is one of those for me?" he squealed.

Laughing, I knew he was looking at the big bag with dinosaurs in Santa hats all over it. "Maybe it is, buddy."

"Jack! Sorry, Thea." My sister-in-law, Marsha, scooped up her four-year-old and balanced him on her hip with a grunt.

"He's getting so big," I said. "You're going to be bigger than grandma next year."

"No way!" Jack squealed.

"Let me get the door for you." Marsha's eyes moved to Devin, who stood behind me on the walkway and she gave me a wink. *Good job,* she mouthed, and I was ready to melt with embarrassment when I remembered a moment too late that Devin could feel it vividly. He tried to hide the smirk creeping onto his face but not well enough that I didn't catch it.

"Oh, hush," I mumbled, shuffling inside. After setting my gifts under the tree, Devin took my bag. I busied myself by pulling my coat off; it was making me sweat despite the freezing cold outside, but I had to keep up appearances or Mom would throw a fit about me not wearing it.

"There's my girl!" Mom came out of the kitchen, wiping her hands on her apron.

Hanging my coat on a hook quickly, she was on me in seconds.

"Come here, sweetie." Mom wrapped me in a fierce hug. The wind was knocked out of me as my eyes burned with sudden, welling tears. This was it. This was the mom hug. Possibly the last one I could risk, ever. Wrapping my arms around her tightly and maneuvering my antlers that were there whether my family could see them or not, I took a deep breath, inhaling the smell of my mother and committing it to memory.

"We lost reception there at the end of the call. How was the drive?" she asked.

"Snowy." I forced a smile, reluctantly letting her go and taking a step back. "But we're here now."

"That you are," she beamed and turned to Devin. "I'm Maggie, we're so glad to have you join us."

Devin reached out to shake Mom's hand. He was wearing gloves that I didn't even see him pull on between leaving the van and arriving at the door, but it was suddenly such an obvious way to minimize touch that I was mad I hadn't thought of it sooner myself.

"Lovely to meet you," Devin said, that charming side coming out. "I've heard nothing but good things about your family."

My mother blushed. *Blushed.* Once they noticed we had arrived, Dad and George pulled themselves away from the TV long enough to introduce themselves while Marsha and I corralled Amy and Jack away from the new piles of presents under the tree. When the doorbell rang, Mom pushed past all of us. "Pizza is here!"

Dad helped her take in the boxes while Mom slipped the cash to the delivery driver. At the mention of pizza, Jack went ballistic and two-year-old Amy fed off his enthusiasm, not knowing why but ready to get in on the excitement.

"Let me show you where you can put your things," I said, picking up my duffel bag.

"Oh, Thea," Mom said over her shoulder, "your Grandma Fern will be staying the night in the guest room." She passed the last pizza box off to George, who took it to the kitchen with the others before turning back to me and Devin at the foot of the stairs.

"Okay," I said, realization hitting me. That was the room I was going to put Devin in.

Mom watched as the last of the family drifted into the kitchen before turning back to look between us. She shot me a knowing glance.

"You're twenty-three, sweetie. I can't tell you what to do anymore, but while you're home, I'd prefer no hanky-panky."

"*Mom.*"

"Of course, we don't have another room so you'll be sharing a bed." She put her hands on her hips.

"*Mother*," I hissed. "Nothing is going to happen."

"I'm just saying, you're a grown woman now," she started. "And I respect that it's your body and your decision, but while you're under our roof—"

"*Stop*, Mom. Stop. I understand. Just, please stop."

"Okay, sweetie. Come down when you have your things settled." She gave Devin a smile, then went into the kitchen.

"Jesus, Mother." My face was probably a tomato after my mother's words, but Devin was obviously more amused than anything else.

"Let's put these away and join your family," Devin said. "That's more important than a little motherly embarrassment."

And my posture softened. He was right. She could embarrass me all she wanted this year; I was determined to soak in every moment with her.

"Come on," I sighed. "Let me show you to my room."

Devin's warmth was almost overwhelming at my back as I stopped at the top of the stairs. My bedroom was the first door, and my mind raced to remember what we might find in there. Was there anything that needed to be hidden away? What bits and baubles from my childhood were about to be unveiled to the fae behind me?

"Thea?" Devin asked.

Squaring my shoulders, I resigned myself to opening the door no matter what was behind it. Pushing it open, we stepped inside.

An era of horses and boy bands plastered my walls, and I closed my eyes as it all settled in. Mom had made a new yellow quilt for my bed, which I appreciated, because it was an improvement over the fleece blanket with running stallions that had been there since I was a kid.

I plopped my bag on the desk, suddenly aware of how small the room was. Devin stood by the door as his eyes roamed over everything—a couple of academic awards, some posters, photos of my family and friends.

"I like it. Very . . . human teenager."

"I used to be one, you know."

"Does your door have a lock?" he asked.

"Why?" I asked, suddenly flustered at the string of thoughts that ran through my mind.

"For your glamour, darling," Devin mused. "We can't have your mother walking in on you while you're asleep. You don't have that firm of a hold on your glamour yet, unless you want to show off your antlers."

"Ah. In that case, yes, it does lock." I wasn't sure if he could see from my expression what I was thinking, but the bond probably gave me away regardless.

His eyes crinkled, that look of mischief that drew me to him at the gallery plastered on his face. "I'm curious, why does a young girl in a town like this gravitate toward a history degree?"

Fair question. I guess it was time to open up, considering our unique situation. Making a mental note to ask him about a million history questions on the way home, I pulled a book off my shelf and tossed it on the bed. "There's not much to do around here. And if I'm being honest, any of my old classmates who stayed here are now doing some kind of farming or minimum wage job or have already gotten married and are keeping house."

"But that's not what you wanted."

I shrugged while Devin opened the journal I'd tossed to him. Inside was a carved bone button, taped to the front cover, and a collection of handwritten notes and badly drawn sketches.

"George had decided he was going to become a famous treasure hunter; got a metal detector for his birthday and everything. We spent a lot of time digging through dirt, and I found that button behind the church. I was convinced it was from a wagon train or something. Obviously, it's not nearly that old. But it did make me realize the history right under our feet—just a couple hours south of Seattle and there's so much history here. So I started keeping records of things I found or facts I learned. I was hooked."

Devin nodded, flipping carefully through the pages. "Even as a child you were a meticulous researcher."

I laughed and took back the book. "Don't you start—Candace teases me enough as is."

"I would never tease you about it," Devin said, his mouth a slight frown. "It's an important part of who you are."

Shelving the book, I traced the spine of it fondly before turning back to Devin. "I guess we should go down to dinner. I'm starving, aren't you hungry?"

"I'm hungry for something," he said. A hot flush of lust hit me, and I couldn't tell if it was coming from him or from me or from both of us. That damned sly smile that fluttered my heart. He leaned forward. "I want you to enjoy your time with your family, but I also want you to know where I stand."

He leaned closer, and the flush of heat between us kept no secrets as my eyes drifted to his lips. I know we both leaned into it when his lips crashed into mine.

My body relaxed a fraction after the initial surprise. Was this what I had done to him just to get rid of that stupid pull? There was a very right feeling with Devin, like we were made for each other. I was starting to understand the intensity of the bond. Beyond the kisses he stole on my fingers, this was more passionate. More intense.

I paused for breath. We locked eyes, and I felt in that moment every-thing he felt. I had been with a couple of guys before, but this . . . I wasn't ready for this. For him. His ferocity would swallow me whole. Lifting my fingers to reach for Devin, a dangerous decision was forming in my mind when—

Thwack.

A plastic dart from a toy gun smacked the wall behind me. Devin shot up on high alert but was able to rein himself in fairly quickly.

"Aunt Thea." Jack stomped into my room, a plastic gun in one hand and a half-eaten slice of pizza in the other. "Daddy says he's going to. Eat! Your! Pizza!"

I looked at Devin. His face was as unreadable as ever, though I could feel the annoyance rolling off him, but his expression was forgiving and warm. "Go ahead, spend some time with your family."

I beamed at Jack. "I know where your daddy's old remote-control cars are."

Jack's eyes grew wide. "No way! No way!"

"Come on, let's go, buddy." Standing up, I gestured for Devin to come too. "Let's see if Daddy can steal my pizza while he's chasing you and his favorite monster truck."

Jack barely let me finish my pizza before dragging me around to get out the toys, much to Devin's amusement. He was a handful, and it wasn't easy trying to keep the remote-controlled cars contained in the square of the linoleum foyer. It was the only place in the house I thought he couldn't break something. Almost immediately he proved me wrong by accidentally denting the umbrella stand by the door just as my Grandma Fern was arriving, and then the commotion started all over again as we greeted her and got her settled with the last of the pizza.

More than once I got emotional as we went through old traditions. Mom played carols on the piano, and I cried. Dad read the kids *'Twas The Night Before Christmas*, and I cried. Even when Marsha and Mom piled a plate high with the cookies Jack and Amy had made, I cried as they came up with a story for the kids about Santa visiting Grandma's house early. I knew why I was so overwhelmed, even if the rest of them didn't. George teased me, but Devin wordlessly took my hand, rubbing his thumb over mine in quiet comfort.

Devin didn't stay far away, but he didn't bring any attention to himself, either, only speaking when spoken to and watching me the rest of the time. I appreciated that he was here, and that he was letting me focus on my family.

When Amy started yawning, the evening turned to bedtime routines, and I was exhausted after an eventful day. Devin excused himself first, and after I told the kids goodnight, I went upstairs as well.

I opened my door to find Devin staring at the shelf above my desk. On it, amid various books and personal knickknacks, were several pictures of me growing up: George and I splashing in the pool at Grandma's house; me with several of my friends at middle school graduation; the day I got my braces removed.

"Enjoying yourself?" I muttered, embarrassed by the godly figure admiring my awkward teen years.

"Don't be shy. I love seeing your room." He looked at me. "I want to learn more about you." He set down a framed picture of me at graduation, and his expression was soft. "Are you all right?"

"Yeah," I said. "Sorry if I'm a crier. Looks like becoming a fae didn't change that."

"It's cute," he said, and then that empathetic face shifted away, replaced by heat. It was too much for me.

"Do you shower in the morning or at night?" I asked, changing the subject. "I was thinking about showering now, but you can go first. If we wait for the morning, the hot water might run out."

"I shower at night." He stood up. "In fact, if we need to conserve water—"

"Don't you dare."

A purr of satisfaction rumbled through the bond as he laughed. "I know, I won't press you. You shower first. I will wait." He kissed my forehead, careful of the antlers. "Is that slow enough for you?"

"I'm not dignifying that with an answer. You have a filthy mind." I dug through my duffel bag, pulling out a shirt and pajama bottoms. I tucked anything personal in the shirt so he wouldn't see. He chuckled as I headed into the bathroom. I turned the water on lukewarm; I didn't need to heat my body up more than it already was.

Showering fast, scrubbing absently, my mind eventually wandered back to the thing on the road. I'd be much better off back in my apartment, hours away from that thing, whatever it was. I shuddered.

I contemplated wearing a bra to bed, but I wouldn't be able to sleep. Instead, I threw on the shirt with pajama bottoms and wrapped the towel around my wet hair, entering my room with my arms across my chest. Devin was sitting at my desk.

"Your turn." Then, remembering the only bed in the room, I realized we should solve the problem now before we ended up with another situation like we had back in the city. "Maybe we should talk about the sleeping arrangements first."

His eyes darted to the bed, which in all fairness was plenty big for the both of us. "I will sleep in the van."

"You can sleep in here," I said before really thinking it through. I glanced around the small bedroom, feeling hesitant.

"Are you sure?" he asked.

"We're two adults. Two . . . mated adults." Groaning, I ran a hand down my face. "That did not come out how I wanted it to."

"You're flustered," he mused.

"I have extra pillows, we'll just make a wall. Is that okay?" I asked.

"We'll do it your way," he said. "This is awkward for you."

"And it's not for you?" I regretted the words the moment they flew out of my mouth.

That heat, that insufferable heat between us, felt thick and heavy with the desire that I wasn't ready for yet; at least, not ready to move as fast as the bond wanted to go. Devin closed the distance between us, a hand rising as though he wanted to reach out to me before stopping himself.

"No, it's not. I've always known this was a possibility. The only thing I could never have pictured was you, but now that I know you I couldn't imagine it any other way." Then, he stepped back as he picked up his bag, leaving a cold emptiness around me in his wake. "I'll be right back," he said, slipping out the door.

My heart was beating hard, leaving me breathless, and the look in Devin's eyes told me he could feel it. I took a deep, steadying breath, which only turned into filling my lungs with the scent of him and making my desires deepen.

Grabbing extra pillows from the hallway closet, I flung them down the bed as I heard the water in the bathroom turn on. I dried my hair and threw the towel over my closet door to dry. With nothing left to do, I turned out the lights, leaving Devin a small bedside lamp, and tucked myself onto one side of the pillow wall. Maybe if I pretended to be asleep we could just settle in for a peaceful night.

Ignoring him when he came back in, his wild scent mixed with soap and his hair hanging freely around his shoulders, I pressed my thighs together a little tighter and willed myself to sleep.

Sleep. Come on, *sleep*.

The click at the door told me he locked it, keeping my secret safe even if my glamour slipped while I was sleeping. I could feel his amusement, even as he climbed into bed next to me. He took me by surprise when he leaned over and kissed my temple before lying down, and it was everything I could do to keep my eyes shut.

He chuckled, the sound low and sensual as it dragged down my spine and I shivered. The lamp clicked off, and Devin's warmth settled next to me, a scant pillow-width away.

"Goodnight, Thea."

It took a very long time to find sleep.

CHAPTER TWENTY-TWO

THEA

Waking up to a dark room, I realized I had never slept so soundly before. It was a welcome surprise—I should have stayed up all night worrying about the wild fae in my apartment or the creature on the road. But I didn't. It would seem up-all-night-worrying Thea wasn't here today, and instead I woke up fully rested, lying on a firm, warm bed. Firm, warm, and with a gentle heartbeat.

What?

My eyes fluttered open. I was in my bed, but I wasn't alone. Devin was under me, my upper body splayed across his bare chest. My movements stirred him, and he opened his eyes with a sleepy smile.

"Good morning," he rumbled.

Heat flooded me, and I was more than keenly aware of his tousled hair and that playful, sleepy smirk he wore, and the way my nipples hardened against his chest, even through my thick shirt. Sitting up and backing away, I gaped at the bed. The pillow wall, which I had all but kicked off the foot of the bed in my sleep, was gone. I'd somehow managed to wedge one of them behind me and the pillow for my head was replaced by Devin's chest, which was bare as it appeared he only slept in a pair of loose cotton pants and nothing else.

"Oh my god." I pulled some of the blankets around me, as though they could protect me from my own mortification.

"You really couldn't make up your mind last night. First, I come in to find you curled on the bed as far away from me as you could get. Then when I finally manage to fall asleep with my untouched mate lying next to me," he said, giving me a heated gaze, "she rolls right through her wall and onto me."

"This has to be the bond—I don't roll around in my sleep." I covered my face with a pillow. "And I certainly don't throw myself on men I've known only for a matter of weeks." I'd never thrown myself at men at all, to be honest, but Devin is not high school puppy love material, and he's no college fling that was never meant to be. If anything, he was straight out of the calendar Candace kept on her fridge.

"Not that I was bothered by it. In fact, I wouldn't mind a repeat."

I threw my pillow at him and covered my face as he laughed. "Please forget that happened."

"Absolutely not." He pulled my hands from my face. "It was charming, don't be upset."

He leaned forward and the rest of the blankets fell away. A burst of lust ran through me as my eyes wandered south, and I couldn't tell if it was from me or Devin or if it even mattered because now we were both acutely aware of it. I groaned and covered my face with my hands.

"I'm all yours to look at, you know." Devin gently pried my hands from my face, taking one of them to press against his chest.

"I'm not ready," I said. "I'm still not used to this yet, and there's the fae that broke into my apartment, and . . ." I trailed away, knowing I was making excuses.

"Then I will be here when you are ready." His cool confidence was astonishing.

"Just like that?"

"Just like that." Devin reached out, playing with a flyaway lock of my hair, his eyes following the line of it up until he settled on my face again. "I hope you don't think I wasn't attracted to you before the thread of fate. I would have pursued you regardless."

Tightening my thighs together, I didn't admit out loud that I had hoped for the same thing. Still, under my parents' roof was too much.

"Breakfast!" I clapped my hands together. "We should go get breakfast. Like, right now."

"That's not what you were hungry for a moment ago." He smirked, beginning to wind the bit of hair around his fingers loosely, as if it was the most fascinating thing in the world.

"Am I able to help cook today? None of that faerie food stuff going on?"

"Making faerie food is a very intentional act. Just remember to maintain your glamour, it will be fine."

"Oh good." Moving, Devin let my hair slip from his grasp and offered me a hand. I took it and stood, but he kept my fingers as he brought them to his lips, pressing a kiss on them in that same, enticing place. As if to hold onto the memory of how this all began.

And all the while I couldn't do much more than remind myself to breathe while the intensity of those green eyes pinned me in place. A thousand unspoken words passed between us, and then he released my hand.

"Go. Be with your family, that's why we're here."

"You could have fooled me."

Devin flashed his fangs, the points of his ears suddenly catching my attention, the grin that was ever so slightly wide in a roguish slant. Something about how he chose to be in that moment reminded me how very inhuman he was, and then all at once it disappeared, replaced by the man I'd brought home to Christmas, who'd charmed my mother and settled into my casual family pizza dinner.

And, shit, if I didn't want a piece of him anyway.

"Keep your glamour in check, darling," Devin mused. "I'll join you shortly."

My jaw tightened as I managed a nod, not trusting my mouth at that moment. I grabbed fresh clothes, changed in the bathroom, and went downstairs to the smell of bacon, eggs, and potatoes sizzling away on the stove.

"Good morning, sweetheart. Sleep well?" Mom had her favorite apron on and she was hovering over the stove while Marsha fed Amy little pieces of chopped-up fruit. "Grab a spatula, I could use a pair of eyes on those potatoes. I've got to get this bird in the oven."

"Yeah, I slept great." I could feel the heat still on my face, but if my mother noticed she didn't comment on it as I pulled out a fresh utensil and took up potato hash duty.

"After breakfast, Dad is taking the kids to see a movie so I can cook. If you leave the house, just be back by noon. Grandma Eve and Grandpa Bill are on their way now. We're going to video chat with Aunt Cathy and her clan in Hawaii real quick before we eat. So, family time, lunch, then . . ." She glanced at Amy. "*P-R-E-S-E-N-T-S.*"

"Got it. I'll stay and cook," I said.

"I'm warning you now, I'm going to make you peel eggs," Mom teased.

The stairs creaked and Devin came down in fresh clothes, his hair now neatly in place as his heated gaze found me at the stove. With a smile, I turned back to Mom.

"Even if you make me peel eggs," I said.

"Better you than me." George came in from the living room with Jack, carrying the giggling preschooler upside down before righting him and setting him on a chair with a booster seat.

"Leave Thea alone, George," Mom said, not even looking up from turning bacon. "You're snapping green beans."

George scowled and I snorted a laugh. Devin came up from behind, catching me off guard and kissing the side of my neck as I gasped. I turned my head to face him, and I could tell he was absolutely trying to get a reaction out of me.

"I'm stepping outside to make a few work calls."

"All right," I said, and he left, pulling out his phone before stepping out the front door.

"Okay, Thea," Marsha pulled my attention back into the kitchen. "Where'd you find *him*?"

George grunted. "I'm right here."

"Yeah, and she found a freaking model," Marsha quipped, teasing my brother, then turned back to me. "Is he a keeper?"

My grin fell, but not into a frown. Giving it a moment of thought—real, honest thought—I pushed the attraction and the bond aside. Devin and I had been on the same wavelength before, and I would have thought being pushed together like this would irritate me but it didn't turn out to bother me at all. Devin was exactly what I'd ask for on paper if I had to describe someone I could see myself with. I was glad he was the one by my side through the strange happenings that had plagued me lately, and I knew that, given enough time, I could be comfortable around him. Too comfortable.

"Yeah," I admitted out loud. "I think he is."

I wasn't as weepy cooking all morning as I had been at dinner last night. I got in my final hug with Dad, the kids, Marsha, and even George before lunch, and I even got in a few games of domino with my grandparents. Devin kept himself scarce while I soaked up my family, staying just on the edge of all the action and ready to jump in with me if I started losing my calm.

Mom took the turkey out of the oven. The smell immediately drew the rest of the house to the dining room. Dad carved the bird while the rest of us looked on. Devin and I sat together at one of the two card tables, between Marsha and Grandma Eve. George and Grandpa Bill got into a heated debate over their favorite college quarterbacks while the kids told us about a movie they'd seen that afternoon, none of it making sense but clearly it had enchanted them. Mom and both of my grandparents went on about the food and upcoming church activities while my heart ached through the meal. Devin had been quiet, for the most part, and I felt guilty that he was subjected to my family's Christmas dinner when he could be doing whatever it was he would have been doing as the Lord of the Winter Court.

"You okay?" I nudged Devin's foot under the table.

"More than okay." His warm expression sent a ripple of happiness through me. "You could say this is a rare treat for me."

That took me back. "Really?"

"Really."

"Who wants pie?" Mom stood, taking an empty casserole dish from the table.

"What kind?" George and Dad asked simultaneously, and I laughed even as I got up to help clear the table. The food was good, the pie was good, and as I watched Mom package up all the leftovers, I knew those would be good too. Once everyone was absolutely stuffed, the peace was joyously broken by an announcement.

"Okay! It's time for presents," my dad said.

"PRESENTS?" Jack squealed.

"Daryl." Mom slapped Dad's shoulder. "I told you to spell it out in front of the kids!"

"Well, it's too late now." He chuckled and hugged Mom around the waist. "We better get to it."

Arranging ourselves in the living room, some still holding plates of pie, we watched as Jack and Amy tore through their gifts with abandon. After a bit, as they settled into a pile of toys and destroyed wrapping paper, the rest of us exchanged gifts. My highlights were a new pair of boots, the name-brand yoga mat I'd had my eye on, and the ornaments Jack and Amy had painted for me. They were hideous and perfect.

Devin surprised everyone with a set of nice scarves for the adults and a large set of coloring books and crayons for the kids. My mother, not to be outdone, had pulled out one of her recent quilts that didn't yet have a home and had wrapped it up for Devin the night we'd arrived. I stifled a giggle, picturing the Lord of Winter curled up under a blue-and-white patchwork quilt. Marsha and Grandma Fern brought a tray of hot chocolate around as we sat in the living room, enjoying each other's company. The kids actually fell asleep on the floor and George had the unfortunate task of waking them up so they could pack to start their long drive to Marsha's parents' house in Idaho.

Overall, it was a perfect holiday. I knew in my heart that I had to cherish these moments while I could, before my changes were so much that I couldn't blend in anymore. As far as I knew, I would look twenty-three for the rest of my life, or at least for too long to be normal.

It was late into the afternoon by the time Devin and I went upstairs to pack. Tossing my clothes in my bag, I could feel through the bond when Devin came to stand next to me.

"How strange," he mused. I stood up, facing him. "It looks like one box was left unopened." He placed the little box in my hand and I peeled the silver paper away.

"Oh wow, Devin. This is too much." I pulled a little velvet box from the paper and popped it open. Inside was an emerald green deer on a delicate silver chain—the same green as his eyes, and the subtle nod to my antlers didn't escape me. "When did you even have time to get this?"

"Believe me, I would do more if I thought you would let me."

Holding the gift, my heart warmed to him. Slightly. "I don't know what to say."

"Don't say anything; I saw it and wanted to give it to you."

I closed my fist around the little deer pendant. "I didn't even get a chance to find you a gift."

"I didn't expect you to." He brushed a thumb over my chin, nudging my bottom lip. "Though, if you wanted to reward me with something . . ."

"You've gotten away with enough of that here," I teased. "Maybe on Christmas day."

"Perhaps," he mused, then his expression turned soft. "I suppose now we go back. Are you ready?"

"Yeah," I said, and I was. I'd made whatever peace I could with this final family holiday. Yes, the last day had been good. It made me forget the mysteries that had been following me around. Tomorrow it would end. Tomorrow I would try to find more answers. What had happened in my apartment? Who was *C* and why were they leaving me cryptic notes? Candace? I didn't think so, but maybe I should ask her. And what exactly was on that farm? Why was I able to hold the iron bar with no consequences? And how was I supposed to fit into the Winter Court as Devin's mate?

Too many questions. Too many for today, at least. Devin and I packed, said our good-byes, and returned to the city. My last human Christmas was over.

CHAPTER TWENTY-THREE

THEA

Parking in the lot at the car wash, I got out, pulled on my coat for pretense, and walked to the office. The letter of resignation in my hand was probably a bit much for a job at a car wash, albeit a nice one like this, but it felt right, or at least it felt like something I would do. Devin was a little reluctant to see me run the errand, but since it was so quick and so deep in Autumn territory, he reached out to Lady Artemis, and then deemed it safe to go.

Being with Devin was comfortable. Was working with a romantic interest smart? A fae mate? Probably not, but the long drive back from my parents' house had given me more than enough time to consider his offer to work at the gallery. The more I thought about it, the more right it felt, putting my actual passion to use—and not having to ever ask anyone if they wanted a wax and detail again was a huge bonus. Almost the moment we got back I borrowed Devin's printer, typed up the letter, and left to quit my job.

I dropped my letter in the locked box so my boss would find it when things opened up again after the holidays and went back to my van.

Starting the engine, I paused, my hand frozen on the keys. On my passenger seat was a note written with familiar, delicate handwriting.

The Lord of Winter can keep you safe, but do not show him my notes.
Don't believe the ones that came before you.
Don't trust the rotting one.
I'll find you on New Year's Eve.
Your friend,
~C

I practically jumped out of the van, walking all the way around it and searching for anyone who could have gotten in and out of my locked vehicle in the scarce five minutes I was away from it. Doubt clouded my suspicions. How would they find me on New Year's Eve? I didn't even want to know who the *rotting* one was.

"Fated of Devin. Thea." The voice was assured and calm and familiar. Breathing in the scent of autumn leaves and smoke, I was wrapped in the essence of the Lady of Autumn even before I turned around and found her standing nearby. Her words were so oddly phrased, but Devin had told me she was the oldest of the court leaders, so it made some sense. On her they seemed to fit.

"Lady Artemis." I awkwardly bowed my head as I had seen others do for Devin.

Her hands were folded neatly in front of her, a deep red peacoat falling nearly to her knees over a long white dress. She commanded every ounce of elegance she'd had on the solstice as she walked toward me in the parking lot.

"I sense unease here," she said, her eyes moving calmly around as she spoke. "I sense something feral."

That sent a chill down my back. "Feral? Like wild fae?"

"Perhaps," she answered, then moved her attention from the scene around us to me. "You would be wise to leave, back to your mate. It would seem I have work to do here."

"What are the chances of a dangerous fae getting this far into the gate?" I asked. The map Devin had given me came to mind, and this was deep in court fae territory.

Her expression was gentle, motherly, but still worried. "My reign will not fail, snowy one. Do not be burdened with concern where it is not due. Go, travel well."

"I will follow your advice," I said, careful not to thank her. "Be safe."

She smiled before turning to walk away. "And you."

As Artemis left, I climbed into my van and locked the doors. Something odd was happening if fae that didn't belong here were suddenly trying to get to me. I shivered, starting the van, when my phone lit up, vibrating in my bag.

Let's go out soon. You, me, food, dancing, hot pieces of ass,
Club Glo

If I wasn't in such a solemn mood, I would have laughed at Candace's text. She had changed, and at the same time she was exactly the same. I didn't know what Club Glo was, but it sounded like sweat and alcohol would be involved. Still, I missed her, and I had her Christmas gift wrapped and ready to go in my van.

The first message surfaced in my mind.

Don't trust them.

Maybe she was getting these too? It was worth a shot. After all, she had changed when I did.

When?

Pick a night, any night. Talk later?

Ok

Dropping my phone in my bag, I started the engine and made my way out of the parking lot, back to the Winter Court. My warm, fuzzy bubble with Devin had been officially burst, and now it was time to get some answers to my mysteries.

—

By the time I pulled up to the house, I could feel that warm, magnetic feeling that pointed to Devin. And it pulled. I noticed when I drove away that it wanted me to go back. To be near. It wasn't overwhelming but it did remind me a little of a magnet, as Devin had described it before. Now that I was in the driveway and I could feel him upstairs in his office, I was getting the hang of feeling out how far away he was.

The moment I opened the door I could feel him move in his office. I quickly shoved the note from *C* into my bag just as Devin came down the stairs. Closing the front door behind me, I turned to see he had showered and changed. He was all business.

"How did it go?" he asked, leaning against the wall with his arms across his chest and those biceps just bunching under his sleeves in a way that straightened my spine to look at him.

I opened my mouth to mention the notes, but something stopped me. It wasn't that I thought Devin was the fae to watch out for, but what would happen if I told him? Would he be the type to help me figure out who was contacting me and what they wanted to tell me, or would he just shut it down entirely?

"It's done. Any news on the fae that was in my apartment?"

His face darkened. "No, but the moment I find whoever it was, I'll make sure they can't approach any of my court again."

My mouth formed a grim line, picturing what a being like Devin could do. He was all charm and sex for me, but I'd read the stories. Saw the others at the solstice. They all had the potential to be something frightening, and it didn't sound like he would be open to talking to whoever was leaving me these notes.

"Is everything all right?" Devin asked. "They can't reach you here, I promise."

The fae from my apartment. He thought that was what had me upset.

He closed the last steps between us, wrapping his arms around me, and I realized he had misinterpreted my distress as a fear of the intruder. While that violation still bothered me deeply, I knew I was safe here. Right now I was more concerned with finding out who *C* was and what they wanted.

"I know what may help. Do you want to see what you're working with at the gallery?"

I pulled back enough to face him. "Now?"

"Why not? We're closed through the holidays, so we have the place to ourselves." The innocence on his face dropped away. "And you can do with that information what you will."

Someone is in a playful mood.

But it wasn't me. I was thankful Devin respected the time I'd spent with my family, but I did have to admit the longer I spent next to him the more frequently I was thinking about what our relationship was and what the next step would be. With the notes from *C* and quitting my job, I was feeling the opposite of sexy. If anything, a new project could give me time to think.

"I'd love to see it," I said. "Let me grab my laptop."

This time there was no avoiding taking Devin's car as he drove through the city toward L'Atelier Rouge. By the time we pulled up to the empty parking lot, my excitement had built to the point of nearly bursting. This was something I had wanted for so long, and now it was here: me, in charge of an archive, setting up the display cases, posting a timeline for the guests to explore.

Inside, the motion lights flickered to life as Devin walked us to a far corner of the building.

"The door at the end of this hall leads to the basement," he said, pulling something out of his pocket. "Here we go." He tossed me a key ring, which I managed to catch before it hit the ground.

"Keys?"

"The smaller one is for the basement, that square one opens the gallery doors. I want you to come here whenever you'd like. Are you ready to see it?"

Absolutely I was. The stairwell didn't look like it was used very often—the paint was still nice, and I didn't see any smudges on the walls or marks on the stairs. We went down to the basement, where we were greeted by a metal door with a simple placard and *AUTHORIZED PERSONS ONLY BEYOND THIS POINT* in bold black letters.

"Here we are," Devin mused. "Most of these things belonged to Marcel or are old records from the courts. Obviously the latter won't be included in the gallery displays, but they could use organizing all the same if it suits your mood."

I didn't know what to expect—my excitement was bubbling over and I was positive Devin could feel it. Sliding the key in, I pushed open the door to my new project.

The basement was an absolute mess. Furniture and who knows what else beneath large sheets. Cabinets full of documents and letters loosely lined up in aisles. Things thrown haphazardly on top of the furniture. Everything under a layer of dust and cobwebs.

"Do you like it?" he grinned with absolute satisfaction. Amusement prickled through the bond.

"No!" I yelled and smacked his arm in panic as my eyes swept the room.

He took a step back. "What?"

"I mean, yes." I ran to the nearest shelf and started sifting through the papers. "But this is no way to store these things. Oh my god, I'm going to need gloves for this. I hope there aren't any windows down here shining sunlight. I'll need blackout curtains for those. What are these sheets made of? I hope they're all cotton."

"Slow down, darling." Devin laughed as I hurried, flustered and muttering, from shelf to table to cabinet. "Do you want to spend some time here?"

I stopped in my tracks. "Yes. No. I mean, not right now. I can't touch anything yet but I need to start on a plan to tackle all this."

He nodded. "Would you like to take anything with you to work on at home?"

Moving between the shelves, my fingers traced the spines of the oldest looking books. "What are these?"

"Old accounts the courts used to keep." Devin waved a hand. "Small notes of events and an account of numbers that means little to us anymore. You're welcome to them."

Turning to a stack of rolled canvases on a table, I cringed at the state in which they'd been stored. "I can make a list of things I'll need, though. Let me make a few notes, take a few pictures. There's a lot to organize before I can even begin to do something with it all."

"I'm glad you're so enthralled," he mused. "Let's get you some food and head back so you can work at home."

"Okay," I mumbled, not paying much attention as he led me away. I was too busy looking through the room and making notes of what I could see.

I would need a desk, that's for sure. Maybe some better lighting too.

"Thea."

Cleaning supplies first—the state of the basement is horrendous.

"Thea!"

"Oh, sorry, what?" Devin had walked us right out the building and to the car and I hadn't noticed.

"I said, what would you like to eat?" He chuckled. "Never mind, I'll pick something."

This project was exactly what I needed, and the idea that old fae records were mixed in? Even better. I was itching to learn more, and maybe the answers to *C* were here, right under my nose.

CHAPTER TWENTY-FOUR

DEVIN

Standing in a few inches of fresh snow I watched the sleepy street wake up from my front porch. My fae were starting their day, and Thea was no exception as she holed up with her laptop and a spread of papers from the gallery across the bed upstairs.

My mouth spread into a slow grin. *My bed.*

The fact that I wanted her was no secret. Even without the obvious thrills of lust that the bond fed me when her eyes fell hot and heavy on mine, I could practically taste it in the air that she wanted me too. But I'd been here when these lands had been nothing but the birds and deer and the pull of the faerie gate; there was no excuse for me to grow impatient now. The move was hers to make. At least, that was what I kept reminding myself as I'd spent another night sleeping in my office. Instead of crawling into the bed with Thea like I wanted to, I gave her space while I took a morning coffee outside.

"Rough morning?"

I was so distracted that I had allowed someone to sneak up on me. I tilted my head in the direction of the approaching Winter fae. "Arthur," I grunted. "You have no idea."

"I have *some* idea."

"Heather," I mused.

He looked to the sparkling white yard around us. "I think we're all feeling an extra something lately. The air feels charged, like we're on the edge of change."

"Can't argue with you there. After everything that's happened lately, I can't imagine the courts are going to remain this unbalanced. Have you found where the wild fae have been hiding?"

I moved inside, Arthur following me to my office. Closing the door so as not to disturb Thea at her work next door, if that was even possible, I sat at my desk.

"They *were* hiding out in a warehouse near Elliott Bay, but by the time I found it they had gone. I don't know where they've moved to, but I have a few ideas."

"Focus on our territory. If wild fae are hiding out in the other courts, it's not our responsibility to smoke them out. I'll be addressing it with the other court rulers shortly." I motioned for Arthur to take a seat.

He remained standing. "They've been more active since the solstice. It's a good thing you brought her here—we found evidence of more tampering at her apartment."

"Explain."

"The door was unlocked and there were scratch marks near the handle. It's possible it wasn't a fae, but I have my doubts. Do you believe Thea is their goal?"

I exhaled slowly and swept a hand over my head. "I don't know. I can't deny that her presence changes things."

"For the better?"

"Definitely. Surely you've felt proof of that."

"Lord Devin, the whole *court* is feeling the effects of it."

A thrill of excitement. Thea had found something interesting in her work, and I smiled at the warmth coming from her direction. "What could the wild fae possibly use her for?" I wondered out loud.

"If they didn't attack us on sight, we might be able to ask them. As it stands . . ." He shrugged.

"I know, I know."

"Anyway, I'll proceed with trailing the wild fae in our parts of town until further orders. Unless there's anything else?"

"No, continue as you have been. I'll update you if anything changes."

Arthur bowed his head and walked to the door.

"Wait." He stopped. "One more thing. I want to know the mood of the other courts right now. How they perceive our . . . new situation."

"You think they resent you?" Arthur leaned against the doorway.

"I'd be shocked if they didn't. What I want to know is what they plan to do about it."

Arthur scratched his head. "Lady Georgina will be the most upset that you've pulled ahead of her in power. The Lord of the Winter Court has a bond mate? Even the other courts can feel all of Winter's collective rise in power. You're having a ripple effect on the rest of us."

"Probably."

"But the gate has its way of balancing us all out. Each court has, until now, been equally balanced, for the most part. I wonder what the others are going to do to prepare for whatever new balancing is thrown their way."

"I'd rather not venture a guess just yet. Keep an eye out for anything unusual."

Arthur nodded. "I'll see how the regular fae of the other courts are feeling."

"You do that." I leaned back. "Send me a report if anything of interest comes up. Keep an eye on the wild fae, but don't make any moves without alerting me. I've got a few theories of my own to test first."

"Of course, Lord Devin."

"I'm thinking of having a small welcoming party with just our court on New Year's Eve. Would you come?" I asked.

He froze, only slightly turning his head my way. "Will Heather be there?"

"You know she will," I answered softly.

"I'm not ready."

"You can't hide from her forever," I called as he walked away. "It's been over fifty years, Arthur."

"I know," he replied, followed by the soft click of the door.

CHAPTER TWENTY-FIVE

THEA

A knock on the door startled me. It wasn't Devin because I had gotten used to the feel of him approaching. Pages of notes, pictures I had printed out, a furniture catalog, and my laptop were spread across Devin's bed and floor. Tiptoeing between the mess, I opened the door to see Heather.

"Is it already noon?" I asked, stepping into the hallway and closing the door behind me. Checking the time on my phone, I swiped past the replies to my Merry Christmas texts to Candace, Alan, my family, and Heather, who was now standing in front of me. Time had flown right by; I hadn't stopped working since last night when Devin had shown me the gallery.

Dressed in sweatpants with her hair pulled back, Heather beamed at me while holding up a bag. "I brought snacks for after."

"I'm nervous."

"Don't be," she said. "It's been a couple of days now; it's time to find out what powers you might have before they show themselves in more unpredictable ways."

My face tightened at the image of losing control of something I didn't even know I had. Before my change, magic was exciting and my curiosity surrounding it was strong, but now my heart raced at the thought of it. I'd already seen the fae in action, Devin in particular with his ice powers. As hard as it was to see and believe, it was even harder for me to accept that I could do something like that too. Devin thought it would be best if a friend like Heather came over to help, and thus, my plans for the day were magical exercise.

At the bottom of the stairs I saw Devin in the sitting room, as he called it, talking on the phone. Probably talking to Arthur, the fae I had heard plenty about as Devin's primary aid in the court but hadn't seen yet. Devin spotted me as we passed by, and I let myself admire the cut of his suit and how he wore it.

"All right, Juliet," Heather nudged me to the back door. "Leave Romeo here, we have work to do."

The backyard opened to the other backyards of the townhouses where the court fae lived and held a large windowless building. A lot of curious eyes watched me as my attention wandered from windows to decks to sidewalks. Now separated from the other courts, I could see definite Winter Court trademarks: Any skin outside the natural spectrum was tinged blue, purple, white—an aurora borealis of fae. Metallic glints appeared here and there, reminding me of Heather. Antlers like mine poked out of one or two foreheads. Bright eyes came in every color, some of which I couldn't describe. Some were dressed, some were very much not, but thankfully I could see they were so glamoured that human eyes would end up rolling right over them without being noticed. That was a skill I hadn't mastered yet, but at least I could hide my antlers.

Heather took us into the building, which on closer inspection looked like it was made of shipping containers covered in wood boards so the fae wouldn't accidentally touch the steel. Inside, the walls and floor were lined with padded athletic mats, and the far end of the room had squared columns with targets painted on them.

"Whoa," I said, looking around at the room filled with faes doing target practice and sparring. Licks of snow and ice were common on the walls and equipment, and the room smelled of sweat and burned plastic.

"Issa!" Heather called, waving to a short, winged fae.

She turned and waved back at us with a big smile before returning her attention to the painted targets. Shooting her arm in front of her in a blur of movement, there was a sudden pop in the air when a chunk of ice launched itself at the bullseye, hitting it perfectly.

"Holy crap," I whispered.

Heather laughed, steering me to an empty range. "Let's do some breathing exercises first."

In that way, it was a bit like yoga. We breathed, we talked about the theory behind how to summon magic, and we watched the room around us as others were present, giving me an up-close look at how it was done.

Okay, it wasn't like yoga. But with Heather it was comfortable learning with a friend and Devin had made the right call to arrange this.

He made a lot of right calls, actually, and I dwelled on the thought when I felt his presence enter the room at my back. That magnetic heat was becoming insufferable the longer I stayed away from him. But I kept my eyes on Heather and the demonstrations she was pointing out around the room, not letting Devin distract me. *Much.*

Heather stood up, pulling me with her and leading me to one of the targets. "Now I want you to try. There's not a clearer way to explain it; you just have to feel it out."

My mouth formed a grim line as I squared my shoulders. Breathing in through my nose and out through my mouth, I put my hands in front of me and willed something forward. All I managed to summon was a frustrated grunt.

"No one gets it on the first try," Heather said. "Give it another go. It took me a couple days to figure it out, but that's on the longer end. You can't let me outdo you, can you?" She elbowed me and I laughed. "All right, again."

We spend a good hour going back and forth between me trying to make something happen and watching the other fae honing their own skills. It was a fascinating thing, and unsettling knowing that the only reason they had to stay sharp was because of the wild fae that would attack on sight. Remembering the thing in the road and the yellow eyes at the farm, I shuddered.

"One more go," Heather urged. "One more go, and we can break for snacks."

It took effort, but I made myself stand up and face the target again. "Okay, one more good try."

Breathe in, square shoulders, breathe out, aim. My focus was wholly on the red painted bullseye in front of me, my vision tunneling as blood thrummed in my ears. I felt charged, like when you're about to touch something that will shock you, only it was my whole body. The hairs on my neck stood up, and my palms heated as my fingers prickled.

In a flash, white strings jumped to life, dancing between my fingers before fizzling out as I yelped.

"What was that?" I squeaked.

Some chuckles and scattered applause reminded me I had spectators. As the newbie, it was easy to be a point of curiosity—as the court lord's fated mate, even more so.

"Lightning," Heather murmured thoughtfully, then her attention turned to the approaching warmth from the back of the room. "How long have you been watching?"

"He's been there a while," I answered, then turned to meet Devin's puzzled expression as he strode over.

"Curious. Most of our court express something a little colder than that," he said.

My palms weren't warm anymore, but the ghost of the feeling lingered as I looked down at my open hands. "Is that bad?"

"No, no. It's not even unheard of. Just interesting." Devin slipped his hands under mine, also looking down at my palms. "Now that you have the feeling of it, do you think you could do it again?"

"Good question." Pulling my hands free of his, I looked back at the target.

"Try it out," Heather said. "I want to see it."

Repeating all the steps I took before, it was even easier this time to feel the warmth, the charge, and the release as more white strings of electricity jumped between my outstretched fingers, but nothing more. I turned to them and shrugged.

"Maybe after some practice," Heather suggested. "At least you've gotten this much figured out."

"Right," I said. "And if I run into any wild fae I can just defend myself with my pipe." I took a mock swing as if I had a baseball bat in my hands.

"Pipe?" Heather asked.

Devin's expression darkened. "That's another unanswered question. I still don't understand how the iron doesn't burn you."

"What are you two talking about?" Heather's voice was full of concern.

Devin held up a hand, looking around the room. "Not here," he said. "Let's go inside."

"Perfect," Heather added. "I'm so hungry right now."

We maneuvered through the building, a few congratulations thrown my way as we left through the front door, walked across a snow-dusted yard, and made it back inside without too much snow trailing in with us. My feet were glad to kick off the ice and leave my shoes at the door, but it was more about the annoyance of wet snow than the cold.

Heather busied herself setting up the kitchen table with boxes from her bag while Devin pulled down plates and glasses. Settling in, I was offered a plate now piled high with bite-sized fruit tarts, cream-filled horns, peppermint-dusted chocolate, and other things I didn't have a name for. Devin poured a tart-smelling wine for each of us while I ogled everything.

"What is all this?" I asked. "I thought when you said snacks you meant popcorn or something."

"It's faerie food. I brought some from friends in other courts, and I made a little bit infused with Winter Court charm." Heather grinned and popped a bite of something chocolate into her mouth. "What's this about a pipe?"

"Did you know Thea has been carrying around an iron pipe in her bag?" Devin asked pointedly.

Heather's face jumped to life. "An *iron pipe*? How?"

They both looked at me and I sheepishly picked up one of the cream horns and picked off a flake of pastry. "I had it before I found out about everything. I saw something in the parking lot one night and . . ." I shrugged. "It seemed like a good idea at the time."

"I'll say, that would have done some serious damage if you'd hit one of us with it," Heather said.

I looked remorsefully over to Devin.

"She did hit someone with it," he added. "And what I want to know is, why it didn't hurt her bare hands."

Heather stared at me for a moment, then tilted her head. "Have you gotten hurt at all since your change?"

"No, not that I can think of."

"Would you try . . ." Heather searched the table and picked up a knife. "Would you try pricking your hand? Just enough to make a little cut?"

"Heather." Devin had a warning tone in his voice.

"Why?" I asked.

"I want to see how quickly it heals," she said.

"That's nothing but a legend," Devin said. "Don't you think if it were real we would have seen them by now?"

"Seen who? I don't get it," I said, eyeing the knife. "Why would I want a cut on my hand?"

The Lord of Winter ran a hand down his face. "There is a nonsense legend at this particular fae gate claiming that four fae have an unusual abundance of powers. The Four, as they're called. But it's a rumor, a legend, there's no discernable proof that The Four have ever existed."

"I don't think it's all gossip," Heather countered, "and if she has the healing, it's proof!"

"You want me to prick my hand and prove I can heal myself?" I confirmed, picking up the knife with a sour expression.

"Don't." Devin looked at me. "It's nonsense."

"It's not nonsense," Heather insisted. "How else do you explain her touching the iron?"

Taking a breath, I put the point of the knife to the side of my hand where I thought it wouldn't hurt as bad. "There's no reason to argue about it. Let's just get an answer one way or another."

Wincing, I pricked a short line in my skin and set the knife down. All three of us watched as a bead of blood welled at the cut, then stopped. Taking a napkin, I wiped it away and underneath there was no trace of a cut. No scar, no line, no nothing.

"Holy shit," Heather whispered.

"Can't you all do this?" I asked, feeling the blood draining from my face at the unnatural sight of the missing cut.

"Not that quickly," Devin murmured, then his eyes met Heather's. "Not a word to anyone until we figure this out. There's a rational explanation that doesn't involve old."

Heather huffed but nodded. "Lord's orders. I won't say a word."

"If there are four of these people, what about the other three?" I asked.

None of us had an answer, and that gave me goose bumps. Rubbing the sight of the cut absently, I forced my eyes away, looking for a distraction as I picked up the cream horn again. Taking a bite, I moaned.

A mistake. The sound came out more impassioned than expected, and Devin turned a heated gaze to me. Sharply aware of the heat between us, I swallowed my bite and set the rest of it down.

"Faerie food," Heather explained, blissfully unaware of the pulling feelings flying between Devin and me. "There is a skill to it where you enchant it as you make it. But the taste is elevated over anything you'll eat made by humans."

My attention back on the food, I gave Heather's words a quick assessment. "You're right. I think you served faerie food at the gallery, didn't you, Devin?"

"Yes, we did. When I gave Georgina those tickets, I thought she would be bringing the changeling herself. The fact that she let the change-ling bring a plus-one in her stead changed things. I wouldn't have had faerie food present if I'd known."

"Little did we know we would get two changelings in the end any-way," Heather added, earning her a sharp look from Devin."Well, we did," she muttered, then switched gears and pointed out more of the food. "Hey, try those chocolate bites. I made them myself."

Gingerly, I reached for another bite from my plate, choosing what looked to be some kind of brownie with mint candy topping. Chocolate and mint flooded my mouth, and the feeling of magic that I had started picking out in the presence of the fae.

"Each court has a few skilled fae that like to make it," Heather added. "It's basically enchanted, and you can even make them do things like turn warm in your mouth or disguise a flavor. There's more but I don't know how to do the advanced stuff."

"That's amazing," I said, reaching for the wine glass. "This too?"

"That too," Devin said. "Every change of season, Artemis gifts the other court leaders a bottle."

Taking a sip, there was a hint of sour cherries but it wasn't over-powering and the rest of the flavor was almost that of a mulled wine or a cider. I could see it being addictive.

The rest of the snacks slowly disappeared as the topics changed from the tense iron discussion to lighter things like Heather changing the menu at work, Devin's newest art collection coming in next week, and my finds in the gallery basement. But no matter how much we distanced ourselves from the conversation, I couldn't stop myself from rubbing the place where a cut should be, and Devin couldn't stop himself from stealing glances at it.

When we had finished off the snacks and Heather left for the dinner shift, Devin and I cleaned up the plates. A familiar quiet settled between us. I was full of fae food, content and warm, and with an appetite for something else entirely. It was time to address this heat between me and Devin.

He wanted to check something in his office, so I went up to move all of my papers and pictures that had been scattered around the bedroom. His bedroom. Despite his previous offer I know he'd never bought another bed, and I wasn't sure how much actual sleep he had gotten in his office. Even though I had tried to bring up the sleeping arrangements, he was trying to be a gentleman about it. Too much of a gentleman, because he ended up dodging my line of questions before I could even begin asking them. Moving the last stack of pages on the bed, I set them on top of the nightstand just as a light knock sounded from the door.

"Come in," I answered, ending in a yawn. It felt awkward to say, knowing full well who was on the other side of the door to his own bedroom.

Devin let himself in, moving toward the closet. "Just grabbing something for tomorrow. It sounds like you need to go to bed early. Did you even get any sleep last night, or were you pouring over Marcel's old things?"

Maybe I was tired, but there was something I wanted to get off my chest before I fell asleep. He didn't really wait for an answer, though, pulling a shirt and pants out of his closet as he moved toward the door again.

"Wait," I said, reaching out to touch his forearm.

Devin stilled, his eyes settling on mine with sharp attention. Suddenly, that magnet wasn't just a mild annoyance anymore as I felt drawn to take a step closer. I did, and he turned to face me.

"Is everything all right?"

"Yeah." I licked my lips, a stall as I searched for what to say, how to begin. He watched the movement at my mouth, then his gaze moved back up to mine. The heat between us growing too comfortable, a siren song to close the distance and find out how he would feel pressed against me. The way his lips tasted on mine when we kissed the night I changed. The way we almost went further than kissing at my parents' house if not for

Jack's antics. But he wasn't dropping me off at my apartment now, and my nephew was hours away, not a plastic dart gun in sight.

Filthy things were suddenly on my mind, and whether they came from the bond or from me I couldn't tell. What Devin would do with me naked on his bed just a few feet away, what he looked like under those sharp suits. How delicious the fall of his hair was when he let it down on such criminally rare occasions, and what my fingers would feel like running through it.

The bond, of course, shared every needy beat of my heart with Devin—his answer through the bond was immediate and primal. It hit me as a wave, knocking my feet out from under me. I grabbed his arm tighter to keep from falling over. He took a shaky breath while his eyes roamed over me. His eyes met mine and I felt the rush of heat between my legs. "You need to let me go, darling, before we start something I intend to finish."

My eyes met Devin's and darted away. "I can't take it anymore. I know this is the path we were on before . . . before. And this wasn't how I pictured us getting here, but I want this. That is, if you do too?"

He closed the distance and wrapped his arms around me. The air left me in a rush as he lifted me off my feet and took me to the foot of the bed. Falling on my back, I was caged in his arms as he leaned forward.

"Now, don't you feel ridiculous asking?" His low voice was playful as he looked down at me, hungry and fierce.

The heat between us was an inferno, and we were teetering on the edge of it. I knew it, he knew it, and whoever made the next move would break the dam and it would all come rushing out. Of the things I wanted to do, I picked one at random as I snaked a hand around his neck, gently pulling the tie on his hair as it fell forward.

That did it.

He leaned down, kissing my collarbone and making his way up my neck, peppering in heated words as he went. "Feel free to touch, darling. It's all yours."

He nipped at my ear and a thrilling shiver ran down my spine. A sound escaped me that only proved to spur Devin on. His hand moved to my hip, squeezing, and brushing the skin above my leggings with his thumb, leaving a trail of inferno in its wake.

Moving my hand over his, I tucked his thumb in the band of my pants and helped him tug them down a few inches, an invitation as I moved my other hand to the top button of his shirt. When I got caught up on one of his buttons he reached up to help me undo the rest, shrugging off his shirt before going back to my lower half and removing the rest of my clothing. We parted long enough for him to undo his pants and for me to shed my sweater and bra, throwing it goodness knows where across the room.

When we were both done undressing, my eyes didn't know where to look. I reached up, touching his chest, stopping at his navel even as my eyes continued down. Devin sank down, one of his legs a steel trap keeping my thighs from closing. Heat wasn't the only thing pooling at my core.

"Devin," I panted, trying to swallow enough air to not drown in the heat between us. "I can't wait much longer."

I wrapped my arms around his neck as his hand moved down my stomach. Lower, lower, until he crossed the line of no return, his hand on me with one finger resting at my entrance.

"Let me know what feels good," he said, and slid his finger inside. I took a sharp breath as a buzz of pleasure spread through me. He rubbed my core in a slow, tantalizing rhythm. Wind rattled the windows as he kissed my neck. The tension in my body was building, drowning out everything but the bond itself, pulsing with need.

He grazed a fang across my collarbone and I shivered. The building pressure had me on the edge and teetering. It was absolutely ridiculous that I was so close to orgasm with only a few strokes of his fingers, but Devin managed to pull it out of me as I grabbed the sheets at my side and pressed the side of my face into the bed. The heat slammed into me in waves. It was all I could do to hold on for the ride, letting out a senseless sound of pleasure.

He pulled his hand away slowly, kissing my forehead. "More?"

"No," I breathed. "You, now, please." I pulled him down and kissed him deeply. He shifted how he was leaning over me, scooting me up the bed as he did it. As he pressed himself firmly against my entrance, I was ready to beg for it if I had to. I wanted Devin. Now.

He slid himself just inside. A sharp breath, my eyes widened. The nostalgic pinch of being stretched open surprised me.

"I'm all right," I breathed. "It's just been a while."

He pressed in a little farther. I dug my nails lightly into his back, and he growled in approval. He grazed my neck with his fangs and a soft noise escaped my lips; he licked and kissed my skin on his way back up to my mouth. An ice-cold breeze whipped past us. I held on tighter as Devin thrust deep inside. I screamed as the waves of pleasure hit again, somehow even harder than before. I removed my nails from his back when I realized how deeply I had dug them into his skin, but he didn't seem to notice. Everything felt like jelly. Content, unwound jelly.

I rolled on my side, catching my breath as Devin curled me into his body, one hand lazily stroking my stomach. "How do you feel?"

"That was intense," I breathed. "Is it always like that with fae?"

"Too much?" He nuzzled into my hair. "You seem tired."

"Gee, I wonder why." I let out a breathy laugh.

"Sleep. It's late." He kissed my temple and pulled the blankets around me.

My hand flew out to catch his wrist. "Will you stay?" I asked. "This is your bed, and at this point it would be ridiculous for you not to sleep in it."

"I was rather hoping you would say that. How unseemly would it be for the Lord of Winter to beg?" he teased.

Nearly choking on the laugh that burst out of me, I turned to face him. "You wouldn't have begged just to stay in this bed."

"Don't be so sure. For you, I'd do a lot of things that would shock the courts."

When I yawned, he pulled the blankets tight around me again. "Sleep, it's getting late."

I leaned into his chest and pulled the covers up around me. "Yes, Lord Devin." I yawned.

"Brat." He slapped my butt and I laughed.

"Goodnight, Devin," I whispered. A warm glow hugged me through the bond as Devin whispered goodnight in my pointed ear.

CHAPTER TWENTY-SIX

DEVIN

Thea was the most beautiful creature I had ever seen, and she was naked in my bed. I gently kissed her hair and carefully backed away so as to not wake her. She stirred some, then hugged the pillow and resumed her rhythmic breathing. I walked to the window.

Things might have gotten a little out of hand—snow now blanketed the city, a direct result of my power entwining with Thea's while we were otherwise occupied. I glanced at the phone on my nightstand—forty-seven texts, five missed calls. I'd deal with them later.

I went downstairs to shower so I wouldn't disturb her, and by the time I came back upstairs she was awake. She stood with her face pressed to the window, the bedsheets wrapped around her.

"We're snowed in!" she said, turning to me and pulling the sheets around her tighter. She came over and sat on the bed.

"Whose fault do you think it is that we're snowed in, love?" I sat next to her and glanced out the white window.

"Yours?" she asked.

"Not just mine. I can't do that on my own."

She blinked once. Twice. "You think I had something to do with it?"

"Darling, I know you had something to do with it." I watched in amusement while she processed this new information. "You've seen what happens when I lose control. It's nothing like this. This is the culmination of two impressive powers of the Winter Court."

"No way . . ."

"The whole city knows what we've done."

She turned bright pink. "You're kidding me! Oh god, Heather's not going to let me hear the end of this. *Candace* isn't going to let me hear the end of this."

"If you like, I can order Heather not to tease you," I mused.

"That's a little much, don't you think?"

"She's one of the few who pushes back against me. I like to tease her from time to time as retribution."

Thea pressed her palms to her temples and took a deep breath. "I need a shower to clear my head. I'll be right back." She went into the bathroom and shut the door. She opened it again a second later and stuck her head out. "You'd better not be messing with me."

"Of course not." She shut the door again, and I chuckled.

Waiting for her to finish, I could feel her emotions flutter up and down during her quick shower. I picked up my phone then and started scrolling through the texts. Mostly my court either asking what had happened or congratulating me, depending on how quickly they'd put two and two together. Georgina and Nikola complained about how we'd disrupted their courts, but I ignored them. I had two missed calls from Heather, one from Artemis, one from Arthur, and one from an unidentified number. I frowned and opened my voice mails.

"Hey, it's Heather. What is goi—"

Delete.

"Damn it, Lord Devin, is Thea okay? The snow—"

Delete.

"Devin, it's Georgina. We need to talk. You and me, then all four of us."

Delete.

"I have news, Lord Devin. Get in touch when you can."

Delete.

I played the last message. A muffled voice crackled through the speaker.

"Don't let her leave your sight"—*click*.

There was no doubt in my mind that *her* was referring to Thea, and the voice on the other end of the unidentified number reminded me of the break-in at Thea's apartment as well as the near run-in we had on the road. I clenched my fists, ignoring the urge to check on her this very second. The cryptic message bore investigating.

The bathroom door opened, and Thea came out in another one of her massive sweaters and damp hair wrapped in a towel. She sat next to me and pulled a brush from her bag.

"Pleasant shower?"

"Yes," she sighed. "I needed that after . . ."

Mischief slipped onto my face. "After?"

"Shut up." She threw a pillow at me. "Don't make me regret it."

"Would you really?" I leaned in and tucked a curl of hair behind her ear. Her expression softened.

"No." She kissed my cheek and returned to her hair.

Setting my hand on her leg, I rubbed a lazy circle with my thumb just above her knee. "I'm going to have a small party for you on New Year's Eve. A Winter Court affair to meet more of us. I typically do this with any Winter changelings within a few days of the solstice, but we had some delays."

"We really did, didn't we?" She bit her lip, and I knew she was thinking about that night at her apartment. Then she frowned. "What does it mean for us to be together?"

"It means whatever you want it to mean."

"Yeah, but everyone knows we have this bond between us. Won't they make assumptions?"

"Let them make assumptions. I don't want the preconceived notions of a mated pair to make you feel pressured." I shrugged. "If you prefer to grow whatever relationship we have a little slower, so be it. You have the Lord of Winter at your complete mercy, I hope you know that."

She laughed, but I was serious. "How do I dress for a New Year's Eve party with the Winter Court? Do I need to dress up?"

"No, dress comfortably. It will be in the backyard though." I nodded to the window. "So dress for the outdoors. We have lovely decorations for it."

Thea scrunched up her nose. "I guess it's going to take me a while to get used to the idea of hanging out in the snow for fun."

"Don't the humans want a white New Year's? We can make that happen." I slid my hand off her leg and around her lower back, leaning in to kiss her neck.

"It's a white *Christmas*." She laughed, looking out the window, the gentle rush of traffic in the background just beyond our private street the only indication that the city outside of our little world had moved on with its day. "And I think we've already done that. Well . . . a white Boxing Day, at least."

"Hm." I leaned in and kissed her neck. "I think we can do better."

"Devin . . ."

"Yes, darling?" I let a hand wander, feeling the goose bumps down her arm.

"We can't spend all day in . . . in bed."

"I have a few ideas that won't require a bed."

"You're incorrigible," she said, turning red as she tried to hide her smile. "Fine. Let's have a snow day."

CHAPTER TWENTY-SEVEN

THEA

There was still snow on the ground from our snow day three days ago. Not that the Winter fae were complaining. I saw several of them playing in the snow or making elaborate snow sculptures, some enchanted with small movements of wings or heads, giving the yards along the street a magical effect that I decided the moment I saw them I would never get tired of.

"You look lovely." Devin rubbed my shoulders as I stood in front of the mirror two days before the New Year's Eve party. I was wearing a simple white sweater and the emerald deer necklace he'd bought me for Christmas.

"I always look like this."

"You always look lovely."

I nudged him. "Tease. It feels like I haven't seen Candie in forever, but I guess it's only been a week."

"Catch up with her, have fun, and next time we can show her how we do things in the Winter Court."

"Stop it." I chuckled as he nipped my ear. "We're supposed to pick up Heather in a few minutes."

"You can't blame me for trying." He kissed my temple and backed off. "Let's get going then, before I change my mind and decide to have you for dinner instead."

The heated look he gave me told me how serious he was about it. I pushed his shoulder lightly as I passed, heading for the car. "*No*, I've been looking forward to this."

The cool air was refreshing. The more I played with my fae powers the more connected I felt to the cold. I could sense the fae around me better too. They each had a different . . . feel? Flavor? It was like a fingerprint that I could inspect from yards away. Each one was different. Devin warned me that I'd learn to dread summer now, but for the moment I was glad to bask in the winter chill.

Devin opened my door for me before getting in and starting the car. I rolled my window down as we sped to Heather's apartment. Passing the time watching frost melt on the windshield, I laughed as fat snowflakes began to fall, courtesy of Devin.

Heather was already outside waiting for us when we got there. She looked elegant in an all-black outfit that matched her long silky hair. She wore a pair of black leather stilettos, unconcerned by her already-towering height. I was more than a little jealous of how good she looked.

Devin drove us to the meeting place and dropped us off at the door. Fae stares followed us through the streets that I recognized to be under Georgina's care, but clearly word had gotten out about tonight's arrangement, and no one said anything as Heather and I stepped onto the sidewalk.

"I'll be a couple blocks away, in a coffee shop getting some work done. Call if you need anything." He looked sharply at Heather. "You as well—I know she might try to handle things on her own."

"Got it, boss." Heather winked at Devin and grabbed my arm, dragging me inside. My eyes flew by the two hulking Summer fae at the door, then inside the dark depths of the nightclub Candie had talked us into.

The building pulsed with a bass that made me wince and the lights were dim, save for flashes of yellow that strobed with the beat. The floor tiles looked like something out of an old disco-era movie, each square lit with a different color that changed and shifted to the rhythm.

"About time!" Candace squealed when she saw us. Pushing past sweaty bodies, she threw her arms around us in a rum-scented hug.

"You're adapting well," Heather said, bending over so the short Summer fae could reach her better.

"Yeah, it's great." Candace flashed her white teeth. "I've never been more comfortable than I am now. The mansion, the Summer Court, all of it."

"The mansion?" I shifted aside for a waitress who walked by with a tray of strange purple drinks.

Candie barely looked at them before swiping one off the tray, walking to the side of the dance floor where we would have a little space to talk. "Georgina's mansion and the home of most of my court. I get my own huge room and a ton of other amenities there."

"I'm happy for you, and I'm really happy we still get to hang out like this." I scrunched up my nose. "Well, maybe not like *this* every time."

She just laughed, taking a long sip from her purple drink. "Tell me all the scandalous *details*. I want to know everything! How big is he?"

"*Candie*, oh my god."

"Inquiring minds want to know if the rumors are true. It's Devin, right?"

Heather cracked up laughing, trying to cover her mouth but absolutely failing any attempt at subtlety as she nearly stepped backward into a sunny Spring fae who was on her way to the bar.

My eyes shifted to Heather. "Well, I—"

"I knew it!" Candace shouted, slapping my arm. "Tell me everything."

The heat that rose from my neck to my face was immediate and intense. "You're worse than when I had my first boyfriend."

"Yup, not sorry. So, tall, dark, and snowy. How is he? Did you like it? I kinda assumed after the way word spread around the mansion, but damn, girl. Finally."

"What do you mean 'finally'?" I sputtered. "I just met him this month!"

"That's nothing for the fae." She elbowed Heather. "Spread the love and spread it fast."

"How is that any different than before for you?" Heather tilted her head teasingly.

Candace laughed. "No arguments. I live how I live."

"And we wouldn't have you any other way. The introverts need to party vicariously through you," I mused.

Candace winked. "You two did the deed and snowed-in the city."

I reddened further. "I guess we did."

"Damn, *Lady* Thea, huh?" Candace grabbed a bread stick and bit off the end, pointing to me with the rest of it. "Guess you're a big shot now."

"Not really. That's Devin. I don't know the first thing about running a court of fae."

Heather stroked my hair and shot Candie a look. "You're gonna have Lord Devin in here in a heartbeat if you don't stop making her uncomfortable."

"You gonna text him or something?" She put down her bread stick.

"He can *feel* everything she feels," Heather explained. "They're bonded."

"Oh, right. Hey, sorry, Thea. Up for a dance? That's why we're here!" Candace didn't really wait for an answer before taking my wrist and Heather's and dragging us deeper into the thrumming music and writhing bodies.

"This place is going to give me a headache!" I yelled.

"Shut up and move that ass!" Candace bumped me onto the dance floor with her bony hip and Heather caught me in a low dip.

"Paranormals only in here!" Candace yelled. "It's bewitched, so be as loud as you want! Flash your powers—go wild!"

"Para-what?" I yelled back, not quite understanding her.

"Witches, vamps, shifters, but mostly fae. Don't worry about it, just have fun!" Candace flashed her fangs.

Heather grabbed some random but instantly willing guy with rubies for eyes and pulled him in to dance. Candie didn't need to find a partner; they swarmed her the moment her heels hit the floor. The two of them were nothing but energy, ready to go all night long. I wasn't much of a dancer when I was still human and even with my new identity as fae, I wasn't the most comfortable in a club. I moved like a rusty doll, trying to keep up next to Candace and Heather, but it gave me an opportunity to look around.

Strange faces were here. More than just the bits and pieces stolen from nature that adorned the fae in colors and wings and fangs, but things that gave me the chills. Things that didn't feel like fae, more than one feral grin in a pack of men who howled and growled, a bloodless face with more intense fangs than I had seen on any of my people so far, a woman who smelled for all the world like a human but maintained an aura of magic pressure that was anything but.

The heat in the room was stifling, but most here seemed to thrive on it. An hour passed, and finally it was too much for me. "I need air!" I shouted in Candie's ear. She nodded. I wandered to the door. A few drunken eyes perused my body, and I heard whispers of my name. The threat of Devin was enough to keep anyone from approaching me.

I went out into the cold and walked around the corner. I sighed as I sank into a snow-covered bench. Anyone passing by would probably stare, but the cold felt too good to pass up.

My phone buzzed. I looked down—a text from Devin.

Enjoying yourself?

I grinned.

Yup, lots of hot guys here

A sharp sensation, the magnetic warmth we shared, heated with annoyance.

I'll show you why I'm better than them when we get home

Jealousy is unbecoming. You're the only one I'm interested in. The snowplows are going to be busy tomorrow.

I heard laughter and suddenly felt an oddly familiar presence behind me. I was getting good at recognizing my friends and my new court, but this I couldn't place. I returned to the corner and looked past the club's entrance to where a group of fae was huddled around something on the ground. A terrible, urgent feeling came over me.

"I wouldn't go back there." The bouncer held an arm in front of me as I approached. Something definitely felt wrong. I took a deep breath, ready to bullshit my way through.

"Do you know who I am? I have Georgina's permission to be here today," I said coldly, more bravado in my voice than I actually felt.

"Yes, but—"

"Then let me through, before I take this up with Georgina." Still he was hesitant. "Or I can take this matter into my own hands." I flexed my fingers and sparks flew. He jumped out of my way and I continued down the alley. He didn't have to know that so far sparks were the extent of my control.

"Wow, this one's a real mess." A yellow fae kicked a figure on the ground.

"Wonder who did it?" a female murmured, clinging to the yellow one's arm.

"Hey!" I snapped. The four fae at the back of the alley jumped and turned around. The largest of them cracked their knuckles and stepped forward.

"You got a problem here?" he growled, sniffing the air. "Winter bitch."

The female's hand shot out to his arm. "That's her," she hissed. "That's the new Lady."

That stopped them in their tracks.

"What are you doing in Summer territory?" one of them asked nervously.

"I have an agreement with Lady Georgina to be here tonight," I said. "What's going on?"

"Some elf-struck human, *Lady*." The yellow one bowed his head, and the other three followed. I didn't miss that the big one looked angry about it.

"A human?" My insides twisted. "Let me see."

All four took this as an opportunity to leave. *Fine*, I thought, *just stay out of my way.*

The man on the ground wore a leather jacket and black jeans, a light dusting of snow on his fluffy red hair. My heart jumped when I rolled him over.

A crack of thunder tumbled overhead.

Alan.

"Alan?" My voice trembled. I reached out and brushed the light dusting of snow from his hair and beard. He was unconscious but still breathing. A sharp metallic scent hung around him that I couldn't quite place. It wasn't iron, but it wasn't like anything else I knew either. His core temperature couldn't have been high; his extremities were freezing.

"Oh my god." I picked him up and hung him over my shoulder, thankful for my newfound strength. "Please hold on in there, please, please, please."

I managed to carry him to the door of Club Glo and glared at the bouncer. "Let me in."

"No humans. Lady Georgina's orders."

"Let me in," I seethed. We stood there for several long seconds, as if having a staring contest. The door opened then, hitting his back with a dull thud that didn't seem to phase him.

"What the . . .?" Heather's voice crept through the crack. "Thea! What's happening?"

"Let. Me. In." Thunder rolled overhead. I was shocked to feel a connection to it, like the charge overhead and I were running parallel. Possibly something to do with my powers reaching out to their natural counterpart.

"Hey, let her in!" Heather pushed through, and the bouncer finally stepped out of the way to make a call. Probably to Georgina.

"Get him inside." My voice strained as Heather took Alan's weight off my shoulders.

"We need to call an ambulance," I said.

Heather sniffed the air. "He's elf-struck. They won't know what to do with him."

"Elf-struck?" I paled, pages and articles filtering through my memory. *Elf-struck: a dementia-like state where the victim can't recognize things around them, and any movement is motivated by a desire to be closer to fae magic, like a sunflower moves to face the sun. Brought about by unregulated exposure to the presence of faerie magic.* "We have to warm him up," I insisted. She took us to the nearest booth. A drunk faerie was passed out on the table, surrounded by glass bottles. I picked him up and placed him in the next booth over, much to the displeasure of the couple practically having sex on the other side of the table.

"Get over it," I snapped. "Heather, what can we do for him?"

"What's going on? Wait, car wash guy?" Candace had come over now, and a good portion of the dance floor was quietly watching our commotion.

"He's going to go into shock if he warms up this fast, isn't he?" Heather pressed her fingers to his neck.

"I don't know, I don't know anything about hypothermia or whatever." I hovered over them. "How's his pulse?"

"I don't know, I've just seen them do this in movies." She scrunched up her face. "I guess it's harder than it looks."

"Why is he here?" Candace looked pale. "This is a no-human zone."

"Some Summer Court fae were messing with him in the back of the alley." I reached out to hold his hand. "Come on, Alan. Snap out of it."

The pit of my stomach tugged at the door; I ignored it. "Is there such thing as a fae doctor?"

"I mean, we already heal fast. There are plenty trained in first aid kind of stuff, but not for humans."

"Only mostly human." Candace bent over him. "He smells funny, like, halfway between us and them."

"Oh no," I groaned. "Be okay, Alan. Please be okay."

"Maybe we should get his jacket off?" Heather suggested. "Rub the heat directly into his arms or something?"

"Why would taking his coat off help?" Candace asked.

"I don't know!" Heather huffed. "What's your big idea then?"

We stared. His breathing was shallow, his lips turning blue. I felt the tug again, and a twinge of panic ran through me. The bond.

"Devin," I whispered, turning around just as the Lord of Winter burst through the door.

The quiet club now exploded with whispers. It tickled my ears but I was too focused on Alan to hear what was being said.

Devin ran to my side, taking in the scene before us. "What happened? I felt you panic and it hasn't subsided."

"My friend, Alan, he's in trouble." I pointed to the unconscious human on the table. Devin stared at him before closing his eyes and taking a deep breath.

"Let's get him somewhere else." He lifted Alan with one hand and grasped my hand with the other.

"Show's over, folks, nothing to see here!" Candace barked, clearing a path for us. Heather followed us outside into the cold.

"Where's the car?" I asked.

"A few blocks away," Devin said curtly, clearly upset. "I ran to you when I felt your distress. And when I heard the thunder, I knew something was truly wrong."

"Where are we taking him?"

He clenched his jaw. "I don't know."

Devin's pace was fast, but we kept up easily. We slowed down only when a car drove by.

"Hey, guys, I'm going to leave this to you." Candace stopped. "I should talk to Georgina. Thea, text me later, I want to know if he's okay."

After I agreed, Candace took off in the opposite direction, pulling her phone out of her pocket as she went. The snow was falling in thick, fluffy clumps, and we were left with only the streetlights to see by as I fussed over Alan.

"What can I do?" Heather asked nervously.

"Thea, who is this human?" Devin asked.

"He was my coworker at the car wash," I answered, fervently trying to rub some warmth into Alan's hands. "I haven't seen him since my change."

My stomach twisted as I remembered that strange dinner. The fae was never there to mess with me. What if he was messing with Alan? "Oh god. I think he could have eaten faerie food."

"How long ago?" Heather asked.

"It was the night before solstice." Pulling Alan's coat tighter around him, I made sure the zipper was as closed as possible, pulling all the heat he could retain into it.

"Where does he live? We should see what signs of fae tampering we can find."

"I'm not sure where he . . ." I trailed off. "There's a new restaurant east of Sammamish, near Soaring Eagle Park. It's about half an hour from my place. It looks like a ski lodge. His cousin Ron works there. He looks just like Alan, you'd know him if you saw him."

"Heather, go there and find out how long this human has been missing from his family," Devin directed.

"Got it," she said and sprinted off in a different direction.

We reached the car and Devin laid Alan across the backseat, taking a blanket from the trunk and throwing it over him.

"Where are we taking him?" I asked, my voice shaking.

"We have to minimize the fae exposure, so our place is out of the question," he said. "Your old apartment is close—is that all right with you?"

"What about the wild fae? The break-in?"

"We'll set up a watch at a safe distance, plenty of eyes on the building for safety."

"Yes." I sighed with relief—we at least had a plan. "Good, okay. What can we do for him?"

"Has he been exposed to anything fae that you know of besides the one instance of food?" He gripped the steering wheel, freshly replaced a few days ago courtesy of Arthur. I told Devin that I hadn't seen him since the week before I changed. "How did you find him?" Devin reached over and took my hand.

"He was in the alley." I took a deep breath, trying to calm myself. "Four Summer fae were around him, but I'm not sure they knew what was going on. He's one of my only friends in the city. Please, I have to help him!"

Devin sighed, his gaze on me heavy with consideration. "We can try to turn him completely, but without knowing how attuned to the faerie gate he is, we might just succeed in driving him mad."

"Oh no." I squeezed Devin's hand and then let go, reaching back to warm Alan's again.

The rest of the ride was quiet but tense. We pulled up to my old apartment and Devin walked in first, deciding if it was safe to bring us inside while I stayed with Alan in the car. Once Devin gave the all clear, he took Alan from the car and I followed Devin to my bedroom. Thankfully it still had at least the bed in it, but little else. With Alan safe on my old bed, Devin began checking for vital signs.

"Weak but steady pulse. He's breathing, he's cold. Get me all the blankets you can find. Does this building have a laundry room?"

"No." I ran to my closet and pulled every clean piece of bedding off the top shelf.

"Hair dryer?" he asked, stripping Alan's wet clothes off him.

"No."

"Where are your towels? I'm going to try to heat them over the vents in my car. It might not do much but it's better than nothing. And where's your thermostat? I'll turn that up too."

Devin returned soon enough and leaned over Alan to check his temperature again.

"How will we know if he's better?" I asked, standing in the doorway.

"He will either act as he normally does, or he will be a babbling fool and cling to whatever fae presence he can find," Devin said quietly. "Like a moth to a candle."

I hugged myself nervously and asked Devin what we do now.

"We wait," he said.

I slumped against the wall and slid to the floor. "I must be the world's worst friend."

"What makes you say that?" He sat beside me and I let my head sink against his shoulder.

"I've barely given him a thought since before the solstice." I rubbed my temples. "We had that weird dinner and I suspected he'd eaten faerie food, but when I texted Alan the next day to thank him for the dinner he said he was fine, so I put it out of my mind."

"It would have taken more than that one instance to affect him like this," Devin explained. "Whoever was involved would have to have done more to him in the following days."

"I should have checked in on him more." My throat tightened. "I really am the worst friend in the world."

"You are most certainly not a bad friend." Devin wrapped his arms around me, rubbing my back. "So much has happened to you, don't be so hard on yourself."

"I nearly forgot about Candie too." I sniffed. "Who's next? Heather?"

"Hardly," he snorted. "She's been stuck to you like glue since your change. At least you'll always have a friend in her, and I'm here for you too."

"Yeah, but—" A faint cough from the bedroom drew our attention. I looked at Devin and we shot up, hurrying to Alan's side.

"Alan?" I leaned over him. He was breathing, but he wasn't awake yet.

"I'll check on the towels, see if they're warm. Stay here and keep an eye on him," Devin said.

I did as I was told. Devin returned a moment later and piled them on Alan and we waited a while longer.

"We need to change him," I insisted.

"It's pretty risky, and I would have to recommend we make that decision when we know for sure if he's fully elf-struck. Overexposure to our magic in a short amount of time is what put him in this state; if we feed him even more of it we could truly push him beyond the point of no return. Give him a little time." Devin kissed my forehead. "I'm going to get you something to eat, stay here."

"Okay." Devin left, and I was alone again with Alan and my thoughts. What if he never woke up? What if he *did* wake up? What if he hated me for being fae? What could I have done differently to prevent this? What if . . . what if . . . what if.

Alan stirred a little. I scooted over to him and waited, but he didn't move again. What if there wasn't anything I could do? I pulled my knees to my chest and buried my face in my hands. So much for being a powerful fae. What's the point in having changed? Learning to control my powers? Being tied to a fae lord? What's the point in giving up my humanity if I can't even save my friends?

CHAPTER TWENTY-EIGHT

THEA

Hours ticked by.

Devin brought tea and soup from Heather's café. I sipped on both until the pink of dawn poked through the blinds. I even spent an hour meditating, hoping it would pass the time. It didn't. Devin, for his part, prodded me to drink, eat, and take a short nap. He never stopped holding my hand.

"There are fae of our court standing guard to keep an eye on things if you'd like some fresh air." He stroked my cheek.

No matter how many people he had around here, I wouldn't feel good about leaving Alan. "No, I need to be here when he wakes up," I said. "Do you know if Heather has been able to talk to his cousin yet?"

"No. The restaurant was closed when she got there. She's waiting for it to open."

My stomach knotted. It wouldn't open for hours yet, and she had been there all night.

"Don't worry over it," he said. "Heather will be fine, the snow means nothing to her."

"What if someone from the Summer Court did this?" I asked softly.

"But at the restaurant all the food reminded me of fall. Nothing really summertime."

"If they did, then they have broken one of our most important rules about interfering with humans, and will be punished accordingly," Devin said simply.

Fidgeting with my hair, I couldn't sit still and kept pulling strands free, requiring me to rebraid it. "If you need to go to the meeting with Georgina, I can stay here with someone else."

"I would like you with me, if you think you're up for it," he said. "You were, after all, central to the events of last night. But you're not comfortable leaving. Would it be all right to invite her here?" He noticed my hesitation. "Or I can call in one of my most trusted fae to come watch Alan while we see her," he offered. "But if you really don't want to go, I will meet with her alone."

"No," I said. "I'm being stupid. Anyone you trust to watch him I trust too. Will they call me if anything changes?"

"Of course." He leaned down and kissed my forehead. "I'll have Arthur come now."

I watched Alan while Devin sent a series of texts. He stood after a while and offered me his hand. "He's here, let's go."

We were outside and on our way to Devin's car a moment later. A white jeep I hadn't seen before had pulled in next to Devin, and Devin walked to the driver's-side window to talk to Arthur. I got into Devin's car and stared up at my bedroom window while I waited. Devin got in a moment later.

"Georgina is expecting us." He started the car and we sped away. I looked back to see Arthur entering my old apartment. I was glad to know Alan wouldn't be alone if he woke up while we were gone.

"Is there anything I should know about meeting the other court rulers?" I asked.

"At my side, you're on the same level as Georgina. If the gate paired your fate to mine, it means something. Your part to play here is significant, whether we've figured it out or not. Our court already senses your worth, your power, your value among us. Don't be intimidated by Georgina. Stand your ground and you will be fine. I'll be there with you."

A crack of lightning skittered across the gray winter sky. I was startled to feel a connection to it, feeling its charge in the air. I pressed my head against the cool window to be even closer.

"Everything is going to be okay," Devin promised.

It wasn't until we'd pulled up to Georgina's that I sat upright again. I looked up at the stone mansion, more castle than home. Devin led me to the front steps. I paused when I thought he was about to knock, but he simply opened the door and walked in like he owned the place.

The scents of Summer were overwhelming, blasting my senses— freshly cut grass, blooming roses. But I quickly recovered, squaring my shoulders. I needed to put on a good face next to Devin and trust that he knew what he was doing. After all, he'd dealt with Georgina for who knows how long by now.

We walked side by side. He gestured for me to raise my chin high as we made our way through the mansion. Curious eyes followed us from inside extravagant rooms until we arrived at a pair of glass French doors. Devin knocked once before opening, not waiting for a reply. Georgina was seated behind a modern red desk, the room decorated in simple, clean lines and minimalist art. In the Lady of Summer's hand was a glass of something amber.

"Devin." She nodded to a set of plush chairs opposite her. "Thea. Let's get down to business." She tucked a stray red wisp of hair behind her ear—a delicate movement that didn't match her stern face.

"Four of your court were seen with an elf-struck human." Devin sat, making himself quite comfortable. I followed his lead, making sure to keep my chin up.

"Seen with, not causing it to become elf-struck," she retorted.

"He's not an *it*," I asserted.

"Fine, the human." She frowned. "Your court was seen with it as well."

"If you are referring to my *mate* and her escorts, one of which is your brand-new changeling by the way, then yes. Our court was also seen with the human, but only after yours."

"What do you want me to do about it, Devin?" she snapped. "Whip all of them until they confess?"

I flinched at that. Somehow, I didn't doubt that she would do so.

"Have you even questioned any of your court?" he asked calmly, tilting his head.

"Obviously," she growled, the temperature spiking a few degrees. "I have no answers for you."

"No answers for me, or no answers at all?"

"No answers for *anyone*," she spat. "Do you think I want to spend extra time in your esteemed presence? I have enough on my plate right now. Nice job with the blizzard the other day, by the way. It's been lovely trying to keep my people warm."

"You are most welcome, my *dear* Georgina. I'll be sure to send more your way soon."

The top of her desk exploded beneath her flaming fists. I screamed in surprise but Devin didn't move, not one muscle. Chips of wood scattered across her pristine office and tendrils of smoke smoldered on her skin.

"You disrespect me in my own court, Devin!"

"Was that really necessary?" he drawled.

"Stop!" I blurted. "This isn't doing anyone any good. If we don't work together, we will never find out what happened to Alan or why."

Georgina's fire extinguished as she tilted her head, assessing me. Her smile turned cloyingly sweet, her blazing eyes a constant reminder of her inhumanity. "I can grant you the *favor* of my court investigating the matter."

A shiver struck my spine and I sat up straighter. If her court would cooperate it could really help get to the bottom of things. "That would be—"

Devin's hand shot out in front of me. His gaze remained on Georgina but he gave me the smallest shake of his head. "No, no favors. You'll help because if I drag Nikola and Artemis over here for a vote, we both know whose responsibility it will be," Devin warned.

Georgina's carefully crafted expression dropped to a sneer.

"We'll be looking into it too," I told her, taking Devin's lead. "But we either need access to your territories or to Summer fae willing to look into it."

Georgina frowned but remained civil. "I can commit a couple of fae to help investigate the cause. Is that what you want?"

"Yes, considering this all happened in your court," Devin said. "Have them contact Arthur, he has all the details. We'll leave you to your busy schedule. Come, my love."

I wasn't sure if he was demonstrating some kind of united showmanship or an earnest show of affection, but regardless, I took Devin's hand like a lifeline as I rose to my feet. I was as ready to get out of there as Georgina was to have us leave. The door slammed shut behind us, nearly catching my heels. Devin put a reassuring arm around my shoulders and steered us through the building.

"Don't mind her, she gets cranky in the cold months," he said.

"I can't wait to spend my days with you in July," I muttered.

"Now, let's get you home before you start leaking sparks. If you get too upset you could start influencing the space around you with unintentional magic."

Sucking in a slow, deep breath, I tried to do as Heather had instructed to keep my abilities in check. "Go home? We need to go to Alan."

"We can't," Devin said softly. "You're still seeping too much faerie influence around you, and I'm not just talking about your elemental grasp. It's the same part of you that you control when you glamour, but finer. Less noticeable. When you cast a net of glamour around your appearance it's like catching rocks in a net; what you're leaking now would be like asking you to hold in sand. You'll do more harm than good by spreading it around Alan."

"What can I do for him if I can't be there?" My voice cracked as my eyes threatened to water. "I can't sit and do nothing."

Devin didn't answer as we made our way out of the mansion again, but as we reached the car again and he opened the door for me, he tilted my chin up with gentle hands, placing a warm kiss on my lips. "We go home, you continue to fuss with work like I know you will while I try to make you eat and sleep, and we wait."

CHAPTER TWENTY-NINE

THEA

We didn't go back to Alan after Georgina's place. Not that I didn't want to, but there was no denying that Devin was right, and endangering Alan any more than he already had been was out of the question. So, I decided to handle the stress the best way I knew how: by throwing myself into my work.

Devin took me by the gallery after we left Georgina's, and while he was upstairs taking care of some gallery business, I was in the basement grabbing every record of the fae I could get my hands on, including the recorded logs of the early days of the gate. If they had anything that could help me figure out the cryptic notes from *C* or how to help Alan, I needed to know.

New Year's Eve had arrived, and for another year in a row I had my nose in a book. I traced letters as I read every word on the page in the little green book.

Now, the bedroom door opened, and I froze on the bed like a deer in the headlights, waiting with bated breath. Devin entered, shaking his head. "No news, I'm here to get you for the party."

Alan had remained more or less the same since yesterday. His temperature had come up, but he hadn't woken up. My mood sank further when Heather had reported back after finding Alan's cousin. Apparently, Alan had dropped off his Christmas gifts and left early, not feeling well. A red flag that I could have caught if I was keeping in touch better. But while Alan's condition had remained the same, the rest of the world was moving forward. The dark sky through the window behind me told me the New Year's Eve party was close.

"Thirty more minutes?" I asked, papers spread all over my lap.

"You said that a half hour ago," Devin said. "You also said you would ease up on your work before the party."

The document in my hand was practically burning a hole through my skin, ready for me to learn something useful. But my burning questions would have to wait, because meeting the court was important, and if my last cryptic note was true, I would find answers to C tonight. "It will only take me ten minutes to get ready."

"All right, I'll meet you downstairs."

Devin left and I had to give up on my papers and books. Setting them on the nightstand, I stretched my stiff back and looked around. A few boxes of my things were scattered on the floor—apart from the furniture, which I didn't need anymore, Devin had had my things packed up and brought over since there were already fae at the apartment anyway. I was officially moved in. The next step would be to tell Mom, but I wasn't quite ready for that yet. Not with everything going on.

Keeping things simple, I wore my nicest dress and easy accessories. I'd always preferred easy, comfortable clothes before I'd become fae—that hadn't changed—but now I also had to consider items that I could get over my antlers.

Downstairs, I found Devin looking sharp in a black suit and silver tie. He kissed me softly on the lips and brushed a stray hair from my cheek.

"Beautiful."

"Am I underdressed?" I looked down at my outfit.

"Thea, we will never be underdressed or overdressed in our own court. They will try to match us, not the other way around."

I smoothed the fabric over my stomach, making sure any wrinkles were gone. "I guess I'm as ready as I'm going to be."

"Very well." Devin took my arm in his and we left through the back door.

The yards between the townhouses had been cleared of snow, with a ceiling of lights strung overhead. Underneath, tables and chairs were scattered about, with sprigs of holly as a centerpiece at each. There was an outdoor buffet with refreshments. As soon as we entered the space, faces turned our way with a mix of interest and merriment. Suddenly feeling shy, I felt my movements grow stiff.

Devin put his arm around me. "They're just eager to get to know you. Are you ready to see your court?"

"I hope so," I mumbled. He led us to a small arch of red flowers with two armchairs under it. As I sat down a short white fae appeared. White eyes, white hair—I was even surprised to see a white tongue as he spoke.

"Good evening! I'm pleased to finally meet you, Thea. I didn't want to crowd you on the solstice." His movements were stiff and formal, but his expressive face was jovial.

"Yoseph, I'm glad you stopped by," Devin said. "Thea has begun to manifest an ability similar to yours."

Yoseph's eyebrows jumped up as he turned back to me. "Is that so?"

Holding up a hand, I focused until I could call up a few sparks, though it took all of my concentration to do it. I shrugged.

"I was hoping you could try to help her along," Devin added.

"Gladly. I can come to the practice facilities most mornings, does that work for you, Thea?"

"Yes, I appreciate it." Tucking my hands in my lap, my eyes moved to the training building in the far part of the yard.

Yoseph beamed, and we fell into easy conversation while other

191

bodies began to drift over. Fae of every Winter shade began milling around the yard. All of them glanced my way at least once, and several came to meet me directly. I tried to stay alert for anyone who could be *C*, but so far no one had revealed themselves to be my mysterious note writer. Those who didn't come to say hello to Devin or me were mostly ones that said hello at the solstice, and while I wasn't the type of person who enjoyed introducing myself to stranger after stranger, I did find myself enjoying watching the party.

There were a couple dozen other changelings in the Winter Court, and most were at the party. The idea of others with my shared experience felt nice, but I got the feeling their background would be similar to Heather's, so advice on how to keep in touch with my family was out of the question. Still, every one of them I met was pleasant and happy, a good sign for my own future. Other fae chatted up Devin, and several included me in on the conversation as well.

Heather came dressed in a cute jumper and boots I was absolutely going to borrow at some point. The moment I didn't have a fae coming up to talk to me she pulled me into the yard where music was starting up. Some who came brought instruments, many of them antiques. A portion of the yard was quickly taken over, tables removed, chairs scooted into lines, and an impromptu orchestra thrown together. The first song was a complete mess until an agitated fae with small thorns up and down his arms grabbed a fork and began conducting.

Devin held back for a few songs, enjoying his time talking while Heather trapped me in a long string of dancing punctuated by breaks for a fruity wine that left me breathless and giddy. After a while, the alcohol loosening my shy tension, I was fully enjoying myself and wrapped in the music of the court. It was nice, just to enjoy myself as one of them and not be under some kind of spotlight like being next to Devin or when I'd changed in front of all the courts at the solstice.

And just when I thought I couldn't take another step, that warmth from behind me approached as one song ended, and Heather passed me off to Devin in a spin before she moved away to find a new dance partner.

"Are you enjoying yourself?" Devin mused.

"I am!" I admitted, a little louder than necessary but it earned me a few nearby chuckles and a dazzling smile from Devin.

"Good. Under normal circumstances you would have been enjoying yourself and making acquaintances much sooner than this. Circumstances being what they are, I'm glad we got to hold this little party tonight. Everyone seems to be enjoying it."

Willing my emotions to even out, I kept any telling distress from slipping across the bond as I remembered the circumstances at hand. Alan, who was still unconscious while I was here making friends with the fae. And *C*, who didn't want me to trust any of them.

Over the past days I had nearly told Devin about the anonymous notes more than once, but his immediate aggression to the wild fae and his hardened mask against anyone from outside of the Winter Court would ensure that I wouldn't be meeting this *C*, or at least not having a conversation with them. But even if they were one of the wild fae, I should be safe here, surrounded by my court.

As if on cue, the song ended and I dropped my hand from Devin's shoulder as we stood in the middle of the group of other dancers. "I think I want to look around a bit."

"All right. Be careful with the wine: I know Heather's been heavy-handed pouring it for you." He kissed my cheek and let me go. "I'll be sitting down where you can find me."

"See you soon." Wandering away from the dancing, I made my way to the food tables so I could look around and think. If this was the party *C* had meant to meet at, then it was time to go searching. Unfortunately, being new to this world meant nothing and no one looked out of place to me, though I could see how a strange fae could hide in this crowd. The presence of all these fae was so overwhelming that it was hard to separate one smell or magical presence from the rest. Eventually, I snagged a tiny quiche and some kind of cider from the buffet table on my way inside the townhomes. The kitchen was an absolute mess. I set my glass on the counter and went to find a bathroom.

193

When I came back for my glass, I found a napkin folded up and tucked under it. I looked around but didn't see anyone. The napkin flopped open when I picked up the glass. My heart accelerated—I recognized the hasty scrawl immediately.

Meet me behind the training shed for answers.
~C

C. It was finally time to meet them, whoever they were. I tore up the napkin and dropped it in the trash, spilling the rest of my drink on it to blur the writing.

I tried to recall my list of questions.

Who is C? Can I trust C?

Who is the rotting one? Who exactly are the ones that came before me? What does Devin not know?

How do I know if I have other powers? What is my role in the Winter Court? Where do I belong?

Moving slowly, not wanting to make an obvious dash to the darker part of the lawn, I drifted away from the celebration. A few fae stopped to say hello, but finally I made it to the edge of the party and hurried to the darkness behind the training shed.

I was pulled around the corner by tiny but strong hands. I would have stumbled were I still human, but I managed to keep my balance and backed away from the unknown figure.

She was petite, with an orange pixie cut and bright, wild eyes. She wore a leather coat and smelled like cinnamon.

"You're *C*," I whispered.

"Caroline." She stuck out a hand. I took it, and she pulled me close.

I was not ready for the kiss. She pressed her lips to mine and held it for a moment. I pulled away from her. She licked her lips. "What the hell?"

"Your kisses pack one hell of a punch, do you know that?" She receded into the shadows so as not to be seen. "Listen, I don't have a lot of time. I don't want my scent to linger here. I know you have a lot of questions, but we're going to have to do this quickly."

"What was that?" I wiped my mouth with the back of my hand, scowling at Caroline. *C*, Caroline. The name tickled something in the back of my mind, but I didn't have time to unpack it while she was here.

"Just a bit of an episode, but I'm better now." She fiddled with something in her pocket, eyes darting around nervously. "I've got some life-or-death stuff to pass along to the most powerful changeling at the gate."

"Why is it life and death? Is someone after you?" I took a step backward.

"No, not me." She paused. "Well, yes, I'm a wild fae after all. A lot of you court fae would kill me in a heartbeat. Your mate in particular."

"I should call for Devin," I said, but Caroline reached out and grabbed my wrist, shaking her head.

"Devin would kill me before I can finish recovering my mind. The life and death I'm talking about is your own," she said quietly. "You have to hear me out—you're the one who can crack this whole gate wide open, I know it. Give me just one minute."

I stared at this small but intense fae in disbelief—a wild fae, no less. "Okay, you get one minute."

"War is about to be waged between true fae and changelings. The fight you've been told is between the wild fae and the courts here? It isn't what it looks like."

"Why would someone wage war against the changelings?" I asked slowly. "The fae need us for their population. We're all fae in the end."

"Do they?" she asked. "Do they *really* need changelings?"

Devin, Heather, and several of the texts from L'Atelier Rouge told me that the fae were creating changelings to increase their population. When it was this hard to get pregnant, numbers were bound to dwindle eventually, especially when a run-in with the wild fae could be dangerous. Devin couldn't lie and Heather wouldn't. So Caroline was the liar, right?

"Can true fae lie?" I asked.

"No." She fidgeted again with whatever was in her pockets. She struck me as a very nervous person. Or paranoid.

"Who is the rotten one?"

"Not rot*ten*, rot*ting*. Names carry weight here. I can't tell you unless I want attention on me again, which I don't. You'll know when the smell hits you." Caroline shifted her eyes. "I know you found the green books in the gallery basement. I need you to look into them, they contain census logs and the proof you'll need to show the court fae."

"Proof of what, exactly?"

"I could tell you the wild fae aren't the enemy, and the changelings aren't needed, but you wouldn't believe me. Not as I am now. I'm still unwell. I need you to see it for yourself. And if you can figure it out, you're worth saving. If not . . ." She shrugged.

Goose bumps crawled up my arms. Flashes of a figure in my apartment flitted through my mind. The horror I felt, the violation from the break-in. If that wasn't the wild fae, who would it have been then? My mouth went dry at the memories, and at the nightmares I was still having over that night.

"You know I can't believe you over the people I love in my life. No more games. What is it you want?"

"I want retribution, a life for a life." She said. "I want my home back, but it's too late for that now. I'll settle now for the rotting one's head on a platter."

I flinched at the imagery. "What's wrong with you?"

"I told you, I was having an episode, but I'm getting better now," she insisted. "Read the book—the changelings were never needed."

The thought was chilling. Sacrificing my humanity never needed to happen. Mine, and every other changeling I'd met. But I wouldn't know Heather, I wouldn't have met Devin, I wouldn't know Issa or Arthur or any of the other fae I'd met so far. So many lives would never have been disrupted, and most of those were disrupted for the better.

"How do I know I can trust you?" I asked.

She thought about it for a moment, then smiled. "I'll give you a little present. Knowledge of sorts. Kiss your sleeping beauty. If he has stars in his eyes, he'll wake up all better. If they're black as a new moon, he's a lost cause."

And she dashed out of sight.

"Wait!" I tried to catch up, running after her through the neatly manicured lawns leading away from the party, but it was dark and I lost her.

"Dammit," I hissed. A pulse of concern vibrated down the bond. I cursed the whole situation—I had to get back to Devin before he noticed anything was amiss.

I made my way back to the party. It was almost midnight and Devin was going to give a toast. What should I tell him? Caroline seemed to have my interests at heart—was it right to keep her a secret? There was no avoiding it. At least long enough to look into her "present." Sleeping beauty had to be Alan. But what was this business of stars and moons? Was he going to wake up blind? Or seeing spots?

My pace increased with my anxious heartbeat. If Alan was going to wake up, I needed to be there.

"There you are," Devin said, seeing me approach. He pulled me into a tight hug that would have sent a delightful shiver through me a short while ago and kissed me deeply. "You taste like cinnamon."

"Oh." *Caroline.* "It must have been the mulled cider. I'm worried about Alan. Can we call whoever you have watching him?"

"Of course, darling." He checked his phone. "It's nearly midnight. How about we toast the court and go straight there?"

"Thank—I mean, I would appreciate that. I don't mean to skip out on the party early."

"Don't worry about it." He dismissed my concerns with a wave of his hand. "We've been here long enough for you to meet some more fae and enjoy yourself. Have a seat, I'm going to get drinks to toast with."

Devin walked away, and I sighed, sinking into my chair.

"Hey." Heather walked over, a glass of wine in one hand and a cookie in the other. "Missed you on the dance floor—er, grass." She laughed loudly, her drink sloshing to the ground.

"You're drunk." I grinned.

"Pfft, I had better be for all the wine I had earlier."

"Here we are," Devin said, handing me a glass. "Are you ready?"

I nodded. Issa came and pulled Heather back into the crowd as the other fae stepped forward, giving us an audience.

"Good evening, children of the Winter Court! I hope you've enjoyed the party so far." His words were met by cheers of approval. He waited for them to quiet before continuing. "I'm glad you could all come tonight to celebrate the New Year, and to meet my mate—Thea. The newest member of our family."

More cheers. My face heated under the attention. "Our night with you is nearing its end, but feel free to continue in our absence." He checked the time on his phone. "Perfect timing. With midnight upon us, I'd like to lead us all in a toast, to a new year and a new court!"

Glasses raised high, mine included, and at the wave of Devin's hand the Winter Court drank to the new year. He clinked his glass with mine, and I drained the bubbly in my hand.

The party quickly resumed while Devin and I made our way out from under the flowery arch and through the excited crowd. We went around the houses to his car and got in. I felt relieved to be out of the spotlight. Devin pulled out his phone and clicked a contact. Eventually, someone answered.

"Hey, Arthur, I'm going to hand the phone to Thea. Be nice." Devin handed me his phone. I stared at it briefly before putting it to my ear.

"Hello, Arthur. It's nice to finally talk to you. How is he?"

"Hello, Lady," answered a gruff but not unkind voice. I frowned at being given a title but Devin had warned me that many would see me on equal footing with him, and this was not the time to nitpick. "No changes, his temperature is good. I'm not sure why he hasn't woken up yet."

"His . . . eyes. What do they look like?" Devin shot me a curious look.

"His eyes?" Arthur questioned. "They've been closed this whole time, but I'll check."

I tapped my foot while I waited. I heard some rustling on the other end, and eventually Arthur picked up again.

"His pupils are pretty dilated," he said. "They're almost completely black."

My heart sank. If Caroline was right, that meant it was too late. Alan was a lost cause. But did I believe her? There was clearly something wrong as she spoke to me, but she hadn't misled me yet.

"But it's strange." Arthur's voice commanded my attention again. "There's a rim of color, red, with little white specks in it. Kind of like a galaxy."

Stars. There were stars.

"What are you—" Devin began when the phone buzzed in my ear.

I checked the screen. "Arthur, we're on our way now but I have to let you go. There's another call."

I hung up and passed Devin the phone. He glared at it—the caller ID read *She Devil.*

"What?" he answered gruffly. I was able to hear the other side of the conversation.

"I've got new information. Where can I meet you?" Georgina said.

Devin eyed me. I nodded. Even if she knew where my old apartment was, it wasn't going to be in use much longer. Tonight would end with Alan waking up, one way or another.

"Heather's Café, off the highway, maybe ten minutes from the gallery. There's an apartment building next to it. Meet us there."

He hung up without waiting for a response. I rolled my eyes—he could be so childish when it came to Georgina.

"What's all this about his eyes?" Devin asked.

Lying didn't seem like a good way to maintain a new and complicated relationship like ours, but I couldn't risk Caroline's safety if what she said was true. "A . . . book from the gallery has given me some ideas. I need to try something to see if it will help."

Devin seemed to accept that, and he sped most of the way there. Arriving at my old building, I was unbuckled and out of the car before he'd even turned off the engine. Georgina was there, too, sitting in a pink convertible. Top up and heat on, of course.

"Thea," Devin called, but I was already headed inside.

"Alan," I said, bursting into my bedroom. He was there still, on the bed right where I'd left him. Standing over him was a tall fae, taller even than Devin. He was the dark figure I had seen inside the white jeep— a deep plum color with long hair and brown eyes. I'd heard his voice plenty of times through Devin's phone, but the soft, low voice didn't fit with his intimidating physique.

"No change," Arthur said.

I sat on the bed next to Alan; his red beard was getting unruly and his cheeks were sunken from days without food. I took a deep breath and peeled back an eyelid. It was just as Arthur had described—almost entirely black but for a rim of red with little white starbursts.

"What is it you're trying to do?" Arthur leaned in to see better.

My heart was beating fast. I didn't have an answer for him, or for anyone. Maybe I was crazy. Maybe Caroline had rubbed off on me. Either I trusted her or I didn't. I lifted Alan's head gently in both hands, closed my eyes, and kissed him.

It was really awkward, like kissing a CPR mannequin.

A loud crack snapped through the room. Setting Alan's head on the pillow again, I whipped my head around to the noise. Arthur and I turned to see Devin, standing in the doorway, fingers so deep in the door frame that they'd snapped the wood.

"What . . . is . . ." Devin was as uncollected as I had ever seen him, a mix of surprise and disbelief across his face.

"Devin," I started, standing up and walking to his side. "I was just . . ." How to explain Caroline without mentioning Caroline. "My new powers, I'm using them on Alan. The idea occurred to me earlier tonight. The ones we talked about with Heather."

Realization hit him, and his attention moved to the bed. I hated lying to him. But if this worked, really worked, I owed Caroline's words more faith.

Suddenly, the most unexpected sound caused everyone to freeze.

A groan.

"Alan!" I started forward, but Arthur's hand shot out. He grabbed my wrist.

"Please, Lady," he grunted. "Do not do that." He pulled me away, no doubt for Devin's sake as well as my own as we watched. We all paid close attention to the human on the bed.

No, not human. Alan groaned again, clutching his stomach as he started to gently glow. Just like I had at the solstice.

"Impossible," Georgina breathed, appearing behind Devin.

"It's not the equinox yet," Arthur murmured. "Who is this human?"

"Alan," I said again. His beard grew wilder, his skin bronzed. His fiery red eyes popped open and locked on me. No, not on me—behind me.

Georgina gasped, clutching at her heart as a flare of glowing heat rolled off her and lit up the room. "The thread!"

And if Devin hadn't been holding me so fiercely, I would have crumpled to the floor. Clutching his arms, I was dimly aware of the sparks flying off me as Devin's chill worked to fend off Georgina's heat.

It was too much for any of us at that moment as realization sunk in. Alan was fae.

CHAPTER THIRTY

DEVIN

My heart was thunder in my ears. I held Thea close, trying to calm the link between us. The human writhing on the bed had changed completely. I have never in all my years seen a change so long after a solstice, and somehow the marvel of a changeling at my side had done it. Thea had changed this human. After the initial shock of walking into the room and seeing Thea's lips pressed to another, I recognized the significance of what this could accomplish if she succeeded. Heather's theory of the four fae powers was little more than urban legend, and yet, here we were.

What none of us were ready for, however, was Georgina.

"*The thread*!" she gasped.

Thread?

Was she serious? I held Thea tighter. She sank into me; she was as shocked as I was. "Georgina," my tone warned. We had no knowledge of this human. He may react poorly to a sudden profession of a fated mate, and Georgina was just rash enough to barrel headfirst into such a moment without even trying to assess things first.

"The balancing," Arthur muttered.

Of course. The balancing. This was how it was to be done? What in the hell was going to happen to the Spring and Autumn Courts? More mates, or something more dire? I laughed—I couldn't help myself. Changeling mates, two in one solstice, and both to fae rulers.

Arthur darted his eyes between me and the human. Georgina didn't look at me at all; her eyes were locked on her mate. The changeling just stared at us.

Georgina pushed past us and rushed over to the bed. She ran to this changeling's side and helped him sit up, then sank to her knees.

I snorted—I'd struggled to compose myself in front of the four courts upon discovering that Thea was my mate. And here Georgina was, kneeling on the floor and reaching out to the mate she hadn't even been introduced to yet.

"Thea?" Alan's voice cracked. His eyes roamed the room in bewilderment. "Where am I?"

She looked up at me. "I won't surprise you again."

"Be cautious," I warned her. "Not everyone comes out of their transformation as intact as you did."

"Good to know," she said quietly. "I'll be careful."

She went to Alan's side. I dug my claws deeper into the frame but did my best to maintain composure.

"Yeah, it's me," she said quietly. "We're in my apartment."

And we weren't strongly glamoured, I realized. For the most part, we had collectively lost our focus when he'd changed and we hadn't put it back in place yet. Thea in particular looked very fae at the moment.

"What's wrong with you?" He squinted at her, probably still reconciling what his eyes were now showing him. "A costume?" A grunt strained from me as my focus stayed locked on the human. The insinuation that anything could be wrong with Thea sat poorly with me. Flexing my hands, I did my best to set aside my urge to intervene—I needed to let Thea take care of the situation the way she wanted to.

"Nothing is wrong with me, but I've changed." She sat next to him on the bed. Georgina stiffened. "And you've changed, too, Alan."

He looked down at his hands. Then his arms. He touched his beard and glanced around the room again. "I . . . have. Yeah, I have. What's going on?"

Thea took a deep breath. "Do you believe in fairy tales?"

Alan stared at her small antlers. "If I didn't before, I get the feeling that I should now."

"Yes, about that . . . I've become something new. Something no longer human."

"And what would that be?" Alan said cautiously.

"I'm fae now. A being both natural and supernatural."

"What does that even mean?" He laughed coldly. "I can believe some supernatural bullshit has happened to you or me, but to not be human anymore? Were you ever human or was this all a trick?" He leaned away from her. "Have you been this, this, *thing* the whole time?" My body tensed, watching Alan speak to Thea this way. Whatever relationship she'd had with him was the only thing saving Alan from the ire of a fae lord right now.

"I don't—I don't know how to explain it any better." Thea looked around frantically for help. "I know you're upset but try to calm down, we'll figure this out together. You went through a change, and now you're one of us."

Georgina said his name slowly, like a delicacy. He looked down at the Lady of Summer on the ground in front of him. "And why do you feel so different from the others?" he asked her.

"Alan," Thea said cautiously. "This is Georgina; there is a good chance she's going to be a special person to you."

"He is my bonded," Georgina's words hissed out like a knife, sharp and purposeful as she moved a fraction closer to Alan.

Alan looked past Thea. "And who's *that* one? And what the fuck does that mean, bonded?"

"I am the Lord of the Winter Court," I said as evenly as I could. "Master of ice and snow. I'm centuries older than you and mated to my beloved Thea. Do not insult her again—this will be the only warning *you* receive."

Georgina stood suddenly and burst into flames. "Hold your tongue, Devin, before I rip it from your head!"

"Shut up, both of you!" Thea was shaking. Thunder cracked in the distance, and I was taken back to feel strings of it flowing from Thea. "None of this is helping Alan. Either calm down right now or get out!"

The tension in the air crackled in the silence that followed Thea's words. She let out a slow breath, and with it, the charge in the room flowed away as she looked to the new changeling.

"Alan, we should get you accustomed to your new body and explain a little more to you before we make any court decisions."

Alan, who had been silently watching this whole time, stood up off the bed. "I'm sorry, Thea," he said. "I didn't mean to upset you. This is a lot. I'm . . ." His words trailed away, his eyes bobbing around the room, not willing to settle on any one of us but not willing to look away completely either.

"I know," she said quietly. "And we'll figure it out together. You're still my friend, no matter what."

Alan's forehead wrinkled, looking from Thea to me. I stiffened. He had feelings for Thea. If he didn't have Georgina right now, I wasn't sure what I'd do. Thankfully, Thea seemed oblivious to it, and I wasn't about to complicate the situation all four of us were in by pointing it out.

"I think I need some time to process all this. And some food—I'm starving," Alan said, staring at his bronze hands. "I'll have some questions after that."

"Yeah, of course." Thea grabbed his hand. "Do you want to get some food now? Or—"

"Alan," Georgina interrupted. "Would you like to come back to my mansion? You can rest there, and I promise you we have the best chef in the city. I can take care of anything you might need."

"Thank you for the offer," Alan said slowly. "But I think I want to talk to Thea first, before leaving with someone I don't know."

I cringed at his thanks and saw Thea do the same. We would need to teach him the rules sooner rather than later.

Georgina embodied a snuffed-out candle, tendrils of smoke wafting from her. "Of course," she said. "Take all the time you need. I'm only a call away."

The Lady of Summer stood up straight and walked toward me. "There is news about the fae who did this to him. We'll talk later." She gave one last glance to her mate before brushing past me on her way out.

"Maybe I should just go home." Alan gave a nervous laugh. "Maybe this is all just a wild dream and I'll wake up in my own bed."

Thea looked at him sadly. "Someone did this to you. We still don't know why or who, until then you have to stay with us. We have to keep you safe. Do you remember anything out of the ordinary?"

"No," he said slowly. "Everything since Christmas is fuzzy."

Thea glanced at me, then Arthur, then back to Alan. "Alan," she said, "it's January first." His jaw dropped. Thea took his hand. "Let's go get you some food. We have a lot to fill you in on."

Outside I helped Thea into the car and closed the door. I caught Alan's arm before we joined her.

"Do not pine for what cannot be," I told him quietly. "But know this: any friend of Thea is a friend of the Winter Court. Do not abuse her friendship and you will have a powerful ally."

Alan stared at me for a long moment. "I understand."

We got in the car and I started the engine.

"Are you cold?" Thea asked him as we pulled away.

"Freezing," he said. "How are you not?"

"I guess you could say I'm attuned to it. And from the look of you, I'm betting you won't be able to overheat anymore."

"Definitely Summer," I agreed.

"What does that mean?" He looked down at his new body.

"Summer Court," Thea explained. "There's so much to cover, let me see if I can explain it clearly."

As she launched into an explanation, every revelation about the fae brought a new degree of anxious concern to Alan's face. Thea did a good job of it, covering what I would have covered with the new changeling under more normal circumstances as I had been doing for a long time. As it stood, never in all my days had we created three changelings surrounding a single solstice. Especially not three who'd had ties to one another beforehand.

The party was still going on when we pulled up to the house, but we avoided it completely and made our way into my house. Thea settled Alan in the sitting room with plenty of blankets and a lit fireplace. We didn't have any spare bedrooms and I wasn't about to put him in the main Winter house next door.

I went to my office for a stiff drink while Thea talked to him. I knew my presence wasn't helping. My phone buzzed—a message from Georgina. I drained my glass before reading.

I have the bastard that did this to Alan. You have one hour to get here before I flay him alive

Georgina was nothing if not dramatic. But she was also dead serious.

on my way

CHAPTER THIRTY-ONE

THEA

The days that followed felt strange and disconnected from the rest of my time as a fae. Devin was in and out at odd hours, working on the mystery of what had happened to Alan. He never took me with him, but I suspected he'd been spending time with Georgina. I threw myself into a morning routine in the training facility out back, but it wasn't the welcome distraction I'd hoped it would be. At least I was getting better, according to Heather. Thankfully, Alan was open to listening. The only thing I left out was my strange healing powers—Devin wanted me to keep that a secret a little longer.

I started bringing Alan with me to the gallery basement, so we could spend some time together while the others worked.

"How tall do you want this thing?" Alan sat on the basement floor, assembling a work desk that Devin had bought while I was busy dusting everything I could reach.

"Tallest setting for the desk, short for the chair. I like a high work surface."

"Got it." He fiddled with some screws on the legs.

"I appreciate the help." I coughed as a cloud of dust billowed into my face.

"I like working with my hands." He shrugged. "And I really need something to do while I think about everything." He wasn't quite himself yet, but no one really knew who Alan was supposed to be after becoming fae. He'd been lighthearted and easygoing before; hopefully he would keep some of that.

He'd checked in with his family, and the contents of his apartment—which were surprisingly few—were in his truck in our driveway. He said he didn't want to keep his apartment anymore, muttering something about the lease being up next month anyway. But he was my friend, and I was worried about him.

"Hey, did you end up using Georgina's number?" I asked.

The sound of a screwdriver dropping to the floor rang through the basement. "I—what? Shit, where'd the screw go?"

Leaving the shelf I was sifting through, I came over to help him find it. "I didn't mean to catch you off guard," I said. "Just curious."

Moving aside a pile of cardboard and Bubble Wrap, I kept looking on one side of the desk as Alan looked on the other. Alan broke the silence a moment later. "Yeah, I messaged her."

"You did? How did that go?"

"Well," Alan started off slowly, "she's actually pretty funny."

Georgina? Funny?

I jerked my head up so fast I whacked it on the desk. "Ouch!"

"Are you okay?" Alan stopped what he was doing, but I already had a hand up, waving him away.

"I'm fine. So, you had a good time talking to her?"

He shrugged and went back to searching for the screw. "I guess. It's pretty complicated, isn't it?"

Now that I could understand. "It can be. Has she been trying to explain the thread of fate to you?"

"Yeah." Alan rubbed his chest absently. "I want to say I'm open to the idea of it, it's just so weird, you know? And the pully feeling, it's incessant."

"That it is," I muttered. "A-ha!"

Lifting the screw from where I found it in the pile of Bubble Wrap, I handed it over to Alan.

"Great, I should be done pretty soon." Shooting me a lopsided smile, he popped the screw in the hole and began to thread it in. "Don't mind me, I'm sure it will all work out. Maybe you can show me some of your floor sign poses so I can stop thinking so hard."

With a laugh, I tossed a piece of cardboard at Alan, who dodged it easily, and just like that he was back to being a clown.

I went back to taking inventory on a new shelf I'd uncovered—a working inventory was the best way to start with this mess. Devin got a laptop just for my work in the museum, connected to the gallery's network with access to all the calendars, spreadsheets, and equipment.

The shelves were lined with books, papers, photographs, and smaller antiques. Every time I found a green book, I set it aside, keeping Caroline in the back of my mind at all times. I'd pored over the books that I'd brought home already, but there were more here that I hadn't gone through yet and I was nothing if not thorough.

"Do you trust these guys?" Alan asked.

"Who, the fae?" I glanced at him. "I trust the ones I know so far. I've also been friends with Heather for several years. Other than the whole fae thing, she's been very open and truthful with me."

He finished putting the legs on my new desk and stood, wiping his hands on his jeans. "What about the Summer Court ones?"

I looked to see him wiping at smudges on my new desk. "It's Georgina, isn't it?" I asked, stopping what I was doing. "You miss her."

"What? Not really, I just—"

"Can't stop thinking about her? You can't fool me, Alan, I went through the same thing." The big difference being that I'd already liked Devin. Poor Alan would have to figure that bit out on his own. I grabbed the pile of green books and sat at my newly assembled desk, gesturing for Alan to do the same.

"I just don't know how you expect me to feel about it," he grumbled. "I don't want to be told who to fall in love with."

"It's not about how I expect you to feel about it, it's about you. Do you want my honest opinion?"

"See, this is why I like you, Floor Sign. You tell it like it is. Hit me."

"Okay, you don't want to be told what to do? Tough shit. Neither did I, neither does Georgina. But here you are, with a fated thread, connected on the other end to a gorgeous fae who is supposedly your perfect match. Not only that, she's smart, rich, and the ruler of a club of terrifying magical beings. You get a longer life span, you have powers, and you get strength and healing beyond human ability. Suck it up, buttercup. Go get her."

Alan dropped his forehead to the desk and his shoulders started to shake. He burst out laughing. It went on for a while.

"Shit," he breathed, catching his breath. "You're right. I'm being a big whiny baby right now, aren't I?"

"No, I relate. I do. Hell, I think I lasted all of two hours before giving in to the pull and kissing Devin." I blushed and looked away. "But the sooner you go with it, the easier it will be. I think after you break the thread it would be easier to resist and avoid each other if that's what you end up wanting. But that thread is a doozy, there's no ignoring that it wants you to at least meet."

"Yeah, I guess." He grimaced. "I should meet her. Properly I mean. Do you think I should ask her out?"

"Like, on a date? I'm sure she'd love it."

"Sure, yeah. I'll do it tonight." He shifted in his chair. "Can we, uh, keep doing something else for now though?"

"Well, you can help me clean." I glanced over my shoulder at the room behind me.

"What are the books for?" He nodded to the pile of green books.

"If I told you, do you think you could keep it a secret?"

"Of course." He frowned. "What is it?"

I told him everything. The dinner, the letters. Caroline and her cryptic messages. It took a while to get through it all, but Alan listened intently.

"So, she has some stability issues, but she may also have some important knowledge for you." Alan scratched his chin through his wild red beard. "The wild fae aren't the real enemy, but this rotting fae is. Not much wilder than anything else I've heard in the past couple of days. What the hell, let's do it."

"You'll help me look?"

"Yeah, I mean, she did help you wake me up. Weird that it was like Sleeping Beauty. Glad it was you who kissed me instead of Devin or Arthur, though," Alan joked.

"Better me than . . ." Wait.

It *had* to be me. I didn't just wake Alan up; I healed him. I healed him so that he could survive the change. My hand shot to my mouth. Caroline knows about my healing powers.

"Are you all right?" Alan leaned across the desk.

"Caroline. Book." Scrambling to my feet, I reached for my bag, which I'd left on a table by the door, and pulled out my copy of the diary.

"You okay?" Alan repeated, watching me flip through pages of the familiar book until I found the sketch I was looking for. I gasped at what was clearly an image of Caroline. In the drawing she had long hair and her clothes were very dated, but it was definitely her. Under the sketch it read *Caroline Dubois—May 1831.*

"Well, that explains why her name sounded familiar." I moved the book to show Alan. "This is Caroline."

"The painter's daughter?" He frowned down at the drawing. "Weird. I guess we knew she was a changeling, though it stands to reason she'd still be around."

"Do you want to look for more green books while I start going through these?" I tucked the diary away and sat back down by the books I had been gathering. "Now I *really* want to know what it is she knows."

"Sure." He walked to the next shelf and began looking for more green covers.

I hid behind a large green book and tried to quell a small panic attack before it caught Devin's attention. He was busy with Georgina anyway, and I didn't want him coming here while I was snooping for anything that might help with Caroline's clue.

Poring over the old pages with a delicate hand, my focus was half on the text and half on evening out my breathing. In one volume I found a photo album depicting the city in its earlier days. Interesting but nothing fae-related. In fact, most of the green books were useless—a church cookbook from 1902, a guide to local plants and wildlife written before my grandparents were even born, a ship ledger from two hundred years before Seattle was even founded. The original diary of Marcel Dubois, which I had already read through several times but which didn't reveal anything new. There were also several copies of census records, but if Caroline's clue was buried there it would take days to find—even if I could recognize the relevant information.

"Any luck?" Alan called from deeper in the basement.

"Not yet," I sighed, sliding down in my chair. "This is going to take forever."

"Hey, found another one," he said, ignoring my skepticism. Alan brought over a short, thick volume caked in dust and smelling of mildew. I was a little sad about its condition, but it did appear to be one of the oldest things we'd yet found.

"What is it?" I asked as he handed it to me.

"A diary, I think."

I lightly traced its spine. The moment I opened it I knew it was the one. It had several similarities to a slightly newer one I was reading back at the house. Faded gold letters across the front read *Gates & Courts*. The first date inside said *1382* in a loose, scrawling hand.

This had to be it. Flipping the pages gently with a gloved hand, drinking in every word. The older use of English would take me extra time to decipher. With the delicate condition of the book, I needed to scan each page and make a digital copy as soon as I could. For now, I jotted down any important notes in a document on my laptop.

"How's it going?" Alan asked, bringing me more green books from the back of the basement.

"I think this is the one. This is the only book so far to reference anything to do with the fae."

"Do you want to talk it out?" he asked, sitting down. "You look like you could use a break."

"Maybe. Okay, so two things need to be addressed: one, do the fae actually need the changelings for their population?"

"Have you found anything about that?"

"Not much. Some birth and death records. A lot of death actually, fae and changeling both."

"Changeling deaths?" Alan asked. "Like, as in us?"

"Yeah, I guess it's common to not survive the change." I flipped to another page. "It's probably a miracle that you, I, and Candace all changed safely this year."

"What's item two?" Alan scratched his chin.

"Who would want a war between changelings and true fae?"

"Whoever has the bigger army?" Alan offered. "Or maybe a third party—the wild fae?"

Wild fae indeed. I stood, one hand anchoring me on the desk. Particles flew through the beams of light in a swirl of the basement's neglect, and I wondered what secrets would be unlocked down here. What story was at the beginning of the conflict with the wild fae? Did they truly want nothing more than to oust the court fae in their own thirst for power, or was it something else?

"Maybe." I tapped the desk. "If I were crazy enough to chase the wild fae for answers, I wonder what I'd discover."

We remained in silence for a few minutes.

"Let's do it," Alan said, breaking the silence.

"Do what, find the wild fae? They're dangerous and go against the court fae." Saying it out loud, I heard how weak my argument was. Even I was starting to doubt it.

"Have you actually seen one? Talked to them?" Alan stood. "Plus, you're dangerous, too, or so they say. You're matched with Devin because you're on his level, right? So why not? If they've got answers, we should go to them."

"You're really suggesting we find one?" I asked. "You're not scared?"

Alan shrugged. "I'm not saying we don't go in prepared, but I am saying we've been told these wild fae are dangerous, and yet the one you met was helpful. Weird, but helpful."

Alan always had a big build, and if I'd gone from being unable to open a pickle jar to lifting his huge form outside of Club Glo, what had the change done to him? Plus, he was completely right. Caroline was a wild fae, but she'd come to warn me about something, and she'd told me how to help Alan.

"If there really is a war on the other side of those questions, we need to know what we're dealing with," he insisted. "We're changelings, it concerns us both. I say we go."

"You're right," I said, standing. "Okay, yeah, let's go. But tomorrow. I want a full day while Devin is busy, and I want more time tonight to read this book."

"Okay, good." He nodded. "Tomorrow."

"Tomorrow."

CHAPTER THIRTY-TWO

DEVIN

A light snow fell outside Georgina's office window. It was a small comfort in the ongoing annoyance I had been dealing with for the past two days. She was pacing behind her desk, the air above her shimmering with heat.

"If you're so sure he had something to do with it, compel him to speak," I said.

Georgina stopped pacing. "That's the problem, *Devin*. I *have* been compelling him!" She slammed her clawed hands to her new desk. "He isn't talking, no matter what my fae do to him."

I raised an eyebrow. "What exactly have your fae been doing to him?"

"That's not the point. This fae or whatever group he's with, *did harm to my bond mate*!" Steam rose from her sharp nails as she scorched the wood of her desk. I wondered briefly if this was the desk that had replaced the last one I'd watched her destroy, or if there had been others in between.

"I understand, Georgina." I sighed and pinched the bridge of my nose. "But if we can't find out who helped him, or why it was done in the first place, then throw your suspect in the dungeon to rot for a while and focus on what's important."

"Which is what exactly?"

"Alan."

Her face crumbled. "I can't stop thinking about him. But he . . . he hasn't spoken to me. I haven't seen him. I don't know if he's eating, or sleeping well, or . . . or—"

"Georgina," I snapped, "we're getting nowhere with the fae you suspect. We have traced Alan's steps several times now, and we are no closer to finding out why he was targeted. Step back from the problem and look at it from the outside. Your court is likely worried for you and concerned about the changeling that is now connected to you; that is, if they even know he exists. Go, be with them, comfort them. Prepare for when Alan comes to you, because I have no doubt in my mind that he *will*."

"What if he doesn't?" she whimpered.

"He will," I said. "Even if only to deal with the thread. The rest is between the two of you. And we will find out who did this; I'm only suggesting we give it a couple more days. Focus on your court. And don't worry about Alan, he's perfectly safe for now, and he will be until he decides to join you. Which he will."

She sat down, her anger deflating. "Right, you're right. It's been two days. Should I . . . call him?"

"How about I go home and talk to him first. Plan a dinner with your court, and I'll see if I can get Alan to give you a call. We'll return to the fae in your dungeon in a few days."

"Fine. But maybe I should get his number from you, just in case—"

"Georgina," I warned. "We talked about this. Let him come to you; he has a lot to absorb right now. It will happen, don't push him."

"Easy for you to say!" she roared. "Your mate isn't off hiding in another court's house!"

"Thea had already learned of the fae, and she knew *me*. We had a connection before the bond reared its head, and she's been close with one of my court for years. Alan knew nothing of us or of you until after he had been changed. You will give him *time*, and you will accept my aid and advice that I am so *graciously* giving you. I will remind you that our courts are rarely on such good terms, and that an assault on a friend of my *mate* would be, under usual circumstances, enough to spark a war."

Silence stretched between us. I knew some of her warriors had probably heard every word. Not that I cared—united with Thea, not even Georgina and her best fae could do anything to harm me. She knew it too.

"Get out," she growled. "I will heed your words for now, but get out of this house."

I stood, casually brushing lint from my shoulder. "Lovely to see you, as always."

She hissed as I slowly made my way out through smoldering hallways and past nervous-looking fae.

Good, let them remember who I am and what I can do.

I was glad to breathe fresh winter air the moment I left the stifling confines of Georgina's mansion. The last two days in that suffocating heat pit had been more than enough. Pulling out my phone, I called Thea once I was on the road again.

"Hello?" she answered, clearly distracted by something. I smiled, picturing her scrunched-up nose as she concentrated on her work.

"I'm on my way home, are you still at the gallery?"

"Yeah, but I'm picking out some things to bring back with me now. I'll work from the house."

"All right, I'll see you there."

Ending the call, I made my way home to find that her van was missing, so I went inside first and poured myself a drink.

Georgina was quite torn up about her distance from Alan. I could understand it, though her short patience and quick temper were not going to help her bond with him any faster. My glass was half gone when the front door opened, letting in both Alan and Thea with arms full of documents.

"Do you need help?" I asked, standing from the sofa and setting my glass down.

"No, it's not heavy, just awkward to hold." Thea started up the stairs. "I'm going to put these on my nightstand, just a sec."

Alan followed with the rest of the books, and a moment later they were coming back down the stairs as I polished off my brandy. "Let's sit," I said. "I have a few things I want to talk with you about. Both of you."

They joined me in the front room, moving aside the blankets that Alan had been using to sleep at night and giving me their full attention.

"Did you find out who triggered Alan's change?" Thea asked hopefully.

"You did, darling. When you kissed him." She grinned sheepishly. "But if you're asking who started this whole mess, no, we don't know yet."

"How is, um . . ." Alan cleared his throat. "How is Georgina doing?"

"She's been better." I looked at him pointedly. "That's actually the other thing I wanted to talk to you about. If you've adjusted to your new situation, I think it would be good to give her a call."

"You think she'll want to talk to me after I decided to stay here with you?" Alan asked quietly.

"Of course she will, dummy." Thea smacked his shoulder lightly. "Have you listened to nothing I've told you about the fae?"

Alan glanced out the window. "I think I'm gonna give her a call right now, if that's all right. I'll be back in a minute. Save me a slice, okay?"

"Go get her," Thea said, and Alan left the room with a face almost as red as his wild hair. She turned to me. "You ready to have another mated pair ruling the courts?"

"I'm ready to have my house back," I said. "Someone wouldn't play with me while we had a guest." Placing my hands on her hips, I pulled her in gently for a heated kiss.

"Alan would hear us," she whispered.

"I'm trembling with concern," I drawled.

She smacked my chest lightly, but the playful grin she tried to shove off her face told a different story.

"At least wait until after dinner, okay? I'm starving."

With a wicked grin, I stole a kiss. "Be careful making deals with a fae, darling. I'll be holding you to it."

CHAPTER THIRTY-THREE

THEA

The bed shifted next to me as Devin got up. I groaned and rolled into the warm space he left behind.

"What time is it?" I mumbled.

"Five thirty. I need to take care of some things at the gallery—I've been neglecting my duties there."

"Why so early?" I complained, pulling the covers up over my head.

"I have to meet with a sculptor while he's in town." Devin sat back down and rubbed the lump of covers that was my hip. "Will I see you at the gallery today?"

The sobering memory that Alan and I planned to track down a wild fae today surfaced, and I struggled to keep my emotions neutral. "No, I've got enough to work on here. And a few errands."

"Are you sure?"

"Don't worry about me, I'll see you tonight."

"All right then." He kissed my forehead and hopped in the shower. I pretended to rest as he got dressed and left.

The moment I heard the lock on the front door, I threw off the covers and ran to the dresser. A quick shower and a change into my favorite yoga pants and baggy sweater, and I was ready to go.

"Alan, you ready?" I jogged downstairs, bag in hand, and found him at the kitchen table, eating toast.

"Yeah." He scooted a plate toward me as I sat down. "Just getting some breakfast. What's the plan?"

"I have reason to believe there is a wild fae hideout about an hour from my hometown."

"We can take my truck. If we have to get away fast, it's better than your van."

"Good," I nodded. "Still no idea what your powers might be?"

He shook his head. "But I can feel my new strength, and I've been in a couple fights in my time. Plus I have Miriam."

I gave him a skeptical look. "Who?"

"My hunting rifle." He shrugged. "Even a fae would stop in their tracks with a hole in them, right?"

"I guess . . . Wait, that's not iron, is it?"

"No, iron would be too soft. It's steel, don't worry."

"All right then. At least you'll have something on you."

"And you have powers," he offered. "Do you have any weapons you can bring? I'd feel better if we both had something, just in case."

"Wait, I do have a weapon, let me grab it from the van before we leave."

We ate breakfast while I felt for that thread between me and Devin to be stretched far enough that his bond was more of a vague feeling than an immediate compass. We had already found out that a few miles of separation can ease it, and today it would be working in my favor. Minutes later we were in Alan's truck, ready to go.

"Where to, boss?" he said, starting the engine.

"South." I nodded toward the highway.

I studied the book as we drove. In my lap was the bent iron pipe from George, and behind our seats lay Miriam, an old but well cared for shotgun that apparently Alan was great with when hunting elk and deer with his dad. Would a bullet stop an attacking fae? I wasn't sure, but hopefully we were both right and the wild fae would be more open to talking than fighting.

I spent the first thirty minutes making charts of fae deaths, changeling or otherwise, and their respective courts. Then I began the tedious process of marking which courts the changelings joined. It leaned slightly in favor of Autumn and Summer but was, for the most part, pretty even across the board.

The farm was as broken and run-down as I remembered it. I gripped the pipe, picturing the figure I'd seen in the window that day—someone who clearly did not want company but was our only lead.

Alan pulled up near the house. There was no use disguising our approach, not from fae. Better to have the truck close at hand anyway. Alan carried his gun, and I kept the iron bar tucked in my jacket, having worn it more for concealment than anything else.

"It does feel weird around here," he said as we got out of the truck.

"This is why we travel with company," I murmured. "Don't get caught alone."

"Speaking of which, do we know if this wild fae is alone?" he asked.

"I don't feel much of a presence like I do with a group in the city."

"Will they feel the same as the court fae?"

I didn't know the answer to that. Silence hung between us as we approached the old house.

"Hello?" I called, startling a pair of birds on the roof. "I know you're here, we just want to talk. Peacefully."

Alan and I looked around but were met with only silence. The still winter air was refreshing on my skin, but I knew that Alan, a Summer fae, even though he hadn't yet committed to his court, must be freezing. Alan didn't show any discomfort, though, beyond how nervous we both felt being here.

"Want to try inside?" I offered.

Alan frowned. "Sure."

A small noise inside told me we were on the right track. I knocked. Nothing.

"Can we come in? We know you're there," Alan called, the firmness of his voice not matching his anxious expression.

"I'm a friend of Caroline's—is she in?" I called.

The door swung open. In a flash there were claws positioned at my neck. Not touching skin, but by only a hair. Still, the message was clear.

A man's face moved into the light of the doorway. He was lean, with reddish brown skin and piercing eyes. His yellow fangs were visible as he spoke. "You again. She isn't here," he hissed. "Leave."

Alan stepped toward me, stopping when the wild fae glared a warning. "Please, we have some questions. Do you know where she is?"

"Haven't seen her in weeks, why are you here?"

It struck me then that he wasn't attacking; he was on the defensive. Unlike the warnings I'd heard about them, this wild fae was not jumping at the chance to land the first blow.

"I'm trying to stop some kind of conflict from happening. I need to talk to Caroline." I tried to avoid swallowing, feeling his claws so close. "Unless you know something about it?"

He paused, sniffing the air between us. He snapped his head to Alan. "You aren't in a court."

"No," Alan answered. "Not yet."

"Why isn't a changeling in a court?" He narrowed his eyes at me. "And you, you're one, too, but you're one of *them*."

"If by that you mean I'm a changeling but also part of a court, then yes," I said. "Can you tell us anything helpful? Did Caroline say when she'd be back?"

"Caroline ain't here, and I don't have anything to say to the likes of you," he spat, lowering his clawed hand.

"Wait!" Alan caught the door as it was closing. "Can you at least tell us what you know about why the fae need changelings?"

That made him pause. "What the hell are you talking about?"

"The reason for the changelings in the first place," I said slowly. "Isn't it the low birth rate of fae over the last few centuries?"

"Is that what they're telling you?" He looked between us, his surprise evident.

"Yes," I said, glancing briefly at Alan.

He stared at me, lost in thought. I could hear Alan's heart beating in rhythm with the tension of the situation. The chill of winter at my back felt good, grounding. My skin itched with a building static that I still had little real control over.

"What's the big deal about them telling us that?" Alan asked after a long silence.

"True fae can't tell lies." The wild fae opened his door for us. "At least not knowingly. Come in, but the big one can leave his toy at the door."

As I exchanged a look with Alan, he set his rifle by the door and we went inside. The house was barren. An old leather couch sat in the middle of the living room, cracked and worn with age. Facing it were two metal folding chairs and a milk crate for a coffee table. We sat on the folding chairs, the wild fae on the couch.

"Can I have your names?" he asked, leaning forward, a dangerous glint in his eyes.

"You may call me Thea," I answered carefully, "and you may call him Alan."

"Thea." He blinked and sat up straight, panic in his eyes. "If you're who I think you are, I'm fucked. Shit! Why the bloody hell did I let you in? I need to go."

"Wait! Devin doesn't know I'm here!" I stood, trying to soothe him. "I'm here to stop something bad from happening, please."

"How do you know Caroline? Is she all right? Is she dead? Is she in your dungeons?"

"She was fine last time I saw her," I said calmly. "She found me, not the other way around. She's been chasing me with cryptic riddles since my change began. I saw her just the other day."

"That . . . does sound like her." He sat back down. "Shit. Okay, all right, I might know what she would've been talking to you about. I'm Keegan. I've known Caroline since right after her change."

"She's not an easy one to keep track of, is she?" I asked. "It's been really difficult trying to track down her hints."

"Not surprised," Keegan said. "What did she tell you?"

"She said there was going to be a war between changelings and true fae," I said. "Then she told me to find a green book, which I did."

"What green book?"

I pulled the book in question from my bag and passed it to him.

He started flipping through. "Ha! This brings back memories. Yeah, I see. It's all in here if you know where to look. The old courts used to keep these kinds of ledgers."

"What do you mean by old courts?" Alan spoke up.

"Courts rise and fall all the time." Keegan shut the book and handed it back to me. "Courts form, other fae topple them, then they form courts, then more fae topple them. Eventually the fates land on powerful-enough courts that they stay put for a while. The gate in Ireland has been safe for millennia, for example, while the gate in Brazil has been a mess of revolving-door courts for as long as we've been recording our history. Caroline would know more than I would; I refused to join. Something felt . . . off. It wasn't right."

"What do you mean?" I was baffled. "You didn't join, but you could have?"

He shrugged. "A wild fae could be a fae that wants to join the court but doesn't. They can also be a fae who doesn't feel drawn to join the courts of a gate at all. A wild fae is just a fae who is out in the wild with no allegiance anywhere."

"But I thought all the wild fae wanted the gate?"

Keegan shook his head. "That's a lot of us around here, but not all. And no amount of wanting to be at this gate could convince me to join the courts back then. Plenty of undesirable fae have been disposed of, rather than welcomed with open arms."

"That sounds terrifying," I whispered. "But back to the revolving-door courts: What about two courts of mated fae?"

"Two? I only knew about yours," Keegan whistled. "I'd say the other two will catch up soon enough. Is that what's going on in the city right now?"

"It will be soon," I said. "What's the book say about birth rates?"

"Don't stop at just births, look at deaths too," Keegan said. "You add up those numbers against each other, then you'll see something worth talking about."

"Deaths?" I shared a puzzled look with Alan. "I thought a fae basically didn't die unless they were killed."

Keegan shrugged. "Just look into it. The age at death is . . . interesting, to say the least."

"True fae or with changeling descent?"

"Doesn't matter." He leaned back. "You look long enough and you'll see the problem. Someone wants to chase off or kill as many fae as they can."

"Who?" I asked.

"Don't know, memories about that get fuzzy. Something's interfering. It's not just me, it's all the wild fae."

"But you want to attack the court fae," Alan added slowly. "Don't you?"

Keegan's face darkened. "Tell me, you two who are away from the gate's influence right now, do you feel the desire to go back to it?"

My lips parted in surprise as I looked at Alan. "Yeah, I do. It's mild, a weaker version of the thread of fate."

"You didn't notice it 'til you looked for it, right? That power that seeps out of the gate, this land, it's got its own desires somehow. If it wants you there, it wants you there. Calling to you like a siren's song. It's not calling too hard now but give it a few weeks and that call is going to get louder." The sound of a car rushed by outside, and Keegan practically jumped to the window. He looked out, then pulled the curtains tight. "Now picture this, you're called to the gate, right? But you can't go there because the court bastards would rather kill you on sight than let you step on their territory. After a few months, that call starts to hurt real bad. Enough to drive you wild. You've gotta get to that gate, bathe in its presence, but you can't do it without risking a fight if you get caught. You're better off immediately trying to defend yourself or running away than talking to the court fae."

"Keegan," I said softly. "That's not at all what we were told."

I couldn't read his expression with his back still turned to us, but his arm moved, as though he was rubbing his heart. "If it's not orchestrated by the court leadership, I don't know who's doing it, okay? All the wild fae I know, none of us remember going wild. Hell, some of us can't remember changing, if we were at one time human. That messes you up. Living with this thirst messes you up." He turned, his face painted with contempt. "And now you're at my doorstep, probably drawing the Lord of Winter's wrath my way as we speak."

"We aren't! I swear," I said. "I'm trying to sort out what Caroline's trying to tell me so I can make things better. She seems to know something but she won't tell me what it is outright, and if what she says is true, a war is going to break out."

"Look, Caroline does know things. There's no good explanation with that one, she just knows somehow. Creepy as hell. She's not quite like you and me; something's going on with her mind. Maybe she's finally lost touch, maybe she's going too wild for the gate's draw. Don't know why, since she seems to be the only one of us who can get close enough for some relief, at least for a time. Maybe she wanted you to take whatever you found in that book back to your court, maybe she wanted you to find out who's behind the trouble. All I know is it's not worth my life to sit here with you two and brew up theories. So, kindly leave so I can get out of here and find a new place to stay before I'm found by more of you court people."

"Keegan—" Alan began.

"Nope, go find Caroline. That book has some pretty shady numbers in it that don't make sense. My guess is that you need Caroline to fit it all together. So, do whatever other scheming she has up her sleeve without me."

With that, we were unceremoniously shoved through the door and

Sabrina Blackburry

left to the cold, the creaky farmhouse door slamming shut behind us. Wind rattled the creaky porch, adding to the abandoned feel of the peeled wood and the desolate yard. If Keegan was squatting here, he'd probably leave this place now that we had approached him.

"What now?" Alan asked.

"I guess I'm going through that book again," I sighed. "Come on, let's go home."

228

CHAPTER THIRTY-FOUR

THEA

Devin stayed late at the gallery, which was fine by me. Alan and I had been charting every aspect of the old court ledger, and it didn't look like we'd be done any time soon. Unfortunately, the Middle English the book was written in, combined with the lack of actual summaries for each year, made it slow work that I had to double-check more often than not, considering Alan wasn't familiar with any of it.

"Got another one for Spring," Alan said from his seat by the fire. "Stillbirth."

I hovered over several pages of tallied information, trying to piece together what we already had. "What year?"

"Hm." He studied the page. "It says 1382."

"Okay," I sighed, adding another tally to the right place. "So many poor babies."

"Keegan said the ages would reveal something." He got up and looked over my shoulder at the data we'd collected so far. "Geeze, half the deaths here are stillborn fae. But no one talks about that being a problem, do they?"

"I've only been told that they rarely get pregnant at all. Why do all these records have so many pregnancies, and so many complications? What changed?" I twisted a piece of hair between my fingers, thinking. "I guess I can ask, but I don't want to raise suspicions with any of the true fae."

"Aren't there any changelings you can ask?"

I smacked my forehead. "Duh, Heather!" I pulled out my phone and called her. She picked up on the third ring.

"Hello?" I heard the clattering of dishes in the background—she was at the café.

"Hey, I've got a strange question. Have you ever heard of a stillborn baby fae?"

"That is a strange question." She hesitated. "No, can't say I have, and I've been around a few decades now. Why?"

"Doing some research for Devin, for my new job. This was a big help, though, I'll talk to you later." I ended the call and leaned back over the ledger.

"If it was a problem in the past, we can see that from the numbers," Alan said. "But even if there haven't been any stillbirths, we still have a population problem on our hands."

"Right, and Caroline said something to the effect of the fae not really needing changelings at all. But if they don't need us, then why is the birth rate so low?" I flopped back onto the floor in frustration.

"Do you think we could find Caroline?" Alan suggested. "Maybe we should just ask the source?"

"Maybe . . . I know Devin tries to keep an eye on where they go when they come into the city itself but I don't think it goes beyond that. Maybe we could find something in his office."

"You're okay with snooping behind his back?"

"Not when you put it like that," I groaned. "Wait, I have another idea." I grabbed my phone again and scrolled until I found his number.

"Lady Thea?"

"Hi, Arthur, yes. You're still tracking the movement of wild fae in the city, right?" I held my breath. I'd heard Devin talk to him on the phone while he thought I was asleep. The question was whether Arthur would tell me anything or not.

"Does Lord Devin know you're calling me about this?" he asked slowly.

"Does it matter?" I tried to put a little confidence in my voice. If he wants to call me Lady, I could see if it would work in my favor. "Your Lady asked you a question."

There was a long pause. "You're really playing this game?"

"I am," I said, my voice losing some of its bravado.

"Yes," he said reluctantly, "I'm still tracking their movements."

"Good," I let out a breath; I wasn't sure I'd get this far. "What's the last place you knew them to be?"

"Lady Thea . . ."

"Please, Arthur. It's important."

Arthur sighed. "The abandoned trade school a few blocks from Georgina's magazine building, near the south part of Lake Washington."

"Good job, Arthur." My excitement slipped through. "Keep this between us, that's an order." I hung up before he could say anything else. "Get your truck," I said. "We're going to the old trade school."

The school was a bit of a drive from the heart of the Winter Court. We cautiously got out of the car at the crumbling parking lot. I kept a hand on the iron pipe in my bag, just in case. Light snow crunched underfoot as we made our way inside. Broken windows and graffiti lined both sides of the doors.

"Miserable place to hole up," Alan commented.

"Not a bad choice for someone who wants to stay out of sight, though." I turned on my phone's flashlight and checked every hall before we entered. Our footsteps echoed.

After a twenty-minute search of the grounds, we found ourselves at the front doors once more.

"Nothing," I huffed, turning off the light and pocketing my phone before the battery died.

"They've moved on." Alan shrugged. "We knew this might be the case. It doesn't seem safe to hang around, even if they're desperate to be in the presence of the faerie gate."

I scanned the ruined lobby around us and sighed. "Yeah, I guess."

"We may have hit a dead end here, but we can keep looking into the ledger. You're clever, Thea. You'll find something." Alan opened the door for me and we headed back to the truck. "You figured out the fae thing on your own; I know you'll get this too."

"I don't think I figured it out on my own," I said, getting in the truck. "Devin put clues right in front of my face and it still took me far too long to understand."

"What clues—the creepy fae paintings at the gallery?"

"That and a diary pretty much telling the tale of a changeling being taken. I should lend it to you, it's interesting stuff. Changeling one-oh-one."

"That still doesn't solve . . ." He stopped and looked into the rear-view mirror. "This jeep has been following for a while."

"Jeep?" I twisted in my seat, peering through the back window. "Arthur!"

"Arthur?" Alan frowned. "Do you want me to lose him?"

"I don't know if we can. He's Devin's tracker. I don't know what his powers are, but I bet he can still follow our trail even if he loses sight of us."

"What do you want me to do?"

"Take us to Heather's," I said, and pulled out my phone again, frowning at the flashing red battery symbol.

"Hello, Lady Thea," Arthur said when he picked up.

"Why are you following us?" I demanded.

"Devin would skin me alive if I let you wander into danger."

"Don't be so dramatic. Go back to doing whatever you were doing. We didn't even find a wild fae at the school," I huffed.

"Good," Arthur said. "I'll leave you alone for now, Lady. But don't underestimate Devin. He's outlived many others for a reason, and he would do anything to protect you."

Click.

"Arrrgh!" I threw the phone into my bag, annoyed.

"What do you think he meant by that?" Alan asked quietly.

I thought about it. "I don't know, and I honestly don't want to think about it."

It scared me to think about it.

I looked out the back window as Arthur slowed and turned down another street. I turned to Alan after a few minutes, satisfied he'd left us alone. "He's gone."

He nodded. "I'm almost to Heather's. What do you want to do from there?"

"I don't know," I sighed. "Maybe we should bring her in on our plans; after all, she's a changeling too. And she was willing to go against Devin for me before."

"A partner in crime, huh?" Alan thought. "If you trust her, I trust her. Three has to be better than two. Besides, she's gonna ask you about your weird stillbirth comment from earlier."

"Ugh, I forgot about that." I sank into the seat as we pulled up to the café. "Yeah, we're going to have to fill her in on everything. She's not going to like that I met with a wild fae and didn't tell her. Or Devin for that matter."

"Do you think she's going to insist you tell Devin everything?"

"Probably," I said as we got out. "But she'll side with me in the end. I'm sure of it."

We walked up to the entrance. Heather was working alone—it looked to have been a slow night, so she probably sent Melanie home early. I watched for a moment, her back to us as she juggled three coffee cups and a slice of pie to a table of college students.

"Now or never, Thea." Alan nudged me.

I took a deep breath and we went inside.

"Take a seat, I'll be with you in a second!" Heather called sweetly.

In fact, she sounded way too sweet. She was pissed. I could feel it. I cringed. Whatever she was mad about I hoped could be taken care of easily, because I really needed her on our side for this. I turned and headed for my usual booth. That's when I caught it—cinnamon. An orange head whirled around, a cup of coffee at her lips. She put it down on the saucer with a gentle clink.

"Hello, Thea, word on the street is you've been looking for me," Caroline said with a wide grin.

"That's her?" Alan whispered from behind.

"Yeah, that's her." I looked to Heather, approaching us with a terrifying glare.

"Shit," Alan breathed. "She looks pissed."

"Yeah," I murmured. "She can get in line."

"*You*," Heather stalked up to me, copper eyes blazing. She prodded my shoulder with one sharp finger. "*Booth. Sit. Stay.*" She turned on her heels, a sweet, plastic smile plastered on her face as she bounced over to hand a customer his bill.

"Charming." Caroline sipped her tea, having witnessed the whole thing. "Why don't you join me for a little chat? We have some catching up to do."

I slid in across from her. It was going to be a long night. She was . . . different. She carried herself differently, the wild spark in her eye more under control now. Her clothes were neater and her hair had been brushed.

"You've changed," I said flatly.

"All thanks to you." Another cryptic answer.

"Are you Caroline Dubois?" I asked.

Her eyes turned wistful for a moment before her eyes focused on me again. "I suppose I am still a Dubois, even after all this time."

So, she was Marcel's daughter. The one that had been changed by the fae, the account of which in Marcel's diary had led me to all of my initial suspicions about them. She had clearly been through a lot since her father kept his diary; it was no wonder I hadn't recognized her from the sketches. Her long hair was gone; her expression, so youthful and innocent when captured by Marcel's charcoal, now sharp and calculating.

"I found the ledger." I tapped my foot anxiously under the table. "There used to be more births, but the death toll during birth was high. Now we don't seem to have the stillbirths, but the number of babies born is still low. Why?"

"Ooh, someone has been studying." She winked at Alan. "And this handsome fellow, has he been helping you? I'm sure the Lord of Winter won't like that."

"You're the one who told me I couldn't tell Devin!" I snapped. "I'm tired of the games, Caroline. Give me some answers."

"All right." She set down her cup again. "Here's one for you: you want to know how I knew how to wake this one?" She nodded at Alan.

"Yes," I said immediately.

"I know what you're keeping secret. I'm like you, but different. One of my four senses is . . . sharper . . . than the others." She waited for realization to dawn on me. I took in a quick breath when I figured it out.

"I thought there were five senses?" Alan muttered.

"Not those senses," I said. "The four fae gifts. Strength and speed, the enhanced body. Then there's your element or nature power or whatever. There's advanced healing, and—"

"Glamour," she finished. "Though, mine comes with a little more oomph than the average fae possesses. We'll get to that in a minute. The strength of glamour that can both disguise and conceal to my liking but also see through everything else. So much so that I can see glimpses of what can happen. Flashes of the future, even."

"That's how you knew I had healing powers," I breathed. "Holy shit."

"What does that mean?" Alan asked.

Caroline studied him. "Oh, how amusing. I'll give you a little gift— would you like to know what your power over nature will be?"

Alan nodded cautiously.

"Water," she beamed. "A fresh summer rain. I might note that your beloved's power is the flame. That should make your reign quite interesting."

"But how do I use it?" he asked.

"It will happen in due time," she assured him, then turned back to me. "So, Thea, has the Lord of Winter been suspicious of your recent actions?"

"I don't think so," I said. "But hold on, I'm not done with the glamour thing. Devin doesn't even believe in this four powers stuff, I still don't think he wants to address my healing. And here you are with the same thing! How have you kept it a secret? Why are we like this?"

"I kept it secret by staying on the run," she answered solemnly. "So many of the changelings go mad with the change; it was easy to pretend to have gone mad and get away."

"You were only pretending this whole time?" I asked, shocked. "I really did think you were hallucinating or something, you know."

"Oh, I was," she admitted. "At first it helped me keep away from the court fae. But I think I was just a touch elf-struck to begin with. Combine that with something so strong as my glamour powers and, well, my mind did begin to crumble. That is, until I found you."

My fingers shot to my lips. "The kiss."

She nodded. "Hopefully I won't need another, now that I'm fully in control of myself, but at least I know just where to find another dose of medicine." She winked.

"So, you two have enhanced gifts—more than normal, I mean?" Alan asked.

"Yes," Caroline said. "Thea is coming into power with her healing. I'm at constant odds with the magic of the gate to keep on top of mine."

"Why is that?" I asked.

"I wonder . . ." She gave a sly look. "No, not yet. I will answer questions about the fae population, though."

"I think I liked you better before," I mumbled.

"Is low birth rate a problem everywhere?" Alan asked. "There are other gates around the world. Does this happen there too?"

"No," she said. "The faerie gates are . . . unstable. No two act the same way. They are as volatile as the creatures they attract. You can't expect a problem at one gate to be reflected elsewhere."

"It's the gate doing this?" I asked.

"I didn't say that. I also didn't say there was even a birth rate problem."

"If there isn't a problem," I asked, "then why do fae need the changelings?"

"At this gate?" Caroline tapped her chin. "They don't, I guess."

"All those people. Torn from their lives, some elf-struck, some dead, for no reason," I murmured.

"Oh, there *is* a reason," Caroline said carefully. "But I don't think you're ready for it yet."

"I've already gone this far for you," I argued. "Why would I not hear you out again?"

"The matter at hand is very . . . delicate. I'm still sorting out more of what I know so I can be sure I have it right."

Heather huffed in a sour note of disbelief from behind the counter where she had been wiping down the surfaces. I waited to see if she had something to say, but it seemed she was intent on staying out of it until we were done.

"Why lead Thea on this wild chase for answers?" Alan asked slowly. "What do you want us to find?"

"I'm not entirely sure yet," she answered quietly. "Unless the books contain enough to incriminate the one behind everything, it won't be easy to convince the courts to take action. I'm prepared to do the unspeakable to accomplish my goal. All I *am* certain about is that you can sway the Lord of Winter into seeing the ledgers in a new light."

Caroline continued. "Just know who you can trust. Trust your mate and trust your closest friends. No one else."

She stood, finishing off her coffee and putting her money on the table. "I have to go; I've been here too long as is. I have friends on my side, and we're ready for a rebalancing. You'd be wise to prepare as well. The rotting one will not wait much longer."

"Seriously?" I snapped. "You can't leave without scattering more questions in your wake, can you?"

She paused but didn't turn around. "I am who I am." And she left, the gentle bell above the exit signaling her departure.

"Should we follow?" Alan asked.

"She ditched me pretty easily before," I said, plopping back down in the booth. "Let her go."

Heather had already flipped the sign on the door to *closed* and let the rest of her business trickle out naturally. It wasn't long before the other customers were gone. She locked the door then and joined us in the booth.

"What brought *her* to my door?" Her voice was low and strained.

"You know Caroline?" I balked. "How?"

"Everybody knows her! They spent forever looking for her when she disappeared."

"She disappeared?" I asked. "Hold on, I thought she was a wild fae?"

"She is now, but she wasn't always. She went feral. I wasn't around when it happened, but I do know that Devin and the others tried to find her and never did. And now she shows up to my place waiting for you!"

"I didn't mean to leave you out; she said not to tell anyone," I explained.

"Apparently they kept looking for her for a long time," Heather said. "Fifty years or so. And now she's resurfaced, bringing back who knows what trouble with her. You've been digging around in some kind of mess without me after promising we'd stick together?" she snapped. "After that mess at Club Glo I stood outside all night to help find *his* family. *For you.*" She jerked a thumb at Alan, who flinched. "I *fought* with Devin when he first began to change you." Tears were flowing now. "Not only do you jump into danger and scare the shit out of me but you don't see fit to tell me?"

"Heather." I pushed Alan out of the booth, so I could scoot in next to Heather and wrap my arms around her. "I'm so sorry. I was coming here to tell you everything, I promise. I didn't know Caroline would be here."

"It's true," Alan interjected. "We were coming here to tell you everything; we had no idea Caroline would already be here."

"Stop, just stop," she said, blowing her nose with a napkin. "I'm just in shock. Don't do that again, no more secrets."

Tightening my hold on Heather, I buried my face in her shoulder. "I promise, no more secrets."

We told Heather everything. The ensuing emotional roller coaster prompted a series of texts from Devin, and I sent him a picture of me and Heather to let him know I was just fine so I could get back to telling Heather our story. She was shocked at some of the things we told her and didn't seem surprised at others.

"Many years ago, before you kids were born"—Heather teased—"when I was a wee thing, a new fae only a few years into my change, I was approached by a small faction of changelings that wanted to help welcome me into their world. There were faeries from every court. It was kind of like a support group, I guess.

"I still see some of them from time to time, but we don't really talk. All they asked was that I don't tell the true fae about them. Something about not wanting to make them feel that changelings were ungrateful or something."

"Do you think these changelings would help us?" Alan asked.

"No," she said slowly. "Maybe. My first thought was, if there's a problem brewing, there has to be two sides to it. They're already a tight-knit group that wants to keep secrets. At the very least maybe they know something."

"Can you put me in touch with them?" Alan asked. "I haven't picked a court yet. I changed under unusual circumstances—I'm probably a poster child for a lost and confused changeling."

"I don't know," I said. "Are you sure you want to do that? I could come too—"

"I don't get the feeling they would want the Lady of Winter in their little club—no offense." Heather patted my shoulder. "You took to the fae world like you alone were made for it. You don't really need their brand of companionship to keep it together."

"Please don't start calling me Lady when Arthur is already doing it."

Heather's face dropped. "Arthur? Yeah, he would, wouldn't he?"

"So you shouldn't go, but I think I could," Alan said. "Not many people know about me and Georgina yet."

"Doesn't the whole Summer Court know?" I asked.

"She was going to tell them at a dinner tonight but I asked her not to do it yet."

"Why?" Heather asked, surprised.

"I guess, I wanted to be sure I really wanted to . . . go through with everything. Not just being connected to Georgina—I don't think I can hold out much longer anyway—but joining the Summer Court at the side of their leader."

"That all makes sense. Heather, while you take Alan to these guys, what am I doing?"

"Preparing for a fight," Heather said. "Just in case. Grab your pipe or something."

I smiled and played with the hard shape in my bag. "Okay, yeah, I'll do that. Can I borrow your truck, Alan? I think I'm going to go to the hardware store and pick up some more things."

"Here." He tossed me his keys. "Don't think I won't bill you if you scratch my girl."

"Your truck is safe with me. Are you good to give Alan a ride, Heather?"

"Sure." She patted Alan hard on the back and he choked on his coffee.

"Good luck, guys." We parted ways, and I planned out my next stop. It was late when I looked at my phone. I only had about twenty minutes to get to the hardware store before it closed. I hopped in Alan's truck and took off. Luckily there were very few other cars on the road. I pulled into the parking lot with ten minutes to spare.

I ran inside, grabbing a plastic shopping basket and tucking it under one arm. The bored teenager behind the counter grumbled under his breath.

"Sorry," I mumbled as I passed him. "I'll be quick."

True to my word, I made a beeline for the pipes at the back. Now that I recognized my powers and the touch of iron, I felt every one of them in the aisle to find the purest, most harmful pieces. I grabbed two more so I could start keeping them on me and in the van. Checking out, I was outside again with three minutes to spare. It was then, while walking through the parking lot, that I felt that heavy presence.

My boots crunched through a light snow as I came to a stop. It felt as if I were suffocating in bonfire smoke and fallen leaves. It was potent, but very pleasant. I had always liked the fall. My heart fluttered slightly as I realized only one being could embody so much Autumn. I turned around to face her.

"Artemis." I bowed my head.

She was dressed in all white, her ebony hair pulled into an intricate bun, a rich wool coat to her ankles. She approached slowly, her face the same calm mask.

"I was nearby when I felt a Winter fae within my borders," she said, her features sharp and noble—proud. "I'm quite surprised to see you out here alone, Lady Thea."

"Oh, Lady Artemis, I'm just Thea," I insisted. "I'm in Autumn territory? I didn't know, I'm still trying to memorize the map Devin gave me. I'm just picking something up from the store."

"Do not fret over it, snowy one." She smiled, putting my spiked heart rate at ease. "You are merely on the border, and I sense no ill intent from you. I am simply investigating."

"Oh," I sighed. "Good, I wouldn't want to overstep my boundaries."

She waved the thought away with a long, elegant hand. "You have made no transgressions here. But while I have you in my presence, may I congratulate you on your new status. You should wear the badge of Lady proudly—the faerie gate would not have matched you to Devin without matching you in power. I sense you will be a good leader to your people, I do look forward to seeing you in action."

"Oh, no," I blushed. "It's Devin who knows what he's doing. I'm only trying to be supportive as best I can."

"You do not see it yet, but you already put your people at ease." A sly grin tugged at her ruby mouth, almost like a laugh. "I wonder if you might even surpass Devin—his temper can get the best of him sometimes. You will be good for the court."

Good for the court. Would I be? I did feel like a part of it by now, and I wanted to help wherever I could.

"Can we expect a tiny fae underfoot soon?"

I turned about five shades of red. "No, I mean, well, we aren't using protection. Not that you needed to know that. But the chances are so low. I'll just . . . stop now."

She laughed, a light, smoky sound. "I am only teasing. You have caused quite a stir, you know. We will all be faced with a balancing soon enough, thanks to you. The gate will right what should be made even. I'm sure the powers are shifting even now, one way or another."

Was she talking about Alan? I didn't know what to say to that.

"Oh, it will be all right," she said. "It was bound to come someday. Nothing stays the same forever."

I remembered what Keegan had said, about courts toppling all the time. This set of courts had been here for five hundred years or so, but I had no idea if that was long or not when it came to fae. I took a breath. "Are you concerned at all that some kind of balance shift might negatively impact the city?"

She stared at me a moment with a hard mask of indifference, as though she could look right through my insignificant form and see something much bigger than the two of us. In fact, the stretch of time grew uncomfortably long as she thought. Maybe she saw me as a child with wild concerns, maybe she thought I was elf-struck after all.

Maybe I shouldn't have said anything.

"You are wiser than I gave you credit for, snowy one," she said finally. "I have given your question thought, and I will answer you with honesty."

I swallowed hard. Her smile remained warm but her words terrified me.

"All things fall eventually. Perhaps it is the nature of my court to think so, but it is true. My answer to your question is this: I would be surprised if we did not see a tremendous change in the near future. You have a good head on you. I pray you survive what comes."

She nodded ever so slightly—a sign of respect—and walked off in the direction from which she'd come.

I shivered, and it had nothing to do with the cold.

CHAPTER THIRTY-FIVE

DEVIN

I threw my jacket on the sitting room sofa and untied my tie as I walked to my office. It had been a long day; I was tired and wanted nothing more than to see Thea and hear what she had been doing in every direction of the city all day. She said she took Alan with her, but I still paid attention for any concerning activity or emotions through the thread. Pouring myself a drink, I sat down at my desk. Mixed feelings of regret and upset shot my way, and I almost dropped my glass. I sent her a text, relieved to get an immediate answer. Bourbon in hand, I settled in to get some more work done. With only a little more business to take care of, maybe Thea and I could have a day in tomorrow.

Oh yes, a day in would be nice and peaceful. We could have breakfast in bed. And lunch. And dinner.

I drained the rest of my glass. That was a dangerous train of thought to go down if I actually wanted to concentrate right now. I woke my computer and pulled up my work emails.

Time ticked by. It wasn't until my phone buzzed that I noticed the late hour.

"Arthur?" I unlocked my phone.

Is Lady Thea home yet?

That was . . . concerning.

No, why?

I stared at the screen, waiting.

Can't talk, just curious

I poured myself another drink and sat back in my chair. Arthur wouldn't have asked about Thea unless he knew she was out of the house. He had to have a reason for not telling me what was going on. He obviously didn't mind me knowing something was up or he wouldn't have sent such a suspicious message. He must have been compelled to not say anything more. And yet, the only ones who could compel him should be one of the fae leaders. Unless . . . perhaps Thea had come into more abilities we hadn't noticed before.

Then, as if she knew I was thinking about her, I felt the warm pull of my mate nearby. Standing, I left my office to meet her at the front door.

"Hello, darling," I opened the door.

"Hey." Thea looked tired but managed to give me a warm look of reassurance before she headed up the stairs.

"Is everything all right?" I asked, following her.

"Yeah." She set her bag down by her nightstand. "I'm just tired."

She looked tired. "Did you by chance run into Arthur tonight?" I asked, careful to not let concern slip into my voice.

She hesitated briefly then kicked off her shoes and busied herself in the dresser. "I did. Why do you ask?" She grabbed some clean clothes from her drawer.

"He was just asking if you'd made it home."

She walked to the bathroom and stood in the doorway. "Here I am."

"Was there a reason for him to be concerned with your whereabouts?" She slipped a large sweater over her head.

"I don't think so, he just saw me in a part of town he didn't like. I picked something up at the store and it turns out I was close to the Autumn borders. I also want to talk to you about something in the morning. Right now I'm exhausted."

She began peeling off her pants. Whatever Arthur's concerns, she was safe and in one piece. One very sexy, beautiful piece. Heat flared through the bond and she sucked in a breath.

"Planning on taking a shower?" I approached slowly, my face revealing every intimate thought on my mind.

"I—yes." Her exhaustion was lifting, replaced with a knowing smile. "Is that a problem?"

"Not at all." I closed the distance between us, removing my shirt. "In fact, I might just need a shower myself."

"Do you want to go first?" she teased. "I'm in no hurry."

"No, no, I won't delay your shower." I wrapped my arms around her, unfastening her bra. "Why don't we take one together?"

A playful smile crossed her lips. "I don't know, that seems terribly inefficient."

"Nonsense." I helped her remove her bra and then slipped the panties down her legs. "I will show you just how efficient I can be."

She moved a hand to my chest, catching her lower lip with her teeth. "Well, you can't shower in your suit."

She leaned up to kiss me, her fingers working on my buttons as I laughed against her mouth. "Eager?"

"Shut up."

I scooped her off her feet as her laughter carried through to the bathroom, where I planned to assist her in a very slow and inefficient shower.

Thea was clever, curious, her heart was wide open, and she was more than I deserved. Holding her close, I realized that my heart was already hers the moment she wanted it. Would it be burdensome to tell her? Perhaps. Still, I would tell her tomorrow. Thea, my darling.

My love.

CHAPTER THIRTY-SIX

THEA

I must have nodded off sometime after dawn, because I woke up with an arm draped over my hip. My eyes fluttered in the harsh morning light. Our scents were intertwined. Stretching just a bit, I didn't want to disturb Devin though my efforts turned out to be unnecessary. His hand moved down my hip and gently squeezed my thigh.

"Good morning." His voice was gruff and still heavy with sleep.

A dry laugh escaped me as I rolled to face him. "I'm tired. Can't we take a nap first?"

He grumbled incoherently but kissed my neck and let me settle back into his arms. His phone buzzed and he cursed at it. I yawned, ready to fall back asleep when he tightened his arm around me.

"What is it?" I woke up fully, feeling the tension rolling off him. "What's wrong?"

"Heather." He tossed the covers aside and went to the closet.

I jolted upright. "What's happened?"

"I don't know, she isn't coherent in her message. I think I need to get to the café."

"*We* need to get to the café," I said and threw off the covers.

—

We raced to Heather's. Alan was still sleeping so I shot him a text on the drive, which was otherwise spent in strained, anxious silence. Nearly there, I heard the sounds of approaching sirens and felt my heart clench.

"Devin . . ." He reached for my hand but said nothing.

We turned a corner and were met with a horrible sight. Bright, raging fire consuming the café, licking the walls and billowing dark smoke into the winter sky.

"No!"

Devin swore and pulled over. I saw Heather by one of the fire trucks. She was in hysterics, a fireman trying to calm her down.

"Heather!" I called, running to her. She whipped her head around and I could see the tears streaking her face, and it broke my heart. She opened her arms wide and wrapped them around me, knocking the air from my lungs.

"What happened?" Devin questioned one of the firefighters.

"We won't know until we knock it out," she grunted. "An old building like this? Could be electrical."

Devin nodded and came over to us. "What did you see when you got here?" he asked.

Heather sniffed. "I got here early to start the soup and rolls. I thought something was off when I pulled up. There are markings by the back door, and they don't look like regular graffiti. That's when I smelled the smoke, then a window burst and I-I messaged you."

I hugged her tighter. "It's going to be okay, you're safe and we'll help you."

"Show me the markings," Devin said, voice tinged with suspicion.

Heather took a deep breath, and I started taking them with her as she watched me. After a few more breaths, she finally calmed down enough to speak evenly. "This way, but they won't let me get close with the fire right now."

Devin waved a hand. "I can glamour enough that they won't notice me. Just point it out and I'll take a look."

We walked around from the front sidewalk to where Heather could point out some markings on the wall next to the lock on the door. Devin walked closer to inspect it, and Heather leaned down to murmur in my ear.

"I'm worried about the note at the door; it didn't seem like it was meant for me."

"What makes you say that?" I asked.

"The message says something like 'how dare you come to the gate, I will find you,' so I don't think it's meant for me," Heather said.

"You're right. That sounds like it was meant for a wild fae, and the only wild fae that's been here is Caroline." The café hadn't caught fire; it was arson. Someone knew Caroline had been here—this was retribution.

"Have you told him yet?" she asked.

I shook my head. "I wanted to last night but we got distracted. I'm going to tell him about the books this morning at least, then ease into the rest."

Devin's footsteps caught our attention as he came back from the doorway, the rush of activity at the front of the building dying down as the fire was growing more controlled. "Any idea what the message means?"

Heather shook her head, looking to me for help.

"Thea, what's wrong? You look pale," Devin said.

"There's something I wanted to talk to you about. I need to get something from the house first." I slipped an arm around Heather's lower back. "Once this is sorted out, can we talk?"

He frowned, but his attention moved to the people in uniform, cleaning up the fire. "This has to be handled first, but I can do that. I'm still a cosigner on the building, correct?"

"Yes," Heather answered.

"I should be able to file a report and contact the insurance. Thea, you take Heather home. Get her wrapped up in blankets, watch a movie, make breakfast. We'll talk once I'm back."

Alan's truck pulled up as Devin was walking away. Devin stopped to say something to Alan, who nodded, then pulled his phone out and began to make a call.

"Hey," Alan jogged over to us. "I got your text. What happened?"

"The café, it . . ." Heather glanced over her shoulder.

Alan put a hand on Heather's arm. "Devin told me to take you guys back to the house."

"Yeah, that's the plan. I have the books in my bag back home, we can organize the talking points then we need to show Devin everything," I whispered. "If something is going on, the courts need to know but we should start with Devin since Caroline specifically said we could trust him in this."

"Shit, yeah, you were in bed already when I got back," Alan said, blushing. "I need to catch you up on last night—the changelings group."

"Do you think this is related?" Heather asked.

"I don't know." He glanced back at Devin's car. "But I think we need to get out of here to discuss it."

"Let's go," Heather said, and we followed Alan to his truck. Devin was still on the phone, but he did wave when he saw us going.

"To your house?" Alan asked, closing his door.

"Yeah, I can grab everything and get ready to show him." I slid into the backseat with Heather so I could hold her hand. "And then we fix up Heather like Devin said."

"Got it." He pulled out, dodging several pedestrians just standing around and observing the fire, and we sped off.

"Okay, let me tell you about last night," he said as we turned down another street. "So, Heather takes me to a bar in neutral territory, way outside of town. I don't know if the fae lords and ladies even know about it—it's run by changelings."

"Weird," I frowned.

"That's not the weirdest part. They talked about the whole thing like their situations were the fault of the fae."

I snorted. "They were."

"Yeah," Alan said. "It's the way they were saying it though, like they were complete victims. I got the feeling they felt the fae had abused their power for too long."

"That's . . . ominous."

"I don't know, maybe they're not behind it, but if there is a war coming between changelings and true fae, I sure as hell know which side those guys are on."

A chill ran down my back as we stopped at a red light near a park. That gut feeling telling me something was wrong but I didn't know what. Heather's hand slipped out of my fingers as I turned and pressed my face against the window.

"What is it?" Heather asked.

"I feel something strong in the park, but we're close to Winter territory and this doesn't feel familiar." Gasping, I smacked the window with my palm. "Alan, pull over!"

"What? Why?" He asked.

"Someone's on the ground, they might be hurt! Oh my god, it looks like Keegan!" Alan pulled into a turning lane and moved ahead to a parking lot.

"Hold on, I see him now," he said.

"Why's he here?" I asked, unbuckling and sliding out the door.

"Heather, can you watch the truck? Keep it running?" Alan asked.

"I don't like this," she said. "Something feels off."

I agreed, but I didn't say it out loud. "If he's hurt I just want to take him to a safe place where the court fae won't attack him." Or worse.

Pulling the iron pipe from my bag, I made my way with Alan through the crunching grass to the still figure under the trees. The closer we got, the more certain I was that it was Keegan, and I began running.

Dropping to my knees next to him, I rolled him over. The side of his face was one big bruise and he seemed to be unconscious.

"Shit, he looks rough. Why's he here?" Alan asked, kneeling at Keegan's other side.

Leaning down, I kissed Keegan on his bruised cheek, hoping that would work as well as the lips. I was more than done with kissing people I wasn't dating on the lips.

We watched as the bruise began to fade, and Alan stood with a frown. "Hey, do you smell that?"

"Is it Caroline?" I perked up, hopeful but still concentrating on Keegan's recovery.

"No, it's like damp leaves. It's a really strong forest floor kind of smell."

It hit me as soon as he said it. "Artemis."

"The Lady of Autumn?"

"What's she doing out here?" I asked.

Movement to the left, deeper in the trees, brought our eyes to Artemis, backlit by the bright morning light. She wore a fitted red dress and matching heels and strode elegantly through the frosted grass. Two fae accompanied her, following close behind. The one on the left was familiar in a way that raised the hairs on the back of my neck. A huge frame and red eyes that glowed just like when I saw them in the parking lot of my apartment before I had even changed. He was obscured by fog or mist or maybe just his glamour at the time, but I was sure this was the same fae. So what was he doing here with Artemis?

"Thea." She seemed confused by my presence before sneering down at Keegan. "What are you doing here?"

"He was hurt," I said slowly, knowing what it would look like to the courts to be helping a wild fae.

"What a coincidence—I am looking for someone as well." She tented her hands. "Does Devin know where you are? He will surely be missing his mate all the way out here."

My heart sank. There was something suffocating in Artemis's presence that was cutting it off, and I didn't know if it was just her strong demeanor or something more intentional. Devin wouldn't be able to locate me right now. Alan looked at me, the same silent question painted on his face, one hand rubbing his chest.

Artemis stared at him and subtly sniffed the air. "Lady Thea, who is your friend? I do not believe we have met." Her tenor seemed calm enough, but something about her question remained unsettling.

"This is Alan, another changeling," I said. "And if you're doing something here, we'll leave. This one needs to leave the gate anyway."

Alan looked relieved, clearly as uncomfortable as I was. Fae intuition, I suppose.

"A moment, Thea." Artemis's words stopped me in my tracks. The two fae stepped out from behind her. Alan's heartbeat picked up. I glanced at him; he was staring at the other fae that had come with Artemis, something registering in his expression.

Recognition?

I looked too. Something about the fae seemed off.

"A changeling?" I murmured. But Alan didn't know any changelings except myself and Heather. Then I realized: he must have been one of the disgruntled changelings Alan had met.

"Artemis," I whispered, staring at her unnerving company. "Who is it you're looking for?"

She closed the distance between us in long, elegant strides. Leaned in close, stared.

Her scent was potent. An overpowering mix of wet leaves, fallen branches, forest fungus.

"No," I breathed.

It wasn't only fallen leaves; it was the undertone of autumn. The ground, cold and near death.

Rotting.

I was so focused on Artemis then that I didn't notice as one of her changelings snuck up behind us. Blunt pain shot through my head, and—

CHAPTER THIRTY-SEVEN

THEA

The first thing I realized upon waking was that I was not on a bed. Wherever I was, it was hard and cold. Cold enough that I was glad for my Winter affiliation—this couldn't have been good for a human.

My eyes darted around the dimly lit room. It resembled a large concrete basement or possibly a warehouse with walls of bars like in an old west jail.

I sat up slowly, my body stiff. The jingle of chains—I looked down and saw my ankle in a metal cuff attached to the wall. I briefly panicked. Not only had they chained me to a wall, they had removed my boots and made sure the metal was against my skin—which could only mean it was iron.

I searched the room then and saw a dozen more bodies—fae—inside the other cells.

"You're awake." A whisper from my left—a cute little yellow fae with big round eyes. She sat with her knees drawn up under her chin.

"What is this place?" I asked.

"The Autumn Court prison," she replied. "You've been here a couple of hours."

"Alan!" I gasped. "Was I brought in with another fae? A little taller than me, big red beard?"

"He's over there." She pointed behind me to another cell.

I whipped around. Alan was on the ground, unconscious. Somewhere in the room I heard the distinct sound of vomiting—iron sickness, most likely.

A small jingle of chains brought my attention back to the yellow fae.

"I'm Gabby," she said.

"Don't talk to her, Gabs. She's one of the court fae." A hiss of displeasure caused the hair on the back of my neck to stand up straight.

"Then why is she in here with us?" Gabby protested. "Maybe she has news from the outside."

"The *outside*? How long have you been in here?"

A mixture of answers ranging from days to weeks came back to me. Gabby cleared her throat. "Mostly recent, some of us much longer if keeping us serves a purpose."

I tried to stretch out my sore back, wondering how long they planned to keep me in here. "I'm Thea."

Gabby wore an expression of surprise. "I've heard your name before."

"Me?" I asked. "Who would have been talking about me?"

She blinked and turned to a far corner of the room. "Keegan! Are you awake?"

"Keegan?" My mouth hung open in surprise.

"I am now." His familiar voice echoed from the dark to my right.

"Thea is awake," Gabby said.

He swore loudly. I could see him scuffle around the cell in the dim light. "About time. Why the hell did you get captured?"

"I didn't plan on it," I said. "Are you okay? What about your face?"

Keegan sat against the wall, holding his stomach. "How'd you know I was hit in the face? 'S fine though."

"Alan and I found you on the ground out cold," I said. "We pulled over to help you and then we were captured."

"Nice try, but it sounds like the same bitch that hit me got you too. That's why we're all here." He grunted uncomfortably. "And I've been questioned on Caroline's whereabouts."

I glanced at his stomach, which he clutched gingerly. Dried blood hung in the air.

"*Dammit*, Caroline," he grunted. "If her ass ends up in here too . . ."

"Get off it with your hard-on for Caroline," growled a turquoise fae from another cell. "She's basically rabid, there's nothing a loon like her can do to help us."

"She's getting better!" Keegan snapped.

"Not helping, guys," Gabby added.

I could feel a headache coming on, and it had nothing to do with the iron around me.

"Since we're in this mess together now, will you fill me in a little more on what's going on?" I was well aware that everyone in the room was focused on our conversation.

"Fine. What do you want to know?"

"Why? Why is Artemis doing this?" I couldn't keep the tremble from my voice.

"Isn't that the million-dollar question?" Keegan laughed, empty and joyless. "A tale as old as time—revenge."

"Revenge?"

"Yeah, Caroline filled me in. She's got clarity now, that's why I came. To tell you what she saw."

A moan just then—Alan.

"Alan," I whispered. "Are you okay?"

"Ugh." He rolled onto his side. "Shit. Fuck."

"The Summer fae you were with before?" Keegan asked.

"Yeah?" I scooted the short distance to the edge of my cell.

"He's not going to handle this cold well," Keegan warned.

"He hasn't joined the court yet, shouldn't that help?" I asked, trying to see Alan's face in the dark.

"A Summer fae is a Summer fae, no matter their allegiance," Gabby said defensively. "I can tell you're a changeling. I don't know how fresh you are, but don't believe everything the gate fae tell you."

Before I could ask anything more, we were interrupted by another agonized sound from Alan. I turned to him again. "Alan, can you hear me?"

"Thea?" He groaned and tried to sit up. "Holy shit, what's wrong with me? I feel like I have the flu but worse. So much worse."

"There's an iron band around your leg, it's making you sick," Gabby said.

"I think I can fix that." I reached through the bars, careful that Alan didn't touch any more iron than necessary. "Can you grab my hand?"

"What do you mean you can fix it?" Keegan growled.

"Come on, just a little more." I ignored Keegan, concentrating on Alan as our fingertips connected.

"Does this make any difference?" I asked, trying to will my healing into him.

"Maybe a little." He still sounded very uncomfortable.

"Can you scoot any closer to me?"

"Hey!" Keegan shouted. "What the fuck do you mean you can help with his sickness?"

"I can heal him, okay?" I snapped. "Something that will probably get me killed one of these days and I'm shouting it out loud for you. Congratulations, asshole."

He swore. Several others began to murmur.

"This is good," Gabby piped up. "Thea, once you've healed your friend, do you think you could heal another?"

"I can try, but I want some damned answers in exchange, without any more bullshit." Alan seemed to be doing better. "Can you scoot any closer without touching the bars?" I asked.

"Yeah, hold on." He slowly dragged his body across the floor. Only once we were face to face, just a couple of inches from the iron bars, did he stop.

"I think I need to . . . kiss you," I whispered, thankful that the dark room would hide my blushing.

"What?" Gabby asked.

"Yeah, it's the strongest way to do this. It's how I, uh . . . woke Alan before."

To Alan's credit, he simply leaned forward and closed his eyes, though I could sense his discomfort.

I pressed my face to the bars, as far as it would go, tilted at an odd angle thanks to my antlers. Barely feeling a tingle from the iron's touch, I pressed my lips to his and I willed my powers into him.

I pulled away and he sagged backward.

"Holy shit, that's better," he said.

"You really did it," Gabby breathed.

"Yeah, real fun party trick. Now tell me what you meant by Caroline has clarity now—all of it."

"Okay, all right," Keegan said. He hunched forward, still clutching his stomach. "First of all, you're one of the four, aren't you?"

A murmur rippled through the room.

"You mean my healing?" I asked quietly.

"Yes. Did Devin tell you nothing?"

"He doesn't believe in it."

"That's impossible," Gabby said. "The whole reason the court fae keep us out is so they don't have to share the power, and that includes the four."

"I don't know what you're talking about. The court fae aren't keeping anyone out; they defend themselves against wild fae because you attack them on sight, right?"

The silence in the room swelled uncomfortably.

"She doesn't know," Keegan said. "Fuck, that bitch is keeping the gate's gifts under wraps, isn't she?"

"What do you mean?"

"There are always supposed to be four fae like you, with enhanced gifts beyond our own."

"What is the point of the four?" I asked.

"It's hard to say what the gate meant for the four to do. Most likely another measure for keeping the balance," Gabby explained. "However, with power comes jealousy."

"Yeah, I assumed that much." Alan fidgeted next to me. I reached through the bars to hold his hand. Maybe I could keep the iron sickness from coming back.

"The four's powers are coveted, but by none more than the rotting one," Keegan added. "She's able to keep the details of your existence away from court fae because she's the oldest being here, and that adds to her power."

I looked around the room. "Are none of you from the city?"

Every one of them shook their heads.

"Anyone who knows her truth is ostracized. Hunted down. Killed or used for other gains," Gabby said sadly.

"She convinced the current court that you're enemies," I said. "You never were, were you?"

"Why do you think this is the only gate in the world with our kind of wild fae around it?" Keegan asked bitterly. "We belong here, we're bound to it. No other gate would feel right or have us. We stay as close as we can while trying not to get killed by her."

"If I'm part of the four, as is Caroline with her glamour-truth-thing, are the other two close by?"

"Wait, Caroline has a glamour thing?" Gabby asked.

"Yeah, her visions. You know, seeing through glamours, seeing bonds." I hesitated. "You did know, right?"

"She's right," Keegan spat. "Caroline's got something, and it's going to get her killed."

"She's not the only one in danger," Alan grumbled. "We're in a dungeon right now."

"I knew she was sick and had been cast out of the city, but I didn't know shit about her clairvoyance until recently," Keegan growled. "That's why the rotting one wants her so damned bad."

"Because she's one of the four?" Alan asked.

"Wait, you don't think . . ." Gabby gasped. "Keegan! It's just like Dublin!"

"Shit, you're right." He groaned. "Some gates can take their gifts away if they're being abused. I'd bet anything the rotting one is losing power as Caroline gains it."

"Shit, that means the rotting one held the power of glamour before Caroline. For centuries and long forgotten since, I'm sure," Gabby said.

"When Caroline was changed," Alan said, "Artemis started losing her touch, didn't she?"

The room shushed him at Artemis's name.

"Yes, that has to be the reason her power has declined in recent decades," Keegan said. "She's clinging to it even as she knows it's going to Caroline. That tricky bitch."

"So, the rotting one wants her out of the picture," I said slowly. "But the rest of the four—"

"She wants in her pocket," Keegan finished. "Every time another is born or changed, she either controls or kills them. Decades later, another is born and she does it again."

"And she can see on sight who they are." I closed my eyes.

"Wait, then why didn't she know about Thea from the start?" Alan asked.

"Her power is failing—badly," Gabby said. "Perhaps she can no longer sense it at all."

"Caroline's been having a really bad time with headaches the last few years. I guess they were never headaches to begin with," Keegan mumbled.

"This is so much to take in." I rubbed my now-throbbing forehead. "So, what does this mean? Nothing will return to the natural order of the gate until the rotting one is gone?"

"That's the theory," Gabby said sadly.

"Kill . . . rotting . . . one . . ." rumbled a new voice from the dark to the other side of Gabby.

"All this time and now you speak?" snapped another fae, next to Keegan.

"No reason . . . 'til . . . now," said the low voice. "I . . . help."

I peered into the cage, attempting to make out the hunched form that had started to move. "What do you mean help?" I asked slowly.

With a grunt, the large shadow shifted in its cage. Gabby moved out of the way. I gasped when I saw him, covered in iron bands from head to toe, angry red welts on his skin where the excess of iron had poisoned him.

"I'm Jude. I'm . . . number . . . three."

The room was silent, even by fae standards.

Another of the four, and he'd been right here all along.

"Gods," Keegan whispered. "This just might work."

CHAPTER THIRTY-EIGHT

DEVIN

It took longer than I would have liked to arrange a deal with Heather's insurance and a contractor for repairs, but eventually it was resolved enough that I could return my attention to my court. Leaning against the hood of my car and checking my emails, I sent a list of things for my secretary to do in my absence, then gave Yoseph instructions for the fae in the main house to help prepare the inside of the café when work on it was finally completed.

It wasn't until my phone rang, Heather's number lighting up the screen, that I had an ominous feeling.

"Lord Devin," she answered breathlessly, as though she couldn't get it all out fast enough, "there's something I think you should know."

"Go on," I urged.

"Thea has had a little mystery on her hands, and due to circumstances out of her control, she was sworn to secrecy."

"*Go on.*"

"Really I don't know what I would have done differently in her shoes." She was beginning to babble, a telltale sign of overwhelming anxiety from Heather. "It's for the safety of everyone in the court, really. I mean, she needed some answers before she could bring them to you. And Alan is helping her, and of course two powerful changelings are much safer than one—"

"*Heather.*"

"Right. I think Thea's in danger!"

Then it hit me—Arthur. "Hold on."

Dialing Arthur in with us, he picked up on the second ring. "Yes, Lord Devin?"

"I command you to tell me whatever Thea commanded you to keep secret," I said. Even through the phone my compulsion would be stronger than hers.

"Finally," he grumbled. "Lady Thea has been poking around the city for wild fae. I don't know who she's looking for exactly, but she was around the old technical college and who knows where else. I think she went out of the city the other day too. Gods, Devin, you have no idea how powerful her compulsion is. She really is your equal."

"That will be all," I said. "Be ready to move at a moment's notice."

"Will do." Arthur hung up, leaving me on the line with Heather again.

"Was . . . was that—" Heather stammered.

"Yes, it was Arthur. Now, *explain.*"

"Right." She swallowed again. "Thea has been in contact with Caroline."

My nostrils flared and my claws poked through my glamour. "She isn't dead?"

"No, and she's not elf-struck. Not anymore at least. It sounds like she got Thea to cure her."

Thea *cured* someone who was elf-struck? "Impossible."

"You know better than that, Lord Devin," Heather whispered. "Nothing about fae is truly impossible. Our gate does what it wants. It's unstable—some kind of balance is being restored here, and I'm scared that Thea is in the middle of it."

"The note on the wall . . ."

"Yes. I didn't realize it at first, but Thea did. My café, it's . . . I think it's retaliation for Caroline being here."

I stiffened. "She was here?"

"Yesterday. She's been in contact with Thea for a while, but I don't know all the details. She says a fight is coming—a battle between true fae and changelings. Thea is trying to stop it. Caroline wouldn't give her any answers if she told you, so she kept it a secret."

"Where is she?"

"I was with her and Alan," Heather said. "They saw someone they knew, I think it was a wild fae. He was hurt, we pulled over, and they went into the trees where the fae was down on the ground. I could tell someone approached them after that, but I couldn't see who it was from the truck, then in the cover of the trees and fog they were gone."

"Where are you now?"

"That park on the way to your house by the light and across from that ugly gas station."

"I know the one." Then I realized: I couldn't feel her. The bond was empty, missing. I couldn't even feel the directionless pull that told me she was in the city. Either she was too far away, or something was interfering. "She's missing. I can't even sense her."

"What?" Heather sputtered. "Not even with your bond?"

"Stay there, we'll meet you. Arthur's coming. You're going to put aside your petty bullshit and work with him to find Thea."

She sounded strained as she answered. "Okay."

"Stay on the line, I'm adding Arthur."

He answered instantly. "Find me in the park to the south of the main houses."

"Lord? Is she—"

"Thea is missing. Get your ass over there now. I want word out to every Winter fae, and I don't give a damn whose territory we have to cross looking for her. Groups of five or more for safety. Heather will help you. Text the other leaders, tell them I am breaking the boundaries in search of my mate. They will understand—it's a clause we made when drawing up the territories."

"Alan," Heather whispered. "Georgina will . . ."

"Georgina will be in a rage," I seethed. "But it won't come close to the havoc I intend to scatter across this gate until I find Thea. You two will handle Georgina, and you will do everything I have ordered you to do without failure. *Do you understand?*"

"Where will we find you?" Heather asked.

"Every fae in this fucking city will know where I am until I find her. If you hear anything, come tell me yourself."

Ending the call, I left my car behind and opted to run the distance so I could try to sense Thea on the way. Snow tumbled around me as I covered the area, spreading outward. The bond had to be here somewhere; since she'd kissed me at the solstice, I had not been unable to feel it, no matter how faint. If I could get close enough to her somehow, if I could just latch on to that tether between us, I could find her.

I made my way to the park, catching her scent as I got there—hers and Alan's. But no pull. Alan's truck was parked nearby, a light white dusting beginning to cover it. Heather was in the grass under a copse of oaks, probably where she last saw Thea. She looked up at me silently as I approached, scanning the area for anything of note.

Whatever scents were there were muddled by strong smoke—someone had burned away what they could of Thea's presence. At my feet I saw a patch of black where lightning had scarred the ground. Thea. She had been in the training facility most mornings, often with Yoseph for guidance, but her efforts were not enough to stop whoever she was with.

I crouched and smelled the area. It was faint but she was definitely here. There was nothing, however, to tell me what had happened to Thea or where she was. But someone had been poking around this gate and stirring up trouble, and she would probably have a damned good idea what was going on.

Caroline.

CHAPTER THIRTY-NINE

THEA

"A little closer," Gabby encouraged, sounding downright cheerful since I'd kissed her, relieving months of pain caused by the iron chains. I had tried to break the chains themselves with my powers, but they didn't budge. I just didn't have the same grip on the tricky lightning that Yoseph had.

My leg was slender enough to fit between the bars of Gabby's cell. I needed to get one of my limbs far enough into her cage that Jude could also reach through and touch me somehow.

"Jude, do the bars burn?" Gabby asked.

"No more . . . than . . . chains . . ." he grunted.

"He has a point," I mumbled, stretching a little farther.

"Hold on there, you two," Gabby said. "You're so close!"

Jude was on his side, reaching both arms, chained together, into Gabby's cage. His legs were the size of tree trunks, so that was definitely out of the question. I could hear Jude's panting, the pain in his lungs as he willingly dragged more skin across the iron bars clamped around his thick muscles.

"Jude, if you move your hands just a bit closer to me . . ." Gabby was acting as our eyes since our odd positioning made it difficult to see what we were doing.

"Oh!" I jumped as a pair of cool hands brushed against my toes.

"Great!" the yellow fae exclaimed. "Now, Thea, concentrate on your healing. Imagine it flowing through you and straight into Jude."

"How do you know it works that way?" I grunted.

"I don't, but you've got to try something," she answered.

Fair enough. Closing my eyes, I took deep, meditative breaths. I could do anything if I just tried—I was a freaking faerie, for crying out loud.

Jude grunted, but I ignored it. I just kept picturing that gentle healing sensation flowing through me.

Gabby gasped.

"What? What's happening?" Keegan demanded.

"Jude! You're feeling better?" Gabby said.

"Mmm . . ." he groaned in approval.

I heard but didn't dare stop what I was doing. This was the most progress I had ever made from touch alone, and I needed to concentrate. Maybe someday, with enough practice, I could stop kissing everyone.

"Are you sure you're ready?" Gabby asked Jude.

Ready for what I didn't know, but I didn't have to wait long to find out. I heard a groan of metal—he was bending the bars. Quickly his hand moved up as far as my ankle, grasping at as much of my skin as he could.

"Shit," Keegan hissed. "He's really doing it. The power of strength then."

"How you holding up, Thea?" Gabby patted my leg. "Ooh! That's stronger than before."

I let out a breathy laugh. "Good."

More creaking bars, more fingers crawling up my leg. He pushed my leggings up as far as they would go, to access more skin, until his arms had wrapped entirely around my calves.

I peeled my eyes open and watched Gabby climb through the bars into Jude's cage.

"Okay, Jude, you've got the biggest chains in the room anchoring you to the wall. I'm going to count to three, and we're going to pull together. Got it?"

He grunted.

"Okay, one . . . two . . . three!"

Gabby yanked as Jude growled and pulled his leg forward. A massive bolt popped out of the wall, then another, then the whole base of his chains tore free of the concrete and clanged against the cold floor.

"Holy gods, you did it!" Keegan roared.

Jude crawled closer to me, and I withdrew my leg. At least, I tried to.

"Jude, baby, you've got to let Thea rest for a minute, okay?" Gabby had crawled back into her cage and was murmuring soothing things into Jude's ear. "She's got to move so she can kiss it and make it all better."

I cringed at her phrasing, but it did get Jude to release his hold on me. Grudgingly. I quickly repositioned myself so I could press my face to the bars, as far as I could with my antlers in the way.

"That's it, just a bit farther." Gabby brought Jude right up to my cage. She was practically bouncing with excitement.

Jude's eyes were closed, the pain on his face evident. As soon as he was near enough, I reached out with my lips and we kissed.

The healing flowed through me, rushing into Jude's massive form as if running water. We stayed like that for a long minute, crouched at the bars, lips locked in the most uncomfortable interaction I'd ever had with a stranger. Then, one by one, Jude ripped the chains coiled around his body as if they were paper ribbons off a birthday present. They hit the ground and were quickly cast to a far corner, where they could no longer do any harm.

"You did it!" Gabby squealed.

Jude stood, stretching his limbs as though he had never felt the sensation before. He was absolutely massive, a wall of muscles under a mess of wild brown hair that hadn't been combed in a long time. I healed the damage to his skin, but he had scarred, giving him the look of a seasoned gladiator.

"*Thank you*," he said. His voice had a gentle quality to it when he wasn't struggling against the iron.

A few hushed gasps fluttered through the room. A chilling tingle ran through me, otherworldly and somehow liquid as it settled into my skin.

Thank you.

"Don't mention it." I stood, not completely ready to unpack that baggage yet. "Get us out of here and we can throw a damn party."

He nodded and pulled the bars between us. It was almost effortless for him—in a matter of minutes my cage was demolished, my chains broken from my ankle.

"What now?" I asked no one in particular.

"Call Devin," Alan suggested as Jude freed him.

"With what phone?" I asked. "Even if I had one, I don't have his number memorized."

"Then we make a run for the café," Alan insisted.

"The rotting one will chase you," Keegan added. "We're under her stronghold now."

"How do we get out?" I huffed.

"We can get out together." Gabby placed her hand on my forearm. "But it might help if we were all . . . in better condition first."

Cringing, I recognized the pained fae that surrounded me. My hands were sufficient given enough time, but a kiss was quicker. "Right, line up then."

Gabby gave me a dazzling smile and a quick peck to top herself off after assisting Jude. Then Alan, a fae I didn't know, Keegan, and the rest. Jude made quick work of the iron, and I made quick work of their ailments. My last kiss was for Jude, to fix any damage done by freeing the other prisoners.

"Now what?" Alan asked.

We all looked at each other.

Think: What would Devin do?

"First, we get out. Together—no one gets left behind," I said. "We can go our separate ways then, if you want, but anyone who wants to follow me to the Winter Court is granted full protection until we can sort out this whole mess."

"You can't promise that," one of the fae said. "Devin will tear us apart on sight."

"She can *too* promise that, Jerry," Keegan growled. "She's Devin's mate, dipshit—she's the Lady of Winter."

I heard several sharp breaths. My status was still new enough that not everyone knew. That, or they'd been down here a while.

"I want to put an end to her," Jude growled. None of us had to ask who *her* was.

"Me too," I said. "But she's probably surrounded by a small army. We need backup."

"We need Caroline," Keegan insisted.

"Can we even trust her after all this?" Alan asked.

"Yes," Gabby clasped her hands together. "You don't have the whole story yet. Look, we can talk about this later. We need to get out of here, fast. Who has a plan?"

A willowy fae named Shae suggested ambushing the guards that came around each day at midday to torture and dole out food. There would be three of them, and with any luck they would tell us how many guards we could expect between here and the exit.

It wasn't a strong plan, but it was what we had.

"Whatever you do, don't eat the food," Gabby warned. "It's faerie food, and it's been tampered with. Poisoned or something."

Some of the fae returned to their cages, careful not to touch any iron. We needed the guards to think at first glance that everything was normal. The rest of us waited on either side of the door. An hour stretched into two, and I was certain we were nearing three before we finally heard noise beyond the door.

"Wake up, wretches," sang a fae as he entered the cell block. "Dinner and a show! Who's first tonight?"

He was several steps into the room when he finally noticed something was different. By then, a second guard had come in behind him, and a third with a tray of old bread heels. The moment the final fae crossed the threshold, we shut the door behind them.

"What the fuck?" the first one screeched as Jude lifted him by one arm. He punched another in the face, sending them into Gabby's waiting arms. She tore off their jacket.

"This will smell like them," she said. "I'll take a quick peek and scout ahead." She hurried upstairs before anyone could protest.

The group made pretty short work of the guards. The one Jude left conscious told us how to get to the exit. He didn't know who or what we might run into on the way—it wasn't his normal route. He was a true fae, I could smell it on him—his words were honest.

Gabby popped her head around the corner. "All clear."

We formed a long line, Keegan bringing up the rear and Jude and I in front, ready to bulldoze anyone in our path.

And there were indeed a few obstacles along the way. We ran into four fae but made quick work of them. Jude knocked out each with ease. I don't think he killed any of them—they'd all wake up to broken bones, though.

Following the guard's directions, we wound through several hallways and up a couple sets of stairs before finally spotting a window. It was large and had bars on it, but that was no obstacle with Jude on our side.

"Keep going or get out while we can?" I asked.

Alan snorted. "Get us the hell out of here."

Everyone agreed, and Jude smashed our way to freedom.

We couldn't pile out of the window fast enough, landing on each other as we tumbled through. Immediately, I felt the bond buzzing again. Devin. Our connection was alive and well, but we were still too far apart for me to pinpoint his location. I sighed and rolled over, relieved.

"Shit, now what?" Keegan huffed.

"Anyone coming with me, get ready," I panted.

As we caught our breath, I was hit with a delicate waft of cinnamon.

I looked up. There, in the bushes in front of us, was Caroline with a line of fae behind her, all wielding various tools from bolt cutters to hacksaws.

"Hello, dear." A wild grin spread across her face. "Now we're cooking with gas. Ready to go?"

A gust of wind picked up, shoving us all to the side. The scent of leaves and burning scorched through the air, and some unseen sense in me could feel the anger rolling off of a very powerful fae.

"Go," I said, sharing a look with Alan. "Go, go, go. Now."

It was probably a stupid move, but damned if all twelve of us didn't follow her.

—

We left the Autumn Court apartments behind, scrambling for some distance. Of course, they weren't just apartments. Like the Winter Court on their own secluded street, the Autumn Court hid their people collectively in these apartments. We headed somewhere more suburban, where apartment buildings gave way to neatly trimmed lawns and two-story cottage-style houses that surrounded us.

We stayed silent the whole way, moving as efficiently as possible while Caroline covered our tracks and scents with a sweep of her own windy abilities. She led us to an old school bus parked outside a post office. We piled in behind her and she began barking orders.

"Thomas, where are the two we intercepted earlier?" She sat behind the driver's seat while the one called Thomas started the bus.

"Hazel took them back to base," he answered.

Caroline shot an unreadable look my way. "Good. Jen! Send Hazel a message to treat their injuries before they wake. Also, have Zara start the food. Richie, did you obtain the list?"

"Yup," said a smiling, slender fae seated in the back of the bus with a laptop. "Can't believe their firewall. The old fae really don't keep up with technology, do they?"

As Caroline asked a few more details from her people, I noticed just how many of them were wild fae. She made her way over to where I was trying to rest beside Alan on the cracked bus seat. "You got out on your own. Good job."

"I was only there in the first place because I was helping

Keegan—someone burned down Heather's café as a message. A message for *you*."

Her attention flicked to Keegan in the seat behind mine. "Yes, I heard. I am sorry about that, but they were the actions of a madwoman. The blame can only fall to her."

I narrowed my eyes at Caroline. I wasn't convinced she wasn't still mad as well.

As if reading my thoughts, she said, "I got better. I wasn't going to involve you in this step, but now that you've been on the receiving end of her schemes, maybe I can trust you."

"She kept your stupid secret all this time," Alan spat. "You'd better trust her."

"Easy, big guy," Caroline chided. "I've learned to be cautious over the last couple hundred years. It's how someone on the rotting one's naughty list stays alive."

"What exactly are you doing?" I said impatiently. "You wanted me to make my own decision in this fight? Well I can't until I have all the facts. What I do know is, I'm one of these four special 'gifted' fae, and you need me to win. I got your proof for you, lying to my loved ones in the process!"

And there, it hit me. I had grown to love everyone I'd deceived. Heather, of course, was already a friend. But now she was closer, through our shared experiences and the care she had shown me, fighting for me behind the scenes, guiding me through the choppy waters entering the faerie world. I did love Heather—she was like a sister to me. And Devin, how could I explain what I had with Devin if it wasn't love? The realization was jarring. He really was like my matching puzzle piece, and I had lied to him to get to the bottom of this mess with Caroline and the rotting one.

"Caroline, fill me in or let me go. I've done my part for you, and I want to stop others from getting hurt, but I need to be by Devin's side. He's been kept in the dark long enough."

She studied me a moment, crossing her arms. "All right, I suppose you do deserve an explanation, now that I'm all put back together up here." She tapped her temple, then shifted her attention to Keegan. "You too. I'll explain everything."

"You're an ass," Keegan spat. "One of the fucking four, and you led us to believe the rotting one wants to kill you because you're the next Lady of Autumn."

"You're what now?" Alan asked.

"Shit." I rubbed my aching temples. "All right, everybody stop. Let me make sure I have this right. There are four courts, four fae leaders, and four gifted fae. The Autumn Court is corrupted for some reason, which you still didn't tell me about, Keegan, and the gate made Caroline to bring balance by overthrowing it? Do I have everything straight?"

"That's the bare bones of it, yes." Caroline tilted her head to one side. "But she is old, and she is powerful. I need every able-bodied fae I can get."

"Why not come clean with Devin? Or one of the other fae leaders?" Alan asked.

She scrunched up her nose. "Bad history with Devin. He'd be pretty pissed if he found out I was still kicking. Actually, I left with a pretty big 'fuck you' to all of them."

Keegan snorted. "Like it or not, you're going to have to involve them—the rotting one is going to start this fight anytime now. Our escape might even trigger it."

I cringed at the possibility of bloodshed being a direct result of our actions, but there wasn't anything I could do about it.

"Right, so we prepare for the fight." Caroline sighed and turned to Jude. "Well hello, who do we have here?"

Jude, who'd been mostly quiet since his release, just stared back at her.

"I see. Well, I know you've seen her plans for the four. Will you join me?" she asked.

"I want her head," Jude growled, the intense sound of his hatred shaking a chilled path through my bones.

"No can do, I have to kill her to take her seat. You know how this works." Caroline wagged a finger at him.

"Fine, but I want blood."

"You'll have plenty." She turned to Keegan again. "Are you on my side?"

"You know I am," he said. "But I'm not happy about how you went about this."

"Noted." She turned to Alan and me. "And you two, are you fighting or stepping back?"

"This sounds like an Autumn Court issue," Alan said. "Should we get involved?"

"If she doesn't go down, nothing changes. The changelings will continue to be made."

"More cryptic bullshit," I scoffed. "Of fucking course."

"Tell them, Caroline," Keegan demanded.

"Fine," she huffed. "But not here. I've finally got it all straight in my head and you lot can't be patient for another hour."

I looked at Alan—he seemed as puzzled as I was. Caroline looked out the window in silence, her back to the rest of the bus. We let it go for now and spent the rest of the ride thinking about everything that had occurred so far. Houses turned into buildings, then the busy center of the city, then something more rural.

I reached out to Devin; I'd hoped we would pass close enough that I could feel him, but nothing came of it. Finally, after half an hour, we reached an old Victorian-style house that had been converted into a bed-and-breakfast.

"This is your base of operation?" I said, staring skeptically at the yellow building with a neatly trimmed rose garden and a blue porch swing.

"It belongs to some friends who are letting us use it," said one of the fae that had accompanied Caroline. "You know the fae who aren't drawn to a gate? Wild but not like us?"

"I didn't know there were any like that here, I thought all the wild fae in the area were . . ." I said.

Looking around, I didn't know what was safe, or even accurate, to say. Caroline shrugged. "Well, now you know."

She led us inside to a large dining space laid out with bowls of vegetable stew. A petite little fae with a baby on her hip smiled at us from the kitchen. Another fae, a burly one, had his arm around her shoulders as they watched us file into their home. Most of the fae stared in awe at the little one rubbing his eyes as though he had just woken up from his nap.

"Hello, Zara, Ben," Caroline said. She leaned in and cooed at the baby. "Hello, Sammie, how are you today?"

The baby wriggled and reached out to try to grasp Caroline's extended finger.

"I see you found some more," Ben said. "Is it time?"

"Close," Caroline said. "I've got some business to tend to upstairs, then it's story time. Grab something to eat, I'll be back." Caroline put on a playful grin, winking at me and Alan before exiting.

We didn't have to be told twice. For the next several minutes, only the clinking of spoons could be heard as we shoveled the delicious food into our mouths. About halfway into my stew, I realized I might have a way to contact Devin. I got up from the table. Alan gave me a curious look—he would hear my idea soon enough.

"Excuse me," I approached Zara, the fae woman with the baby. "Do you have a phone I could borrow?"

"Sure, dear." She pointed to a phone on the wall by the sink.

I didn't know Devin's number by heart, but I did know Heather's. I dialed it quickly and held my breath as I waited for her to answer.

"Hello?" Heather answered.

"It's me," I said. "Is Devin there?"

"Thea!" Heather gasped. "Shit, no, he's not here. He's tearing through half the city looking for you, and Georgina is tearing up the other half looking for Alan."

"Oh no."

"Yeah, Georgina kinda blew up her own office, and now they're shrieking about some escaped guy and Alan, I don't know. It was amazing. But where are you? What happened?"

"I don't think it's a good idea to tell you everything in case Devin makes you tell him—I know you can't avoid that. I can't have Devin starting this confrontation until I get there, but I promise to explain everything. Can you tell him I'm with Caroline? And Alan is here, too, we're safe. There's about to be a challenge between her and Artemis for the Autumn Court."

"Holy shit, why?" she spat. "Yeah, I'll try. Where are you exactly? He'll want to know."

"I'm not sure, but I get the feeling I won't be here long anyway. Have him ready to meet near Autumn territory in a few hours."

"Do we need backup?" Heather asked.

"I don't know. I'm about to hear Caroline's side of the story. All I know is, her enemy is my enemy."

"Devin is going to kill me," Heather mumbled. "Listen, I already told him about Caroline, since we were about to anyway. And I showed him the books."

I winced. "All of them? Everything?"

"He's all caught up," she confirmed. "He seemed pissed, especially with Caroline."

"Yeah, they have bad blood." I paused. "But he's going to have to suck it up and help her cause."

"Got it. Anything else?" she asked.

"Not that I can think of. Just be careful out there. Don't trust the Autumn Court, but don't tell Devin that if you can help it. I don't want him poking around blindly and getting hurt without having the whole story. Just . . . wait for us," I pleaded.

"Got it. See you soon." Heather hung up. I turned to Alan, who was listening from his seat at the table. He had heard it all.

"So, we're with Caroline now?" he asked.

"I'm not sure, that's why I told him to wait outside the territory." I returned to my seat. "We need to be ready for whatever happens."

"Smart move, but your help might turn the tide in our favor," Keegan said. "And trust me, you want Caroline to win."

"We'll see." *If she ever tells me her story.*

The stairs behind me creaked then, and I turned to see Caroline coming down, followed by a familiar set of designer heels.

"Candie!" I shrieked, launching out of my seat.

"Thea?" She nearly shoved Caroline out of the way and pulled me into a hug. "Wait 'til I tell you about my fucking day!"

"What are you doing here?" She was scraped up and her makeup was a mess. I ran my hands over her arms, her face, checking for anything worse than a surface scratch.

"I don't even know." She pulled back to look at my face. "Some assholes were going to kidnap us."

"Us?" I asked, and she gestured behind her.

I looked past Candie and saw the vaguely familiar features of a fae with startling violet eyes. I stiffened and pushed her protectively behind me.

"*You*," I hissed. "From the restaurant!"

"Whoa, calm down." Alan came over and put a hand on my shoulder.

"It's the freaking waiter!" I spat. "He gave you faerie food that night at the restaurant! You couldn't see him because you were human, but I could!"

Shoving myself between him and Candace, the fae paled and stepped back. Alan's hand tensed on my shoulder.

"Did you do this to Alan?" I asked.

"Back off!" Candace tugged at my other shoulder.

"He attacked Alan! He could have killed him!"

She pulled my arm back enough to come up next to me, both of us facing the fae who was giving Candace a sad look.

"How can you defend him?" I asked.

"Thea, he's my mate."

My muscles softened, and she let go of my arm when my defenses fell away. "Your *mate*?"

"Mates? They're popping out of the bloody woodwork!" Keegan threw his hands in the air and walked away.

Studying this new fae for a long moment, I had to admit he looked as rough as Candie. No, rougher. They had been through something together, and then I remembered what Heather said about Georgina's fit of rage at the Summer Court mansion. Burn marks and worse littered this fae's limbs, a large welt across his wrist carried the light scent of iron.

"Why did you change Alan?" I asked, still in disbelief.

The fae turned away, ashamed.

"Because I told him to," Caroline said, inserting herself between us.

My expression darkened. "More of your schemes."

"Why?" Alan asked.

"I knew then what you are, what you could be," she said quietly. "Come, have a seat. I'll tell you everything."

"Do I have your word on that?" I asked, knowing full well that it would become an oath she couldn't break.

Caroline gave me a long look before sighing. "Yes, I swear it."

Shivering as the prickly sensation ran through me, I knew she would be bound to tell me and I would be bound to hear it. Caroline led us to a sunroom that had once been a back porch. It had since been windowed in, with a cozy electric fireplace installed. The fireplace flared to life when we entered, and I took a few steps away from the overbearing heat of it. Caroline sat on an overstuffed green armchair and waited patiently for us to take our seats.

"I will tell you my story from the beginning," she said, scanning the room. "I was born the daughter of a painter. My mother died when I was young, so it was just Father and me. But my father . . . he loved me as a parent, but he did not understand me. Not really. We grew distant as I reached adulthood. He threw himself into his work while I . . ." She paused and looked out the window. It took her a while to collect herself. Then she looked me right in the eyes.

"I was young and stupid. I wanted to dance. I wanted to be wild. I wanted adventure. And when a handsome stranger took an interest in me, I flung myself into his arms. By then I was already estranged from my friends. They were all leaving their youth behind, settling down or moving to the city. Mind you, that didn't mean here—there was no city in these hills then." Her eyes clouded over.

"I continued to meet my dark stranger. He would give me occasional gifts. I laugh at them now, knowing it was faerie food and trinkets meant to draw me to the gate. He must have sensed a compatibility in me and was easing me toward the change. At the time, I thought they were the most romantic gestures. I was a fool in love. I believed he was, too, but looking back now, I knew deep down that this was a fling for both of us. He told me as much, but I didn't want to hear it. Winter drew close, and of course I was beginning to change. I was seeing things. Hearing things. I don't even remember much about the ball anymore—what dress I wore, what music I danced to. I remember the change, though. I'll never forget that."

I had to agree with her there.

"After the change, my world turned upside down. It wasn't seeing the fae that did it, oh no, it was the wretched court I put myself in. Of course, I chose the Autumn Court. It drew me in like a moth to a flame. I was made for it. For Artemis."

Keegan and a few others snarled at her name.

"At first I flourished in the court. Finally, beings who shared my adventurous soul. The ties to my father faded long before my change, but if there was even a string of familial regret in me it would have disappeared the moment I landed under Artemis's wing. I learned my magic quickly, which pleased my lady. However, despite her warnings, I continued to see the handsome fae who had turned me. She warned me not to, but I did so anyway. She was upset with me, but not so much that she forbade me from seeing him. I started meeting him in secret, so as to lessen my lady's displeasure."

"Who was it?" Alan asked. "Which fae were you seeing?"

My stomach sank as pages of small, tight handwriting filled my mind. Sketch after sketch of what her father was seeing before he lost his daughter completely. I knew the name before it even crossed her lips.

"Devin Grayson, Lord of Winter." She looked my way, probably assessing my feelings on the revelation. But I had known, deep down. The weight of it hadn't really hit me until now, but I knew Devin had coaxed her into the courts. My mouth was dry and I didn't trust myself to speak, but my face was neutral enough and in the end he was bonded to me now.

He had already made it abundantly clear he was happy with what we had.

But would he still be happy once he found out I'd deceived him?

"It was a long time ago," Caroline continued. "And if anything the memory is bitter for both of us. We were never really compatible, he knew it then and I know it now. It's the next part that he never knew about that tipped my world end over end. The day I realized I was pregnant."

A gasp escaped my lips. Murmurs rippled throughout the room—I was not alone in my surprise.

"I never got the chance to tell him. Artemis took one look at me and knew. Of course she did—she had the powers I have now inherited. Her bright new changeling was with child, a distraction. What made it worse was that the child was sired by her enemy, though at the time I didn't know it. And in the end, I was poisoned."

"Poisoned?" Alan said.

"It's in the faerie food," Caroline said softly. "It's always been in the faerie food. You can enchant it any which way and we can't really tell, can we? It just tastes like magic mixed in, but that's what makes it taste good. And it's only the food she gets her hands on, but how easy is it to pass to the other courts? Plenty easy."

I touched my lips. "The infamous Autumn Court wine."

Caroline nodded sadly. "The poison killed my baby. I was a wild changeling to begin with, some say elf-struck. My bitter loss made it worse, and I completely lost my senses. I came to my lady, begging for guidance, for help. That's when I caught her in the lie."

A lie?

"True fae can't lie," I whispered.

Caroline gave me a sharp look. "That witch is no true fae. She is a changeling as surely as you or I."

"How did she become Lady of Autumn?" Alan asked.

Caroline chuckled darkly. "That was a hard one to figure out. She is old. Very old. The oldest thing I have ever encountered. And she is twisted in hate. However she came to power happened many centuries ago, and it doesn't really matter now, I suppose."

"How do you know all this?" I asked.

Caroline shrugged. "Glimpses of the future, glimpses of the past. I've uncovered many secrets with my powers, some of them very old."

She adjusted herself before continuing, glancing out the window at the falling snow. It grew heavier than it had been when we arrived, and I wondered if any of it was from Devin as guilt hit me. I had to get through this story, then I needed to see him.

Caroline continued. "Artemis had been touched by the fae somehow, though she didn't know it at first. She brought the fae touch home to a husband and daughter. Her love for them was deep, which is what makes the whole situation so tragic."

"Oh no," Gabby whispered.

"She drove him elf-struck, along with their child. Can you imagine what it must be like to watch your family tormented in that way? To grow old and die in that state? That's what happened."

"That's awful," said a fae from the back.

"Before you grow too much sympathy for her, let me draw you back to the present," Caroline said. "I was poisoned and my child was lost."

"You said you caught her in a lie?" Keegan prodded, though I feel like he already knew this story.

"I did, which is the moment I realized, simultaneously, that Artemis is not who she pretends to be, and that I have the power of glamour. Truth, perhaps, would be a better term for it. Oh, at first I didn't know exactly what it was, but I recognized its significance. So, naturally, I tried to kill her."

"How are you not dead?" I asked, shocked.

She shook her head. "I'm not, that's all that matters. In my grief, I lashed out at her in front of everyone. Some struggled to find an assailant, not knowing I was fighting Artemis. Others who recognized what was happening fled or stood guard. It was a bitterly short fight. It ended when I called her out for her lies, accused her of poisoning me, and demanded retribution. The courts thought I was lost to my grief, but Artemis knew the truth. She knew I had seen through her glamours, her pretty lies. Her mask. We both realized that I would have to die for her to keep it up."

"Yeah, so seriously, how are you not dead?" Alan asked.

"I am not dead because I escaped. And I used Devin to do it." Her attention slid to me. "I called for him. He came to me and I ran. In the confusion, he held off Artemis's pursuit. It was enough. In the state I was in, I never did get to tell him any of it. I don't think he would have remained at my side, but the fact that the rotting one killed his chance at a child, something the fae don't get often . . ."

And he didn't know. God, he'd had a *baby*, which Artemis had killed, and he never even knew. Young fae meant everything to the courts, and it was a life extinguished before it could even begin. A wet streak fell down my cheek, and Alan wrapped an arm around me. I clung to it for comfort. On my other side, Candace slipped an arm around my waist and leaned her head on my shoulder.

"I have sought her truth ever since," Caroline said quietly. "Thanks to your powers, I've finally pieced it all together. She collects changelings, particularly disgruntled ones. She poisons most of the offspring from ever seeing daylight. And you'd never know, if she sees more true fae are going to be born, she takes care of it before the parents would even know. She captures, kills, or banishes mates before they can meet to lessen the odds even more."

"Why?" Gabby asked, crying.

"To what end?" I asked. "Why do this? She knows the pain of that loss, how does that help her revenge?"

"The fight?" Alan asked. "You said there would be a battle between changelings and true fae . . ."

"Yes," Caroline replied. "Her revenge is the total slaughter of the fae race, so that her travesty can't be repeated. She would be left in the end only with changelings who would never desire to turn more humans, eventually destined to die out."

My stomach churned. "You're kidding. She's repeated it time and time again herself!"

Caroline laughed darkly. "I've seen enough over the last few cen-turies to know that this is the most fertile gate in the world. Children are conceived all the time. Bonds are littered across the city like matching pieces in a children's memory game, only to be plucked away by her."

"Why didn't you take this to the other leaders? You could've stopped it, they . . . they would . . ."

"They would what?" she scoffed. "Believe me? The elf-struck changeling? Artemis has been in power longer than anyone here has been alive. And after attacking a fae leader, all four courts wanted my blood." She paused. "But with the arrival of Thea and her abilities, I could finally see clearly enough to find an end to Artemis."

"And how do you see this ending playing out?" I asked. "Start a war with her? There has to be another way."

Caroline shook her head. "A war is my last resort, but I'm afraid that's how it will end anyway. First, I want to challenge her just as any fae has the right to challenge a court lord for their seat. Technically, I'm still a fae of the Autumn Court, after all. But if I go in there with no backup, it will be too easy for her to play dirty and kill me quietly. I've seen it happen." She tapped a long finger on her temple. "I need backup if things go poorly."

Thoughtful quiet settled over the room. Eventually, Jude stood up.

"I stand with you."

Silently, fae and changeling alike stood behind him in solidarity. Almost none remained seated. Caroline met my stare.

"I will do what's in my power to make sure the Winter Court stands with you," I pledged, a tremor to my voice. "Artemis must fall."

CHAPTER FORTY

DEVIN

A blizzard bombarded the east side of the city as I crossed through it. The humans noticed the blizzard pretty quickly and the streets soon emptied. Hope filled my chest when the bond sparked to life, albeit faint, and I could sense Thea again, but I still didn't know where she was. What we had was still new and needed time to grow.

Failure filled my thoughts. I'd failed her, after all my promises to keep her safe. The insatiable bond drove me wild, but even more than that I had failed one of the Winter Court I was bound to watch over. Without keeping my word, I was unworthy of my position. Unworthy to guide the Winter fae, unworthy to watch over the faerie gate, unworthy to be by Thea's side. Without his word, a fae is nothing, and it fueled me in the desperation to make everything right again. If losing her was a correction of the gate trying to maintain balance, I would give up anything to take her place.

In my state, I had completely lost track of time. All I knew was that at some point, I sensed a faint thread of hope, of surprise. Something had caught Thea off guard. I spun, trying to grasp at a direction but failing. I decided to make for the center of the city in hopes that I could either sense her again or that Heather or Arthur had found something to go on.

I was in a park when I felt fire claw through my icy aura, knocking me off course.

"Devin!" The Lady of Summer, in all her fiery glory, stalked toward me. To her credit, it did stop my rampage. Momentarily.

"*Where is he?*" she screeched, her crimson hair flailing in the force of our combined powers. "You were watching over him! How could you lose my bond mate?"

She launched a stream of fire at me to drive her point home. I dodged it, but she set a car on fire behind me. I put it out immediately, before the gas tank could explode. I clenched and unclenched my fists, trying to control my emotions.

"In case you missed the *point*, my dear, Thea is also missing."

Georgina snarled at me. "Fix this, Devin! Find him now."

"I'm trying!" I took a deep breath and the snow lessened. Slightly. "You can help, or you can get the hell out of my way. Your choice."

She tore past me, heat rolling off her, melting my snow in her wake. Presumably she was conducting her own search, though with the newness of her own bond it was unlikely she would succeed. Until they bonded in heart, body, and mind, it would be like finding a needle in a haystack.

"Devin!" I turned to the sound, barely audible above the tumult; it was Heather, with Arthur right behind her.

"Lord Devin!" she called again. The wind whipped her hair around wildly.

I covered the distance, the storm dying as I got closer.

Heather held her hands up. "She's safe."

"*Where?*"

Heather looked to Arthur, concerned. "She doesn't know."

My temper flared briefly. "Tell me everything."

"She called—she'll be on the move soon. She's . . . with Caroline. She wants us to gather the Winter Court and hold a position in neutral territory but close to Autumn. She says she will meet us when she can."

Heather took a knee in the snow and bowed her head. "Just tell me what you need from me. Whatever part I played in keeping Caroline quiet . . . We will get her back."

"Lord Devin," Arthur spoke up. "I can gather the Winter fae who don't live at Court. Just give me a location." He followed Heather's example and showed his penitence.

I took a long breath. My people didn't need a rampage right now; they needed the Lord of the Winter Court. "Arthur, bring the solitary fae to the park at the border of the Winter and Autumn Courts, and await further instructions. Heather, send out a message to the others. Have them meet us there. Have the fae from the main house bring the emergency packs with them. I want Yoseph to take a small scouting party of his choosing to set up a moving perimeter, to search the city for Thea, Caroline, or any suspicious movement by groups of fae. If Thea wants to meet me in the city, she can't be that far away. I'll meet you both at the park in half an hour."

The pair of them took off. I glanced around at the ice and snow that coated everything. I stopped any more from falling and blew some of it away, though I left enough ice to deter the humans from leaving their homes until this was over.

I would have her again soon, and whoever took her would pay.

And if Caroline was responsible, there would be a frozen hell waiting for her.

CHAPTER FORTY-ONE

THEA

Standing in the heavy snowfall felt good for me, a place to breathe after listening to Caroline's story. I was absorbing all that had happened, and the weight of what had to be done. Alan eventually came after me, despite how cold he must have been.

Alan rubbed my back. "It's going to be okay."

"We have to bring Artemis down, and we have to keep Caroline and Devin away from each other until I can fill him in."

"You think he's going to handle that well?" Alan asked.

"No, I think he's going to throw the biggest piss fit I've ever seen." Looking up into the falling snow, I wondered if that part had already started. "I just have to make sure it's aimed at Artemis."

"He's about to find out one of his coworkers is a murderer. He's kind of got a right to throw a fit," Alan added. "I'm going to go back inside, figure out when we're leaving." He started back toward the house. I grabbed his wrist.

"I'm coming with you." I hesitated. "I can't waste time freaking out. I should be in there, planning. I volunteered our people after all." A wave of sickness hit me suddenly. "Oh god, I volunteered our people. Some of them are going to get hurt, aren't they?"

"Maybe." Alan held my hand. "I'm not gonna lie and say that won't happen, but you're doing the right thing. You're going to help save so many lives from that monster."

Wiping a stray tear with the side of my thumb, my shoulders straightened and I tipped my chin up. "Let's go then."

Inside was a beehive of commotion. Caroline was at the dining table with a map and a red marker. Jude and Ben were with her. Candace was in the corner with the fae I'd almost attacked earlier. Her mate. Was this how she'd felt seeing me and Devin? It was like my best friend had skipped an entire stage of dating, and now she was serious with someone. A first for Candie. He was on a couch, and he looked to be in pain still from injuries I couldn't see.

"Where are you going?" Alan asked.

"I have to make sure Candie is okay. And I think I need to make amends." I made my way to her.

She had a look on her face like I'd never seen before. Being a fae had changed her, but at her core she was still my friend. Right now, though, I almost didn't recognize the love I saw in her as she stared at her mate.

"Hey," I said. She didn't look up at me. "I'm sorry about . . ." I glanced at the fae on the couch.

"Donovan."

"Right, I'm sorry I almost attacked Donovan. I didn't know." I noticed his wrists and winced.

"No harm done—you didn't actually attack me," Donovan murmured, reaching up and tucking a strand of hair behind Candie's ear. He flinched as he bent his injured wrist.

"I can heal you," I offered. "You've probably heard by now about the healing thing."

Candie sat up straight. "Sort of, you can do that for him?"

"I can try. It's still new to me."

Candace exchanged a look with Donovan, and he showed me his wrist first. Tracing a finger along the angry red mark, my heart tightened. "What happened to you?"

He grunted at the contact to his pained skin, and I lightened my touch. "The Summer Court happened."

"Georgina," I whispered. "Oh my god, you're the one who turned Alan, her mate. You're the one she told Devin she had caught."

Candace scowled at the mention of her former boss and current Lady of Summer. I wondered how damaged their relationship would be now that Donovan had surfaced with his connection to Candace. But that was a problem for later; right now I had to try to move that healing magic through my fingers again, because this kissing business was getting old fast. I moved my hands over his wrist just as I had the fae in Artemis's dungeon, willing that cool sensation of magic into Donovan's wrist. When it appeared to ease his pain, I moved around his arms, back, and neck to other places he pointed out while Candace clutched his hand tight.

Donovan wore an expression of amazement as he stared at his wrist, turning it this way and that. "So, it's true. The Four . . ."

She studied Donovan for a minute, then back to me. "We have some catching up to do, don't we?"

That was an understatement. "After this is over, we should spend some time together. I'll even go to one of your spas."

Candace laughed darkly. "You really must be tired." Then her expression sobered. "Are you going to be okay? They're talking about a fight."

"I'll have to be. Will you be okay here?" Scrappy as she was, Candace wasn't a fighter and didn't belong anywhere near a battlefield.

"I'm coming with you," she insisted. "I can help clear people away or clean up messes. I can't heal like you, but I can summon small amounts of water. I can clean up cuts."

Donovan nodded. "I'm drawn to Autumn magic, even though I'm not allied with the court here. My fire is nothing compared to Lady Georgina's, but I can keep her from freezing in the winter air, and I'll watch her with my life."

And I knew he would. This bond was serious, and the fae were serious about it. Wherever Candace stood about it, I knew Donovan meant it when he said he'd put her life before his own.

"Thea," Caroline called from her map.

I turned to the table behind me. "I've got to go."

"Okay," Candace said. "Be safe."

I walked over to the table, a dining room complete with china cabinet and family pictures on the walls had been transformed into a place of strategy and planning.

"So glad you could join us." Caroline looked up from the map.

"I was mending relations with a neighboring court."

Caroline snorted. "Already speaking like a diplomat—Devin would be proud. Now that you're here, I'm going to give you the quick and dirty."

I nodded, inspecting the map.

"It's pretty basic. I'm going to be here." Caroline pointed to a parking lot down the street from the Autumn apartments. "There isn't much in that area, so we're looking at minimal human casualties."

Nods of approval bobbed around the table.

"I'll be there with a handful of wild fae; the rest will wait downwind until Artemis is in the open. Hopefully we won't need more than a few to flex our point and she'll just accept the challenge. Her mind has deteriorated—I can sense the torment in her. She's been chasing me for so long, to finally have me in her sights should drive her out."

"And if it doesn't?" I asked.

"Then we pummel wave after wave of her people until she has no choice." Caroline shrugged. "It's not an elegant plan, but it's what we have."

"Where does the Winter Court wait?" I asked.

"Here." Caroline pointed. "This is our fallback. We need a safe haven for the overwhelmed and injured to fall back to. I'm leaving that to you. Once we leave here, you'll have to gather your people quickly. Do you think you can do it?"

My eyes widened. That was one hell of a commitment, but it had to be done. "Yes—I don't have much choice. I'll be there."

"Okay," Caroline stood back from the map and clapped her hands. "You all know your jobs. Be ready to leave on the hour. It's time."

—

The bus was loaded up once again, with even more fae and gear than before despite the rage of the swirling snow.

I spent the last few minutes before leaving trying and failing to control my electric powers. I eventually gave up and took my seat at the front of the bus next to Alan. Candie and Donovan took a seat near the back, deep in discussion. I'm sure they had a lot to work out. Zara made sure everyone was on the bus, her mate Ben staying behind with Sammie and a few others that weren't joining the confrontation.

"There's too much snow," I heard the driver of the bus tell Caroline. She had to sift through all the fae on the bus to find those with ice or wind powers strong enough to clear the way, and much of the bus was shuffled around to allow these fae into the front seats to help. More than once I wished I'd had an easier power to control, and the feeling of helplessness was uncomfortable.

"How are you holding up, Floor Sign?" Alan asked once we had settled into new seats.

A laugh mixed with disbelief and stress bubbled up. "Still? I'm still Floor Sign even after all this?"

He nudged my shoulder with his. "Yeah. You're still you, even with the new accessories." He tapped one of my antlers and I shook my head. "No luck with your powers?"

"No."

"Me either." He wiggled his fingers. "Caroline said I have water abilities, but I don't feel anything at all."

"Maybe it's too cold for you to feel it? I guess we're both going to be next to useless in a fight—I can barely make sparks at will even after practicing every morning. Anything bigger than that has always been by accident."

"Maybe it won't come down to us using powers."

"Maybe."

Caroline stood at the front of the bus and clapped her hands. "This is it, folks, we're crossing into the court territories. I'm glad you all appreciate the importance of what I'm trying to do here, and that's as close as I'm going to come to thanking any of you."

A few on the bus chuckled.

"I will do my best to keep this confrontation between me and Artemis, but if I can't keep it contained, there will be backlash. Be ready."

The rest of the ride was quiet and contemplative. Many of us watched out the window for any sign of court fae; with a whole bus of wild fae energies we were bound to draw some attention. Seattle was coated in snow like I'd never seen before, and I was past the point of doubt that Devin was behind it. Every mile we climbed into the city was a fight against the weather, snow slamming against the sides of the bus as we went. The only reason we were moving at all was thanks to the efforts of the fae in the front, pushing the snow out of the way.

The bus finally pulled into the driveway of an empty church next to an expanse of empty space where nothing had been built, or maybe it was a park. It was hard to tell under the blizzard, but that same swirling ice and snow was also what had emptied the humans from sight. Good, the last thing we needed was human casualties, because once a fight broke out all glamouring would be out the window.

"This is it!" Caroline called over the howling storm once the doors were open. "Keep your Summer friends warm; this is our stop."

My oversized clothing preference was coming in handy as I slipped my university sweater off, helping to pull it over Alan and leaving me in a tank top. Thank goodness for being a Winter fae, because I couldn't imagine how uncomfortable the others were going to be out there. We filed off the bus and I sucked in a breath. We were close enough now.

"Devin!" I turned in the direction of the bond, now picking up that telltale heat that pointed to the other end of our shared thread of fate.

"Go!" Caroline shouted after me. "Fill him in and try to stop him from wringing my neck until after I find Artemis!"

"Keep Alan and Candie safe!" I shouted, then left, running through the heavy snow as best as I could, trudging a small canyon through it on my way to Devin. An overwhelming aura of comfort hit me—I didn't realize the hold that the court had on me until it was gone—and at the center of it all, that specific magnetic pull. He was close. At the edge of the park, heads turned toward me from every direction. Familiar faces popped into view, many of them relieved to see me. The feeling was mutual.

"Devin!" I called. I knew somewhere in the crowd and the snow he was waiting for me. Almost immediately they parted and he appeared.

"Thea!" He ran for me, meeting me halfway, the snow falling away from him as if it was nothing, and scooping me into his arms. My breath hitched, he held me so tight. I shut my eyes and inhaled his scent. Cold tears tried to fall down my cheeks before freezing on my skin. Devin pulled back just far enough to cover my mouth with his. His taste on my lips caused my heart to erupt in a burst of warmth. All around us, the raging snow slowed. No more swirling wind, no more shards of ice. When it was down to a trickle of snowflakes, Devin pulled back to look at me.

"Tell me what's happened," he demanded. "Was it Caroline? Where is she?"

"Caroline *saved* me. Well, we saved ourselves, but she was obviously coming for us. Heather showed you the ledgers?"

Devin's face darkened. "Yes, did you find out who is behind it?"

Nearby fae came closer. Some were from the main house. Heather and Arthur were there. Yoseph was a few steps behind me. I gave Heather a weak smile—she looked relieved to see me.

I looked to Devin again. "Artemis."

Shock rippled through his features, then confusion. "You're certain?"

"I was in her dungeon," I said quietly.

That didn't sit well with the court. They had taken to me pretty quickly, and to hear now that I had been captured . . .

"Why would Artemis do this? How could she have anything to do with the ledgers?" Devin asked.

"She wants changelings to blame the fae for turning them. She wants discontent in the city. And the wine from the Autumn Court? She's tampered with it, specifically getting poison into the hands of potentially mated fae. She's using it to prevent or kill fae that haven't even been born."

A range of sounds echoed around me, everything from growling to sharp intakes of surprise. "What does she want us to do, die out?" shouted someone.

"Yes," I stated. And then I explained everything, spilling it all out in front of the whole court, in front of Devin. The only part I couldn't bring myself to share was why Caroline attacked Artemis that day, but it seemed I didn't need to for the court to be enraged by Artemis and her deeds. Devin wore a mask of hard indifference as I admitted to all of it. Deceiving him, meeting Keegan, chasing after Caroline. But despite the mask he wore, I could feel the hurt from him as a sharp stab to my heart. What I had done would be very hard to repair and it would tear me up, but it would have to wait. Because as I explained what happened and the budding rage from the Winter Court grew to outrage, Caroline was starting the confrontation.

A crack sounded in the distance. All heads snapped toward it.

"Devin," I begged. "We have to go now!"

With a hard stare in the direction of the conflict, he tightened his jaw, then turned to the fae around us. "Yoseph, call your people back from the perimeter search. Thea, where do we need to be?" His grip softened.

"The far end of this street if we keep going, next to that gray brick church. We're the fallback line."

He nodded again, roaring loudly for all to hear: "We follow Thea's direction for now. Arthur, go ahead, you're my eyes. Those strongest in defense form a marching border and watch for outside attack. I need a set of three trained scouts to report to me once we move out. You have two minutes!"

The Winter Court scrambled beautifully. I made a mental note to have Devin teach me these procedures as soon as this was all over.

"You're never leaving my sight again," he grumbled as we watched the activity around us as we began walking. His storm had calmed, but the snow was still above my knees.

"I'm sorry," I said.

"We'll figure it out later." He put an arm around my back, as though being able to touch me would prevent me from disappearing again. "You scared me."

Another crack sounded in the distance, followed by a flash of red light and a boom like thunder.

"It begins," Devin murmured. We closed in on where Caroline would expect us to be and watched the scene unfold in front of us.

The temperature fluctuated. Lights flashed and sprays of water erupted here and there. The piles of snow were scattered and disturbed where fighting broke out and wind or fire pushed it out of the way. Caroline stood in front of a group from the Autumn Court with only a few fae at her back. Caroline's band of wild fae had very successfully gotten the attention of the Autumn Court and had become surrounded.

"Come out, Artemis!" Caroline shouted. "It has to end, you or me!"

Still gripping Devin's hand, I looked up to see a calculating expression on his face. Ahead, a group made up of Autumn Court fae parted as Artemis herself stepped through.

"*You*." Artemis's eyes were blazing. "Finally. After all your slipping away and hiding, you're in front of me as though you have a right to anything here. You will not get in my way."

"Bullshit. As if you haven't done that and worse a thousand times over," Caroline spat. "I challenge you for the seat of the Autumn Court, Artemis. To the death!"

The Autumn fae shifted around. Some were surprised, but many were not. Artemis's face was a blank mask, cold and cunning.

She surveyed Caroline and her group. "No."

Devin stiffened beside me.

"What?" I asked.

"It is not a request, Artemis cannot refuse the right of challenge," Devin answered. "No fae lord can, in the same way that we're not built to lie."

"She's not a true fae," I said softly, holding my breath as I watched on.

Artemis raised her hand slowly and smiled. "Autumn Court, I command you: bring me Caroline's head." Chaos erupted. The court could not disregard their Lady's command, and even those distressed and confused by what was unfolding found themselves moving forward to defend her honor. Caroline cursed and ran at Artemis, and the clash began.

In the middle of it all was Jude. A beast among monsters, he was lightning fast for his size.

As the initial skirmish began, another wave of Autumn fae, accompanied by changelings, hit the field. They immediately overwhelmed Caroline's party, and Keegan and Ben responded with a raging fire and lightning from the south.

"I'm going in," Devin snapped. "Artemis had no right."

"No!" I grabbed his sleeve. "Caroline said she needed us here. We have to trust her."

"She can't be trusted with the Autumn Court, Thea. Artemis will pay, but not at Caroline's hand."

"You don't understand," I hissed. "She's meant to be the Lady of Autumn. You might not like it, but every fae standing behind her accepts the role the gate gave her. I do too."

A massive gust of wind blew through the field. It would have knocked me over, as it did others, had Devin not caught me. It came from the battlefield, and I could only imagine the force of it up close. The air reeked of rotting leaves, choking the air with venomous intent.

"Artemis," Devin snarled, eyes wild. "I'm ending this." He stepped forward.

I grabbed his arm. "Devin, forgive Caroline," I pleaded. "Let her have Artemis. Just support her. Please!"

"She attacked her own court when she fled. She is no leader."

I didn't want to tell him like this—it wasn't my story to tell. Also, I had no idea how he was going to react. But I was out of options. "She attacked Artemis that day when she caught her in a lie and knew she wasn't true fae. Caroline lost her baby the same way the other fae had. Devin, she was poisoned."

The story I saw on his face broke my heart into pieces.

"Artemis . . ." His voice was ice; I almost didn't hear him over the wind.

He let go of me. Stepped forward.

He'd figured it out. Ice veined the ground around him, overwhelming the snowdrifts and transforming them into sharp blades rising from the ground. It spread from him effortlessly, coating everything, even climbing up my boots.

"Artemis will die."

"Devin!"

"Stay here," he commanded and then took off. He moved quickly, propelled toward Artemis's eruption. He was out of sight in the blink of an eye, the only indication of his presence the patches of ice where his feet had briefly touched the ground.

"Shit." The urge to run after him, to help somehow, was strong. What kept me back was knowing that I had not mastered my powers—and I'd promised Caroline I would hold this location. Turning around, I could see all of the Winter Court staring at me expectantly.

"What happened?" Arthur hurried over following Devin's departure.

"Devin is going to fight Artemis," I said.

"What would you have us do?"

Well shit. Guess I'm in charge now.

An eruption of heat to my right caused me and several others to turn away. Clouds of smoke puffed toward us. I couldn't see what was going on in that part of the city, but from the red glow I could only assume it was Georgina's fire. I prayed Alan would find her soon.

Several fae were on the ground now, injured and exhausted, the fighting having shifted.

"Everyone . . . " I started.

"Attention! Your Lady is speaking!" Arthur bellowed.

All eyes turned to me.

"Thank—good job, Arthur." I cleared my throat and addressed them all. "I need volunteers to retrieve fallen fae from the battlefield! I don't care what court they are, I don't care what side they're on; if they're injured, we will help them. Any takers?"

Immediately two dozen battle-ready fae stepped forward. It was easy to come up with tasks, and the court was hungry to help in the conflict. Some of us cleared space in the snow to receive the injured, some of us kept watch to guard this safe place to fall back to, but I prayed Caroline wouldn't need to. We readied ourselves as quickly as possible, and almost as soon as we laid out tarps, jackets, whatever we could find for bodies to be laid on, it was time to use them.

The first wave of fae had returned with burns, cuts, and broken bones. I flinched as they were carried past me—a wild fae covered in thin cuts with a clearly broken arm jutting out at an odd angle, an Autumn fae with scorch marks down half his body.

"Where are the worst ones?" I asked the fae bringing in the injured.

The moment I had a direction to go, I ran to anyone I could help. I crouched over the nearest one—a young fae with a bad gash in his side. He was breathing heavily, his hands weakly attempting to stanch the flow of blood. His eyes were shut, his brow slick with sweat.

"I'll take the worst ones, just keep sending them to me," I said loud enough for everyone around me to hear. My court was going to discover my healing powers one way or another; it might as well be now. I leaned over, careful not to disturb the wound further, and pressed my hands to any wound I could find. He took in a sharp breath, and a moment later opened his eyes in wonder.

I helped him sit up, and he tore away the remainder of his shirt and inspected his torso. His body was still slick with blood, but underneath was a clean white scar.

He stared at me. "The Four . . ."

We seriously needed a better name than that.

Giving him a grim nod, I moved on to the next in line. I didn't have time to go through that moment of realization with each fae I healed. My hands crossed over several more bodie s. Broken bones, burned flesh, lacerations so deep I was scared that even my abilities would not be enough to save them.

When a fae I recognized from the Spring Court appeared before me I was taken back. Helping her with a badly broken arm, I turned to catch sight of the fighting.

"Is the Spring Court here?" I asked.

"Some," a fae I didn't recognize coughed from down the line. "Lord Nikkola noticed the commotion and sent some of us ahead."

I nodded, glad they had chosen our side of this chaotic fight. Or maybe they hadn't, maybe they were injured in the confusion and just so happened to land in this field where we were treating the injured. Either way, it felt like every fae in the city was going to be involved before everything was done. I healed the broken arm, did what I could for a torn-up wing, and moved on from the Spring fae in search of my next patient.

At one point, a pair of hands crossed over mine on a new fae, washing away a pool of blood that prevented me from seeing what I was doing. I looked up and met Candace's hard expression, and we silently finished our task before moving to the next.

Between patients, my thoughts drifted to the battle. Realistically, only minutes had passed, though it certainly felt longer. The bond told me that Devin wasn't far. I had just finished taking care of burns on the last of the severely injured when a wave of warm air hit the clearing. The skin on my hands and face, the most exposed parts of me, tightened with the sudden onslaught of heat and most of the court had to crouch to not be blown over by the force.

"I got him!" I couldn't see Heather, but I heard her familiar voice. A moment later, she came over, one arm around Alan.

"What happened?" I asked.

"Georgina's joining the fight," Alan answered, his face flushed as sweat beaded on his skin. "I'm here, can I help?"

I shook my head. "Stay safe; if you can get your water abilities to work, conjuring something to clean blood and soot would be useful. Candace is around here somewhere doing the same thing."

Alan nodded, and Heather pulled him away just as more shouting kicked up. "First wave, move forward!" Yoseph called. Twenty fae ran to the field in sync with one another.

"Good luck," I called after him, then kneeled next to a fae with a bad gash through their spine. We needed Georgina to help turn the tide.

CHAPTER FORTY-TWO

DEVIN

The clashing of fire, ice, rock, and everything else under the sun painted a gory scene across the empty lot where Caroline had decided to provoke her fight. A challenge to Artemis, one that the ancient witch had been able to refuse. A changeling. This entire time, a changeling.

A rage boiled within me. To think, I had missed any signs of her betrayal. That Artemis, the oldest of our courts, could sit on her lies for centuries while the rest of us struggled to hold everything together. Every false tear she'd spilled for our losses crossed my mind. Every tale of losing a changeling to the wild fae. She would pay for every one of them.

A line of asphalt launched upward from an Autumn fae, one I recognized to be at Artemis's side many, many times. Rock pushed upward, unearthing utility lines from under the street as it raced my way.

It was easy enough to press forward with ice in my step and wrath in my heart, covering the gap as I closed the distance between me and the offending fae.

"You follow a betrayer," I spat, his face contorting in anguish.

"I do not," he grunted. "She gives us no choice."

Realization hit me: she could orchestrate all of this with orders even if they didn't agree with her. Her whole court was at risk of dying in a fight they wanted no part in.

Rushing forward, I hit him square in the chest, knocking him onto the ground a few feet away and covering his sprawled limbs with ice. "Stay down."

He let his head fall back, closing his eyes as he panted. "Thank you."

There wasn't time to acknowledge the boon that just formed between us; I had a feeling more than one of the Autumn fae would be grateful to be taken out of the fight without dying. Giving myself a heartbeat to look back at Thea, assuring myself that she was with the rest of our people, I moved on.

More than once, I found the presence of Spring and Summer. The battle had spread enough that it gained the attention of the other courts but my focus remained on Artemis and her court as I scoured the area.

I found more of them, defending the space where Artemis and Caroline were locked in their own struggle. Moving forward, each expressive face told me what side they were on. The ones who were fighting for Artemis against their will I pinned in place by thick ice, but the ones loyal to Artemis received less mercy—I took them out of commission with shards of ice through each hand.

The moment they were out of the way, I could turn my attention to the heart of the chaos. Artemis looked rough, a crazed glint in her eye that reminded me of many an elf-struck changeling through the years. Her usually pristine appearance was now tatters and scratches, her hair and clothes long forgotten in her own windy abilities.

Caroline was little better, mostly as I had remembered her but with much shorter hair. Her narrow shoulders were heaving with effort as she buffeted her own wind at Artemis. There was no love lost between us, our fling long since discarded for anger—she had attacked the court fae and fled to become wild. I suppose now I know why, not that it mattered. She was an unfit leader. Still, today we shared an enemy.

"Artemis!" I yelled over the gale being slung between the ancient fae lord and the petite wild changeling. "I will have your heart in my fist for what you've done!"

Artemis feigned a blow to Caroline, then knocked her completely to the side with another gust of wind, pulling ash and debris from the rest of the battle to batter Caroline as it knocked her away into a tree with enough force to snap the thick trunk. She landed in a crumpled heap on the ground.

Artemis turned to me, fueled with a rage that marred her face in a way I had never seen before. "You don't deserve life, *Lord of Winter,*" she spat. "You change human after human, every year another tragedy." A chilled hatred overtook me as I stared her down.

"You know why we do it!" I snarled. "You were there when it was decided!"

"I will end you, Devin. Thea will be a better Lady of Winter than you ever could, and the changelings will see the end of the fae!"

With a ferocious growl, a giant of a wild fae charged forward, fists raised as he slammed into Artemis from behind.

The Lady of Autumn shrieked, turning to throw the big fae off her with her aged and honed powers. A huge gust whipped around Artemis, readying her attack.

"Move!" I called, thrusting ice under his feet to drop him to the ground before he could be thrown in the air.

Artemis screamed her fury, shifting her body at the last moment and launching her massive attack my way, when I was nearly at point-blank range. My body was thrown, shoved into a hurricane until I went flying back. I caught a glimpse of the big one tossing Artemis down the street before his attention turned to Caroline. Then, my vision blurred as I landed in a tilled-up crater that should have been a street.

White-hot pain hit me, and the feeling of something breaking through my back. My weight and the weight of the blast shoved me down onto something that pressed its way through my body like a needle through silk until I was pierced completely, my flesh burning. Every breath I took was like swallowing nails, and my strength failed as I reached for the shard protruding from my chest.

It was iron.

CHAPTER FORTY-THREE

THEA

I fell to the ground, a sharp pain in my chest. Heather pulled me to the side before I could fall on my latest patient. Arthur and Yoseph were immediately at my side, helping me back up.

"What is it?" Arthur demanded.

"It's Devin." I reached through the bond, struggling to catch my breath. "Something's happened to him. I have to go."

Yoseph and two others helped me walk quickly toward the fight. Our side was holding their own but only barely. More Autumn fae were streaming forward from the direction of the apartments. I was worried we would soon be overwhelmed. Sickening sounds, screams, surrounded us.

"There." Arthur pointed to an absolutely destroyed retaining wall where Artemis and Caroline were exchanging blows of powerful wind magic at blinding speed.

Artemis's face was contorted, her once beautiful orange dress in tatters, sliding off one arm with the bottom hem torn off at her knees. Caroline was a bruised mess; her clothes were marred where embers had burned through, but she stood proudly wearing the soot and ash that coated her face and hair, staring down the Lady of Autumn. The two of them seemed evenly matched. Caroline, probably not paying one bit of attention to the rest of us, flung a huge gust of cinnamon wind in our direction, knocking me off balance. Yoseph steadied me, but I was already prying myself out of his grasp.

"Devin!" Caroline had pushed me in the direction of a crater of asphalt and dirt. At the bottom of the hole was Devin, on his back and bleeding.

I threw myself into the crater. Dirt and rock scraped my skin as I tumbled toward him. He had abandoned his shirt at some point, his entire torso one giant scrape of blood. Sweat ran down his neck and his eyes were clamped shut. He clutched his ribs.

"I told you to stay," he protested softly, wheezing as he drew breath.

I shook, seeing white bone beneath his fingertips. An impossible amount of blood was flowing from between his fingers, spilling onto the ground. I cupped his jaw with both hands and he leaned into my touch. Relief flooded his face and he slowly opened his eyes.

"Caroline is the rightful Lady of Autumn. You were right," he said.

"Just shut up and kiss me." I leaned down and planted my lips to his. The kiss tasted like salt and blood. An icy tug—I felt my magic flowing into Devin, and I was alarmed at just how strong a pull it was. I held our kiss for what felt like ages.

Finally, I broke our connection. "It isn't working," I sobbed.

He closed his eyes again, brow creased in pain. I gently lifted his hands to inspect the wound. An iron pipe was protruding from his chest, a piece of bone grating against it, surrounded by tattered flesh.

"No." It came out a hoarse whisper. I tugged at the iron protruding from him, realizing with horror that it was jutting from the ground and I couldn't pull it out. Devin grunted out a hoarse, pained sound, my fingers slipping off the pipe from his blood.

A shuddering then and the ground beneath us crumbled, broken pavement falling around me. A pair of snow-white hands pulled me away. Arthur crouched over Devin as Yoseph helped me to my feet. A bright red flare nearby briefly distracted all of us. It had to be Georgina—hopefully she knew the truth by now. Arthur shifted Devin a bit, and the Lord of Winter hissed in pain.

"He's lying on it. We need to lift him," Arthur said.

"Then lift him!" I pleaded. "Get it out of him!"

"I wouldn't do that if I were you," hissed a cold voice from the road above.

I whirled around. Artemis stared down at us. She was covered in blood and her clothes were in ruins. Her eyes blazed with hatred, her once-neat hair now a wild eruption.

"You did this to him!" I snapped.

"You could have been great, Thea," she spat her words in contempt. "They deserve this fate, feeding off the humans with their deceit. A plague upon the Earth."

"It's over. The Winter Court knows about your betrayal." I glanced at Devin; he was struggling to breathe.

"Betrayal," she laughed. "It's the fae who have betrayed *you*, my dear. Their treachery ripped you from your life! An accident, Devin will tell you, but his mistake all the same. I know how you must have hated him, hated all the fae, for taking your choices from you."

"That was before," I said, my voice wavering. "Before we bonded . . ."

"Ah, but does it matter? The betrayal will always be there. If your own mate can't be trusted, how can you trust any of them?"

My fingers trembled at my side. I didn't have an answer for her. But that didn't mean she was right. I trusted Devin with my whole heart.

He'd made mistakes—big ones. But I wanted to hear him out. I needed to work this out with him, and if I were to have that chance then he had to live. If I turned my back, she would likely attack us all. But if I didn't help Devin soon . . . I had to keep her talking.

"I'm sorry about your husband," I yelled. "But more death won't bring him back!"

"No," she said coldly. "But it will stop this from happening again."

"So, you kill off all the fae at this gate? And then what? There are other gates, more fae."

"I will kill them all if I have to," she growled. "I'll spend eternity extinguishing their filth from this world!"

"These are not even the same fae that hurt you!"

Artemis lunged, and Yoseph shoved me behind him in time to take a forceful blow to the face. He fell to the ground in a heap.

"Yoseph!" Arthur lunged at Artemis. "Thea, run!"

"No!" I screamed. I looked up to see the blazing hell fires of Georgina. She was stark naked, her clothes burned away as she appeared above us cloaked in flames.

"You will kill none," she said. "Not one more living thing. Artemis of the Autumn Court, I strip you of your titles and condemn you to death."

"I'd like to see you try!" Artemis hissed. Her winds mixed with Georgina's flame hurricaning around us.

"I was hoping you'd say that." Georgina grinned and sprinted to meet Artemis head-on.

"Lady Thea!" Arthur hissed, back at Devin's side. I ran to them. "I'll lift him if you can take it from there." Arthur waited for my nod. "Then I'll take Yoseph back to the court."

"Okay," I breathed. He swiftly raised Devin off the pipe, a pitiful trickle of blood now dripping from his back.

Immediately I pressed my lips to Devin's. My healing flowed into him. It took my breath away—his need was like an ocean current pulling me under. He had to have been close to death for it to be so strong. I took over holding duties and Arthur disappeared to help Yoseph. My head swam with all that Devin had siphoned from me, so much so that I didn't notice when our roles reversed.

He opened his eyes and gasped for breath. "Thea . . ."

"I thought I'd lost you," I cried.

"Not that easily, darling."

We looked up then, at a rush of heat, and saw Georgina and Artemis locked in deadly combat.

"We have to find Caroline and end this," he said, "if she isn't already dead."

He helped me to my feet. My head was spinning, but I made it up the slope of the crater.

"There." Devin pointed to a pile of rubble. Caroline was alive, on the ground and trying to catch her breath. Her left leg was twisted at an unnatural angle. Jude was beside her, whispering something. I ran to her side and wasted no time in kissing her. Her sweet cinnamon scent ignited, and her eyes snapped open.

"Holy fuck that hurt," she gasped, pushing me off her. "Wonderful, you're a peach. Got to run now."

"Hey!" She shoved past me, heading straight for Artemis. Jude gave a stiff nod and ran after her.

Devin helped me to my feet. "Are you all right, love? Stay here." He gave me a tender kiss. "I'll be right back."

He rushed toward the fiery storm ahead—Georgina was lobbing a constant barrage of fire at Artemis, who was expertly dodging each volley. She'd also noticed Caroline and was carefully building up a shield of fierce wind between them.

Devin strode forward with purpose, gravel and cracked pavement underfoot giving way to dried winter grass as he stepped onto the field. Artemis didn't seem to sense him. He stopped a respectable distance away from the fight and placed both hands on the ground. Instantly, ice shot across the ground and ensnared Artemis's feet. She snarled in fury but still managed to twist her way free while avoiding Georgina's attacks. Caroline was pressing closer, Jude right behind her. Devin continued his onslaught of ice, but Artemis's struggling and Georgina's fire were making him work for every inch he could get. Ice freezing flesh, melting away as fire burned, only to be extinguished by a new wave of ice as they vied for control.

In a moment of clarity, it seemed like everything around me slowed. I raised my arms in front of me, palms out, fingers spread. I took a deep breath, my shoulders relaxing as Yoseph's advice rang in my head: *Breathe. Relax. Let it go through you.*

Artemis locked eyes with me, and in that moment, I felt her pain. Her loss. Her years of torment.

I also felt for the ones she had killed. Poisoned. Run off. I let go.

My hands ignited the night. A strangled cry escaped me as the lightning surged through my palms. I was but a vessel for the raw, white force erupting forth—so much more than the scant sparks that Yoseph had helped coax out of me before.

Artemis screamed. Her defenses were all but gone. I'd distracted her enough that Devin's ice was able to snake up her body and ensnare her. Georgina's fire engulfed her immediately, illuminating the entire street. The scent of burning leaves was overwhelming. Jude threw Caroline the rest of the distance.

And with a smooth swoop of a sharp blade of wind formed in Caroline's hands, she removed Artemis's head from her body.

It was over. I dropped my aching, stinging arms as exhaustion took over. My eyelids drooped.

"Suffer in hell," Georgina hissed, erupting Artemis's body in white fire until there was nothing but scorched earth where the twisted fae once was.

Devin looked to me and, sensing my exhaustion, ran forward.

I wanted to tell him I was all right, but I couldn't as I fell into a comfortable darkness.

CHAPTER FORTY-FOUR

THEA

A headache like I'd never experienced thrummed in my skull. I opened my eyes reluctantly to a bright light and the blurry faces of Heather and Devin. I looked around—we were in an unfamiliar room. It was too warm and I was in a bed, propped up by some rather comfy pillows, so it wasn't all bad.

Groaning, I tried to move so the offending bright light wasn't in my face.

"Thea!" They both said it at the same time as two pairs of hands reached for me. Gentle motions halfway between a hug and not wanting to touch me too hard grounded me, waking me the rest of the way up.

I swallowed painfully—my throat was dry. "How long was I out?"

"A few hours," Heather said, her expression strained. "Before you ask, we're both fine, Candace is fine, Alan and Georgina are fine."

Sighing through my nose, my body relaxed. Good.

"You're healing at a remarkable rate." Devin leaned over to take one of my hands. If Heather looked strained, Devin looked worse. "But I suppose that was expected."

Heather handed me a bottle of water, and I began to drain it desperately.

"Caroline is now the Lady of the Autumn Court," Devin explained. "There were few objections. It would seem Artemis had bullied most of them into submission. Her philosophies about the true fae have died with her."

"Good." I leaned back. "What about Yoseph and Arthur?"

"Injured, but recovering well," Devin said, and I noticed Heather turn away from us.

Okay, this had gone on long enough. "Heather, why do you hate Arthur?"

She stiffened, turning back to me. "It's not that I hate him."

"Heather, you were both in the wrong," Devin said, softness in his voice. "What if you had lost him today?" His grip shifted to my hand, holding it tight as though I would disappear at any moment. Heather's eyes followed the motion.

She nodded and stood. "I'll go talk to him. Feel better soon, Thea."

Heather left, and I looked to Devin. "What is going on between those two?"

Devin pulled at my hand, placing it over his own heart. "They have a connection, but they never did anything about it."

Devin's heartbeat was a steady pounding under my touch, even as my own emotions spiked. "Seriously? For how long?"

He shrugged, his thumb moving slowly over mine in his hand. "Decades. Since her change."

"What happened between them to wait this long?" I asked.

"I'm afraid that's not my story to tell."

Sinking into the pillows, I cleared my throat to do what I wish I had gotten the chance to do properly before the fight. Knowing what I almost lost, not willing to wait another moment before getting it off my chest, I faced him. "Devin, I'm sorry."

"Don't. I understand why you did it. I spoke with Caroline, she made sure I knew the position she'd put you in. I don't blame you for any of it, darling."

"That doesn't make it right. If you had known sooner, all of this would have turned out differently."

"You don't know that," he said. "I probably would have hunted for Caroline, and we never would have uncovered Artemis."

"Still . . ."

Sighing through his nose, Devin gave my hand a squeeze. "Then let's make a promise not to hide anything else from each other. We won't have a repeat of the situation. Deal?"

"Deal." My throat tightened, threatening tears. After everything I had been through, I guess I'd still always be an easy crier. "Devin, I love you."

His face briefly turned to shock before he engulfed me in his arms. "And I love you, Thea. I wanted to tell you yesterday, but then everything happened."

I choked out a sound so strange that I didn't even know what it meant but my heart swelled, and through our connection, I could feel Devin's overwhelming concern. We had almost lost each other when our story had just begun.

"I'm never going to keep secrets from you again," I insisted.

Devin rubbed my back until I calmed down, then pulled away from the hug to wipe my tears. "Shh, we can talk more later if you want."

"Yeah, okay." Finding tissues by the bedside table, I wondered whose room I was in but decided I didn't want to know. Silently thanking the bed's owner, I cleaned up my face and swung my legs off the side of the bed. "What now?"

"The other court rulers are meeting to discuss matters. We should join them."

I took his hand. "Lead the way."

Devin navigated us through the Autumn Court's halls until we reached a large room that could have been a lobby for the apartments. The way the tables and chairs were set up told me it was likely used for court business. Georgina, Alan, Nikola, and Caroline sat at a long table at the end of the room, and I wondered who'd had to fill in the Spring Court on what had happened. Large groups of other fae had shoved their way inside but were careful to not crowd the table with the fae lords and ladies. Everyone looked haunted and filthy, some with heavy blankets. Most likely the Summer fae.

Walking into the room, an uncomfortable number of eyes fell on me. I swallowed my protests as we took our seats across from Caroline. Alan was to my left and Devin to my right.

"Thea, I'm glad you're feeling better," Caroline said, as if I were getting over a mere cold.

"What's been discussed?" Devin asked.

"Not much," Georgina said, drumming her fingers on the table. "You know little can be done without all four courts represented."

"Then by all means, let's begin." Devin put on a face that I knew he used just to annoy people. Particularly Georgina.

"I'll begin," Caroline said, smiling sweetly. "My first motion is to abolish the annual changeling process."

Gasps swirled around the room.

"But the changelings—" Nikola started.

"Are no longer necessary," Caroline insisted.

The argument was not short. Alan and I voted alongside Caroline. Devin stayed quiet until near the end, at which point he agreed to abolish the changeling process, provided human mates could still be changed. Only Caroline would be able to identify mated pairs, but she agreed so long as the intended human also agreed.

The next order of business was to integrate the wild fae into the courts. Every last one of them wanted in. We removed the table and arranged our chairs in a similar fashion to how the thrones were at the solstice, when Candace and I had chosen our courts. Alan and I stood uncomfortably to the side, not wanting anything to do with the throne situation but not wading into the rest of the crowd. It took two hours to go through the line. It wound up being a fairly even distribution across the courts, with Summer technically gaining the most new fae by four.

Keegan was accepted into Caroline's court and immediately given a position of power. Jude, the strongest fae and our third of the four, with his enemy slain and his anger subsided, was once more a gentle giant. He was brought into the Spring Court with no objections. Gabby went there as well. One by one the fae landed in whatever court they were called to, and at last the conflict with the wild fae was over.

After the fae had been sorted, a sad cloud seemed to hang over the crowd. The four rulers read off names of the fae who had died in battle. Someone from Autumn Court must have gathered the list for Caroline. She did a good job stifling any resentment she might have felt while reading off the lost Autumn fae.

Following that, certain chosen, trusted fae were sent to bury the dead in the forest. They would quickly become trees, ready to give back to the nature from which they were birthed.

The last order of business was to introduce myself, Caroline, and Jude as three of the legendary four gifted ones, a title that Caroline absolutely hated and vowed to change. Caroline did all the talking, which we were happy to let her do. We held our breath at the end of her speech, hoping the last one would step forward, but no such luck. We quietly agreed to look for them on our own later.

It was nearly dawn before we'd finished everything. The fae rulers waded into the crowds to meet their new court members and arrange housing. Devin had made the calls earlier, before I woke up, so our new fae were all set with a warm meal and a bed as soon as they were ready to head to the townhouses. Luckily there were a few empty ones, a buffer between us and the human neighbors on the next street.

I spotted Heather and Arthur talking in a corner most of the night. There was anger, tears, and a few punches thrown—by Heather. Whatever had happened between them, I hoped she'd tell me someday.

Candace made sure to find me before going home. We had a lot to catch up on and I still didn't have the whole story between her and Donovan, but that could wait for a calmer day. I did leave Donovan with a harsh warning about consequences of hurting her, and Candace laughed at me for the attempt at sounding tough.

Speaking of mated pairs, the wild fae that had integrated into the courts started finding mates among the city fae. The second the official business stopped and the mingling started, several couples formed and began making out. Some had the decency to find a private room after a while, but several pairs had no qualms about mating right there in the main hall—an aspect of the fae I may never get used to.

Devin and I left with a procession of Winter Court fae. It was lovely and cool outside. A light fog was lifting as we walked back to our court, and Devin made sure to glamour our path as sleepy humans began to emerge from their houses, braving the remnants of the snow with shovels and scrapers. I was curious how the humans had written off the strange events of yesterday, but between the glamoured fae and the unexplainable events, I'm sure human nature would find a way to write it off as something easier to believe.

I glanced back over my shoulder, smiling at the faces behind us. Happy conversation, laughter, new friends, and tired soldiers, all. Our Winter Court.

When I turned back around, Devin was watching me. His warm smile melted my heart.

There was a lot of hurt to heal, but right now, I was content to hold Devin's hand and walk with our people. Home.

AFTER

THEA

"Can we hang that any higher? I want people to be able to see it outside."
I directed Devin and Arthur from the front doors as they hung the banner
for the brand-new Dubois informational exhibit. Thankfully the cool air
was cranked up to a Winter Court level of comfort while the three of us
worked in the summer heat.

"Here?" Arthur asked.

"Perfect."

My stomach was in knots, somewhat nervous but mostly excited for
tomorrow's unveiling. I even had a field trip from an art club coming next
week when I would be giving my very first tour.

"If that was it, I'm going to head out," Arthur said. "Good luck
tomorrow, Lady Thea."

"I really appreciate the help. Tell Heather I said the lunch she sent
was delicious."

"Yes," Devin drawled, "Go home to your bond mate. Let's be quick
about it this time, shall we?"

The usually calm Arthur looked as though he could smack Devin's
head right off his shoulders, but he didn't say anything as Devin laughed.

Six months later and Arthur was still hearing about how long it took them to reconcile.

"Don't tease him!" I smacked Devin's arm lightly. "Arthur, I appreciate the help."

"Of course, Lady Thea." A name I still couldn't get him to shake. "Farewell."

With Arthur gone and everything else set up, all the tension in my shoulders fell away as Devin stood next to me, an arm around my shoulders.

"I need to pick up that outfit from Candie before tomorrow." Chewing my lip, my mind wandered to other last-minute errands I could do. "Maybe we should have picked up extra napkins for the reception too."

"It will be fine."

"I don't know if I ordered enough pamphlets."

"Thea."

"I shouldn't have designed them in color; I could have just printed them here if they were in black and white."

"*Thea.*"

"Then again, what if our printers can't handle the glossy paper I chose? Maybe next time I should test that out first."

"*Thea!*" Devin turned my shoulders, having us face each other. "You need to stop worrying—everything will be fine."

"I can't help it, I'm a chronic worrier."

"Believe me, I am fully aware." He leaned down and kissed me, warm and soft. "I do have a trick to get you to relax though."

And I knew exactly what his idea of "relaxing" was. "We're at work!"

"We're *alone* at work," he teased, lifting me off my feet and walking away with me in his arms.

"You're insatiable!" I laughed as he bound up the stairs.

"Only when it comes to you, love."

In his office, he kicked the door shut behind him before setting me on the small couch by the bookshelves. He caged me in his arms and leaned down to kiss my neck.

"What do you think you're doing?" My lips protested, but my head moved to the side, giving him more room to kiss me.

"Are we still trying for a faeling?" he asked. "These things can take quite a bit of time, you know."

"It could take decades!"

"A sacrifice I'm willing to make," he teased.

Wrapping my fingers around his tie, I gently tugged his face down to mine so I could kiss him, reminiscent of our first kiss that had cemented the bond between us half a year ago.

"Whatever happens, happens. I'm not as impatient as you, Lord of Winter."

"Only for you," Devin answered. "Only ever for you, love."

He kissed me again, deeper and hungrier than before, and I wrapped my arms around his neck and melted into him.

Half a year ago I may not have known where I was headed, but I certainly did now.

I belonged in the Winter Court, I belonged at L'Atelier Rouge, and I belonged with Devin. My heart was whole.

ACKNOWLEDGMENTS

So many people had a hand in this book, I don't even know where to begin. *Dirty Lying Faeries* was a lot of "firsts" for me, and it got this far thanks to a lot of kindness and patience from those around me.

First, I want to thank Leah and the Paid Stories team at Wattpad for giving *Dirty Lying Faeries* its start in the world of publishing. I can honestly say that I would have written several more books before trying to publish one if it hadn't been for my experience with you.

I also want to thank Deanna McFadden and the Wattpad Books team, as well as Andrew Wilmot for all the insightful editing. The experience from start to finish has been challenging but rewarding, and I'm so grateful for everyone on the team who had a hand in making this experience happen. Especially Deanna and Andrew, my editors. I promise in my next book to cut back on how much I talk about food. Or at least I'll try.

Thanks to two very important agents on my journey—Amanda Leuck and Ali Herring at Spencerhill Associates—without whom I would have been lost in the world of publishing on more than one occasion.

I want to acknowledge the Wattpad Books authors that came before me as well, especially Tamara, Jessica, and Caroline, who have put up with my incessant questions.

Rodney, you're a mentor to many of us, and you were a rock to me on many occasions this past year. Thank you.

Thank you, Wattpad, for my start. Thank you to the Wattpad friends I've made and the amazing readers who encouraged me from day one. Every vote, comment, and read means so much more to the writers on this platform than you even realize. Thank you.

And finally, thank you to my husband and sister, who dealt with my stress during this process. I owe you both quite a bit, but I hope you'll settle for a nice dinner because it's time to start book two.

ABOUT THE AUTHOR

Sabrina Blackburry is a fantasy author from central Missouri. She has a love for morally gray characters, fated love with a touch of magic, and passionate women finding their place in the world. When she's not writing, Sabrina enjoys adding plants to the collection on her front porch, sewing for the local renaissance festival, and hiking.

Turn the page for a sneak peek of book two
in the Enchanted Fates series.

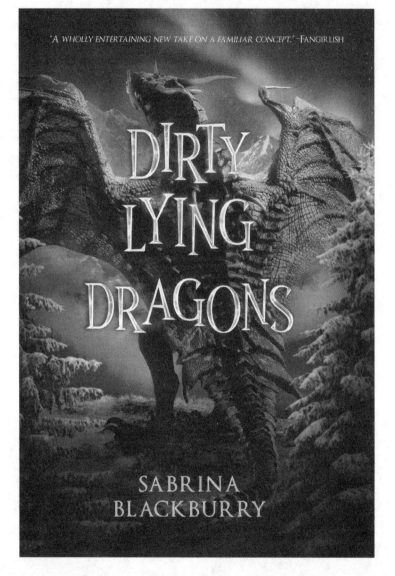

"A WHOLLY ENTERTAINING NEW TAKE ON A FAMILIAR CONCEPT." –Fangirlish

DIRTY LYING DRAGONS

SABRINA BLACKBURRY

Available August 2023, wherever books are sold.

CHAPTER ONE

DANI

There's nothing quite like a burning sensation on your ankle at seven in the morning to get the blood pumping. My eyes popped open and were met with the avocado-green tile of my ancient Chicago bathroom. The bathroom because I had passed out next to the toilet three hours ago, and the retro tile because that's what poses as an inconspicuous and affordable apartment for a witch with no coven and no reliable powers to back her up. Not that anywhere outside of the city was much better; the closer you get to trees and shit the more likely you were to run into a fucking fae, and that wasn't on my bucket list.

"Ow!" I slapped at the charm on my ankle, tucking my fingers in my boot to reach for the delicate chain as it sizzled against my skin and roused me from my night of rum and bad decisions. Staring at my leg for a moment, I registered why it might be burning in the first place. The charm. The charm on my ankle. The charm made by far more competent witches than myself that alerted me to impending supernatural dangers. I shot straight up and nearly brained myself on the toilet bowl. *"Fuck."*

Adrenaline, still the best hangover cure I've ever encountered, fueled my mad dash to the living space as I slid to a stop at the front window, knocking my knees on the windowsill in the process. Thankfully, I hadn't taken off any of my clothes from last night before passing out, including my black leather boots, which were about to get some use.

I couldn't see anything from the window side of the building, but that didn't mean that danger wasn't nearby. There was rapid knocking on my front door, but it wasn't until I heard my neighbor that my stiff shoulders relaxed a bit.

"Dani!" Mary's shrill voice peppered her knocking. "Dani, open up! There's trouble."

Her pale, pink eyes were wide with shock and her matching hair was still only half-curled. The fact that perfect little Mary had left her apartment in her pajama shorts and cami told me everything I needed to know about the urgency of this situation.

"What?" I whipped the door open, resisting the urge to jerk my leg as my anklet started burning again.

"The Blightfang are here," she said. "You need to go before they catch you!"

Fuck. The Blightfang were bad news. Fierce werewolves and merciless bounty hunters doing the bidding of a particularly nasty vampire. I hadn't done shit to them, but if the rumors going around were to be believed, their boss, Apollo, was looking for covenless witches. Mary made a face that told me she knew they were after me. No one else in the building was a covenless witch. A mostly voluntary situation, but right now it made me a target.

I spun around, running for the bed. "What do they want with the covenless witches anyway?"

"How can I help?" Mary offered, coming into my open doorway.

"Lock my door and be safe." I grabbed the keys from my bedside table and threw them to Mary. A locked door wouldn't stop the Blightfang, but it might slow them down.

"Are you going to be okay?" she called. "Maybe Lance can hold them off . . ."

Offering up the services of the warlock she was shacking up with was a nice gesture, but she and I both knew his second-circle ass wasn't going to stop a werewolf, let alone a group of them with a vicious reputation and a bounty in their sights.

"I'll reach out if I can." I offered her a weak smile. "Bye, Mary."

A crash came from downstairs and we both jumped. A door, a wall, a person. Whatever it was, it spurred both of us into action. Racing to my bedroom, I dropped to the floor, stuck my arm under the bed, and yanked out a stuffed backpack. Slinging it over my shoulders, I ran for the window and pried it open. When I crawled onto the fire escape, there was a big car parked out front eight floors down (and definitely in a tow zone, but I had an inkling that the Blightfang didn't care about getting a ticket).

"*Shit*," I hissed and pulled myself up the ladder to the next floor. Up and up I went, straining to carry myself and the huge backpack to the twelfth floor where the ladders stopped, while cursing the building management that kept the interior stairwell to the roof locked. I glanced up to the ledge where I needed to climb onto the roof. It was kind of high up, but I should be able to make it. Probably.

Another crash below drew my attention. My window had been broken, and splintered on the sidewalk below were several familiar pieces of wood.

"My table!" My heartbeat thrummed to the pace of panic and anxiety. How did they find me? They would be on my ass in a few seconds, but with some luck, a few seconds was all I would need.

I jumped, barely grabbing the ledge with my fingertips. Wriggling and squirming until my hands had a better grip, I pulled myself up. After finally throwing a leg over the edge, I rolled onto the roof and came to a stop on my back. Standing back up, I rushed for the center.

A teleportation circle had been painted in the middle of the roof, barely a lighter shade of gray than the existing tar but mixed with a whole host of potent ingredients. Mary had made it—my magic was unreliable—because we thought it would be wise for any witches to have an escape in a pinch, and boy did today count. Mary gave me the code words, something

3

that wouldn't be accidentally uttered by any unsuspecting maintenance workers, and even my volatile abilities shouldn't be able to mess this up. *I hoped.*

Slamming to a stop in the middle of the circle, I screamed. "Take me where my heart wants to go!"

Closing my eyes tight, I pictured my dad's place behind the bar. The familiar couch, the flat screen he had installed crooked and likely still hasn't fixed, the tiny kitchen where we'd spent late nights in deep conversation while he cooked bad snacks and made sinful cocktails. I panted, my breath catching up with me as I stood in the circle picturing my destination and . . . nothing happened.

That's not good.

"Take me where my heart wants to go!" I demanded, stomping my boot.

Nothing.

"What the hell?" I whipped my head around the circle at my feet. At this point my anklet was absolutely scorching. Something was wrong. I turned, looking at the intricate patterns around me when I saw it: four huge gashes slid through the roof, tearing up and breaking the circle. Claw marks.

Panic rising in my throat, I swept my eyes across the roof. The only hiding spot was the large air units in the far corner. A low growl rippled through the air and sent a chill down my spine as a giant wolf prowled from its hiding spot.

The gray beast shook its head, giving what must have been the wolfish equivalent of a cruel laugh as it stalked toward me. Sickening cracks popped through the air. Disgusting, crackling cartilage and splitting tendons as bones reshaped the beastly form. Claws shrank into fingers, the snout shortened to a human nose and mouth, and the fur retracted to bronze skin and a cloud of soft black hair. The only thing remaining to hint that this naked woman had been a wolf was her glowing yellow eyes—which I could only see thanks to my mother's witch's blood—and sharp white fangs.

"What a pain in the ass." The wolf shook her head, rolling her shoulder. "Why do the weak ones always try to run?"

Four big guys were climbing up to the roof. Stumbling away from the edge, I retreated to another side of the roof, but I was being backed into a corner. Bile rose in my throat and I swallowed it down as I gripped the straps of my backpack to keep my fingers from trembling.

"Not too bad, little witchling. You nearly got away." The she-wolf licked her fangs, her unblinking yellow eyes roaming over me. "Clever thing, you would have made a good wolf."

"Sorry, I'm allergic to dogs," I said. "Would never have worked out."

Think, Dani, think. Stall. Run.

The she-wolf growled, a sound that shouldn't come from a human throat. The back of my boot thumped against the opposite edge of the roof and my heart jumped.

"I wouldn't be mouthing off if I were you," she snapped. "Wouldn't want any accidents between here and when I deliver you to Apollo, would we?"

Fuck.

"It's true, then? There's a bounty on covenless witches?" I asked.

Something dangerous glinted in her eyes, followed by amusement. "Blightfang has the exclusive contract. We've got a little deal with Apollo."

"That sick leech can eat a stake," I said, my voice cracking at the end as my bravado failed me.

In a flash, the she-wolf was in front of me, grabbing me by the neck and lifting me off the ground. "Think what you want about Apollo, but he's the one paying for your ass, so get used to his company. He has what we want, and what he wants in return is your kind."

More footsteps crunched over the sunny rooftop. I clawed at the hand on my throat and gasped for air.

"I'm not even . . . a full witch," I wheezed and coughed, pulling at the hand on my windpipe. "I can barely light . . . a candle properly. I'm just part on my mother's side!"

5

The she-wolf leaned in and sniffed me like the dog she was. Wrinkling her nose, she held me at arm's length again. "You like the rum, don't you?"

Pulling back one boot, I kicked with everything I had only for her to dodge it with ease, though her sneer brought me a little satisfaction. My anger was already boiling in my veins; the lives of weaker beings than them were nothing more than a job for these assholes.

"What do we do with her, Amelia?" one of the brutes asked.

Amelia. I'm going to remember you, Amelia.

"It only takes a drop to have witch blood, and she has it. We're taking her."

"Like hell I'm going with Apollo's lapdogs," I grunted. "You're all trash who prey on the weak."

That might get me killed, but being done in by these wolves would be better than whatever a vampire lord had in mind. Apollo's reputation was terrifying. Amelia tightened her grip, snarling. She flung me across the roof as if I weighed nothing, my skin scraping against the rough surface and cutting up my exposed arms and knees as I rolled to a stop.

"Watch your tongue, witchling," Amelia demanded.

My whole body ached, and with trembling fingers I inspected a big gash on my shoulder. My hand came back bright red, smeared with my own blood.

"Any others in the building?" Amelia asked.

"The only other witch was with a coven," said the tallest one, with a buzzed head and a lazy gaze. "I verified it myself. What's the next move?"

The only other witch. Mary. At least they left her alone.

"Do one more sweep to see if any came out of hiding, then meet me in the car. Jack, grab the witchling and let's go."

I swiped my fingers across the ground, panicked laughter taking over. I dug my fingers into my shoulder with a sharp pain, bringing up more blood and smearing it on the roof.

"What the hell is so funny?" Amelia snarled at me.

"The first rule of magic," I whispered, "mind your ingredients.

Nothing can spice up a spell like blood. Like you said, it only takes a drop of magic, and I have it."

I dragged my fingers across the last opening in the circle, closing it. Before the wolves registered what I had done, I screamed out the incantation once more.

"Take me where my heart wants to go!"

The circle flickered to life, and dark smoke puffed up from the roof.

"Stop her!" Amelia screeched as all the snarling, salivating wolves pounced, ripping through clothing and shifting as they lunged.

The magic breathed to life around me. My skin was on fire with it as everything began to fizzle. My body felt a pull like I was going to be sucked up in a vacuum, but I couldn't tell what direction it was coming from. A sharp pair of claws raked in front of my face barely a hair from the bridge of my nose, furious yellow eyes filled with a promise of pain behind them. I sucked in a breath, wrapped my arms around myself, and in a pop, everything obscured to black.

CHAPTER TWO

RYKER

The piece of antler splintered, and I cursed at the half-carved knife in my hands. Nearly everything I'd tried to carve from this particular piece of elk was giving me trouble, and I was about to give up and move onto another antler entirely. Sitting behind my cabin, surrounded by snow with the warm sun on my skin, I reached into the bucket, where more dried pieces sat waiting to be made into something useful.

It was peaceful here, spending my days how I wanted. The snow that stayed for most of the year helped to preserve food so I could hunt for long stretches and then stay put for even longer. Still, something under my skin itched to move. Maybe now was the time to break my routines and stretch my wings. Change was in the air, as it tended to nudge me every so often, and I played with the thought of what part of the world I could visit next, just to see how much it had changed. But as I sat on a stump that served as my favorite carving chair and let my thoughts drift, something was off.

When the scent of whisky and leather hit me, my hand shot from the bucket and threw my nearest knife, embedding it in a thick pine tree just to the side of my cabin. "Show yourself."

A man with a trim red beard and gray at his temples came into view, walking past the assaulted pine. He raised one thick eyebrow in question, his face showing no surprise.

"It's good to see ya too," Gavin mused, his accent a mix of Scottish with a dash of several other European languages that he'd picked up from decades of wandering.

"Still won't learn Russian?" I grunted.

"Still won't wear a fuckin' shirt?" he shot back. I shrugged; jeans and boots were enough. Shirts got in the way.

"I'll get around to it eventually. I've got time." Gavin laughed. "Do you have a lead for a bounty, or did you come here for my riveting conversation?"

"Christ, Ryker, you could offer a bastard a beer before you get straight to fuckin' with him."

Tossing my carving tools in the bucket, I kicked over a nearby log to offer a dry seat and nodded to the pile of snow under the window that had a few rows of glass bottles poking out of it. Gavin leaned over to pull free a beer and sat on the proffered log, popping open the top on the edge of my firewood ax that was half-embedded on my splitting stump next to him. Next would come his pitch. Some story or tip he'd picked up in a seedy bar or off another knife for hire that wasn't after the job. He came all the way out here only if he wanted me to tag along for added measure. Sometimes it was for a second pair of capable hands and sometimes I think he did it simply for the company. If I was being honest, I'd add that Gavin had his own reputation and got plenty of work, but I'd never tell the bastard to his face. He had a big enough head as it was.

"What brings you out here?" I asked, reaching for my own drink.

"A thing or two."

"A thing or two," I said flatly. "On the Central Siberian Plateau."

"Passing through to see Vissic. Thought I'd say hello and make sure yer still a grouchy hermit. Glad to see some things haven't changed."

Vissic was a bastard of a vampire, but he did have a lot of intel that a mercenary like Gavin could make good use of it for the right price. "If you find Vissic, give him a knife to the kidney for me."

"I might." Gavin took a long drink from his bottle. "We'll see how he wants to play it. I'm supposed to be trackin' down some demon who pissed off the wrong bastard, but ya know how tight-lipped Vissic can be."

"No other jobs have you all the way out here?" I asked.

Gavin eyed me. "I might. That depends on how interested y'are. I don't have much worth your time."

I take a swig of my beer. "Hit me."

"There's a rogue warlock in Italy runnin' rampant and the family wants it dealt with quietly." Gavin pulled a finished knife from the bucket at my feet and inspected it.

"Nope," I said.

"The wolf packs in Mongolia are fightin' again. I'm sure either side would pay for yer services." Gavin scooped up some of the snow around him and cleaned up the knife.

"Not really in the mood to play with the wolves right now."

Gavin took a drink, then locked his eyes on mine. "There might be one more. Speakin' of Vissic and vamps, I did hear somethin' interestin' on my way here."

Ah, here it was. Whatever Gavin came out here for was a job bigger than he wanted to handle alone.

"What'd you hear?" I asked.

"There are a few whispers that a house of bloodsuckers in North America is looking for covenless witches."

A dark heat crept up the back of my throat at the mention of it. There was no love lost between me and the vampires. I held a centuries-old vow of hate against most of them and I tolerated few of their kind.

"I don't help vamps."

"Yeah, I know. But this isn't the same bloodsucker that killed Ferox, ya know that."

"Gavin," I warned.

"I'm more curious to see what they're up to, aren't you? Their contacts in Moscow said they're payin' a decent amount per witch. Thought you'd want to hear it." Gavin pocketed the knife. "I like this one, I'm keepin' it."

"Of course you are," I said flatly. "How much are we talking?"

"Ten grand."

"Rubles?" I scoffed.

"Dollars," he answered. "A temptin' sum for easy work."

"What would they even want witches for?"

"Who knows?" Gavin tilted his head and scratched his beard. "Not that we have much of a lead on it but if I hear anythin' I'll pass it along. If this Apollo is making himself known over it, he must really want them for somethin'."

"Don't like the sound of it," I said. "What would a vamp need with a bunch of witches who don't have access to their little book of secrets?"

"I'll poke around for more while I'm at Vissic's. I don't like it either but a dollars a dollar, and more than one ear is willing to listen."

"This is going to come back around and bite our work in the ass." I grunted and pulled myself a beer out of the snow.

"Likely. We'll see a whole batch of new blood tryin' to play the hired hand, and half the jobs are going to be handlin' the aftermath of whatever game this vamp is playing."

And the idea of that pissed me off.

The mercenary drained his bottle, setting the empty one with a couple of others by the back door of the cabin. He stood with a grunt, zipping his leather jacket a little higher. "The fuck are ya doin' out here anyway, ya crusty old lizard? Any colder and my balls are gonna move in with my liver."

"Get the fuck out of here, Gavin," I said, half-heartedly.

"Bah, piss off." He leaned down and took another beer for the road. "I'll come back around in a couple of weeks after this demon business is done."

"Wouldn't care if you didn't."

"That hurts, Ryker." Gavin put his hands over his heart. "Ya wound yer only friend. I'm comin' back anyway, see ye later. Take care, Ryker."

Draining my beer after Gavin left, I moved back to my carving bucket. Finally, it was quiet. Just the sound of the wind in the trees and the scraping of bones on my knife. I was at peace, and alone, which is how it should be.

After finishing a bone knife without cracking it this time, and cleaning up the mess, I watched the sun start its path downward. I removed my jeans and tossed them over a low branch by the back door. Walking down the hill to the base of the steaming natural hot spring, I sank my body into the water, wiping away dust and mess from the carvings.

As I leaned back onto the wooden seat I had built into the spring, I closed my eyes, soaking in the water and letting the cool air sweep across my shoulders as evening set in. The first stars were beginning to shine through the blue sky.

Something was off. Not in the way that I had sensed Gavin was nearby; instead it felt like something with a bigger impact was coming. My eyes snapped open as ripples swirled in the spring. The air overhead grew warmer. I tensed, uneasy, and stood up in the waist-high water. I'd shift if I had to, but there wasn't exactly an excess of room for wings in this clearing.

A puff of smoke filled the space overhead, and a crackle of light. In a flash, a form dropped out of the sky a few feet overhead. *Fuck.*

I dove to catch it, a tiny human in all black that was about 50 percent backpack and a tangle of dark hair. I was fast enough to stop them from smashing their head on the natural rock around the spring, but not fast enough to stop us both from splashing back into the hot water.

Finding my footing and lifting us both up, I held a woman who gulped down air and coughed up water. Her wet black hair clung to her shoulders and her thin cotton dress stuck to her body. Her eyes grew wide, and she threw a hand over her shoulder, wincing. Blood welled between her fingers, running with the dripping water down her shoulder to drip in the water.

"What—?" She flailed back in surprise with fear in her eyes as they darted between me and her surroundings. "Where . . . this isn't Seattle. Who are you?"

"No, it's not."

I vaguely recognized the place name but couldn't recall where it was located. Her accent gave her away: American English. While her shock subsided, I set her down on her feet close to the edge of the water where she could stand up. I doubted she'd want to be in the cool air with wet clothes when the brisk spring day was below freezing.

She clutched her shoulder harder, her face flushed from the steamy water, and I got my first good look at her: short, with black clothing and boots. Her backpack looked like it could topple her over, but her legs were a solid build. Her big brown eyes were pretty, if not alarmed. Understandably so, because she seemed to be as confused as I was.

"There was an accident with the circle and . . ." She swallowed, catching her breath. "God, it's warm in here."

She eyed me warily, sweat beading on her skin. She looked at my eyes, which were silver and not quite human. The fact that she could see them—not to mention her reference to a spell circle—meant she was something more than human herself. The claws trying to poke through the tips of my fingers would give me away as something supernatural if she hadn't already figured it out.

"Stay back! I know kickboxing," she threatened. I was a lot bigger than her, with my muscled bulk gained from a lifetime of fighting every kind of creature under the sun. She was all soft lines with no fight to her pose.

"Yeah, sure you do."

Then a sharp taste hit the air, brushing through my nose and to the back of my mouth. I stopped. Her blood stung the air and tasted metallic on my tongue, but it also carried the taste of magic. There was very little she could be if not one of the Sisters, a non-religious type of witch with magic in their blood. "What is a witch doing in my spring?"

"It was an accident. The portal was supposed to send me . . . not here, wherever *here* is." She brushed a wet strand of hair off her forehead.

"A portal?" I frowned.

"I was . . . going . . ."

She lost consciousness and sank into the water with a splash, the weight of her backpack finally pulling her down.

Shit.

I held her limp body to my chest. She was still breathing, but she was overheating and had lost a lot of blood from that gash in her shoulder. If I wanted answers, I wasn't going to get them from her corpse. Pulling us both out of the spring, I took off for my cabin, grabbing my pants as I went.

Now that she was out of the water, I could see gashes on her knees, though not as bad as the deep one on her upper arm. Her blood dripped down my stomach and onto the ground. I adjusted her weight in my arms, but her backpack was making things awkward. I pulled it off her and carried it on my back instead. Up the hill and into the cabin, I kicked the door open, bringing the witch inside and laying her on the couch.

Away from the water, her scents stung my nose in bursts of strong substances and smoke. Under the layers of rum and tobacco lay a sweetness to her skin—definitely witchcraft from the Sisters. This one seemed to be in distress and very far from home. I toweled her off, leaving the towel under the couch where it continued to catch her dripping wet hair while I looked at her cuts. Then I grabbed a box from under the kitchen counter and began cleaning and bandaging the worst of them. If there were any wounds on her apart from the arm and knees, I couldn't see it for the dress, but I didn't smell blood anywhere else. She moaned once, but never snapped out of her hot stupor.

I tossed her boots and backpack by the fire to dry. Her dress would have to dry on its own; I didn't have anything else for her to wear and in front of the fire she would dry out quickly enough. She had a few pieces of jewelry I didn't bother to remove. I knew better than to mess with a witch's charms; they could do just about anything and usually had nasty surprises for those who touched them.

It had been a while since I had been around humans, even magical ones; other than Gavin, but he was hardly the norm. I remember them being fragile, but I wasn't sure how it was with witches. These injuries would have been more than easy enough for a supernatural being to recover from but could she easily survive?

Her clothes were mostly dry when I carried her up the narrow staircase to the loft and put her in the only bed that the cabin had: mine.

I cleaned up the blood she left on the couch and floor and poured myself a drink, staring up at the loft. The question remained: Was she just a damsel in distress, or was she about to bring trouble to my doorstep?

A witch. Landing, right after learning that a vampire was collecting them, in my damn lap. I was no fan of the bloodsuckers, but I was no friend to witches either. They were crafty devils; at least, the ones that practiced like the Sisters were. Always a trick up their sleeve, nothing was ever straightforward with a witch—they always had to complicate it with their kind of magic.

Magic. I scowled. Even from the lower level I could still smell her. There was something in her blood that spoke of magic. Old magic. Enough for me to sense it. A scent I had all but forgotten. Still, I couldn't quite place the scent. One of the older covens, probably. Maybe I killed some of her ancestors?

The whisky felt good going down.

I could sell her to the vampire and try to glean what he has planned.

That option didn't sit quite right. I'd done a lot for money, but I did have one or two lines I wouldn't cross.

She would make good bait to see what the vampires are up to. They're not collecting covenless witches to have them over for a picnic.

I'm sure I couldn't tell her that. She didn't know me and I didn't know her; I wasn't about to reveal anything let alone any plans to use her to dig for information. If I was going to be an asshole about it, the least I could do was be a smart one. Besides, I wouldn't leave her with them.

Grumbling to myself, I drained the glass and set it in the sink. I grabbed the rest of the bottle and left. The witch would be out for a while, so I could finish my soak in the hot spring and think about what to do.

It had been a while since I had left the mountain, and there was only one way to find out what the vampires were up to. It might be time to remind a few beings that I was still kicking.

CHAPTER THREE

DANI

My entire body ached like one big bruise. Disoriented and dizzy, once I regained my bearings I remembered the rooftop, the wolves, and the nasty gash on my shoulder, which was still throbbing by the way.

Thanks, Amelia.

When I sat up, my head spun from the quick motion. This was not my bed. Could I even call it a bed? It was a loft of some kind with a giant mattress lying right on the wooden floor. The mattress had black wool sheets, but the similarities to an actual bed stopped there. On top, instead of a regular comforter, there was a pile of furs. Actual furs, from animals. Dangerous animals. And in lieu of pillows there were rolled-up sheep fleeces. Weird, but comfortable. It all looked a little too caveman for my taste, which recalled the tall, dark, and questionable man from the hot spring.

I moved a little more and the furs dropped from my shoulders. Air hit my skin and I shivered, my dress barely coming to my knees and not covering my arms. Bandages wrapped my knees and shoulder, telling me I had more scrapes than I had first thought. Someone had taken my wet boots off. And if they took my boots and backpack off they may have removed . . .

My eyes widened, and my hand flew to my ankle bracelet.

Oh, thank goodness.

The charm from my mother was still intact, and the fact that it wasn't burning on my skin meant I wasn't in any immediate danger here. The thin gold chain had a string of stones on it, each with different purposes. I'd worn the anklet for most of my life and I wasn't supposed to take it off. Ever. It was my lucky charm, a memento of my mother, and a magical defense, all wrapped into one.

Wherever I was, it was cold, and it looked rural from my first glance around. Definitely *not* Seattle. The teleportation circle, then the hot water, and then the hulking naked guy. He was huge and there was no way he was human. Not with silver eyes. It bothered me that I couldn't figure out what he was; he was unlike any creature I'd ever encountered before. I almost wish I had stayed to try my luck with the werewolves instead. No matter how hard I tried, I couldn't stay away from the magical world.

I shrugged off the rest of the furs, a chill racing across my bare arms in the cool air, and peeked over the edge of the loft.

The place was what real estate agents like to call 'rustic.' The fireplace was huge, taking up half the wall, but the flames were flickering dangerously low for being somewhere so cold outside. The walls were logs bigger than my thigh. No insulation, and the primitive windows held thick panes of glass that warped the images of landscape outside. They would do nothing to tell me where I was, but they did show me it was night.

I ran my eyes along the walls and ceiling. No electricity that I could find. Instead, a series of lanterns burned in key places of the room, lighting it as brightly as one could expect from firelight in a heavy cabin at nighttime.

The possibility of a bathroom wasn't promising either, as the kitchen sink's water was a manual pump shooting up right out of the floor. I grimaced at what the toilet must be. Some literal hole in the ground, probably. A simple wooden table and an out-of-place modern couch finished off the furniture. When all was said and done it was a pretty basic cabin.

The hairs on my neck stood up as I scanned for something to defend myself with. Just because my anklet wasn't warning me now didn't mean it wouldn't later. If I could find my bag I could find my pocketknife, which was better than nothing. And clothes—I wasn't about to run outside in the snow without clothes.

I stood up and climbed down the stairs carefully, my feet padding across the wood floor. My backpack and boots were by the fireplace, and I began going through my things. Yanking out all my clothes, I laid them out to dry and shoved my pocketknife in the side of my bra for easy reach. Screw the people who made cute clothes with no pockets. The wad of cash I had somehow managed to save up was in a plastic bag and was dry, but the granola bars were ruined. I tossed them and the wrappers in the fire. I pulled the case off my pay-as-you-go phone and tried to dry it out, but I was pretty sure it was a lost cause. My charger and headphones were probably useless too, but I dried them out anyway in case they had miraculously made it through the dip in the spring.

I had a few charms with me for protection and good luck. Cheap baubles from crappy hedge witches, but they made me feel better. But they were ruined too. Tossing them in the fire I sighed, sitting on the stone fireplace. I jumped when I heard a crunch of twigs and snow outside.

I spun, facing the doorway as he came through the door. The man from the spring leaned on the wall and he was even bigger than I remembered. Clothed this time, mostly, in jeans and black boots, every bit of him was either muscles or faded scars. His shaggy head of hair brushed his shoulders and he had stubble as though he couldn't be bothered to shave for a couple of days. His eyes were silver, not giving away what he could be but confirming my first instinct, that he wasn't human. I tried to think of something to say that wouldn't make me out to be a scared little rabbit.

"Did you bring me here?" I asked.

The man raised an eyebrow and crossed his arms over his massive chest. "You're welcome."

My boots were still a bit damp. Certainly, I had worse problems than damp shoes. I had no idea where I was, what he was, or what to do from wherever rural hillside I had landed.

"What is your name?" he asked, the gravel in his voice running a chill down my spine. Like the kind of voice you get after a long stretch of smoking. Whatever it was, it was sexy as hell. Too bad I don't fuck with supernaturals.

"Are you anything I shouldn't be giving my name to?" I asked.

He smirked. "No."

"Tell me a lie, what color are my boots?" I asked.

"White." His words were easy and not judgmental. He knew the games we all had to play in this world, and it looked like he wasn't one of the fae.

"Danica," I said, shoving my boots on. "You?"

He was quiet a moment and I didn't think he was going to answer. Finally, he murmured, "Ryker."

"I didn't mean to drop in on you, Ryker, so I'll get out of your way now." I stood, gathering everything back into my damp backpack.

"Where are you going to go?" he asked.

Did I want him to know where I was going? He had interest in me, and it wasn't comfortable. It would be best to keep it vague.

"The nearest train station, maybe. Can I get a plane around here? I don't have much ID on me." I shifted through my belongings and pulled out a wallet. "Maybe my driver's license will work."

As I rummaged through my belongings, Ryker chuckled.

"The nearest village is about a hundred kilometers that way." Ryker jabbed his thumb out the door behind him. "And I suggest you have a seat, because I'm going to get a few answers from you before you go anywhere."

I paused, my hands still halfway in my bag as I rummaged through my things. "Kilometers? Where am I right now?"

"Siberia. Russia."

The room spun as everything caught up with my head. It explained the climate, his accented English. "Russia? You mean I landed halfway around the world?"

"You did." Ryker tilted his head. "And I want to know why."

As suspicious as I probably seemed, I wasn't surprised he wanted answers—I wanted them too. Groaning, I dropped my bag to the floor for now. "What do you want to know?"

"How is it you got here?" He came into the cabin and closed the door behind him. He walked slowly towards me, looking every bit like a predator. I. Did. Not. Like. That.

Straightening up, my muscles on high alert, the hair on my neck standing up straight, I answered, but maybe a tad sharper than I meant to. "I told you: a teleportation circle."

Ryker raised an eyebrow at me. "I know how they work, and you don't end up in random places. Unless you have been to my cabin before, which I know you haven't, and this was your intended destination, there's no way you could have landed here. There's something you aren't telling me."

When he sat down on the couch, I felt a bit better. It was hard to concentrate with a giant looming over you.

"There was an accident and part of the circle was torn up. I patched it up with . . ." I brushed my fingers over my bandaged shoulder. "With blood."

"That alone wouldn't have done it," Ryker murmured to himself. "What was your incantation?"

"How do you know so much about magic?" I crossed one leg over the other, still seated on the stone fireplace. "Are you a warlock or some-thing? Like, a really beefy one?"

"No, I'm not." He smirked. "Answer the question, Danica."

"Dani, please. The incantation was 'take me where my heart wants to go.' I wasn't the witch who set the circle up, but I trust her."

Ryker frowned. "Take me where my heart wants to go."

"Look, you can't word a spell in a way that someone could acci-dentally activate it. If some random maintenance worker walked over the circle and said 'man, I want to go home' and then they poofed away in a cloud of smoke, how do you think that would go over?"

"Why would the spell bring you here?" he asked.

A good question. A very good question. Maybe I could ask Mary more about it. Because nothing in my heart wanted to be in the middle of nowhere with a dusting of snow outside and a grumpy whatever-the-hell Ryker was in my face.

"Like I said, I didn't set it up. I don't do spells."

Ryker frowned. "But you're a witch, aren't you?"

"Not a practicing one."

"Where were you trying to go?" Ryker sat back now, his posture more relaxed though his eyes still sharp. I had no doubts he could claw my ass up in about two seconds if he wanted to.

"My dad's bar."

"What were you running from?" Ryker asked, expectantly.

"Wolves."

He scratched his scraggly chin. "All right, wolves then. Do you know why they were chasing you?"

"No idea," I lied. A small grin tugged at Ryker's mouth, but he didn't say anything. It was too close to playing games, did he know something I didn't?

"Why don't you stay here for a few days? I have a friend stopping by and he can take you to Moscow. That is, unless you want to go on your own?"

"What's the catch?" I asked.

"Maybe I don't feel like letting a strange witch die in the snow. With what you're wearing it wouldn't take a day."

I clenched my jaw. "Is there even a road from here to that village?"

"No." Ryker shrugged. "And it's going to snow tonight. Really, you came on the only good day weather-wise; I don't expect another one like it for weeks."

I leaned back and rested my head against the stone fireplace. "Guess I'm taking you up on your offer then."

"Why don't I make us dinner and you can use the bathroom," Ryker offered. "You smell like human misery. It's that door over there, I'll have food when you're done."

"It's called smelling like an awesome night out," I quipped. I grabbed my toothbrush and a clean set of clothes and headed toward the bathroom door.

Surprisingly, the bathroom was like something out of a magazine. There was a giant claw footed tub and a toilet. A real toilet, not a hole in the ground like I was expecting. There was a sleek sink, a mirror, and a modern light fixture. I squealed despite myself and stuck my head out the door.

"You have plumbing? And electricity?"

"I have a generator for it," Ryker called from the kitchen. "I haven't upgraded the rest of the cabin in decades, but the bathroom I fixed up when I discovered indoor plumbing."

While the bath was filling up, I brushed my teeth. I cleaned off my face and sank into the water with a sigh. After a short soak and some ferocious scrubbing, I felt much better. I re-bandaged my shoulder, struggling to get it wrapped high enough to cover the injury, and put on a clean black cotton dress. All I was missing now was my eyeliner, but that wasn't exactly a priority. Walking out of the bathroom I felt refreshed, until the second I opened the door and the cool air hit me. "Shit!"

"What is it?" Ryker frowned, setting two plates on the table.

"It's so cold here," I complained. "Aren't you freezing?"

He tried not to smile but he wasn't able to hide it. "I must not have noticed; it takes a lot for me to get cold. I'll throw some more wood on the fire."

I sat down to my plate, and stared. A single steak took up the entire plate. It was thick and looked like it was cooked quite skillfully, but that was it. Just a steak. No salad or potatoes or anything you might expect to go with it. I raised an eyebrow, but since I was the one crashing his space, I didn't complain. Maybe he just wasn't big on vegetables or something.

"That should do it," Ryker said as he sat down across from me. He picked up his utensils, masterfully cutting his meat into large bites.

I followed his lead and began to eat. It was a strange, silent dinner at who-knows-when o'clock. Through the kitchen window, the stars twinkled outside, and a light breeze rustled the trees. And as Ryker said it would, snow began to fall as we were finishing dinner.

When I couldn't take the silence anymore, I scooted my chair back and stretched.

"I don't think it's been that long since dawn for me, but I guess I'll try to get used to the schedule in this part of the world," I said. "Can I have a blanket for the couch?"

"I can give you something, but you're going to freeze down there. You'd be better off in the loft." Ryker took the plates to the sink.

"No. Not sharing a bed with a . . . whatever you are, of unknown origin. I'll take as many blankets as you will give me, and the couch will do just fine."

Ryker shrugged, a smile wide on his face. "Suit yourself, little witch."

I twisted around in the blanket on the couch for the hundredth time. The fire was roaring not five feet away, but it still wasn't enough. I would barely warm one side of me, and in that time the other side would freeze. I felt like a turkey roasting on a spit; I had to keep turning to stay warm.

The walls had small cracks that let freezing air in from outside. They were probably held together by stubbornness and bullshit.

How could Ryker stand the temperature here for months on end? Was he a vampire? I hoped not. No, he found me in the daylight, that's not it. And if he was a vampire, I was in deeper shit than when I'd dodged those wolves. Alone, no resources, with a vampire? He'd probably take a bite and then turn me over to Apollo. My stomach turned at the thought of whatever that sick leech wanted with stray witches. There weren't many that practiced from *The Book of Sisters* without a coven, but I was definitely one of them.

Shivering again, I pulled my arms tight around me. Maybe Ryker was right about the furs; maybe that's how he made it through the Siberian winters. Maybe I could sneak up and grab just one.

Steeling myself against the cold, I rolled off the couch and to my feet. With the blanket still wrapped around my shoulders, I padded across the floor as quickly and quietly as I could. Gripping the blanket with one hand, I reached out with the other to climb the steep stairs to the loft.

Ryker was sprawled across the bedding, ass up and naked as the day he was born. He let out a sleepy hum and shifted a little before settling back down.

Damn. He's chiseled from head to toe, I'll give him that. Wait, I'm freezing my ass off and he's butt naked and content?

From the top step I stretched out my free hand, reaching for a thick black fur that wasn't directly under Ryker. My fingers fell short by several inches.

With a grimace, I climbed off the top step and onto the loft floor. Reaching out for the fur, I gently dragged it to myself as Ryker slept on. I wrapped it over my already blanketed body and drank in the warmth. It was heaven, wrapping around my body, sinking into my bones, caressing my face. My face? The blanket wasn't covering my face, but it was warm anyway. Blissfully warm.

I crawled a little farther onto the loft and away from Ryker and the edge. The last thing I needed right now was to fall and break my damn leg.

I reached out and tested the air with one arm. My eyes widened as I realized it was the air in the loft that held the heat. I shrugged off a little more blanket and I was still perfectly comfortable.

"What?" I hissed.

Ryker stirred, shifting in his sleep and I snapped my mouth closed. Then, in one horrible moment, he flung a leg across his bed and blocked my exit.

No! *No no no.*

I inched forward, seeing if I could reach the stairs at all without disturbing him. I could try to creep over his leg and to the stairs, but I risked falling or waking him up. Neither one of those options was something I was willing to risk.

I resigned myself to a night on the wooden loft floor and laid the fur out in a corner. I curled up on top of it with the blanket, and eventually drifted off to sleep. I was finally warm.